Published by
Harper Grove Publishing Company
45 Plumpton Walk
Bradford BD2 1PD

ISBN 978-0-9562122-0-7
Printed by Ellset Creative Print, Shipley BD18 1BW

INTRODUCTION

This is the story of Antony Heyes' a highly educated intelligent man who is a dedicated conservationist. Disillusioned after years of trying to make the world stand up and see what they are doing to the environment, he çan only see one option, to retaliate against the populace without discrimination. A university graduate and a highly trained pilot, serving in the R.A.F. he has two deadly weapons in which to pursue his goals. To terrorise a nation!

CHAPTER ONE

1986

Herbert Ackroyd paused for a moment and gazed upwards at the arched wrought iron sign above the gateway. 'Joseph Bottomley's Beers, Leeds Ltd'. He sauntered on through the large steel gates of the brewery yard and eyed the rows of empty steel barrels stacked to the side. His mind returned momentarily to the day 53 years ago when, as a fresh faced boy of 12, he'd walked through the same gates on the very first day of his working, life and now it was his last. He eyed the same rows of barrels. The barrels were made of wood then, instead of the steel ones that were stacked up towards the top of the high surrounding wall. In place of the large Volvo lorries that were parked in neat rows, huge shire horses had stood in harness two abreast, four wheeled cart in tow. A flicker of sadness for days long gone flashed through his mind as he neared the red coloured wagon and climbed into the driver's seat. Another man was already sitting in the passenger seat of the 20 ton lorry, his head submerged in the sports pages of the Daily Mirror.

"Morning Bert," said Joe Duckworth, as he lifted his head momentarily to greet his workmate, before returning to his paper. "Nothing but bloody trouble, Col Cluff," referring to the local cricket hero. "Time they got rid of him. Give some youngster a go," added Joe.

"I'll be glad when the summer's over an' we can get back to a man's game, football," replied Bert. The thought of having more free time cheered him a little although he felt doleful on what was to be his last trip. The yard manager came up to the cab window and held a clipboard upwards.

"Sign for your load, Bert, and don't be late back' cos all the lads are coming in early to see you off with a drink." The traditional farewell get together of a loyal and trusted servant of Bottomley's Beers.

"Right '0', Sam," replied Bert as he fired the diesel engine into life and returned the chitty.

"Sounds more like a bloody funeral than a retirement do," said Joe as Bert crunched the gear lever into first and started the lorry out through the gates. The dray wagon turned down a cobbled side street and headed down Hunslet Road and on towards the M62 motorway, for this was Wednesday, Pontefract day, a delivery ritual that had hardly changed for Bert since he started work all those years ago, only then he was a mere horse groom or shit shoveller as they were known in the yard.

Bert was a happy, easily pleased family man, who enjoyed nothing better than drinking best bitter and following the fortunes of his beloved Leeds United Football Club.

Joe Duckworth, assistant drayman as they were called these days was a relative newcomer to the firm. He'd only been at the brewery for just over 15 years, most of it working as a drayman's mate with Bert. Joe led a totally different existence to Bert; he was a single man of 42 who lived with his widowed mother in a small back-to-back house across the other side of the city in Harehills. Joe's main vice was his weakness for gambling, especially the horses and on the whole very rarely placed a winning bet. The two workmates were as different as chalk and cheese. Two simple-minded men who enjoyed life and who both shared a great fondness for a glass of beer. As they drove down the M62 the sun began to shine for the first time that morning. They had three deliveries to make that day and Bert smiled to himself as he thought of the kindness that had been shown to him by the landlords of the various pubs on his very last delivery. Some had presented him with a small gift, others had slipped a fiver or a tenner into his hard worn hand, and then Bert frowned as he thought of the couple of miserly landlords who'd not even bothered to wish him good luck.

Bert pulled the gear lever from third into second as he slowed the big lorry and turned into the car park of the Malt Kiln Inn, a trendily middle-class sort of pub not far from Pontefract town centre. The landlord was ready and waiting for his delivery. He'd already stacked his empty barrels by the side of the open trap doors that led to the cellars below the pub. It was nine o'clock when they started to roll the heavy barrels down the runway into the cellar and by ten twenty five the delivery was complete. Joe and Bert stood waiting in the tap room as Tony Woods, the landlord, pulled the waiting draymen their customary reward of a pint.

"Cheers and good health, all the best for the future," said Tony as he sipped the froth off the head of half a pint, more as a gesture than for the drink. As soon as the draymen had left, his half pint of beer would be poured back into the waiting slop bucket and then back into the barrel to be served later in the day to an unsuspecting customer. This was the country of hand pulled beer, beer sucked upwards through a piston pump, rather than the modern way of pushing the beer up the barrel with the electric pump. It was common practice for landlords to overfill the glasses to leave a good thick head on top of the pint. The overspill went into a tray below the pump and when full was poured into the waiting slop bucket.

A barrel contained 18 gallons or 144 pints of beer. A few unscrupulous landlords were not adverse to adding several pints of water to their beer, diluting the brew slightly whilst increasing their own profits. Bert and Joe were experts in their field and could tell after just a sip which landlord had been overdoing the water.

Bert and Joe downed their beer in a matter of seconds. This was not a good pint. Tony Woods, the landlord, handed Bert a half bottle of Teacher's Scotch Whisky as a thank you gift for his years of endeavour, and after thanking him and a few niceties, the two men were back on the road. The next stop was the Railway Hotel, a scruffy but well supported pub in the tradition of many of the working class pubs; poor furnishings, cheap prices and good ale. The drop was short and sweet due to the landlord, a chronic alcoholic, still unconscious in his bed after a three day drinking bout. The two draymen left the six barrels stacked by the cellar head, refusing to take away any empties much to the annoyance of the publican's wife. "Sorry lass," said Bert firmly but politely, "we're not doing Rip Van Winkle's job for him as well as ours. He should have sorted out the empties and we would have taken them away." They weren't being stuffy but only the landlord could possibly know which barrels were empties and which were slops.

The third drop at midday was one of Bert and Joe's favourite pubs, generally left to the last so that they could squander an extra half hour and relax over a pint or two. The Four Feathers was located in the centre of Pontefract's Main Street. A portly jolly landlord called Jim Smith was the publican, a middle-aged man who was well liked by the majority of his customers. Jim was serving behind the bar in the lounge as the two draymen strolled into the bustling room. His face exploded into a large grin as he saw them coming towards the bar.

"Am I glad to see you lads:" said Jim, a smile spread across his red boozer's face.

"You've not run out again Jim you old scrounger," replied Bert leaning on the bar eyeing the rear end of Brenda, Jims attractive wife, as she stood holding a glass up to the whisky optic. "Do us a favour Bert, sunshine?" asked Jim, "go down and fasten a barrel of bitter on to last empty keg. I'll pull your first two pints free of charge."

"Each," chipped in Joe.

"Of course," smiled back Jim, "and I might even bribe our Brenda to give you a kiss for your retirement."

Bert and Joe quickly unloaded a barrel of bitter into the cellar and connected it up to the draw-off tap.

"Right Jim, we have ignition," shouted Bert up the stairs from the cellar. Bert watched the brown liquid shoot up the clear plastic pipe, signaling Jim's response to Bert's shout. The two draymen abandoned the unloading until later. They sat in the games room sampling their favourite wet lunch. A game of dominoes and two pints later the two draymen were joined by Jim who was taking a short break during a lull in the lounge bar.

"Cheers lads," said Jim as he downed half a pint in one gulp, the same way a slow drinker would take a sip.

"Thanks for putting a barrel on," said Jim, "saved me bacon. Sold out at ten o'clock last night we did, got a party in from the races. Do you know they supped two bloody barrels they did, right good crowd an' all." Before he'd finished talking Jim reached over and grabbed Bert's hand under the table.

"There you are Bert, take your wife out for a drink on me." Bert opened his fist to find a screwed up twenty pound note.

"Thanks Jim but it's too much," said Bert slightly embarrassed.

"Nonsense," exclaimed Jim, "we've not finished, there's our Brenda to see to yet." Jim winked at Bert, a mischievous grin spreading across his jolly face.

Joe interrupted. "Don't mean to be a nag, but have you seen the time? Supposed to be back in the yard at two and it's twenty to now."

"Aye, giving me a colour telly they are and a cheque, better not be late," said Bert downing the dregs of beer from the glass. The two draymen finished unloading the last of the beer. Joe shouted up the stairs to the bar that they'd finished.

Jim rushed out of the room first and was standing at the main door with Brenda as Bert came out up the trap door of the cellars.

"Give us a kiss love," said Brenda before planting a huge kiss on Bert's cheek leaving a large red mark from her cherry coloured lipstick. Bert blushed a little after groping Brenda's sides a little too near her breasts. She smiled gratuitously. She'd been groped often.

"Come see us regularly, you're always welcome, and bring Freda with you." Without further ado the two men left the pub and were soon heading back down the motorway.

Thirty minutes later Bert drove the large Volvo through the iron gates of the brewery yard for the last time. Seventy workmates were waiting in the draymans bar and after the presentation of the small portable television and a cheque for £500 followed by several speeches, the drink flowed free. At six thirty that evening a taxi delivered Bert and his colour T.V. to the small neat semi on the outskirts of the city. Freda, Bert's wife, had to put him straight to bed much the worse for drink. He was sweating profusely and could hardly speak.

Joe Duckworth had left just after Bert and had called for some fish and chips at his local fish shop before he arrived home in his Reliant Robin three wheeler car. His mother had warmed a plate in the oven and she was pleased to see her only son as he sat at the table and tucked into his fish supper. As she enquired about Bert's last day, she couldn't help but notice the sweat that began to run down Joe's face.

"Are you alright our Joe?" she enquired a little worried.

"Fine, Ma," he replied wiping his brow with his handkerchief.

"It's only the booze, laid on a right good spread for old Bert. I'll miss him you know, bloody good sort." He stuffed a large piece of fish into his mouth and his face grimaced slightly. "Tastes a bit funny this fish, Ma, sorta bitter, a bit like aspirin tastes."

"Leave it lad, I'll open up a tin of soup for you."

In the Four Feathers that night Jim Smith was his usual jovial self. He stood leaning against the bar with some regulars whilst his wife Brenda, served behind the bar.

"You okay love," she said as she noticed her husband's usually red face had turned a creamy white, and sweat was beginning to pour from his face. Large stains began to appear on his shirt as it soaked up the perspiration from various parts of his upper body.

"Don't feel too good, I think I'm just starting with a summer chill."

Next morning Freda Ackroyd woke early, a habit of the last fifty years. She turned over in bed to wake Bert for work and she smiled as she suddenly realised she had no need to give him his usual morning nudge. She reached her arm across his chest to give him a loving squeeze, and as she gripped him tight the coldness of his body flowed into her warm skin and she screamed.

"Bert. Oh my God, Bert." She quickly lifted her head off the pillow to look at the blue lifeless face of her dead husband.

Joe's mother, Nellie Duckworth, turned off the gas ring allowing the shrill whistle of the kettle to slowly subside. She walked into the front room and stood at the bottom of the stairs.

"Joe, tea's ready. You'll be late." She returned to the kitchen and spread a piece of bread with marmalade. "Damn that lad," she thought to herself. She carried the freshly filled teapot into the front room and proceeded to fill two mugs with the steaming brew. She picked up one mug and carried it up the stairs and into the small bedroom where her son lay still, amidst a pile of ruffled sheets. She placed the tea on the small bedside table and grabbed Joe on his shoulder to rouse him. Instead of the soft flabby skin, her fingers stayed rigid and firm against the rigor mortised body of her only son.

Brenda Smith had been dreaming she had been making love with one of the young good looking male customers she had her eye on for some time. She opened her eyes slowly and her hand was holding the firm hard nipple on her left breast. Her hand slipped down between her legs and disappeared into the wetness of her arousal. 'No, sod it,' she thought. 'I'll make that fat sod do some work.' She turned from her back onto her side and delved along with her hand. She expertly pulled his pyjama cord loosening the garment. She slid her hand down and made a lunge for his penis. Her hand clawed at the dilated bundle of cold penis and testicles. A sudden fear swept through her. She withdrew her hand quickly pushing herself up to a sitting position. She stared for a moment at the back of her dead husband's head. Then when her courage had increased she felt the side of his cheek with the back of her fingers. His skin was as cold as ice.

"I always said you'd bloody die when I needed you most you rotten bastard," she said as tears welled into her eyes and began to stream across her cheeks.

CHAPTER TWO

The tall slim man walked briskly up the hill. Several newspapers jutted from the pocket of his combat jacket. He turned the corner, crossed the road and turned down the back street between the two rows of Victorian brick built houses. Debris and rotting food littered the cobblestones. The once cared for houses now had been left unrepaired for several years; peeling paint, rotten window frames and leaking gutters were the norm. He climbed two steps and inserted a key into the rim lock of a house near the middle of the row. The ill-fitting door stuck fast and he cursed as he kicked at the lower frame and the door sprung open leaving the frame separated from the wall.

A small, pretty woman who had been watching television in the front room came running into the kitchen and she threw her arms around the neck of the thin, pale-faced man as he slammed the door behind him.

"Damn these fucking dumps," he cursed forcing a smile as he faked pleasure responding to the girl's delight in his presence.

"Any news?" he asked throwing his well worn combat jacket over the rear of the tatty table side chair.

"No, nothing," responded the girl, hovering closely to the man.

"Hey, Sarah," shouted a voice from the front room, "make some coffee. She filled the kettle over the old pot sink and placed it on the grease covered fifties style gas oven.

"Like some, Tan?" she asked. Always eager to please her lover and benefactor. He nodded as he pulled a rolled up bundle of newspapers from the pocket of his jacket and threw them amidst the debris of several meals on the kitchen table. He unfolded the newspapers and began to sift slowly through the pages, his eyes scanning every corner for normally missed small comments. Ten minutes later he stood up and took a sip of the cooling coffee.

"Not a mention," he said to the woman who'd been sitting patiently for the man she worshipped to finish his task.

Tan brushed past and walked into the front room. Sarah followed like a faithful puppy. Two youths were sitting in opposite chairs. The once brocaded upholstery had been worn 'shiny' on the arms through years of abuse by numerous previous tenants, who'd also rented the near slum. Both men looked up from the T.V. and quickly responded to the presence of their leader.

"Is there nothing in the papers?" asked a bespectacled youth of twenty. Tan waved his head. Richard Normans was a drop-out undergraduate who had wasted too much of his time on the picket lines in the miners' strike and various other industrial disputes, where, with other card carrying communist agitators they had enjoyed the confrontation with the police, the representatives of Margaret Thatcher's government on whom they had reeked their vengeance whenever the opportunity presented itself. He was a small, thin faced ugly man with narrow slit eyes and shoulder length brown hair that was matted in long strands through lack of washing. He came from a wealthy background as did most champions of the working classes. His father owned a successful haulage company employing nearly a hundred men. He was a weak willed type who needed the company of contemporaries and like most communists was easily led but staunch in his beliefs. The other man, another slim wiry type, was Philip Sellars, a twenty four year old ex-social worker with a degree in psychology to his credit, and various dismissals from several different councils to his discredit. He was virtually finished in his chosen career because of his petulance and inability to take any form of criticism or advice; a dedicated militant whose heroes were Wedgewood Benn, Eric Heffer and Derrick Hatton. His upbringing too was middle class although he hadn't spoken to his parents in over four years after his father had tried unsuccessfully to get his only son to visit a psychiatrist. But now, free of any form of discipline, was quite easy going and again easily led.

"You sure you put the stuff into a full barrel and not an empty one?" asked Philip as he stubbed out his sixteenth cigarette of the day in an ashtray and immediately lit another. He would rather have been smoking canabis but without any money of his own he could only rely on the generosity of Tan who now and again had given him some to satisfy his needs.

"It was full to the top, I even tasted it in case they filled them with water," replied Tan. "It's only been two days. I think we'll hear soon enough." He sprawled down on the grubby settee and Sarah squeezed in alongside. They sat glued to the television. At six o'clock after the national news, Look North, a regional round-up of local news came onto the screen. Midway through the programme an announcement suddenly made them all very attentive. The reporter stood in the road under the arched steel sign of the brewery gates. He began,"Yesterday two men who worked for Bottomley's Brewery were suddenly taken ill and in a short time both were found to have died in their sleep. The cause of death is not certain although a spokesman for the West Yorkshire Police said they suspected food poisoning. Routine investigations are being carried out."

A large cheer rang around the room. Philip danced on his chair and Sarah threw herself over Tan who sat imperially, a small grin spreading on his face.

"It's begun," he said calmly. "You two stay glued to the T.V. I want to know the exact figures when they're announced." Tan stood to his feet and eyed Sarah lustfully. She understood. They left the room and went upstairs into one of the bedrooms. Tan unfastened her jeans and pulled them down around her ankles and after a small tussle managed to release one foot from the crumpled denim. He mounted her without any foreplay, ejecting his sperm quickly and when he was finished rolled onto his back and stared at the ceiling deep in thought. He felt excited for the first time in ages. He had found the reason for his existence and now it had begun, all the planning and the sleepless nights, the flights of conscience had been won and now he was committed. He knew now that he had to discipline himself totally to his cause. He had to make the people see what was going on and the only way they would listen to him was through fear, the fear of a person's ultimate demise that would make them sit up and take notice.

He wasn't afraid to kill he knew it was the only way forward. He worked long and hard on his plan and spent most of his small savings financing it. He had searched out his helpers, Normans and Sellars, carefully. He'd told them when they could go out of the house, when they had to stay in. He'd sworn at them, threatened them with violence. Then he'd been nice to them and told them why they had been treated the way they had.

"We are going down a long hard road that no one else has ever travelled," he'd explained. "We must stay in line together, one step from the line will form a crack that will grow until it separates us completely. That is why I have chosen you and only you and no-one else. When we start the world will watch and wait on our every move and they will seek us out with every resource possible, but they will not find us because we are disciplined and careful and we have intelligence and cunning and most of all we are dedicated."

He had wondered if he was insane as he lay there. He didn't feel insane, what was insanity anyway? To live by the laws laid down by one's government whether right or wrong, to conform to society's ways and traditions? Were Marx and Lenin insane for their ideals and the latter insane for practising the other's ideals? Was Hitler really a madman or a genius? What kind of man was it who could rise from lowly beginnings in life to lead a great nation and nearly the world? Could he, by fear, also rise from lowly beginnings or would he be hated and despised? Whatever they thought of him he was dedicated to the cause and only his death would release him from his dedication.

Anthony Heyes was a tall, slender but well muscled and proportioned man of thirty two. He came from a working class background brought up by his mother after she'd been left pregnant from a casual affair. Although every birthday a card would arrive with a tenner or a fiver stuffed between the folds from an unknown man who always signed the card, Pop. He'd grown up with a chip on his shoulder and at the age of twelve he was hardened to the ways of the world. He'd practically brought himself up, his mother who worked throughout the day and then was out most nights was rarely in attendance at their small council house on the outskirts of Manchester. He spent a lot of his time trudging the Pennine hills, the backbone of England, as they were known, a vast rugged emptiness teaming with wildlife, an exciting mysterious place for the young Heyes. He did not have many friends as most young boys did, and because of his light brown hair he'd been given the nickname of Tan. Even his mother used that name. As he'd grown older he grew apart from his few boyhood friends and spent more and more time trekking alone through the hills. There wasn't a wild flower he didn't know the name of. To most people the hills were just scrubland and heather, but Tan had seen its beauty and the mysteries of nature had him delving through library books in his thirst for more knowledge. He was intrigued by the kestrel and the sparrow hawk, how it hovered for hours seeking its prey and then swooped like a dart homing in for the kill onto some small animal that had dared to come out of its hole in the ground. He had marvelled watching a fox as it scurried and tore at the earth in the early morning dew and was amazed to find that the fox's staple diet was the common earth worm. He'd watched hares dance and play and had listened to the high pitched sounds, like children's laughter, that they made as they played for hours on end in the warm sunshine.

He'd attended the local comprehensive school where he'd excelled and armed with 13 '0' levels and 4 'A' levels he'd gone on to Cambridge where he'd gained a degree in Biology, but where he'd found another love, flying. He'd joined the Cambridge flying school and had been so enthralled by the thrill of flying he'd applied and found himself accepted to the Royal Air Force's training college, Cranwell. He was the star pupil, awarded the coveted sword of honour and by the age of twenty one he'd found himself with the rank of flight lieutenant, training to be a fighter pilot on Harrier jump jets.

Based at RAF Finningley in the heartland of East Yorkshire he had been forced to quit the RAF after 5 years of service. It stated on his discharge papers that he was mentally unstable for the role of fighter pilot. That was seven years ago and since then his life had been a total mess. That is until now.

Like Hitler, Tan had decided to try and change the direction of society at whatever cost. No matter how many people would die he was determined to succeed.

Sarah reached across and caressed his handsome face with her fingers. She swept back his short cropped hair and it immediately sprang back to its original style. Tan had met Sarah at an animal rights rally in Harrogate about 10 months ago. She was alone and vulnerable and Tan had worked his spell on her. He hated bossy, arrogant women and only ever bothered with subservient types, but they had to be pretty. Sarah filled this requirement with ease. She had a small upturned nose and a well proportioned elegant mouth and crystal clear green eyes that made the onlooker gaze at them incredulously. Sarah was the daughter of a now retired surgeon, and she had qualified as a doctor too. She'd worked in the Casualty Department of the Halifax Royal Infirmary, but couldn't cope with the ceaseless pressures involved when a wrong decision could cost a person's life. She had turned to drugs for release and progressing from amphetamines she was now totally dependant on heroin. Sarah was 26 years old, and she'd completely lost her own identity, left somewhere in the corridors of the hospital. She now became absorbed totally in Tan's ideals and obsessions.

Tan was awakened from his half conscious doze by Richard's screams from the front room. He bounded out of bed still in his underpants and came crashing into the room. A reporter, microphone in hand, stood outside a public house floodlit in the darkness for the benefit of the T.V. cameras, and Tan heard the words, "113 dead so far and who knows how many more. This is David Sebastian for the Ten 'o' clock News, outside the Four Feathers Public House, Pontefract, Yorkshire."

Sarah came into the room rubbing her eyes and Richard shouted excitedly, "Sarah, 113 we've killed, we are now in the terrorist business."

Tan rounded on Richard quick as a flash and grabbed him by his shirt collar.

"Don't you ever use that word again. We are not terrorists, and those people who died are not our enemies. They are martyrs, martyrs in the cause for a better world." Tan's contorted face subsided as he released his grip and pushed the smaller man away.

He placed his arm around Sarah's shoulders and said, "What does it feel like to be part of history? Without you we couldn't have done it." He kissed her gently on the forehead before leading her back up the stairs.

It had been Sarah who had stolen the ricin, the poison

used to contaminate the beer. The television programme 'World in Action' had given Tan the idea. The programme investigated the death of Georgi Markov, a Hungarian defector to Britain, who'd worked for the B.B.C., broadcasting propaganda to his native country. Markov was killed supposedly by the KGB. His leg had been impregnated by a small capsule, a quarter of the size of a pin head, injected from the tip of an umbrella. Contained in the capsule was a poison, ricin. Ricin is an extraction of caster oil plants, a deadly poison, one thousand times more powerful that cyanide. One drop of ricin would be enough to kill over 500 people. There is no antidote. The symptoms are not dissimilar to the 'flu' virus, sweating followed by vomiting and then death. The time lapse between administering the poison and death depends on the dosage. It took Markov two days to die. This had been the weapon Tan had been searching for and he spent weeks researching the poison's whereabouts and accessibility. He found the poison could not be obtained anywhere. It was only kept by the government for purely research work, and then only in small quantities, again confirming to Tan the caution and esteem in which the poison was held. A few weeks after the Markov programme World in Action followed up with a sequel in which they interviewed a Professor Willis who was doing research for the Home Office on the poison. Tan noted the place where the Professor worked, The Department of Forensic Science, situated in the University of Leeds. This alone had brought them to the area.

Tan had sought out Sarah deliberately for the task of obtaining a job as a research assistant. Her qualifications easily found her working in the same section as Professor Willis. The Professor, thinking Sarah was interested in his work, took her into his confidence and they soon became friends. The Professor, an expert in forensic medicine, was in constant demand in other aspects of research and as soon as he had broken off his tests with the ricin, Sarah swapped the ingredients of the small bottle of ricin with distilled water. Although the poison had been kept in a safe, she had no trouble taking the keys from his jacket pocket while he removed his blood splattered overalls after dissecting one of the many cadavers used in his research. Tan was dismayed at the small quantity.

"Probably only enough to fill an eggcup," he'd moaned. Sarah had left the department suddenly as instructed by Tan using the excuse that she'd been offered a job in Africa treating the starving in the Sudan. He knew it would only be a matter of days before the poison was missed.

Tan lay on the bed with the half-naked Sarah draped over his hairy chest. He lay silently smiling to himself in the darkness. "At last, he thought, it's begun."

The scene outside the Four Feathers was pandemonium. The police had set up a mobile portakabin in the car park and several high-ranking police officers sat inside co-ordinating the operation. It hadn't taken long for them to work out the connection between the two dead draymen and the pub, although they didn't know yet what or who had caused their deaths. They only had one thing to go on. All the people who had died had visited the pub in the last two days and after questioning Brenda Smith they'd found that the draymen had eaten nothing at the pub and had only drunk two pints of bitter. Teams of detectives were questioning relatives of the dead, itemising their eating and drinking habits. It wasn't until daybreak the following morning that all the information collected had been fed into a computer.

A tall smartly dressed young man stood inside the doorway of the mobile headquarters trying to look inconspicuous. Other detectives mingled and were busying themselves in their allotted tasks. A large portly man with a red face saw the young man standing by the doorway and studied him for a moment before pushing his way through the cramped room. He came and stood in front of the young man.

"Who the bloody hell are you?" he barked menacingly. The younger man recognised the intimidating frame of Detective Chief Superintendent George Redburn who was heading the inquiry team. He swallowed hard.

"Er, Galbraith, Sir, Detective Sergeant Special Branch." The CSI smirked. "Who sent you out here, that old bloody woman, Forrest, eh."

'Yes, Sir. I'm to offer my services only if requested, sir."

The CSI glared hard at the young Detective. The smell of whisky wafted into the younger man's face as the CSI leaned nearer. "When I need your lot on this I'll bloody well request it, now piss off."

Galbraith nodded and was glad he was near the door as the raised voice of the CSI had attracted the attention of the other officers who watched in silence as Galbraith sidled quietly out of the door. He knew he shouldn't have been there until requested but he'd found out enough of what had happened or at least as much as the CSI and his team knew. His normal duties on the small Special Branch team based in Leeds were guarding important people such as politicians, etc., when visiting the city. Intelligence gathering from subversive groups; The National Front, the Communists factions at the nearby university and any form of terrorist threat that arose. This was the subject on which he had spent long weeks in a special training centre in London. He knew of nearly every terrorist faction from the Red Brigade to the Shi-ite Muslims, Black September, the IRA, the INLA, the Christian Falangists, the Basque Separatists, Bader Mienoff. His research had been endless and the course gruelling but he felt he had learnt what makes each outfit 'tick', which was the underlying reason for the course. Know thy terrorist. The nearest he had come to any such group was when he infiltrated a gang of soccer hooligans who went under the name of the Wrecking Crew and hung out on the terraces of Leeds United Football Stadium. Through his endeavors, where he even had to prove himself by bashing in a few heads of the opposing soccer teams' supporters, he had seen thirty or so vicious thugs safely behind bars.

He came out into the cold morning air. Camera crews and reporters hung about the cordoned off section, desperate for any scraps of the latest news. The young detective smiled as one of the reporters asked him hopefully if there had been any developments. He just waved his hand as he strolled quickly to the white car parked down the road. He climbed into it and set off down the road towards the M62.

Without paying much attention to where he was heading, the Detective Seargeant found himself on Hunslet Road cruising past the huge gateway of Bottomley's Beers. He was amazed to see not a squad car in sight and with a screech of brakes he did a complete 'u' turn and drove into the cobbled stone yard. A great Victorian clock hanging from a large red bricked five storey building, overlooked the brewery as Galbraith noted the time. 7.35 a.m. He was surprised to see a forklift truck loading one of the draywagons. A middle-aged man stood holding a clipboard supervising the work. Galbraith walked briskly up to him and flashed his warrant card identifying himself.

"Surely not more questions?" grumbled the man. Galbraith looked agitated.

"You're not still delivering beer after what's happened."

"Why not, nobody's told us to stop."

Galbraith's tone became angry. "Good God, man, hasn't anyone told you what's going on? Half your beer could be contaminated or poisoned for all we know and you're still transporting it around the countryside."

"Look, I only do what I'm told," replied the man. Galbraith noticed he was becoming agitated.

"Well stop all distributions now."

The man glared at Galbraith for a moment, his simple mind still absorbing what had been said.

"They tested the beer at the processing plant two days ago when Bert and Joe croaked it."

Galbraith realised the man only needed instructing like most prosaic button pressers. "I'm ordering you now to stop any movement of barrels from this yard. Do you savy?"

He glared hard and coldly at the older man, his eyes wide and unblinking.

"What about lorries that have already gone?"

"Call them back, radio them, telephone the drop site, but stop them now!"

"Very well," said the man as he set off running round the yard shouting at various people waving his arms every time he came near a lorry.

Galbraith walked fifty yards across the yard to where the fork lift truck driver sat on his machine smoking a cigarette. "Hello," he said in a warm relaxed tone. The man just nodded.

"I'm a policeman, could you tell me where the lorry of the two dead draymen was parked on the morning of the last trip?"

The forklift driver pointed to a spot near to a large pile of empty kegs stacked against the perimeter wall, at various levels some nearly as high as the thirty foot wall that enclosed the yard. "So Bert's lorry was parked nearest the wall." Galbraith walked over to the spot looking up at the barrels. He took off his jacket and handed it to the bemused man asking him to hold it for him. He shinned up the first row and leapt up barrel by barrel until he was on top of the wall standing on the fourth row of empty kegs. Looking down the other side he saw a small office building with a flat felt roof built into the wall. David lowered himself onto the flat roof, some eight feet below and then down a drainpipe and he was on the pavement. One or two people walking by gave him a peculiar stare. At the bottom of the drainpipe on the stone flagged pavement lay bits of the cement pointing which had been knocked out of the wall by someone climbing up the way he had just come down.

He then climbed back up the drainpipe onto the roof and pulled himself up over the wall and back onto the barrels. He inspected the top of the kegs carefully for any feet marks and found the toe marks of what looked like a training shoe on one of the barrels nearest the wall. He climbed back down and took back his jacket.

"Thanks," he said dusting off his trousers. He thought for a moment. "How many people work here?"

"Near on two thousand all told'.

"Is there any history of this company being threatened, or someone who's left with a grudge?"

"Don't know, not that I can recall. Good firm Bottomley's. Pay's good, nobody hardly leaves. You can get a free drink at any time of day, as much as you want, stops pilfering you see. Most men that work here take a drink."

David replaced his jacket. He strolled over to his car and unhooked the portable telephone and began to dial his office. As the ringing tone sounded he looked around the yard again and a shudder suddenly engulfed him as he wondered if he was stepping well out of line. The absence of any form of enquiry team or even the odd reporter at the brewery niggled at his brain. A click followed by a soft, woman's voice entered the earpiece. He recognised it immediately.

"Barbara, listen it's David." His voice was eager and impatient. "Ring the Poisons Unit at Guy's Hospital. I want a list of poisons that are tasteless, especially when diluted in large amounts of liquid, and ones that produce symptoms of say, shivering and sweating." He paused to think for a moment. "Oh, and the killing time is say between one and two days."

"You want this straight away?"

"I'll ring back in half an hour." David hung up and returned to his car. He fired the engine and throttled hard on the pedal. The sweet noise of the Ford XR2 engine subsided and he drove slowly towards the gate. He turned down the cobbled street and onto Hunslet Road. Across the dual carriageway a convoy of police cars and vans passed on the other side, and he watched in his mirror as the convoy turned left in the direction of the brewery. He was relieved. He knew he was one jump ahead of the official enquiry team. He had a strange feeling in the pit of his stomach, a feeling he had not had since, as a young constable of 19, he had sat-in on a routine interview at Clarks Engineering Works in Shipley, near Bradford. He'd watched a dark haired man with a black beard being asked about his whereabouts on the night a young woman had been savagely murdered. A screwdriver had pierced her eye before entering her brain. She'd been bitten on her breast by a man with a gap in his teeth. The murderer wore a size 7 shoe. He worked in engineering and drove a lorry. The man with the black beard fitted all these requirements. His name was Peter Sutcliffe. He'd killed thirteen women before his reign of terror was over. David had reported to his superiors at the time that this was the man, but for some reason he was rebuffed. He was told by an aide of George Oldfield who had led the hunt that he couldn't be the man because he didn't have a Wearside accent. From that day David's opinion of most of the senior detectives was one of overweight, senile alcoholics, who spent most of the day drunk. He later found all his assumptions to be correct.

As he drove, his mouth tasted bitter as all the frustrations of that time came flooding back as if it was yesterday. He knew he'd only been sent to Pontefract to the Four Feathers to spy for his superiors. He had not been seconded to the case at all. The police force was riddled with men of conflicting ideals. This in turn created mistrust and petty jealousies amongst officers, where clashes of egos and back stabbing was commonplace. He opened a packet of mints and sucked on one, refreshing his mouth and cleansing his breath as he'd not been able to clean his teeth that morning. Twenty minutes later found him parking his car in the car park behind the Forensic Science building in the vast complex of St. James's Hospital at Burmantofts. He strolled through the glass plate door and nodded at a porter he'd seen on many previous visits to this building, for this was where most murders were solved. This was where victims were dissected piece by piece and where implements and thousands of other items connected with serious crimes were examined with intimate care and dexterity. He walked into one of the four large laboratories as if walking into his own office. A large fat man with receding grey hair stood at a bench, a half-smoked cigarette hanging from the corner of his mouth, the long trail of ash about to drop, David caught it in his hand.

"Paddy, me old son," he said in greeting.

"Hello, Chief Inspector, or have you been demoted to Constable," replied Paddy, a smile on his face, recognising the DS and continuing the constant banter they always had whenever they met.

"Only one way for me, Paddy, that's upwards." He peered into a large plastic bucket where several human organs were floating in formulin.

"Naughty, naughty, shouldn't go peeping into Prof's lunch box," said Paddy extinguishing the cigarette.

"Where is the old boy anyway?"

"He's across at Pontefract doing that pub job, thought you'd be in on that one."

"I am, sort of unofficial, will be official soon as all the media disappear and the Chief Constable and all his blue-eyed crawlies go back into the cupboard." Galbraith smiled and walked over to a telephone on the table.

"Can I use this?" he asked, the receiver already in his

hand. Paddy nodded. He dialled his office. The woman's voice said, "Yes."

"Ah, Barbara," he said to the policewoman on the other end of the line. "Did you get what I asked for?" A short silence before she replied.

"No, sir. I've traced a toxicologist from Guys, a Dr. Berson in Middlesex but I've not rung him yet. He's probably still in bed."

"Well do it now, Constable Dawkins." He slammed the 'phone down with a crash. Paddy turned distracted from his work.

"Now, now, petulance, dear boy." David walked up and sat on a high swivel chair next to Paddy.

"Tell me, Paddy, you've worked with the Prof for years now. What do you know about poisons?"

"Someone poisoned the beer eh?" replied Paddy.

"Looks that way." David popped a mint into his mouth and offered one to Paddy who declined. "What would you use Paddy?"

Paddy studied for a moment. "Obviously, it's not got to taste too badly or have a peculiar smell if it's to be palatable. That rules out strychnine and cyanide. Perhaps also the parts per ratio of liquid that it was to be added to would rule out rat poisons, weed killers. What are the symptoms?"

"Flu, sweating but no evidence of vomiting," replied David. Paddy studied again.

"What about a virus, it's not forced to be a poison."

"No, no, retorted David. "It's got to be poison. The whole batch of beer had been brewed at the same time, it would all have been contaminated, not just the one barrel. Besides, they do stringent tests on the finished product. You should see the lab they've got, and the technicians, must be sixty of them. No, it was something poured into one barrel."

Paddy's brain fired again testing David's intellect. "What about the barrel, could the virus be in the barrel casing itself?"

"All barrels are sterilised before they're filled." David yawned, not through boredom but through lack of sleep, but he was enjoying himself. Paddy, although only paid and classed as a research technician was a dedicated and intelligent scientist. Patrick O'Connel was in his late fifties. He was a single man, his zest for knowledge in his chosen field was his life. David knew he was the only man who could or would answer his questions.

"Maybe they missed one," replied Paddy smiling. He pondered for a moment. "Think you're right, Chief Inspector, it's more likely to be a poison than not."

"Well what the fuck is it?" demanded David knowing he was being toyed with. Paddy smiled and then it faded as if a sudden thought had hit him. David saw the change in his expression and rounded on him quickly.

"What is it Paddy, tell me?" A pretty girl assistant walked into the lab and began to settle down to do some work. David gripped Paddy by his sleeve and led him to a corner of the room out of earshot of the girl. "For God's sake Paddy, there's a fucking nutter out there killing people."

Paddy stared at the intelligent face of David. His eyes were large as they pleaded unerringly without blinking back at him.

"It's not my place to tell you this, you should really see the Prof."

David waited quietly knowing if he spoke Paddy might change his mind.

"This is between you and me, David," said Paddy using his christian name.

"Off the record."

"Agreed." He replied.

"I'm not too sure." He paused for a moment still fighting himself, his scientist's brain, which only dealt in pure logic and facts, still searching for another answer, but there wasn't one. It could only be one thing.

"Ricin, it has to be ricin."

David stared in disbelief. He had read the report on the Markov poisoning a couple of years back. He'd also seen the 'World in Action' reconstruction of the case on T.V. He thought for a moment.

"You've heard of it," said Paddy.

"Yes, of course. Tell me where is this ricin kept?" asked David.

"Outside the Home Office laboratories I don't think anywhere. Prof's been doing some research for the Ministry of

Defence on the stuff." Paddy nodded with his head towards a large Chubb safe in the corner. "It's in there." Both men stared at the safe silently for a few moments until David turned to face Paddy.

"You sure?"

"We'll soon find out," replied Paddy as he marched off towards the safe, delving into his pocket for a bunch of keys. He stood in front of the safe and unhooked a long key with no apparent end on it. He hooked a small piece of metal which was the key end and secured in into the shaft. He placed the combined key and shaft into the safe, turned it and then turned the large handle withdrawing the bolts allowing the door to open. David stared at the rows of bottles inside. His eyes scanned back and forth as he recognised several labels from his drug squad days until Paddy blocked his view by withdrawing a small black plastic box with the word 'Poison' in white letters, stamped clearly across the lid.

Paddy placed the box carefully onto the lab bench and he pulled on a pair of surgical rubber gloves before he opened the lid. Packed neatly into a hole in the middle was a small bottle. Paddy eased the bottle gently out of its resting place in the shatterproof box.

His face turned pale as he muttered to himself, "Oh my God."

David stared at the clear liquid, but he knew something was wrong by the scientist's face.

"That's not it, is it Paddy?" Paddy shook his head.

"No, that's not unless it's done a complete chemical change from white to clear." Paddy unscrewed the lid and tore a strip of litmus paper from a card. He tested the liquid with the paper.

"Water," he said. He dropped the litmus completely into the bottle and secured the lid back on. He knew even though the ricin had gone, the minute drops left in the bottle and on the litmus paper would be enough to kill a hundred men.

"Who has the keys to the safe?" asked David.

"Only me and the Prof. Mine never leaves my person."

"Who's been working here lately, any newcomers? Anyone just left?" David's brain working ahead of himself.

Paddy's brain was just as quick, "Sarah Harrison, it's got to be."

"Who?" asked David.

"Oh, some fancy tart of a failed doctor, came begging for work, told Prof she wanted to work in tropical medicine, the Prof's pet subject."

"What makes you think it's her?"

"Easy. Prof went grovelling to the administrators for a temporary assistant. He got her a year's contract he'd put in for a grant for her. He's a great scientist is Prof, but when it comes to people and the outside world. I mean there wasn't even a vacancy, she just came in off the street..."

David interrupted, "But why her? She could be genuine:"

"She's gone and done a runner. Said she'd got a job in Africa, and besides that, I've seen her eyeing the safe, once caught her stood looking at it, I mean you've seen one safe you've seen the lot:"

David grabbed the 'phone and looked down the wall chart till he came to Admin. No. 14. He dialled the number.

"This is Detective Sergeant Galbraith from the Special Branch. I need the address of Sarah Harrison who formally worked in forensic science." A few seconds elapsed until a woman's voice broke the silence, "16 Bexley View, Leeds 6." Paddy stood rambling as David slammed down the receiver.

"I mean we're not even a research lab, why come here to research tropical medicine?"

"Thanks Paddy: I owe you one," shouted David as he raced out through the doors leaving them swinging. He climbed into the car and reached for his A to Z street map. He quickly located the street on the map. He crashed the car into first and sped through the complex and out onto the main road. Bexley View was less than half a mile away and he was there in under two minutes. He pulled up at the end of the street and looked down the scruffy run down red brick terrace. He turned the key in the boot of his Ford allowing the lid to fly open. Lifting the flap covering the spare wheel he reached under and lifted a dirty rag from within. He quickly unrolled the rag to reveal a brand new Smith & Weston 45. Checking to see he was unobserved, he placed the gun behind his belt at the back of his trousers. He closed the boot and set off down the street. Number 16 had been converted into bedsits and he scanned the list of names against each bell. The name he sought was not there. He paused and thought for a moment. He realised he should have radioed for a back-up team, but he knew the place would be empty even if she had actually lived here. He had a feeling something special, something big was happening. These was no random killings but carefully planned and executed. A twinge of excitement flinched in his stomach, as he realised that he was working on the biggest mass murder ever in modern history.

The door suddenly opened and a large black guy stood there looking at David.

"What can I do for you man?" asked the guy in a broad Caribbean accent. "You want a room?"

David smiled, "No, man, I'm looking for my sister. She works at the hospital down the road, they gave me this address."

"What's her name?"

David obliged.

"No man, she ain't here, she pays a month's rent in advance and I never see her again."

David held out a five pound note. "Could I see her room?" The guy grabbed the fiver and it disappeared quickly into his pocket.

"Sure man, but there's nothing there"

David was shown room No 7. The man was right. Just a bed, a cooker and a chest of battered old drawers with nothing inside. No blankets or bedding, nothing to indicate that anyone had been staying there. Just a smell of damp and mould in the air. David returned to the car and wrapped his gun back in the rag before replacing it discreetly under the spare wheel. He'd never had to use the gun although he'd had plenty of instruction. He'd not cared for the weapon but he knew he'd use it if and when necessary. He checked his watch, 11.05. The adrenalin still flowed as he drove back into the city centre. He knew he must share his findings immediately with his superior and the thought depressed him. He liked his solitary role of operating. Most of the men he had worked with before were not as conscientious as him and on many occasions he had found himself sitting alone outside some late night club whilst his colleagues drank the night away. David hardly drank nor smoked, but he did like to grapple between the sheets whenever the occasion presented itself. He had no steady girlfriend, he never found the time. For him his work came first and apart from the odd game of golf which he played off a 7 handicap, his only other pleasure was reading. He'd done the usual round of sports, squash, parachuting, deep sea fishing, but he'd abandoned them eventually. His dislikes were many. He hated students, classing them all as lefties and communists. In fact, he hated anything to do with socialism. How can everyone be the same, he reasoned. All right, take care of the old, the unfortunates and infirm, but the scroungers who just abused the system, gypsies, immigrants, people who came for free handouts, he despised.

He pulled into the rear car park at the police headquarters situated at the south end of the town centre. He set the alarm on the car before entering the modern brick building. He took the lift to the fifth floor and pressed a buzzer on a steel plated locked door in the small hallway. He looked up towards the camera that protected the entrance and smiled. The electric lock release buzzed informing him he could proceed into the rooms beyond. He walked quickly past several doors that ran on both sides of the corridor. A plump WPC saw him go by and chased him down the corridor.

"David, I've got your info," she shouted. He turned and waved.

"Be in soon," he replied. He stopped at a door marked Chief Inspector Forrest. He knocked once and entered. The Chief Inspector was sitting at his desk behind piles of cluttered files. David smiled at the ill fitting toupée that rested like a flattened bird's nest on the man's head. The Inspector's eyes peered at him over a pair of large Roy Orbison type glasses. David was still smiling as he sat down in front of the desk.

"What's the Lone Ranger looking so smug about?" asked the Inspector. "Thought you'd be off home to bed." David's face straightened.

"I've been on the trail of the poisoner, Sir." The Inspector removed his glasses. "Poisoner, so you think it's poison do you? What you got?" David explained his findings.

"The poison came from the forensic science lab. Stolen probably by a Dr. Sarah Harrison. It was poured, or a drop or two was, into a barrel already loaded and waiting to be delivered on the night before the two draymen became ill." David quickly went through his assumptions, clear, clinical and precise.

"You've been busy." The Inspector smiled, pleased with his protégé. He picked up the 'phone and dialed a short number.

"George, where's George Redburn?" he demanded. He listened to a voice for a few seconds. He slammed the 'phone down hard.

"God, who'd put a prick like Redburn in charge of a case like this. He's in transit from Pontefract to the brewery." The Inspector smiled. "That means we've got the drop on them. Good lad Davy boy." The Inspector screamed at the top of his voice, "Briggs, Norris, Reardon, Janice, get in here quick." Doors flew open at the Inspector's request.

"Just one thing," said David as the room began to fill, "the poison stolen is ricin." The Inspector's face stopped smiling, replaced by a worried glance.

"How much?"

"Enough to kill about 5000 people, probably more:"

The Inspector thought quickly for a moment before his glance rounded again on Galbraith.

You 100% sure about the ricin?"

Galbraith returned his glare.

"Stake my career on it."

Forrest pondered for a moment again. His police brain covering all the angles until his mind became ordered.

"Janice," he shouted, "get on to the media at once, release the info about the contamination at Bottomley's advising the public to avoid drinking its products till further notice."

Galbraith breathed a loud sigh of relief. Forrest's eyes rounded on him again.

"If you are wrong about this you're finished young man."

Galbraith smiled back confidently. A slight flush warmed his face, his mouth dried as he tried to swallow, a slight doubt entered his mind. He stood up, walked to the door, "I'm right," he replied without looking back and he left the room.

CHAPTER THREE

Tan rose early the next morning. He turned on the radio and tuned in for the 6.00 a.m. news. The main bulletin was again the deaths in Pontefract. The latest tally was 124 people reported dead and still no information available as to the cause. He smiled to himself as he poured the water from the kettle into the vacuum flask. He screwed the lid on tightly. It was three whole days since he had poisoned the keg. He cursed himself on his lapse and weakness. He'd nearly changed his mind about the woman. Damn it, he'd let her live just because he liked to screw. It wasn't too late though, the first appeal for her whereabouts probably won't come till tomorrow.

Tan walked into the front room. Richard lay on the couch curled up in a sleeping bag. Philip Sellars lay on the floor in front of an unlit gas fire, an old brown rug draped over him in place of a blanket. The air stank of stale beer and the faint smell of cannabis still lingered. Tan shook Richard by the shoulder. He grunted before reluctantly opening one eye.

"Get up," ordered Tan. He kicked the rug. It moved and sat up. Philip sat trying to force saliva back into his dehydrated throat.

"What time is it?" he croaked

"Time to move," replied Tan.

"What about a coffee?" asked Richard pulling his jeans on.

"Drink this on the way." Tan dropped the flask on the couch. "Here's the key and here's the new address. I've drawn a map. I've even noted the door colour for you. There's food and beer in the fridge. I'll be there between six and nine tonight, so be in, okay."

"What about Sarah, is she coming?" asked Richard.

"No She's leaving the country today. I'm taking her up to the airport now." Tan lied.

I'll miss her, nice to have a doctor around. You never know when you've got the clap see,"

"Shut it," ordered Tan cutting Philip off in mid-sentence. He shepherded the two men out to the old Viva parked out the back.

"See you tonight," he said forcing a pleasant smile. He always found it hard to be nice first thing. He watched as they drove away, a cloud of thick blue smoke belching from the exhaust of the ancient van. 'Reptiles,' he thought. Inside the house he tuned in to Radio One for the six thirty news.

"The latest bulletin of the deaths in Pontefract. We now know it was the beer that was responsible. The police have issued a severe warning; on no account must anyone drink Bottomley's Beers of Leeds. I repeat again." Tan turned the radio off. He lifted a pile of magazines from the side of the fireplace and sorted through until he found a copy of Cosmopolitan. He turned to pages 64 and 65 that were glued together to form a large slim envelope. He cut across the corner opening the pages with a pair of scissors and shook out all the white powder onto a waiting saucer. He took the saucer into the kitchen and placed it over a low gas flame. Adding a little water he stirred the liquid into a smooth wet paste. He took the saucer up to the bedroom where Sarah lay sleeping contentedly. He removed the well used syringe from her handbag and sucked up the contents filling it completely. He didn't know whether to wake her or not, but she turned and opened her eyes and smiled at him warmly.

"Hi," she said smiling at him.

"Hi," he replied, "brought your breakfast."

"Thanks, you are good to me."

He gripped her arm and looked for a fresh area to inject the heroin. The skin was pitted and sore through regular use, the tell tale sign of an addict. He nipped an untapped vein with his thumb until it bulged and he inserted the needle slowly watching her face as the euphoria began to rise with every push on the syringe, until finally it was empty. Tan smiled as a whole week's supply, some 1200 milligrams of heroin entered the blood stream for the last time.

"Oh, that's it," she moaned as she kicked back the sheets and lay tantalizingly in front of him with her legs wide apart. "I'm hot," she said, "fuck me." The heroin's power of sexual arousal took over and he watched as she began to masturbate, moaning and groaning until she screamed in climax. The act aroused him and he lowered his trousers and entered her. She writhed and struggled under him and the thought of her imminent death aroused him more and more and he ejaculated almost at once. She struggled out from underneath him as he lay panting on the bed.

"I don't like you any more," she said, "You're cold as an old flat fish. Your breath smells and you can't even fuck." She began dancing round the room singing and then she threw herself onto the floor and began masturbating vigorously again. Her teeth bared and her once lovely face became contorted and twisted as her fingers moved back and forth in her drug-induced frenzy and then she screamed again. Froth began to appear in the corners of her mouth. She stood up and staggered around the bed, where Tan sat fascinated with the spectacle. She stood still for a moment shaking slightly. A smile spread across her face. Tan noticed a trickle of water on the floor and then he realised she was urinating onto the side of her leg and it ran, unseen on the inside of her thigh to join the puddle on the bare floor. She dropped onto the floor and began to convulse as her muscles began to contract. She writhed about, her eyes wide and glazed staring at something only she could see. She began to thrash wildly kicking her legs and flaying her arms, covered in her own urine, and then with a suddenness which surprised him, she became rigid and still, her eyes wide and staring upwards. A trickle of blood ran down her lip from the inside of her nostril and into her mouth. Tan sat watching her, expecting her to jump up again any minute until, after a few minutes he moved nearer to where she lay and he saw she was dead.

He stood looking down at her, his heart was still thumping hard against his chest and he smiled. He felt no remorse. He checked his watch, 7.10. His brain calculated it had taken less that fifteen minutes for her to die. He carried the naked corpse downstairs and dragged the stinking filthy carpet from its resting place in the front room. He wrapped it round her and secured the roll with the television aerial wire. He brought in three strong plastic sacks from the transit van out back. He placed a bag on each end of the roll of carpet, then he split the third one and wrapped it round the middle. He fastened them together with two inch wide sticky tape and stood back admiring the neatness of his handywork. He taped an address on the side of the bundle and lifted it out through the back kitchen door and propped it against the wall of the house. He returned to the transit and lifted three foam filled fire extinguishers from the rear and carried them back into the house. He carried one up the stairs and proceeded to squirt the foam all over the bathroom covering the walls, the doors, all the fixtures, glasses and cups. He did the same in the downstairs rooms, in the hallway, down the staircase, even onto the walls until the whole inside of the building looked as through a snow storm had occurred. The only room he left untouched was the bedroom. Only he and Sarah had used that room. The last room he sprayed with foam was the kitchen and he used a whole extinguisher on that until the foam reached almost three feet from the floor. He closed and locked the door behind him checking he had picked up the large envelope from the kitchen drawer. He placed a five pound note in a copy of the Weekend Magazine and placed it behind the carpet, with a stone resting on it to stop it blowing away. He climbed into the rusting van and glanced over at the motor cycles roped against its side. The van fired after two attempts and he set off down the bumpy back street and joined the road at the bottom.

A mile further on, he brought the transit to a stop beside a telephone box. He glanced at a number from the local advertising paper before dialing. A rough sleepy voice answered.

"Hello."

"Is that Dan's removals?" asked Tan. "Odd items removed for £5?"

"Yes."

"I want a carpet delivered, only a couple of miles. I won't be in as I'm off to work but I've left the money." He told him the details. "Okay." Tan gave him the address of the house and told him the delivery address was taped to the carpet.

"Oh, and another thing, I've packed some household gear inside and some clothes, so it may be a little heavy."

"All right, ten 'o' clockish it'll be though," replied the sleepy voice.

".Just right, thank you. I'll use you again." Tan hung up and smiled as he tried to imagine the faces when they opened the parcel.

Tan looked at his watch. It was 8.10. He checked the large brown envelope and headed off in the direction of the ring road. He made the York Road by 8.30 as the traffic began to ease, and by 8.50 he came to a stop in the centre of Tadcaster. Tan parked the van down a side-street and walked briskly alongside the huge Victorian stone wall. He passed a large gateway that people were entering, about to start their day's work. He stopped and stared at the small brass plaque above the letter box and he read the wording slowly to himself, 'Samuel Braithwaite and Sons, Tadcaster'. He lowered the letter quickly through the well polished brass flap as he checked no-one had been watching him, not that it mattered. He walked across the road and stood where he could see both the door and the entrance to the car park. Several cars entered until finally the bright red Silver Spirit Rolls Royce purred almost silently up the slight gradient and into the car park. Tan smiled to himself, pleased he'd not picked a day when the driver of the Rolls would be playing golf or taking his mistress off on a jaunt in his helicopter. All the waiting and watching over the last few weeks have been worthwhile. He thought, "I hope you have had a hearty breakfast, Braithwaite, you'll need something in your stomach."

Robin Braithwaite had just finished strolling through the grounds of Bradbury Hall surveying his domain as he always did before setting off to work. He'd wanted to see the head gardener especially that morning for he'd had a row with his mistress and wanted a bunch of freshly cut flowers placed discreetly in the boot of the Rolls. The sun was coming up over the roof of the east wing of the magnificent sixteenth century mansion. The wing was an extension built by his great grandfather 180 years ago just as Nelson had triumphed in the Battle of Trafalgar against the Spaniards. As a tribute to the great admiral who had been killed in action, he had christened the extension the Lord Nelson wing. Robin hated it and he had been threatening to have the building pulled down for some time and to build a squash court instead. He walked through the main doorway into the large hall just as his pretty young wife came out from the dining room dressed in jodhpurs and expensive leather riding boots. She approached him and kissed him on the cheek.

"Have a nice day darling," she said as she breezed past the way he'd just come, to go for her morning ride. He turned and stared at her elegant figure watching her smooth behind moving with a sensual swagger until she'd gone. He felt a slight guilt for he had not made love to her for many months, he didn't know why but she just didn't stimulate him sexually any more. He remembered the time when they had first met six years ago when he couldn't keep his hands off her for five minutes, and a twinge of sadness cast a shadow in his mind. Then he cheered as he thought of the two sons she had borne him, a son and heir. A son to carry on the title of Earl of Bradbury, the seventh Braithwaite to do so. The chauffeur announced his arrival by tooting the horn of the rolls. This in turn signalled the butler who appeared as if by magic brandishing a brief case and a black Crombie overcoat.

"Thank you Rodney, but I'll drive myself today," he said, knowing he was to visit his mistress on his way to work. He stopped off as planned and made his peace with the pretty secretary, Susan Marchant, the recent mistress of a long line. He made love to her selfishly satisfying himself only and promising to see her that night before he left to continue his journey to the brewery. She was glad when he had left.

Robin Braithwaite's office was more like an expensive suite at the Savoy. Apart from the great 18th century mahogany desk there was none of the usual office paraphernalia. Before starting work he exercised in the small gym he had added a year ago, mainly for the use of other brewery executives. It was seldom used. He showered quickly following his usual twenty minute stint, after hardly breaking sweat. By 9.30 he was behind his desk checking his morning mail. His normal mail consisted of business correspondence and the regular blind sale letters addressed to an unknown managing director. Mrs. Soomes, his secretary, sifted these from his normal correspondence but this morning a large brown envelope marked 'Strictly Personal and Urgent' on the front caught her eye. It was hand written in neat scrip and acting on the instructions written on the envelope she placed it to the top of the pile.

Robin Braithwaite slipped the gold plated letter opener under the flap of the envelope and removed a large piece of common note pad paper. He began to read.

"Dear Lord Bradbury,

This letter is a ransom demand for the sum of £100,000. Three days ago our organisation poisoned Bottomley's Brewery in Leeds with a small portion of ricin. Ricin is one of the most deadly poisons known to man. There is no antidote. Your brewery is our next target. You will not be able to Stop us. We only need to penetrate one barrel inside the brewery, or for that matter in any one of your many hostelries. I repeat, you cannot stop us. Unless, that is, you agree to our demands.

We think our fee is very modest considering one drop of ricin would completely destroy your whole operation. Just look at Bottomley's, they were selected at random to demonstrate our cause and to prove we care not who we kill, but who will ever drink their beer again.

To prove we are the genuine poisoners of Bottomley's we have deliberately mentioned the poison used. At this stage the police don't know yet, but I'm sure they will before the day is out. Also in case you are in any doubt about our threat we have also executed one of our own people. Her name was Dr. Sarah Harrison, and her body has been delivered to the police by us as another gesture of our intent. If you watch the news bulletins throughout the day all this prior information will be substantiated. You have only until eleven o'clock this morning to make up your mind. When you agree to our demand fly the brewery flag upside down. You must have the money in small notes, no higher than ten pounds, before six o'clock tonight. We will telephone at one minute past six with instructions for the delivery.

If the flag is not flown by eleven o'clock the process to eliminate Braithwaite's Beers for ever will have begun. If you failed to read this letter by that time, we are sorry but your company will serve as a warning to other breweries by its demise.

However, if everything goes according to plan and we receive your generous donation you can rest assured we will not bother or threaten you ever again. Our aim is political and we need funds to finance our enterprise. If you inform the police in any way before you've delivered the money, (afterwards we don't mind) consider the end of your multimillion pound empire.

We will not tolerate any excuses. Your first excuse is your last." The note was unsigned. Robin swallowed a mouthful of saliva lubricating the dryness of his throat. Beads of sweat rested on his brow and he read the letter again and again. He examined the paper on both sides and studied the envelope as if trying to find a clue or a sign of the sender. His first reaction was to believe it was a practical joke but the more times he read and absorbed it, he began to realise it was for real. He opened the antique globe drinks cabinet and lifted a bottle of brandy from inside the southern hemisphere. He poured himself a double. His immediate instinct was to 'phone the police but his intelligent reasoning of the contents of the letter dissuaded him from this course. He sat in a leather high backed Chesterfield sipping the neat spirit, his mind going back to his first thoughts when he'd heard of the disaster at the Four Feathers. He assumed it was something straightforward, a mystery virus or somebody with a grudge against the landlord. But this, mass murder. A shudder ran down his spine as he checked his watch and waited a couple of minutes before turning on the radio for the ten o'clock news.

"Latest reports on the incident at Pontefract now indicate the cause of the deaths was something in the beer. At this moment a team of forensic experts are trying to isolate whatever caused this tragic loss of life. The police are also warning all landlords and managers who sell Bottomley's Beers to restrict sales to bottled beers only. Also the police would like to trace a woman named as Dr. Sarah Harrison. We will keep you informed of any updates on the crisis when....'

He turned off the switch and picked up the 'phone. A shudder ran up his spine!

"Get me the chief accountant. Jenkins, get up here at once." He sat staring at the door until a knock came and in walked a tall thin man of fifty, his head tilted to one side through years of eyeing figures, a regulation polite smile stitched upon his lips, used only when in the presence of superiors. He was about to speak but he only opened his mouth before his benefactor started to speak.

"Jenkins, I want one hundred thousand pounds in small bills up to £10 here in my office by 5.30 latest. Here's a company cheque." He signed one of the numerous cheques in a large pad and tore it free. He smiled at the bemused Jenkins.

"Don't document it, I'll pay it back to the company funds by the weekend." Jenkins stared at the cheque. "Now get on with it man, I need that money today. "Jenkins walked over to the door. As he was part way through his Lordship called out, "If you have any problems raising it I want to know at once. Understood."

"Yes, Sir," he replied as he left the room.

CHAPTER FOUR

Inspector Alan Forrest finally located the leader of the team investigating the poisoning incident. He was at the brewery conducting his enquiries.

"What is it Alan, I'm up to my neck with people wanting to get in on the act?"

"Well George, one of my boys is way ahead of you and if you've got a minute I'll fill you in," replied the Inspector arrogantly, always pleased to put one over on regional. He gave him the details.

"You sure about all this, what's your boy's name?"

"Course I'm sure, and his name's Galbraith, Detective Sergeant."

"Ah, yes," Redburn remembered his presence in the caravan. "Can I have him?"

"By all means," replied the Inspector inwardly pleased to be involved at last, knowing full well his man would report to him as well.

"Bright boy is he?"

"Top man, you'll see."

"What's the poison called? Ricin you say, and it came from Professor Willis's lab?" asked Redburn. "Hope you're right."

"We're right," replied the Inspector, his eyes thrust up to the ceiling as if asking God for confirmation of David's story. "Galbraith will fill you in properly." He hung up.

The Inspector turned towards the eager group assembled in the small room. He rubbed his hands together and a sly smile spread across his face.

"We're in," he said pleased with himself. "David, you get down and report to George at the brewery, but insist on working alone. You must have a free hand, I'll back you up." David stood making the chair legs screech as he pushed away. "Oh, and report here first, there's a good boy." David nodded and left the room. The Inspector turned to face the rest of his team.

"Janice, track down all previous addresses of one Dr Sarah Harrison including parents. Briggs, Norris, get back up to the forensic science lab and interrogate anyone who knew her, where she boozed, who her friends were, you know the scene. Reardon, get up to this address, 16 Bexley View, and take it apart. There may be something, don't forget to quiz the landlord." He leaned back in his chair and lit a cigarette, his mind delving to see if he'd missed anything. "Oh, and if Redburn turns up, just disappear discreetly."

It took David ten minutes to get down to the brewery. Chief Inspector Redburn was marching about the yard when David pulled to a stop in his XR2.

"Excuse me, Sir," he said as he stood behind a group of policemen who were dressed in white space suits and were taking samples from every barrel, labelling them as they progressed. George Redburn turned round and eyed David suspiciously. He hated younger men just for that reason.

"Galbraith isn't it?" he said, "tell me your findings." David went through his story. "You're right about this?" David stood expressionless. "What's your next move?"

"That's up to them now, Sir."

"Them, who the fuck's them?" demanded Redburn.

"The perpetrators, Sir." Redburn look puzzled, Galbraith continued. "What's the point of all this? No ransom demand. No motive. No, in my opinion this is just a trial run for something bigger."

Redburn smiled. His reddened face stared at the younger man and he saw confidence that flowed within. "Confident bugger aren't we, eh? Tell me, who or what are these people?"

"Killers, terrorists, extremists, people who think they have a cause, a cause more important than people's lives."

"Nutters you mean," interrupted Redburn. "You certainly put your neck in the noose." David ignored the last remark and continued to answer the previous question.

"If you like, but clever cunning intelligent nutters." George Redburn placed his hand on David's shoulder and gripped it menacingly.

"You piss off now and do your Special Branch stuff but

you keep me informed if you pick anything up. You're on my fucking team now." He gave David a twisted sadistic grin. "Don't go reporting to that old fishmonger boss of yours till you've seen me." He saw the tiredness of the long night in David's face and ordered him home. "Go get some rest, I've got a feeling I'm gonna need you before we've finished with this business." He watched the young detective sergeant climb into the white sports saloon and waved his head from side to side. Bloody spoilt to death. He thought of years gone by when after ten years on the beat you were lucky to get a bicycle to help you along your patch.

Tan was sitting in a café in the centre of the small town reading reports of his actions in several of the daily papers. His eyes kept a watch on the flag that carried the Braithwaite crest. He could just see it over the roof tops as it fluttered above the building in the warm summer air. He checked his watch. It read 10.30 and the flag had not been reversed. As he watched the green and gold emblem flutter and whip in the breeze it reminded him of the green flag with a white dove that was the emblem of his beloved Greenpeace. 'If only they'd been more aggressive,' he thought. The support both spiritually and financially they had throughout the world was immense. With Greenpeace he had learnt many things; how to organise and plan a campaign. He had enjoyed that side of the work, but when it came to the actual operation the result was nearly always the same, failure. Whether trying to stop the dumping of nuclear waste into the sea, or harassing Russian whaling ships, they'd never succeeded. They only delayed the inevitable. Tan was aboard the Greenpeace ship Rainbow Warrior when it was blown up with two limpit mines in Aukland harbour, New Zealand, killing a photographer who had gone below after the first explosion by the French Secret Service in 1985, only to be killed by a second. This is what had changed him so dramatically. His pent up aggression had finally been released at the same time as the explosion. All they had been trying to do was to draw people's attention to what governments were doing to the earth, destroying the very environment that we all need to survive. He was only slightly bruised in the bomb blast, but he became more mentally scarred when it was proved the French government were behind the bombings. He couldn't understand how a powerful, civilised European government could be upset by a small ship threatening to sail into waters where they were going to test a nuclear device. He couldn't reason why governments could enter another country and kill anyone they felt like, for this is what they had done. If governments could do it why couldn't he?. A president of a country was only one man, a man who if he so wanted could order the destruction of the whole planet. The only difference, Tan thought, between himself and a president was that the president got someone else to do his dirty work, whereas he himself was both president and executioner. A one man country at war with another, a war he could not win. How he hated the French government for what they'd done. He would have his revenge.

His thoughts were interrupted by a waitress who clanked the empty cups as she collected them from the table. He turned to check the flag once more and he smiled to himself as he saw it was flying upside down. He quickly returned to the transit van and left Tadcaster driving the 20 miles to the outskirts of Bradford. A large city of 299,000 people. He pulled to a stop on the side of a main road where to his left a large forest ran some three miles up onto the overlooking hillside.

For most of that afternoon Tan checked and rechecked the designated area where the money was to be paid. There was no doubt in his mind that Braithwaite would pay the £100,000. After all, it wasn't a great deal to a large company who spent that kind of money refurbishing one of their pubs. His main worry was the police. But then he discounted the thought. No, the man would have to be a bloody fool to risk his whole sack of potatoes just for one small one. He was meticulous in his preparations and checked every location carefully until satisfied.

Just before six Tan returned to the van where he switched on the radio to catch an update of the news. Nothing new about the poisoning but at the end of the bulletin the newscaster said, 'The body of a naked woman was delivered, wrapped in a carpet, to Leeds Central Police Station today. Police are still making enquiries, but believe the woman to be one Sarah Harrison who the police have been waiting to question since yesterday.'

Just after six Tan stopped at a 'phone box just off Lumb

Lane in Bradford. He dialled the Tadcaster code and then the number of the brewery. The 'phone rang once then came a click as the receiver lifted, a rich upper class voice answered.

"You alone?" he asked.

"Yes, I'm quite alone. I've told no-one." Good, thought Tan.

"What is the telephone number of the mobile in your Rolls?" Braithwaite gave him the number. "Be in the Rolls at 11.30 tonight and I'll give you instructions where to drop the money. I warn you to listen carefully because I will only give the details once." Tan crashed the 'phone down in triumph. He felt good, nothing could go wrong and he knew the money was as good as his. The money he would need to finance stage 2 of his plan. He climbed back into the van and drove for half a mile before turning left into St. Paul's Street, the heart of Bradford's bedsit land. He saw the old blue Viva parked outside No. 34 and pulled in behind. He'd rented this flat a week ago, another run-down tenement really only fit for the human despondents who colonised these places in their hundreds. People who'd given up their lives either for drink or drugs and would sell you their very soul for the price of a drink or a fix, but he knew he was invisible in their midst.

Tan turned the key and entered the large building, a smell of mould and decay in his nostrils. He walked past several doors until he came to Flat 5. He entered with another key. Richard and Phil were both reading newspapers and they both looked up together, their eyes appealing for a response.

"It's on," said Tan smiling, "we collect tonight."

"Good, then we can leave these dumps behind and move somewhere better," replied Richard screwing his nose up at the smell.

"You eaten?" asked Tan.

"Not since lunchtime," replied Phil always ready to eat. Tan pulled his wallet from the rear of his jeans and counted the contents carefully. There was £45.00 left out of the £4,000 life savings which had gone on financing his scheme.

"Here's a fiver. Go and get us all a Chinese. I'll have the beef curry." Phil took the money and was putting on his coat.

"Get me a sweet and sour pork," said Richard.

"Oh and Phil," said Tan, "go on the motorbike, give it a warm-up for tonight," referring to one of the 2 motor bikes, the

250cc Honda scrambler that was in the back of the Viva van. Tan slumped down in a chair and surveyed the grim surroundings. There was no television or radio in the room. Although Tan had a portable radio in his van he left it behind purposely. He had to break the news of Sarah's death to his two associates. He stared at Richard who carried on reading the paper.

"Sarah's dead," he blurted out. Richard turned in his chair and stared at Tan, a disgusted look on his face.

"You mean you killed her you bastard," he retorted. Tan was surprised at Richard's courage, he'd had him down for an easily led subordinate but he was not now too sure.

"It had to be. She was a threat. The police would track the poison to her in no time. Besides she wouldn't have lasted much longer anyway. What heroin addict does?" Tan appealed to Richard's intelligence. He needed him to help him implement his actions, for Richard had brains. "The cause is too great to allow her to stand in the way. She was dangerous."

"How did you do it?" asked Richard eyeing Tan carefully and wondering if he had any plans for his demise. Tan told him the details and Richard smiled a little at the thought of the police unwrapping the carpet. He returned to reading his paper. Ten minutes later Phil returned with the Chinese meals.

"Bike's okay," he said.,

"Sarah's dead," said Richard hardly giving Phil time to take off his coat.

"Thought as much," replied Phil calmly. "Seen a body's been sent to Leeds Central Police Station this morning. Just caught a glimpse of the northern news on the telly in the Chinese." Tan smiled pleased at Phil's response.

"She had to go, she was a weak link. All main line junkies are fuckin' weak links, you ought to know that Richard," said Phil referring to Richard's previous addiction to heroin.

Tan dished out the meals and they ate in silence. Richard's face told Tan he was still upset at Sarah's death, and he knew he had to straighten it out with him before they left to collect the money.

"Listen Richard," he said as he finished the last of his curry, "we have a cause, a purpose for being alive. I would gladly sacrifice my life if I thought it would change the world's attitude to what these pricks in government are doing to the environment." He paused and lit a cigarette. Richard stared back, the hatred shone from his eyes. Tan continued, "We have a small chance of trying to do something worthwhile. I mean we'll probably all end up dead anyway. What chance do we have, the three of us against the whole fucking country and perhaps the whole world?"

"Up the revolution," shouted, Phil as he threw the remains of his meal down on the table, bits of rice exploding into the air.

Tan sat back in the chair and he could see Richard's expression change a little as he swallowed and tried to smile. Phil leaned across and placed his hand on Richard's knee.

"Look man, the one thing we've got going for us is our anonymity. Once the pigs find out who we are we're finished." Phil lit an old half-smoked splif that had been in his pocket since the previous night. He blew a long line of smoke into the air then sucked a lungful of the relaxing smoke and he offered the stub to Richard.

"Thanks," he said as he sucked on the sweet tasting smoke. "Phil's right," said Tan stubbing out his tab. “We’re already mass murderers anyway. If they catch us they'll throw away the key."

Richard smiled, "You're both right of course, it's just hard to come to terms with, when someone you know dies."
"Man, she died years ago," interrupted Phil. "If it wasn't for Tan here keeping up her supply, she'd have been prostituting herself all over the place." Tan smiled at Phil. He'd had him labelled as the weaker of the two, but Tan's attitude towards him changed to one of respect. He had met the two of them at the same time at the Edinburgh Festival last year, and as Tan was on the lookout for helpers in his mission they agreed to join him, if only to help him spend his life savings. But Tan had won them over to his cause in the months they'd spent planning their campaign of terror. Had he not doubted their sincerity to his cause at any time he would not have hesitated in killing them.

The 'phone rang waking Galbraith from a deep sleep. He checked his watch. It was 6.10 p.m. He lifted the receiver to hear Inspector Forrest's voice.

"Had a good sleep?"

"Yes," replied David his throat dry and still only half conscious.

"Got some news. We've found the girl, she's dead, dumped naked by a removal man, paid to deliver a package to Leeds Central Police Station." Forrest went on to fill in the details. “We've got an address of where she was collected, forensic are up there now giving it the works." David noted the address.

"I'll be in the office in an hour," replied David, "I'll just take a peek at where the body was found."

David pulled up outside the terraced house amidst several other police vehicles. He pushed his way through a small gathering of spectators and climbed the three steps that led to the front door. Inside the long corridor stood George Redburn ankle deep in foam and he smiled as he saw David approach.

"Ah wonder boy," he said.

"Anything here?" asked David ignoring the jibe and looking puzzled by all the white foam everywhere.

"No, just the one room upstairs left untouched, sprayed the foam everywhere but not in that room. What do you make of that wonder boy";" Redburn lit a fag and waited for Galbraith's reply. David thought for a moment.

"Seems like he's an egotist, wants all the glory for himself or he's protecting his accomplices by destroying all the finger prints with the foam. Bet you that was his bedroom, though."

"Good, good!” agreed Redburn.

"Who rented the house?" asked David. "The gir1?" George nodded again. Redburn was beginning to wonder who was in charge of the case, him or the detective sergeant. But what the hell, he would still get the credit.

“We've got a report of two vehicles, a light blue Viva van “R” registered, and a red transit van, no indication of registration. A witness reports seeing three different men,student types, wore combat jackets, parkas, etc. Two thintypes, one shoulder length hair, one large slim frame, fair hair, blood type B, plenty of finger prints from the bedroom." George held the paper he had been reading aloft anticipating David's next question. "Lab report, the post mortem on the girl. she had a fuck this morning before she died. Semen was present in her vagina. She died of a heroin overdose, probably murdered." George smiled at David, "Well we should have them soon enough now."

"How's that?" retorted David much to his superior's surprise.

"All points bulletin on the vans won't take long to track them down."

"Excuse me, Sir," David said politely knowing he was overstepping the mark. "Don't you think they've let us find this place deliberately. They gave us the body. We've still no information on why they killed all those people. No reason, no motive." David eyed George Redburn, waiting for a response as the man struggled for words. The faint smell of whisky still hung on the CSI'S breath.

"Only police work, still got to carry on with ordinary police work," he said as David looked baffled. "Ordinary police work caught the Ripper laddie. Don't you forget it." Inspector Forrest's words came back to David. 'They've put that prick Redburn on the case.' He had to agree as he stared hard at the chubby round reddened face with raised blue and red veins prominent on the CSI's nose. He reminded David of a circus clown.

CHAPTER FIVE

Tan lifted two bundles from inside the transit. One of the edges of the cloth wrapping snagged against the chain of the Suzuki 500 scrambler that was fastened to the inside of the van. He looked down the quiet street and was pleased with his choice of location. He took the two bundles back into the bedsit and unravelled them on the floor.

"Change into these," he said throwing an oil stained denim jacket and a grubby leather jacket at his two colleagues. Philip held the denim jacket up and read an emblem painted across the back.

'The Devils Serpents. Hells Angels'. All three had the same motif on the back of their jackets.

"Leave all your old clothes here, make sure the pockets are empty," Tan said pulling on an old pair of denim leggings over his jeans.

"Is this all really necessary?" Richard moaned.

"Yes it is, I want them to know what we are, that we are intelligent and not some maniac radical group. When we make our demands they'll know to take us seriously and besides it stops cranks getting in on the action. For instance, I could tell them about the mole on Sarah's bottom or the mileage on the vans, which removal man I used to deliver the body, hundreds of small details that prove we are who we say." Tan pulled on his leather jacket and a pair of mirrored sun glasses. "Anyway this is where we leave the trail cold."

Phil moaned, "God these trousers stink, couldn't you have washed them."

"Hells Angels don't wash their tunics, the more worn and filthy they are proves how long you've been an angel," replied Tan. "Where did you get them?" asked Richard.

"They were my father's." Richard and Phil stared at each other and then burst into fits of laughter. Tan smiled.

"Your father's?" repeated Phil hardly able to keep his face

straight. Tan felt obliged to explain.

"When I was about four he just up and disappeared. No one knew where he'd gone and what had happened to him for twenty-five years. Then a copper came knocking on the door telling my mother he'd been killed in a gang fight with another chapter of angels. My old lady told the copper to get stuffed and slammed the door in his face." Tan went on to explain his mother and father had never married but only lived together, and when he died he'd bequeathed everything to him. "Anyway I went to the police station and they gave me this bag with all his possessions and clothes." Tan pointed at Phil's jacket. "See that hole in the left hand side of the jacket, that's the knife hole that killed him."

Phil wriggled his fingers through a three inch split, the blood stains still clearly visible.

"Did you see the body?" asked Richard.

"Yes, I went to the funeral. There were over 500 other angels there. They paid for it all. Apparently he was a general or something, one of their leaders." Tan thought back to after the funeral when one of the other angels gave him a suitcase full of personal things that the police had not known about. That was where he'd got the gun. Amidst piles of photographs, a few Nazi daggers (which Tan sold for several hundred pounds) and the Luger, complete with several rounds of ammunition. The gun was now hidden under the seat of the Suzuki. Tan made a special compartment with a steel flap across the top. A long bolt secured the lid which had been secured very tightly and only on very close inspection was the compartment visible. They left the room checking they had left nothing but their discarded jackets behind. They climbed into the vans and drove a half mile to an old railway arch which ran over a disused canal, here they unloaded the bikes. Tan was expert on his machine, he'd been a motorbike fanatic for years, but Phil was a relative novice and needed all the practice he could get. But at least, thought Tan, he was past the stalling stage. Both bikes were Tan's, but he'd changed the number plates and ground away the engine block numbers. They donned the crash helmets from inside the vans and Tan made one final check of both vehicles before they mounted the bikes. Richard rode pillion with Phil and the trio set off in a cloud of dust. Tan gave the

Suzuki a surge of gas and lifted the front wheel into the air in the sheer pleasure of being on his beloved machine. The front wheel lifted easily off the ground helped by the weight of the camping equipment fastened to the rear. He rode for over a hundred yards or so on the back wheel until the pathway turned left and they followed it down onto the road. It was ten minutes to eight when they arrived at the edge of the wood. Buck Woods was a large deciduous wood that covered an area of twenty square miles. Most of the wood ran along a steep hillside that overlooked the Aire valley. Tan drove expertly through the trees while Phil struggled on behind. Tan knew the area well. As a schoolboy he had camped many times in the wood, swimming and fishing in the canal that ran alongside the river in the valley below.

Tan stopped the bike at the brow of the hill and climbed onto a rock to survey the valley below. Two miles down the hill the wood stopped against the bank of the Leeds-Liverpool canal. A small swing bridge dissected the canal to the west, and a hundred yards lower down the hillside in the basin of the valley a second bridge, a long thin Victorian steel footbridge about seventy five yards long, and four feet wide hung twenty feet over the River Aire. Across the bridge Tan's eyes followed the well worn footpath up and past a small farm,

with fields on either side. 600 yards from the farm he could see the traffic sprinting along the main Shipley road where the path came to its end. Tan pointed out his plan to his accomplices.

"Richard, your job is to stand on this rock and watch for any lights moving anywhere in the valley. If you see any sign of trouble fire a shot in the air from the Luger. I'll give it to you when the time comes. I'll pick up the money from his Lordship. Phil, you will wait by the swing bridge there." Tan pointed to the bridge. "If anyone follows me up the hill from the river get ready to turn the bridge as soon as I've crossed. It only opens from this side. Then you jump on the bike and we rendezvous back here." Tan knew his plan was foolproof. Even if Braithwaite had informed the police, up until four minutes before the pickup they would not know the location and would not be able to lay a trap.

The sun was lowering towards the top of Baildon Moor on the opposite side of the valley but it would be another hour before it got dark. It was still quite warm and as Tan stood surveying the area, a flight of wood pigeons fluttered past, their wings clapping together sounding like applause as they headed off down the hillside. The trees were in full leaf and they seemed to cover the hillside like a green patterned carpet. One or two people could be seen ambling along the tow path by the side of the canal, and a barge lay anchored for the night a mile from the footbridge towards the town of Shipley. "Its a bloody good post is this," said Richard pleased with his role of pig spotter.

"Yes you should only see the one light come over that footbridge and it will be mine. It's not wide enough for a car so if he's got the police with him they'll need a bike to follow me. It's impossible to cross in the darkness without, but when I've crossed it, I'll turn out the headlight." Tan tapped the light on the front of the scrambler. "Keep your eyes and ears open, sound carries a long way down the valley, you'll hear my bike's engine quite easily." Phil eyed Tan admiringly.

"You've put a lot of work into this haven't you?" he said.

"Yes I planned all this when I was in prison."

"How far do you think we'll get?" asked Richard.

"Who knows. If his Lordship fails to show with the money tonight or if he brings the police," Tan stopped quickly.

Will you kill him if he doesn't pay?"

"Yes, I'll kill him," replied Tan.

"Does it bother you all these deaths?"

Tan grinned back, his eyes mocking in anger. "Did it bother Hitler, Churchill or Stalin?" He lit a cigarette and handed the pack to the two men. He sat on a rock while Richard rested on the bike. Phil lay down chewing a blade of grass, staring upwards into the darkening sky.

"Did you know Stalin had over 3 million of his own soldiers executed?" continued Tan as he took a drag on the cigarette "Everyone dies, some sooner than others, but at least we're trying." He paused for a moment. "It's the trying that matters, do you see, at least we're trying to do something." Tan crashed his fist down on the rock. "If one of those fucking nuclear power stations explodes half the country will be uninhabitable for years to come. Not to mention the fallout that will kill millions. What price cheap electricity then." Tan's eyes glared wildly and anger swept over him. "I mean, they just don't care, look at the beauty of that valley, they're going to build a fucking motorway through that, right between the river and the canal." Tan turned and looked down the valley. "I saw my very first kingfisher down there." A smile spread across his face at the memory. "You won't see one down there anymore, a sewage plant further up the river saw to that. That river's one big sewer that runs sixty miles all the way to the Atlantic ocean." He stubbed out his cigarette and stared at Richard who was picking the bark off a small twig. Tan took a controlled breath to stop him ranting. "Does it bother you?" Richard looked back.

"Yes it bothers me. I wouldn't be here if I wasn't bothered. I've come round to your way of thinking." Tan smiled.

"If we can get publicity for our ideals or maybe get the people interested in our fight, we may have done some good."

"Yeh man: Anthony Heyes for Prime Minister," shouted Phil.

"He could make you Minister of Agriculture and you could grow fields of cannabis plants, and give out free reefers on the National Health," replied Richard. The others laughed at his remark.

The Rolls pulled to a halt outside Bradbury Hall, Robin Braithwaite sat behind the wheel reflecting on the day's events that had left him shattered. He stared straight ahead unaware that the front door of the Hall had opened and the faithful butler emerged and was proceeding towards the Rolls. Braithwaite saw him from the corner of his eye and opened the door of the car. The old butler saw the tired expression on his master's face.

"Everything all right Sir?" Lord Bradbury climbed from the car and stared at the old man.

"What is it, Beavers?" He looked at the man as if he wasn't there.

"You all right, Sir?" repeated the old butler.

His Lordship ignored the butler but stared straight past him and his eyes scanned the ancient building, as if he was taking

stock of its value like some estate agent seeing it for the first time. The family dog, a border collie, came bounding from the half open door and began to make a fuss of his master. The act distracted his Lordship from his preoccupation and he rubbed the dog's head, it was leaping up at him as he entered the Hall. His wife came from the large dining room and kissed
him on the cheek.

"Had a nice day, dear?" she asked before adding "You're a little late tonight." Her manner was without feeling, more business like, a duty of a wife to greet one's husband as he came home from his toils.

He forced a smile in greeting without reply. She passed through the hallway and into the corridor for her nightly sauna. He watched her from behind. Her head wrapped in a towel, turban style and a long designer dressing gown hung loosely from her small shoulders. She glanced back catching his eyes for a moment as she turned to enter the hotroom. She'd smiled at him, an empty cold smile. He recocnised the smile as the same one used by Jenkins, the chief accountant at the brewery, earlier. The same subservient smile used by some of his contemporaries whenever they needed something and had come to grovel. He hated it. In that fleeting glance of only a second before his wife had disappeared he had seen inside her for the very first time. He hated her. He hated this old house. He despised its status and what it stood for. He had lived in its rooms man and boy for 52 years and he hated it. But most of all he hated himself. He hated his existence, his shallow empty existence, the years gone seemed suddenly wasted. He climbed the stairs and entered his bedroom. He placed the briefcase on the bed and slowly lowered himself into the gold velvet cosy chair that stood by the window. His thought now returned to the brewery. The brewery established 218 years ago by the 2nd earl. The well founded and run company, that is, up until now. A company that had run successfully for some two hundred years until he had taken charge on his father's death 12 years ago. Was it only 12 years ago that he had tried to bring the brewery and its hostelries into the 20th century. A programme of modernisation, disco style pubs, flashing lights, plastic panels, loud music. He was warned.

"Rural pubs rely on regular local drinkers, steady reliable people, two or three pints a night people, that's been the foundation stone of Braithwaite's." But he'd argued that it was the time of the car, people would travel to the right type of place, young people with money to spend, young people who didn't care about tomorrow. "Get rid of the tenants, replace them with managers. We'll double the profits overnight" and he borrowed heavily. He indulged himself with expensive chattels, the brand new Rolls, the Ferrari, the helicopter and the yacht in Marbella. The discos had flopped. The bubble had burst. Instead of offloading the public houses to private buyers as advised to recover capital, he had tried to reverse the damage he had wreaked and return the pubs to their original state. This had cost more money. The company had debts of over £75 million and assets of only £30 million. Braithwaite's Beers established 1758 were on the verge of bankruptcy. He had been working on several schemes to re-liquidate the company, until today that is. The letter. The threats it contained had been the last straw. He saw no light anymore, no way through the blackness. He was filled with rage, an inner smouldering rage, growing bigger and bigger by the minute. He rose to his feet and walked over to the walnut cupboard by the far wall of the room. He depressed the scrolled beading on the side, a false drawer opened at the front and he reached inside and lifted a heavy canvas holster from the drawer. He pulled on the flap, the press stud gave way and he slid his hand around the shining blue steel handle of the Webley service revolver.

He lifted it clear of its resting place and surveyed the weapon more closely by resting it sideways on his hand. He remembered the last time he used it, he was Captain Braithwaite, then of the Northumberland Fusiliers and the place was Korea in '52. Hill 47 it was, all the hills had numbers in that war, he'd fought for others, defended others but he could remember Hill 47 as clear as yesterday. His hand unconsciously touched his arm where the Chinese bullet had entered, he felt the hot searing pain once again and he transferred the pistol to his left hand as he had done all those years ago. He could feel the heat of its barrel after extinguishing its load into the bodies of the defenders. He inspected the clasp on the bottom of the handgrip where he had brained another Chinese, he had swung the empty gun in the air from the lanyard that had hung around his neck like a dervish, with his ball and chain. He turned to look over his shoulder as had done at the end of the battle and he stared back down the hillside at the multitude of bodies that littered its slopes and he had wondered again as he had a thousand times since how he had come through it all alive. He lay on the bed for a long while, faces of comrades long gone flashed in and out of his mind and the faces of slant eyed men he had killed in close combat. He always remembered their faces. He had once heard a famous footballer on television remark that he could remember every goal he had ever scored. Well it was just the same with him. Every dying expression was impregnated on his brain and would be until the day he died. He raised himself slowly from the bed and could not remember whether he had slept or not. He put on his jacket and pushed the gun into his pocket, picking up his briefcase he left the room. He went into his study where he poured himself a large brandy from the crystal decanter standing on his desk. He carried the decanter and sat behind the wheel of the Rolls drinking slowly. The brandy had calmed him down a little and he sat listening to Chopin on the cassette player. He had been there some time watching the digital clock creep round to 11.30. The bleeping noise startled him.

"Hello," he said lifting the 'phone almost at once.

"Are you alone?" asked Tan who was in a call box on the Shipley road.

"Of course."

"You have the money?"

"Yes, I have the money."

"If anything goes wrong or you have informed the police we will get your wife and two sons, oh and maybe that mistress you stop to visit for a quicky on your way to work." Tan was making sure he knew they had been following him.

"You bastard," shouted Lord Bradbury. "You lay a finger on my sons and I'll,"

"Shut the whining and listen," Tan said, interrupting. Braithwaite quietened. He continued, "drive to the White Cross roundabout near Harry Ramsden's fish shop. Take the Shipley road and park on the left by the garage 50 yards from the roundabout. Wait there for another call while we check the area for the fuzz. You got that?"

"Yes Who are you bas-"

Tan slammed down the 'phone cutting him off in mid-sentence.

Lord Bradbury started the Rolls and it purred into life.

He slipped the automatic gear box into drive and the car eased forward. A curtain opened and the enquiring face of Beavers peered out into the darkness. The gravel crunched and crackled under the heavy car as it eased down the long driveway and out onto the lane. The clock on the dash showed twenty-five to twelve. He reckoned on thirty miles from Wetherby to Guiseley which should take him about half an hour. Tan parked his large machine in the car park of Harry Ramsden's. People were queuing at the take-away section and the car park was half full indicating there were still plenty of people in the restaurant. He watched as the doors were locked at 11.45. At 12, the last people from the restaurant were ushered quickly but politely out of the door amidst sounds of laughter and several 'goodnights'. Tan watched as the silhouettes behind the frosted glass clanked and clashed plates in their eagerness to finish off the last of the washing up. He smiled as he thought of the time he'd worked washing up in a holiday camp in Clacton several years ago. People's faces and names flashed into his brain as he remembered back. Then suddenly his daydreaming was interrupted by a red flash and he lifted his head to see the rear end of the Rolls disappear round the roundabout and pull to a stop by the garage. Tan fired the electric start button and kicked the gear lever into first. He drove back down the way the Rolls had come, then further up on the Leeds road checking for signs of police lurking in the rear. It was all clear. Tan came back round the roundabout and cruised up past the Rolls. He glanced inside to check if anyone else was inside hiding on the floor. He saw the case on the back seat and his heart began to quicken with excitement as he pushed the gear into fourth and roared down the hill touching 70 mph and on the two miles to the 'phone box. Tan checked the road once more. Nothing but the odd car flashed past. He rang the 'phone in the Rolls till he heard the unmistakable voice on the other end.

"Listen carefully, I'll say this only once. Drive straight on down the hill towards Shipley. On your right hand side in exactly one point eight miles is a pub called the Shoulder of Mutton. Fifty yards past the pub on the left is a bus shelter, park just past the shelter and get out. Twenty yards on your left is a track. The track is sign-posted 'To Buck Woods.' walk one hundred paces down the track and stop. A light will shine from further down the track. Drop the case and then return to your car. You have five minutes to maake the drop." Tan hung up.

He climbed on the bike and drove the 200 yards to the track. He switched off the engine and free-wheeled down the slope to where a tree hung over the lane. He propped the bike against the wall and standing on the saddle he reached up and pulled himself into its branches. He could see the road accross the open fields on both sides. Three minutes later he saw the Rolls pull to a halt near the end of the lane. Tan leapt down from the tree and sat abreast the Suzuki. He started the engine and let it idle gently ready for a quick getaway in case of trouble. In the Rolls Lord Bradbury took another large gulp of brandy from a hip flask he'd brought along. He pulled the heavy case over to the front seat. He opened the driver's door and staggered slightly under the influence of the brandy. He picked up the case and looked up at the sign pointing to the woods. He stared down the lane into the pitch black night and stumbled slowly forward, his weak flabby arms were unused to carrying anything heavy. Tan could see the silhouette lit against the background of the iodine coloured road lights as it grew slowly then disappeared into the darkness out of the range of lights. Bradbury felt for the Webley in his pocket. He pulled it clear and still holding it let it hang loosely by his side. It reassured him against the unknown. Tan could hear his steps and the noise of the bag scraping along the ground. He'd been counting up to a hundred to give his Lordship the chance to come well down the lane. On one hundred he turned on the powerful headlight on the bike's handlebars. Lord Bradbury was only 15 yards away from Tan, his pinky white face reflected the light and

Tan could see his angered expression quite clearly. The brightness hit the half drunk man with complete surprise and in panic he raised the gun and fired towards the light. The shot whistled past Tan's ear, he felt the heat of the bullet and heard the swish of its flight like an express train leaving a tunnel. The noise, amplified by the warm still night, echoed. As if by instinct he throttled hard and released the clutch. The bike lifted into the air and screamed away on its rear wheel towards the black shape taking aim again. Another shot rang out and it crashed into the underside of the sump sending splinters of alloy engine block flying into the air. Tan came on down the path, the underside of the bike sheilding him from the bullets, like a stunt rider. He couldn't see his way as the headlight shone upwards high into the sky. Tan felt a thud as the bike hit the man knocking him backwards at the same time as the machine's front wheel came crashing down landing on the man's head with a bone splitting crack crushing it to the ground. Tan was thrown over the top of the handlebars and landed on his chest with a thud 20 feet away from the bike which lay on top of the crumpled man, its engine screaming away as the twist grip throttle was jammed open against the floor. Tan lay stunned for a moment or two before he staggered to his feet and walked back to the screaming Suzuki. He pulled in the clutch disconnecting the drive from the spinning rear wheel and lifted the heavy machine off the crumpled man. The headlight shone down on the ground and it caught the blood red crushed-in skull of the oil splattered corpse, the gun still smoking in its hand. Tan looked about half expecting a mass of policemen to overpower him, but he was alone. His first instincts told him to run but he fought them till he quickly gained control. He lifted the case onto the luggage rack and hooked across an elastic rope. He reached down and pulled the revolver from the dead man's hand placing it down his belt at the front of his jeans. He stared at the dead man for a moment and then he came to a decision. He heaved the body accross the petrol tank of the motorcycle so its arms and legs hung either side. He sat uncomfortably on the seat and drove the machine slowly down onto the footbridge over the river. It plonked and spluttered as the oil began to drain from the shattered casing. He propped the bike against the steel sides of the bridge and lifted the body from the machine. With one mighty heave the sixth Earl of Bradbury crashed unceremoniously into the fast-flowing black waters of the river twenty feet below and disappeared. Phil was hiding by the side of the swing bridge and didn't show himself until he had made sure it was Tan who'd come flashing up the hill from the footbridge.

"What the fuck was all the shooting?" he said as he climbed nervously onto the back of the bike.

"Tell you later," replied Tan knowing this wasn't the right time to hold a conversation. The Suzuki through lack of oil in the sump began to pink and then it ceased.

It was another hour before they located Richard at the lookout point. They'd abandoned the Suzuki at the top of the wood and made their way on foot bumping into trees and stumbling along till they finally located him.

"What the fuck went on down there?" asked Richard relieved to see the return of his two colleagues and eyeing the case excitedly. Tan surveyed the scene in the valley and up to the road. There was no sign of light anywhere within two miles of the path where Tan had mown down Robin Braithwaite. He dropped the case on the ground.

"The bastard had a gun and he tried to kill me."

"I saw the flashes and I saw the bike's light go up in the air. God what a wierd sight," said Richard who still had the Luger in his hand.

Phil knelt down in front of the case and began to undo the two large straps that held it secure. He threw back the lid and eyed the contents.

"Jesus, look at all this money," he said. Richard joined him and they both lifted out a bundle of ten pound notes. Tan came to look. He fingered the neat piles of brand new notes.

"The bastard! They're all new notes, they'll have a list of all the numbers. Then he smiled, we'll have to see what we can do about that"

"'What do we do now?" asked Richard enquiring after Tan's next move. Tan was thinking hard. His bike was finished. He knew the Rolls would attract attention sooner or later parked where it was on double yellows on a busy carriageway, and for the first time he was lost for an answer. He could feel the sticky blood between his fingers and his face and jacket were covered with it as it began to dry. He told the others to wait while he walked a few hundred yards to a small stream he'd seen earlier that day that ran down the hillside to the canal. The cold crisp water felt good as he cleansed himself thoroughly.

He returned to the camp to find Richard and Phil counting the bundles of notes. He'd decided to stay the night in the wood. He knew they wouldn't find the body too quickly, and as he scanned the valley again there was still no sign of life. He checked his watch. It was 2.50 am. If somebody had heard the shots the police would have been on the scene hours ago. He pondered for a moment.

" We're safe."

They bedded down for the night, Tan tired and exhausted was soon in a deep sleep. It was the dawn chorus that woke him, a multitude of birds all chirping at the same time announcing the arrival of a new day. He was cold and wet and it was a moment or two before he realised he was covered from head to foot in the morning dew. It was 5.30 on his watch and he glanced at the other two who were lying side by side with both their heads resting on the small case like a pillow. Tan checked the pathway below. The river was completely obliterated by a thick mist that hung over the lower regions of the valley. The pathway was visible and there was still no sign of activity. A passing police patrol car had noted the number of the Rolls as they passed and did a computer check to see if it had been stolen, but they'd not even bothered to check the vehicle out. Tan woke the other two and they took the Honda and collected Tan's Suzuki and dumped them both in the middle of the canal. The rest of the gear, including the blood splattered jacket they wedged into a crevice beneath some rocks. They walked the two miles to the road and waited, hidden by the edge of the woods. At eight o' clock they walked up into Thackley village and caught a bus along with the group of rush hour workers who worked in the centre of Bradford five miles away. They returned to the bedsit in Manningham and the weary trio were soon asleep again in various positions around the room. Tan had claimed the small bed and lay on top of the covers. The crushed face of Robin Braithwaite kept re-appearing in his mind.

CHAPTER SIX

David Galbraith had left the house and called in a pub on the outskirts of Leeds. He ordered an orange juice and a ham sandwich. He sat in a corner people watching, a little game he played with himself, guessing their occupation or imagining what their names were. Half way through his sandwich the bleeper sounded in his pocket. He went to the 'phone in the entrance porch and dialled his office.

"What's up Barbara?"

"We've got a name and a picture, get in here quick." It took him seven minutes to return to the office and Detective Inspector Forrest was already waiting, a huge smile on his face. He handed David a photograph across the desk.

"That's our man," he said confidently. David stared at the prison photograph enlarged several times. The name on the bottom of the picture read, 'Anthony Heyes'. He stared at the handsome features, the shoulder length blond hair.

"Fingerprint in the house matched his. Ex-junkie jailbird," said Inspector Forrest.

David memorised the face and an excitement swamped over him. At last he had a face, a name. The Inspector handed him a report that accompanied the photographs.

'Anthony Heyes, born Stretford, Manchester, 10.7.56. Educated Manchester Grammar School. Qualifications, 13 'O' levels, 4 'A' levels. Languages, French and German. Enrolled Cambridge Flying School '74. Joined Cranwell RAF Training College '76. Trained on Tornadoes, Phantoms and Harriers. Rank, Flight Lieutenant. Dismissed RAF '79 after mysterious disappearance surrounding Harrier jump jet. Claimed to eject over bombing range in the Wash North Sea. Found floating in dinghy. "No trace of Harrier including 100,000 rounds of 30 MM cannon, 6 rapier missiles never found."

David blew a short whistle into the air and looked up at the Inspector who was smiling back at him acknowledging the contents of the document. He carried on reading.

'Did various jobs around the Manchester area before joining the Greenpeace organisation in May '80. His record from then till '85 when believed to be on the Rainbow Warrior when sunk by an explosion in Aukland, NewZealand. Movements unrecorded till came through Heathrow Airport 6th November '85 on a Quantas flight from Sydney. Found in a confused and drugged state in Holburn Circus underground railway station. 300 milligrams of heroin were in his possession. Sentenced to one year's imprisonment on 12th December '86, released from Strangeways Prison, Manchester, after 7 months for good behaviour. No further criminal record.'

David looked up. It was obvious from the report that someone had been recording Heyes' movements.

"Whose report is this"?" he asked.

"Don't know. Came straight from Scotland Yard, they've probably had him down for a subversive and been keeping tabs on him."

"Is that all there is?"

"That's it."

"Someone's not playing fair!" The Inspector agreed.

"It's the Yard, they want in on the case but till they're asked or we run a blank they've no chance so they'll hold back all the best info."

David got up from the chair and began to stalk round the room. He stopped at the window and stared out at the traffic below. "God," he cursed, "we've got some nutter on the loose out there." He paused for a moment, his brain was still trying to absorb what he'd just read. "I mean, he's no ordinary everyday type of subversive, he's bloody RAF trained bloody nutter with an inordinate interlect for all we know, and they won't give us a full report. Well, we'll see about that then." David gathered his temper under control and smiled smugly at his Chief. He began to make for the door.

"Where are you going to?" asked the inspector.

"I'm off to prison," he replied. "See if I can pick up an old cellmate of Heyes'." He was half out of the door when the Inspector called him back.

"Oh and Sergeant, keep me informed, eh."

David came out of the building and was glad to breath the clean outside air, glad to be free of the smoke filled corridors of the building. He crossed the Headrow and headed for a small tobacconist kiosk across the road and bought a packet of twenty Bensons. The sun was trying to break through small gaps in the thick cloud as he recrossed the road back to where he'd parked his car. He was on the M62 motorway in 10 minutes and after screwing the car at speeds up to 120 mph he found himself turning off at the Prestwich exit. Another ten minutes down the A56 to the outskirts of Manchester city centre he turned into Bridge Street and came to a stop outside a huge grim red brick building. It always reminded him of a French Fort of the 18th century. Built on high ground, its small barred windows and thick solid built walls made it look impregnable. Strangeways never failed to leave him with a feeling of doom and despair and he'd often wondered what kind of man would risk any crime for a term of incarsaration in such a place. His warrant card gave him quick admission and after a delay of twenty minutes he found himself in the records room with the chief warder. He soon found out that Heyes had shared a cell with only one man and fortunately he was still in residence. A man named Raymond Seymour, a small time burglar, who was serving seven years for his most recent crime. David waited in the interview room whilst his man was brought in from the excersise yard.

Raymond Seymour was ushered into the interview room. He was a thick set man of about forty with an immaculate head of well-groomed hair, a large round nose and a set of Clark Gable-type perfect false teeth that didn't seem to fit his mouth.
David introduced himself as Seymour lowered himself slowly into the chair. A prison officer stood impassive at the side of the room. David pushed the photograph across and Seymour inspected it closely.

"Bloody 'eck," he said suddenly, "it's the Prof."

"What do you know about him?"" asked David. Seymour eyed David's fingers looking for the nicotine browned fingers of the smoker and his face dropped. He decided to ask anyway.

"Got any snout?" David smiled. He learned a long time ago not to interrogate a prisoner without the customary bribe of cigarettes. He placed the pack of twenty Benson King size in the middle of the table.

"Ah, let me see," said Raymond leaning back and pretending to look deep in thought. "Yes, the Prof, called him the Prof because he always had his head in a book. Did nothing but read all day in, day out. Knew bloody everthing he did. I remember asking him the capital of Iceland for the Sun crossword and gave us it, just like that." He paused for a moment. "Still can't remember what they call it."

"Rekjavik," replied David smiling at the man's ineptitude.

"That's it, that's the one" replied Raymond his eyes wide in unmistakeable bewilderment. 'Another clever bugger,' he thought.

"What else can you tell me?" David still rested his hand on the cigarettes.

"Good looking lad, remember one or two queers got a grip on him once in t' showers, nearly killed one of them he did. There was fucking blood everywhere. Yes that's it, he was one of them silent hard types. You know the type, don't have to prove anything to themselves or anybody. Confident like. And ice-cold," He said as an afterthought still trying to earn his cigs

"What do you mean?" asked David.

"Well when he done them queers and they were both lying on the floor covered in blood, he walked calmly into the lav, got one of those lavatory brushes wit' long wooden handles and shoved it right up yon queer's arse!" David smiled. "You should have heard fucking scream that came out 'at queer." Seymour's face lit up in sheer delight at the thought. "It were like summat out of one a those horror movies." David released the cigarettes to their new owner. Seymour put them into a breast pocket in the blue prison overall. "That's what near killed him, ruined his insides. He don't queen it anymore that cunt, I can tell you." David had all on to refrain from laughing more at Seymour's unique way of recollection.

"He didn't lose remission did he?" asked David still grinning.

"Nope he was out that wash room quick as a flash. Screws thought queers had done each other in. Ay tell you, it was bloody great. Screws couldn't stop laughing as this queer run round toilet wit' brush stuck up his arse screaming like a woman."

David finally burst into a fit of hysterics as did the warder standing by the wall. If nothing else thought David it had been worth the trip just for a laugh.

After the laughter had died down a little David decided to try just once more to see if there was anything that Seymour had missed.

"Anything else odd or strange he ever say to you?"

Seymour gazed at the wall above David's head and pondered quietly for a moment.

"There was one thing he said." David leaned forward, Seymour pondered a moment.

"Well 1 don't know."

"Get on with it man," demanded the detective.

"It's just something he said one day."

"Spit it out man, what the hell did he say?"

"He was looking out of the cell window this time and a bunch of jets roared past sorta overhead. You couldn't see them like cos of the restricted view. Well the Prof nearly breaks his neck to try and get a glimpse of them and when he climbs down off the chair after the noise had subsided from the jets he glared at me a look that could kill sorta. Then he said, 'When I get outa this place, Retard,' he nicknamed me Retard, says I must 'av been bent over picking my feet when God was giving out brains."Seymour laughed.

"Get on with it. What did he say," demanded David.

Seymour composed himself quickly seeing as no-one else had bothered to laugh with him.

"He said, 'When I get outa here, Retard, you'll hear a noise like that, only this time it'll be followed by a big bang and the whole fucking building will come down on your head."

David sat staring at Seymour's discoloured teeth while he absorbed what had just been said. The colour drained momentarily from his face as he respoke Seymour's words over to himself in his brain. A sudden excitement overwhelmed him as he realised he's just had confirmation that Heyes did have the Harrier Jet stashed away somewhere and it was fully serviceable. 'My God, 'he thought to himself as the picture of a Harrier flashed in front of him, Heyes at the controls.

In Pontefract that day a service was being held to commemorate the unfortunate victims of the massacre. The Prime Minister had attended and she'd visited some of the relatives of those killed. Later in the afternoon she visited Milgarth Police Station in Leeds and checked on the progress being made to apprehend those responsible. George Redburn greeted her and assured her that the man responsible would be under lock and key within the next few days. It had been five days now since the massacre and the British public were in panic as to where the poisoner would strike next. Only the hardened drinkers were still continuing their nightly ritual of visiting their locals. Most people had decided to curtail their drinking habits till after the poisoner was caught. The large breweries were feeling the pinch and debates in both Houses of Parliament centred around the poisonings. A powder keg had been ignited once again under the Houses of Parliament only this time the fuse was still smouldering away.

Tan awoke at 12 o'clock. After checking his watch he jumped off the bed and quickly woke Richard and Phil.

"Right lads now we start work," he shouted at the two sleepy men. "You've been lounging around too long.

"I wish you'd tell us what your plans are," said Phil pulling on his jeans over a baggy pair of underpants.

"Listen I'll tell you everything soon enough." Richard was ready first and Tan gave him a five pound note from his wallet. He smiled at him. "Go and get a handful of papers. I've got a feeling they'll have my picture in it by now." Phil looked surprised.

"How do you know that?"

"Easy. They've got my fingerprints from the house in Leeds. I've got a criminal record."

"You want them to know who you are!" said Richard, "but why?"

Tan smiled, "Listen lads I'll tell you everything maybe tomorrow or the day after, but definitely by then, agreed." They both nodded reluctantly. "Now go get the papers quickly." Richard came back in ten minutes with a bundle of papers under his arm and a worried look on his face.

"The Pontefract Poisoner. Jesus fucking hell, they're on to you," he said as he closed the door dropping the papers on the bed. Tan walked across and placed his arm on the distraught man's shoulder and smiled reassuringly.

"It's all in the plan."

"Was killing Braithwaite in the plan too?"

Tan frowned, "No, but he tried to kill me. His death is neither here nor there, it makes no difference. Look, just trust me and by tomorrow you'll understand everything, okay?"

"He's right," agreed Phil, "He's kept us out of it so far, he's only incriminated himself. Besides, I like the thought of being famous."

"Infamous you mean," corrected Richard smiling again after his daily dose of reassurance.

Phil chirped up, "I wouldn't mind being caught, being on the telly, in all the papers." Tan glared angrily at him.

"Cut that talk out, we're not going to be caught. Ever! Only fools get caught," Tan faced Richard who was catching up on the news. "Right no time to waste. Here's today's plan of action." Tan was writing a list as he spoke. "Take £5,000 each from the case. We're going to launder some money." Tan knew the numbers of new notes were easy to check when they ran in sequence as these bills did. He also knew the numbers were circulated by the police for the public to keep a look out for, usually circulated in the newspapers. He'd worked in a bank for a couple of months after leaving the air force. He knew all about money.

"Now listen carefully, this is very important." He handed round a cigarette each and as soon as he felt he had their attention he carried on. "Change the new notes in sweet shops, betting shops, newsagents, the markets. Don't buy any clothes with it. I'll tell you why later. Go into betting shops and place no more than £50 on the first three favourites in every race. But only one per race per bookies, don't worry about losses, we'll be lucky to get half our money back. Don't collect any winnings till after the last race. That way you'll get notes paid in the races before. Hopefully!" Tan smiled. "When you've placed all your bets go round as many smaller shops and spend no more that one pound. That way we'll be sure of nine pounds change from a ten pound note. But this is important, only buy trivia. Apples, oranges, sweets, papers, small toys, anything."

"What do we do with all the stuff?" asked Richard.

"Dump it discreetly. We must have at least £5000 in clean money by tonight. In between, with clean money only, get yourselves a short, well groomed haircut."

Phil moaned, "My lovely hair man."

"It'll grow," said Richard.

"Then get yourselves some casual clothes each, a suit and tie, I've made a list. Nothing ostentatious, just normal wally wear, okay." Tan smiled and stubbed out his cigarette in an old saucer on the table. "Get me a nice conservative dark blue suit and the trappings. I've put the sizes down." Tan checked his watch. It was 12.35. "Right get going and don't get any taxis, go on the bus there and back." Tan knew they'd have to risk staying there one more night, he didn't want anyone knowing they were there especially some nosey taxi driver. They'd only dumped the vans about a mile and a half away, but he thought the police wouldn't read too much into where they were found. After they left on the shopping trip Tan lay back on the bed and began to scurtinise the newspapers. One of them, The Mirror, was offering a reward of £100,000 for his capture. He finished reading them an hour later and he sat on the bed and emptied the contents of his rucksack onto the duvet. The Luger and the Webley lay in the tangle of papers. He picked up the small radio and tuned into Radio 2 to await the latest news. He lifted up the heavy revolver and inspected the chamber. There were three shells still in the gun. He checked the driving licence and the letters with the name Stanley Rodis written on them. These items that were his father's would now give Tan his new identity.

A voice on the radio announced the introduction of the two o'clock news. Tan listened intently. An appeal was made for the public to be on the lookout for him, warning them he was extremely dangerous and must not be approached. Tan smiled to himself. There was no mention of Lord Bradbury at all. He thought the police would have found the car, but then they would give him time to turn up before taking any action. That would give them a while longer to launder some more of the money.

He located the bathroom on the next floor; an old gas geser attached to a gas meter heated the water. As he stood checking which coin to put in the meter an old man came out of a door along the corridor, pushed past Tan and began to urinate in the toilet basin. Tan returned to his room deciding against using the comunal bathroom. He washed as best he could in the cold water, but managed to boil a pan of water on the old gas oven that stood near the window. After he'd shaved he collected all his old disposable razors, about four in all, and began to shave off the hair down the top of his head.

It was 6.45 when Phil and Richard arrived back at the bedsit. They both were struggling to carry armfuls of carrier bags and were relieved to drop them on the floor. Tan was reading one of the papers and he peered over it exposing his new look to the two startled men. He had shaved the top of his head completely bald, and had trimmed the hair at the sides short. He was wearing a pair of clear brown rimmed spectacles; altogether it made him look fifteen years older and his two comrades stood aghast at the absolute change in his appearance. He'd passed the test.

"God, it's Alf Garnett," shouted Phil with a huge grin on his face.

Richard stood with his mouth wide open, till he said, "That's bloody amazing, you look like a different person."

"I am," replied Tan smiling as he stood up from the chair. He picked up the driver's licence from the bed and threw it to Richard. "This is my new identity." Richard scrutinised the licence.

"Stanley Rodis, who's he?"

"He was my father." Tan went on to explain he had been given his mother's name as his father and mother were never married.

Phil walked round Tan staring at his head.

"God, I can't believe the difference. I would have sat next to you on a bus and not known you."

Tan was pleased with the result, he'd had to make himself look older as his father was forty nine when he died and his date of birth was printed in the top left hand corner of the driving licence.

"How did it go?" he asked as Richard began to empty piles of notes onto the table.

"No problem, we just about ran out of shops although Phil made a profit on the horses." In the excitement Tan had failed to notice the shorter hair cuts of the two men and he thought to himself with a conservative suit they'd look more like tax collectors than terrorists.

The final count of the laundered money was eight thousand and seventy pounds. They had changed £9,650, not a bad loss thought Tan. The next ploy was the casino tonight. Tan explained all they had to do was change money for chips, then back to money again. But only play the odd pound and then wander around a bit.

"But make sure you change it at the gaming tables, not at the cashier's desk. The croupier will deposit your money in a slit in a security box under the table and they don't empty them till they are full." That way you won't get back the same bills. By eight o'clock that night the three men had changed into their new attire. The difference was quite amazing as they clowned around for a few minutes till the novelty wore off. Tan was decked out in a dark blue suit, black shoes, white shirt and a red, yellow and blue tie. He looked every inch an accountant or bank manager.

Richard wore a grey flannel suit with a white shirt and a black tie, and Phil had gone in for a pair of grey flannels and a black wool double breasted blazer.

Phil ventured out for some fish and chips which they all devoured eagerly before all three left the bedsit to catch a bus on Manningham Lane. They arrived at the City Car Auctions next to Valley Parade football ground. Tan had checked the auction starting time earlier that day. An hour and £1,600 lighter they drove away in an eighty-two beige Ford Cortina, and a 1969 Landrover. Both were taxed. Although Tan had decided to buy the

Landrover for reasons he would not divulgetill later, Phil was over the moon proclaiming he'd always wanted one, and he sat in it till all the formalities had been carried out in the payment office by Richard and Tan. They'd used the laundered money to make sure there'd be no trace on the purchased vehicles later on and bought them in the name of Stanley Rodis. Only Richard and Phil ventured into the two casinos in the city centre that night. Tan waited patiently in a city centre discoteque enjoying the music. He couldn't help but notice hardly any of them were drinking beer.

At two o'clock he rendezvoused with the two tired men and with another £7,000 added to the kitty they booked into the Norfolk Gardens Hotel for a comfortable night's sleep, explaining to the receptionist that they were too drunk to return home and would just stay the one night, not that she showed the slightest interest whatever in the three unfashionable men as she handed the keys to the £40 a night rooms.

Thursday. Concern was now growing for the whereabouts of Lord Bradbury. The police had kept a watch on the Rolls for most of the day and as soon as the dawn broke a search was organised along the river bank. At seven thirty in the morning of Thursday 24th July, a Policeman found the body of Robin Braithwaite, the sixth Earl of Bradbury. It was snagged against some trees in a bed of the river about two miles down from the footbridge where Tan had dumped it into the river. A close inspection of the bridge found dried blood stains on the rail and floor. A search from the bridge up the path found the two spent cartridges from the Webley revolver. At lunchtime a team of detectives swarmed into the Brewery's offices in Tadcaster and found the ransom note locked in Robin Braithwaite's safe. The chief accountant, Herbert Jenkins was questioned and he revealed details of the withdrawal he'd made on his Lordship's behalf, for the sum of £100,000.

"He blew a fuse when I told him all I could get was freshly minted notes," stated Jenkins. "He went red with rage and threatened to sack me, called me a stupid old dildo. I've never seen him like that. He kept repeating, 'You've ruined me, you've ruined me."

Chief Superintendant George Redburn arrived at the Brewery and took charge of the investigation. David Galbraith turned up shortly after.

"Ah, Wonder Boy," said George in greeting, "the net's closing, eh." George realised at once that the new notes would be easily traced. "We'll be able to keep tabs on them, even if we don't catch them we'll know more or less where the hell they are."

"They may have changed the money already, this guy, Heyes, is very bright," replied David.

"You piss me off you do," replied George angrily.

"Only suggesting possibilites, what do they teach in police college, 'Know thy man'."

"Do you know him?" asked George.

"No! But they do in Whitehall. Had some MI5 blokes up to our office today, wanted a copy of every document relating to this case." Forrest had informed him when he'd rung in on his return from Manchester.

"Fucking hell," blurted George angrier than ever. I'm only the man in charge of this operation and I know fuck all. Why didn't you tell me?"

"I just did." George threw his head back in disgust and walked away. David examined the ransom note that was carefully enclosed between two pieces of clear plastic film. He stopped at the sentence, 'Our aim is political.' So, they needed funds, he thought, still no nearer the motive behind all of this. The letter told David one thing though besides, Anthony Heyes was a well-adjusted, intelligent man and not the raving fanatic he'd thought earlier. His only misgivings about this man was the way he could kill without conscience and without feelings, perhaps he did care, but his cause was far greater then his concern for human life. A political action more important than human life itself. What could it be? Then David's mind thought back to the MI5 invasion earlier that morning. He knew MI5 dealt mainly with the country's security and not with ordinary criminal investigations. He smelt a rat.

Tan woke by 8.30. He bathed in the luxury of the modern bathroom whilst he listened to the radio. The reports of Lord Bradbury's murder came across the air waves in a special news bulletin.

"A gentle knock came to the door and he shouted, "Who's there?"

"It's me Richard. You up?" Tan grabbed a towel and opened the door dripping water all over the floor. "You don't half look a prick with that head," smiled Richard. Tan smiled.

"Is Phil up?"

"Yes, he's scoffing his bacon and eggs downstairs. I've had mine."

"Go get him, we've got things to do." Tan made himself a cup of coffee with the courtesy kettle and powdered ingredients placed in the room. He was just about dressed when the familiar knock at the door announced Richard's return. He let them in. Tan was ready to confide his plans to them and wasted no time at all. "Today I'll tell you some of the things you need to know, but first there are a few things we need to buy." They left the hotel and crossed the grass island that fronted the hotel and found a sports equipment shop just across from the Town Hall. Tan bought waterproof jackets and leggings, and a pile of sandwiches from the coffee bar next door.

"It'll be a long day," remarked Tan as he tried one of the large flashlights he'd just bought. They drove the Cortina to the bedsit where they changed into their new climbing outfits. They loaded the gear they needed into the Landrover plus a pair of bolt cutters they'd purchased on their way back to the bedsit from a hardware store. Phil jumped eagerly into the driver's seat of his new toy and was pleased the Landrover fired and started first time.

"Where to, Boss?" he said smiling.

"Head out towards Huddersfield and I'll show you from there." They drove on through Huddersfield on out through Holmfirth and up the A635 up into the Pennine hills. Half way up the bleak barren terrain Tan instructed Phil to orive down an old cart track. They bounced and bumped along the pot-holed road for five miles with only the odd sheep crossing their path as they went. They stopped for a moment, Tan got out and checked his bearings. Climbing back in Phil saw a strange glare of excitement on Tan's face. They left the track and with the four-wheel drive engaged they bumped and jostled for a further four miles which took them the best part of an hour. They were now high into the Pennine hills, one of the most remote and unknown parts of Britain.

Tan explained he'd been up here many times as a youth on his first ever motorbike. This is where he first enjoyed the thrill of finding out about nature for the first time. It was a place so remote that only lapwings and grouse and the odd skylark lived there. The higher altitude and strong winds made it difficult for insects which most birds thrive on to survive. Rabbits ran in their thousands, out of reach of their most feared predator, man. Tan had watched large hares play and dance all day in the sun and had likened them to children as they played tag and hide and seek amongst the heather. He'd learnt from them the joy of just being alive on a fine summer's day, before society had contaminated his uncomplicated happy child's brain. A fleeting sadness momentarily engulfed him for those long ago days. But his mind quickly returned to the present, always a realist he knew that the present and future were the only important things; only fools lingered on times long past. The ground began to' even out and they drove easily along a smooth but thickly grassed section about twenty feet wide.

"What's this, an old Roman road?" asked Richard amazed at the smoothness of the track.

"No, it's an old Victorian railway line, a rack and pinion railway I think," replied Tan. "Been closed down for over 80 years."

"Why's that?" asked Phil.

"There's a tunnel up ahead that caved in and blocked the line. It was too expensive to re-open as they realised you can't really build a tunnel under a peat bog as was the case. The water eventually seeped through all the building materials and the whole thing collapsed. I think it carried ore from a tin mine higher up the hills."

"Why are we up here, Tan?" enquired Richard, a little worried by the remoteness of the place and his imagination beginning to think Tan had brought them up here to bump them off. Phil must have read Richard's mind.

"He hasn't brought you up here to bump you off if that's what you're thinking." Tan gave the two men a quizzical stare.

"I wouldn't do that," he said, "we're a team."

Phil smiled sadistically, "couldn't do it anyway cause I've got the fucking Luger."

Tan was surprised by Phil's initiative, but disappointed at his mistrust although he'd not given them much trust in return. He was just beginning to warm to them these last days, having kept them at arms length for most of the time. He decided to be more open with them.

"Look, comrades," he said warmly, choosing the term 'comrade' deliberately, "I owe you a full explanation and in a short while I'll tell you everything. We are in this together and we'll all see it through together, okay." Just as he finished speaking the dark shape of a gaping hole began to grow nearer and nearer till Tan signalled Phil to stop by tapping his shoulder. Tan climbed out and stood looking at the steel struts that spread across the entrance in both directions like a great steel portcullis. The tunnel entrance was about 30 feet across and at its highest point in the roof it stood about twenty five feet high. Signs hung from the steel grid; one read 'Danger Natural Gas Seepage'. Another read 'Danger Do Not Enter Loose Roof Stones'. Tan walked up and began to examine the rusty grid work closely. A smaller inspection gate led through the large obstruction. Tan examined two rusty padlocks that obviously hadn't been removed for years. He smiled as the two men looked at each other bewildered. Another metal strut had been welded down the seam on the gate securing it permanently even if the padlocks had been removed. The grass and small shrubs round the entrance told Tan nobody had disturbed the inside of the tunnel. They loaded up the ropes and climbing gear and donned the protective helmets, Phil and Richard still bemused but both as curious as two children at what lay ahead. Tan collected the torches and he set off to climb the hill by the side of the tunnel urging the others to follow. The hillside was steep and almost vertical, but the three men were all experienced climbers and were soon on the high point thirty feet above the entrance to the tunnel. Tan carried the long bolt cutters he'd bought over his shoulder, a huge smile beamed across his face. It was obvious to the other two he was extremely excited about something. After twenty minutes of hard slog Tan finally stopped and perched on a large circular stone structure not unlike a small cutaway mill chimney. He waited for the two stragglers to catch up to him. They both plonked down. gasping for breath.

"I'm knackered," said Richard.

Tan smiled, "Well we're here now anyway." Richard scoured the surrounding desolate countryside. Where's here?"

Tan nodded at the steel plate he'd sat on.

Phil eyed the structure.

"What is it?"

"It's a ventilation shaft to the tunnel." Tan jumped off the large steel plate he'd been sitting on. It covered the top of the small chimney but was supported by eight long bolts that left a gap so air could circulate. He picked up the bolt cutters and proceeded to cut through the well rusted half inch bolts with relative ease. They snapped easily. The last one severed by the powerful jaws, he pushed the heavy steel plate over the side into the heather. Tan picked up a stone and tossed it into the dark void. Seconds later it crashed to the bottom. A loud pinging noise echoed up the shaft. Tan tied the rope round the chimney and then through a large steel bar that was left especially for this task. A soot covered steel ladder ran down the inside of the shaft but Tan doubted its strength after a hundred years or more of corrosion.

"Come on chaps," shouted Tan as the two men looked down into the shaft. "I'll go first, the rope is a safety net, the ladder will be alright but loop the rope through the steel clasp like this and let the slack out as you descend."

"We're not going to live in a fucking cave now are we?" joked Phil.

"This is no ordinary cave," smiled Tan, "all will soon be revealed."

"Why can't we walk into the other end of the tunnel?" asked Richard not over keen to venture into the shaft.

"There is no 'other'" end, it's collapsed. I told you earlier," replied Tan eager to get down. He strapped the nylon rucksack to his back and without further ado he began to descend into the shaft. Chunks of rust and dislodged soot from the burnt up coal fired engines of years gone fell off the ladder but it felt quite firm and secure, and Tan thought of the Victorian engineers who'd built this tunnel. It took five minutes to descend the 70 feet to the bottom. He had to lower himself the last thirty feet into the tunnel with the rope, the ladder having stopped at the roof. He was covered from head to foot in soot and he'd wondered of his decision to enter the tunnel this way. He shone the torch down into the blackness. He could see mothing but pools of water as the tunnel acted like a giant drain for the rainwater that seeped onto the moor. Phil came quickly down the ladder. His time spent potholing throughout Yorkshire crags showed as he expertly absailed down the last section of rope onto the wet floor of the tunnel. Tan shone the torch on his face. It was jet black with the soot and he laughed as he handed him another torch from the sack. Richard practically fell the last thirty feet Only the quick thinking of Phil saved him from serious injury. But his curiosity stopped him ftom moaning.

"Right follow me," said Tan. His voice carried down the brick-walled tunnel and was amplified several times.

He set off towards the direction of the entrance which was not even visible at this stage; Tan hoped the roof hadn't caved in blocking it off. A few bats screeched unnervingly as they passed and at one point a stream of water seeped from a large hole in the roof where the bricks had caved in, causing a small lake to form for a hundred yards or more. Tan's heart raced against his ribs as he crossed the water and found the rest quite dry. He stopped at one point and shone his torch on the wall. Scratched into the stone was 'T Heyes 67'.

Phil came up and stared at it. "You did that?"

"Yes," replied Tan. "When I was a lad some years ago."

"Hope you haven't dragged us all the way down here to see your etchings."

"Ha, ha," replied Richard, "very good." Tan's torchlight beam picked out a dark shape in the distance and he suddenly became excited and ran ahead, the torchlight casting giant shadows as he ran.

"It's here," he screamed in stereo as the echoes caught up

with themselves. "They've not found it, it's here."

The two men followed in Tan's wake till they came up to a large object almost blocking the tunnel. At first Phil thought it was a roof fall as he shone his torch over the mould and slime that clung on the large canvas sheets and the light followed down onto the ground and its beam caught the uncovered rubber of the tyre. He gasped in amazement.

"What the fuck is it?" asked Richard as Philip stood, his mouth ajar unable to speak.

"Give us a hand to get the ropes off you two," shouted Tan as he bared the wing to reveal the blue circle and red dot that was the motif of the Royal Air Force.

Phil recognised the plane at once and at last able to speak he screamed, "He's got a Harrier Jump Jet. I don't believe it, man, I don't." He suddenly gawped again and his speech faded as the canvas cover fell completely from the wing to reveal three black and white checked missiles hung under its span. The two onlookers began to help unwrap the jet till after ten minutes it was clear of all the canvas. Tan opened the cockpit and lifted out a tool box and then a tungsten grinder, the tool he'd used to cut the entrance bars from the tunnel before re-welding them when he'd got the jet inside. He handed the tool box down to Richard who was shining his torch all over the plane as if he still couldn't believe his eyes. Tan rested the tungsten grinder on the fuselage before lowering himself into the familiar seat. It felt good as he gripped the stick pushing it to and fro as he watched the flaps on the wings move up and down. His feet pressed the two rudder pedals and he smiled as he thought of the last time he'd flown the jet. He hadn't stolen it to keep, just a sort of challenge, a gesture to his superiors to prove it could be done.

He'd reasoned the most effective way of using the vertical take off jet was to scatter them all over the country in independant hides or specially made bunkers with their own fuel supplies and armourments so that in case of a Russian invasion the Harriers could fight a guerilla war from their secret positions. He'd suggested a thousand or so hides could form the basis of a fightback against the invaders.

"Impossible to hide one jet, never mind a thousand," had

insisted the squadron leader. Tan had decided there and then to prove him wrong. The day of the practice missile firing over the North Sea gave him his chance. He'd already taken his motorcycle and all the tools and ropes up into the old tunnel. He'd cut through all the steel bars on the grid protecting its entrance and left it tied by rope for when he'd bring the jet up into the tunnel. Everything was set up. The day of the practice run came. The idea was to fly out to the target boats, fire one rocket, turn away and wait for orders to do a second run, and so on till all six missiles had been despatched. The squadron took off at three minute intervals so as to give each jet room to maneouvre away for fear of collision or the risk of the following jet being caught in the other jet's missile explosions.

The sortie was a low level run, and immediately away from the aerodrome. Tan banked and flew north up the coast at about 150 feet well under the radar scan. Fifty miles up the coast he turned west and came back down on the outskirts of Wakefield down over Skelmansthorpe onto the hills. He radioed he had begun his bomb run and then screamed he's lost control and then cut the radio. His main worry as he circled low looking for the tunnel in dense heavy cloud was a rambler or walker who'd spot him as he landed. But it had been a weekday and he didn't see a soul as he hovered and lowered the jet onto the ground thirty feet from the tunnel's entrance.

The rest had been easy. He cut the ropes and dropped the heavy grille to the ground. Then he taxied the jet as far into the tunnel as he thought safe, although the noise of the Pegasus jet engine was deafening and he'd half expected the roof to crash in on him. He'd lifted the heavy portcullis style grid back into place with the help of an old wooden pully he'd bought and held it in place with chains and padlocks securing them. It had been 2 hours and 15 minutes since he'd left the Base. He would return and weld the bars secure later but his main problem now was to get back to the coast. The 500 cc scrambler had been hidden in the tunnel and he drove like a madman for two hours till he hit the coast north of Boston where he'd hidden the inflatable dinghy. He'd seen two Westmorland helicopters go overhead and other spotter planes so he donned the sowester and large oilskin coat to hide his flying gear. If seen as he propelled himself out to sea the game would have been up, but about seven miles out he cut the motor, slashed the rubber of the dinghy and jumped into the water. Half an hour later he'd waved as the helicopter came to pick him from the water.

An inquiry followed and a frantic search found no wreckage or debris from the place. The only possible solution to the complete dispersion of the wreckage was that a Soviet submarine had been in the area and salvaged the jet intact. A Royal Navy sub had been on the scene two days after the crash and had found nothing in over two months of searching. Tan had been confined to the aerodrome while this was going on after being interrogated several times and threatened with charges of high treason. He'd got in too deep and had to keep silent not daring now even to come clean about his ploy. He'd only intended to hide the jet for several hours and explain his ideas in full, but the way he was treated by his interrogators as though he was some criminal made him change his mind and he began to enjoy the game he'd landed himself in. He was grounded and after nothing could be substantiated he was asked to resign. His ploy had backfired on him.

The RAF had kept all of the inquiry private and as far as the media was concerned had stuck to the original story of the Harrier crashing into the sea. As long as no-one found the jet he was home free. Careful no-one followed, he returned three months later and finished off welding the grid. He was going to blow up the jet by setting fire to it which in turn would have exploded the war heads bringing the tunnel down on the jet, but he changed his mind at the last minute. If he secured it properly it could stay there for years undetected and also in good working order. After all, the controls were all cable powered, there was only the jet engine that would be vulnerable to dust and damp, but he fastened all the open ended air ducts up tightly before wrapping the jet in large canvas sheets used by lorry drivers to cover their loads. He'd even had the sign painted: 'Danger Natural Gas and Deadly Fumes Keep Out' by a professional signwriter just in case some nosey minded person was curious as to what lay behind the grid, just as he had done when he had been a boy, then he'd squeezed through a small opening at the other collapsed end of the tunnel and which had completely collapsed since then, sealing it forever.

After a while he began to notice people were following him making ir obvious he was under surveillance. Then one night he was suddenly grabbed off the street, hooded and bound and taken on a long drive till he found himself in a room. They'd beaten him, given him electric shocks demanding to know what he'd done with the jet. He'd played the part well denying any knowledge of the jet insisting it was somewhere under the sea. After two weeks, whoever they were released him. Still hooded he was pushed out of the car, drugged and dazed, in an empty country lane in Stockport. He'd been in a state of terror since the first day, but whatever they did to him they couldn't break him. He'd won.

That same night he'd filled a case with clothes and slipped out the back window of the flat he'd rented in Moss-Side and made for London. In a wine bar in the East End he'd met some people who worked for the Greenpeace Organisation and he mentioned he had a degree in Biology and also a private pilot's licence. They begged him to join them on board the Warrior to assist them on their pursuance of their defence of the world's environment. He'd jumped at the opportunity and for five years he'd sailed the oceans of the world as an unpaid volunteer interfeering wherever they could in mankind's great crimes against nature. He'd been happy and content. He was doing something worthwhile with his life, as if this was what he was alive for But then came the explosions. He'd been asleep at the time in his bunk. The ship had been in Aukland Harbour in New Zealand. Most of the volunteers had gone for a night out on the town before sailing to prevent the French government exploding a nuclear device off a small island in the Atoll group. The first explosion threw him from his bunk and he'd landed on the floor dazed and shaken. He'd seen Robert, the photographer, rush past the doorway after enquiring if he was all right and then he'd heard the second explosion as the ship lifted high out of the water before setting back down again. He'd found the young photographer's body smashed and disfigured floating in the hold as water poured through a gaping hole in the side. It had been two weeks later when the police arrested two French agents who had planted limpet mines on the ship's hull. No-one could comprehend that the mighty French government could be implicated in such a hideous crime.

Tan had left New Zealand and flew to Sydney where along with some of the others he flew to London to join another ship to carry on their crusade. Through the publicity of the blowing up of the ship the MIS men had been monitoring his movements and were waiting for him as he flew into Heathrow. He'd been stupid to think that they would leave him alone and they repeated the same treatment as before, beating him, not allowing him to sleep, and injecting him with heroin. In the end they dumped him in a toilet semi-conscious with a small amount of heroin in his pocket and tipped off the police to take him out of circulation for a while. The judge had sentenced him to one year imprisonment but with remission he'd finished his sentence in seven months, a mean and bitter man, whose only thoughts were of revenge. Revenge at the sick society he believed ruled and abused the world's rescources, the self-destructive human beings whose lives were wasted in their endless struggle to improve the material quality of their lives. He detested them, the suburban man and woman living in their semi-detached, with their regulation two kids growing up to repeat and live the same unrewarding wasted useless existence of their parents. But now his revenge had taken him over completely, his every being was to put his plans into action and now as he sat in the cockpit of this magnificent machine of destruction he had another weapon with which to fulfil his life's work, the annihilation of as many people as he could, total war against the whole of society, whatever age, sex, colour or creed. There were to be no exceptions; no mercy would be shown in his mission of the cull. He'd thought of the cull whilst laying in his cell as he remembered trying in vain to stop men clubbing the seals as they looked back with large appealing eyes, begging for mercy. Murdered so women could wrap the pure snow white pelts around themselves, uncaring and unconcerned about the previous wearer of the skin. He'd cried openly as he'd witnessed the killing of over a thousand baby seals in one day, their only crime to be born into a world dominated by the human species, man, who in his self-glorification conceives that eveyrthing else on this planet is there solely for his use to do whatsoever he pleases. The same man who will, no doubt, destroy the world or contaminate it forever with his nuclear weapons and laboratory bred bacilli, just because he can't agree with his neighbour. But now it was his turn. It was as if He'd been born just for this purpose. To stop the abuse of the planet.

Tan climbed from the cockpit and jumped down onto the gravel floor. Phil's excitement was obvious as his face beamed in admiration of the man who now stood in front of him.

"Oh, man, this is absolutely incredulous. I just can't find the words, I..." Tan interrupted him. Tan's thoughts of the past had angered him and he was eager to carry out a check on the jet.

"Pass that tool box," he said pointing to a small brown tin box lying on the floor Tan disappeared under the tail section as Richard came down from inspecting the cockpit.

"Will it fly?" he asked innocently. Tam removed a piece of aluminium covering and then undid a couple more bolts before lowering the two batteries from their resting place.

"It will when I've charged these up," he replied checking the batteries that had oxidised badly on the outside.

"You mean those two small batteries are all that's needed to start this thing?" asked Richard.

"That's all," replied Tan.

"You mean ycu start it up just like a car?" Tan smiled, "Not really, unless your car's got a gas turbo starter and a Pegasus engine under the bonnet."

"No, I mean, don't you need one of those big generators they start Jumbo Jets with?" asked Richard.

"The only thing stopping this from being operational is these two batteries," replied Tan, trying to clear the white fungus off the sides.

"Wow," said Phil as he fingered one of the missiles hanging from the wing. "Are these things real?"

"That missile is equivalent to five hundred pounds of TNT," replied Tan.

"Wow, that's all right:" exclaimed Phil.

"What are you going to do with it?" asked Richard who was just about to light a cigarette. Tan suddenly pulled the match from his grasp and glared hard at his comrade.

"You stupid fool," he snapped, "there's over 400 gallons of high octane aviation fuel in there, you'll blow us all to kingdom come." If' it hadn't been too dark in the tunnel Tan would have seen the redness of Richard's face as he flushed in acute embarrassment at his own stupidity.

"Oops, sorry Tan, wasn't thinking." Richard vowed there and then to himself that from that moment on he would give nothing less than 150% to the cause, and as with Phil, was filled more than ever with admiration for their leader.

"Man, what we going to do with this, what we gonna blow up, the Houses of Parliament?" said Phil as he inspected one of the rapier missiles more closely.

Tan smiled, "Something like that."

"It looks okay to me," said Richard checking the rubber on one of the tyres, "although the tyres could use some air."

"We'll soon see," replied Tan as he realised the batteries he'd hoped to recharge were totally beyond reuse. "Next time we come up here, which will be soon, she flies." Tan needed his two accomplices to help him remove the plane from the tunnel. He'd brought it in all right under its own power, but now it faced the wrong way and would have to be towed out backwards with the landrover, and with only the nose wheel to steer and two feet clearance on each wing Tan knew it wasn't going to be easy. They draped the canvas loosely back over the jet, no need to wrap it securely now. In just over a week it would see daylight once again and Tan felt a slight thrill at the prospect of piloting the Harrier one more time. He took a final look at the nose cone before pulling over the covering.

"Don't worry, your sentence is over," he said quietly patting the nose of the jet.

A small struggle and half an hour later they were back on top of the hillside. Tan rested the heavy plate back in its position over the ventilation shaft, and twenty minutes later they were bounding down the hill with Phil at the controls again of his beloved Landrover. On the drive back to Bradford the two men nagged and badgered Tan to tell them what his target for the missiles was to be. Tan just smiled as the two tried to guess.

"Not a nuclear power station," suggested Richard.

"Wow, imagine the havoc, people jamming the roads like ants trying to escape the radiation fall-out. Wow:"

Tan smiled, "No that would destroy the environment for a couple of hundred years, probably contaminate every corner of Britain in some form or another."

"Yeh, man," agreed Phil, "we want to come across as protectors of the environment, not its destroyers."

Tan sat quietly in the rear of the vehicle. His thoughts were now solely on the jet. He was excited and elated that it had remained undiscovered and completely intact. No reason for it not to fly, he thought as he discarded all the problems he'd felt before on whether the jet would still be okay. It was! He now knew it would fly and once more he would feel the delight and wonderment only one who'd flown a supersonic jet could feel. This time though, this time they would feel its sting. This was the sole reason and this reason alone why he had revealed himself to the police. By now they would know everything about him. He smiled contentedly to himself. His eyes suddenly caught Richard's intense gaze and his thoughts were momentarily broken as he saw the admiration and total obedience shine through from within. Richard smiled and nodded once at Tan, the gesture small in movement but Tan read it easily and he smiled and returned the gesture, heightened in the knowledge that this man whom he'd doubted previously was now his, totally and without question. He knew Richard Normans would lay down his life on his command. Now they were two. Two dedicated men who dared to take on the world. Perhaps he thought the only two who were actually doing anything to save the world itself, the planet, the trees, the insects, from mankind's poisons and discarded wastes that poluted the atmosphere and seas by the billion ever single day. Tan gazed at the stuck up hairs on the back of Phil's head as he sat in the driver's seat of the jeep. He knew Phil would never be totally dedicated to the cause although he was dedicated to him and probably more so to Richard who had some strange hold over Phil, but he was satisfied with his choice of accomplices and for the first time all doubts about both of them were gone.

It was 7 p.m. when they arrived back at the bedsit in Manningham. Tan didn't like the place, one or two people were beginning to take notice of them as they were coming and going, and he made a gut decision to leave as soon as it was dark. He'd enjoyed the comfort of the previous night at the Norfolk Gardens Hotel and with the laundered money they booked into the Novotel which was situated right alongside the M63 motorway 3 miles from the centre of Bradford. They didn't attract much attention as they registered in the three star hotel. Phil and Richard shared a double room next door to Tan who, after soaking in the bath for a while, turned on-the television for the ten o'clock news. Tan was greeted by his own face splattered full across the screen. It was the picture the police had taken when he'd been charged in Bow Street Police Station. He smiled at the grubby image of himself, still half drugged and without much sleep.

The picture looked so unlike his present image even without shaving his head.

The newscaster began, "It is now over a week since the mad poisoner struck and police are still unsure of Anthony Heyes' whereabouts. The police have appealed for any information as to his whereabouts believing him still to be somewhere in the Yorkshire region." Tan smiled as the image changed to the booze-red face of a man standing on some steps, a perspex police sign hanging from the door behind him. A reporter held a microphone in front of the man's face.

"Tell me, Chief Superintendant Redburn, what progress have you made in locating the suspect, Anthony Heyes?" The fat policeman fidgeted uncomfortably and smiled nervously at the camera.

"We are making a tremendous effort to locate this man who has obviously gone to ground somewhere, probably in Bradford, or he's still here in Leeds."

"What makes you think that, Superintendant?" asked the contrary reporter. George Redburn gave the man a filthy stare.

"Some of the money that was paid to Heyes before he killed Lord Bradbury has turned up in Bradford. We have several officers, including Special Branch men, working on this now."

"Could we expect an arrest soon before anyone else is murdered?"

"Yes, very soon," barked back George Redburn who hated being interrogated by sharp reporters.

Tan switched off the television and dressed back into his suit. He'd arranged to have a drink in the bar with Phil and Richard at 10.15. The smart cocktail lounge was completely devoid of people as Tan sidled up to the bar and ordered a pint. A tall thin waiter stood reading a paper leaning on the bar.

"Good heavens, Sir, you're the first pint I've served for several days," he said.

"Ah yes," replied Tan, "the mad poisoner. I've just been watching it on the news. Better make that a bottle of light ale." Tan quick to respond to the scare.

"Very wise, Sir, but he still could have poisoned it before it was bottled."

"I'll risk it, he could have poisoned the water supply for all we know as well" Tan took a sip of the frothy brew and smiled at the bar-tender. "Tell me, do you think he's mad this poisoner?" The bar-tender screwed up his face and scowled angrily before leaning nearer Tan's face.

"Got to be bloody barmy he had, 'scuse the language Sir, but he makes my blood boil. If I got me hands on him I'd bloody throttle the bastard. Well wouldn't you, Sir?" Tan pretended to screw up his face and in a serious tone he replied.

"Of course, why yes, I think they should bring back hanging." Tan was glad to see Richard and Phil approach.

"Ah, more brave souls, we are busy tonight," said the barman trying his best to be funny. Tan ordered two more light ales for his friends before they retired to a table well out of earshot of the bar.

"Did you see the news, man. Jesus, what an ugly sod that poisoner is," joked Phil smiling.

"A million pounds, Tan," said Richard inspecting his beer.
"What's that again," inquired Tan.

Richard smiled, "A million pounds reward, put up by a consortium of breweries for your capture. Thought you'd seen the news, that's why we're late down. The news was all about us."

"The world's most wanted man," added Phil slightly jealous of all the media attention on Tan.

"Wait till we've given them one up the arse with one of those cigars hanging from the jet," Phil said taking a sip of beer. "Fucking 'ell they'll double it overnight."

Tan leaned forward,. "Yes and we've only just begun."

If an onlooker had taken any notice of the three men sitting drinking in the corner, it would have been obvious they held some private joke. Their faces beamed with excitement and their eyes shone with an acute awareness as they eyed any stranger who entered the bar with suspicion till they were sure he was no threat to their freedom. Tan could feel the Luger as it rested against his back protruding from his belt hidden from view under his jacket. He wouldn't hesitate to use it. It was 12.30 when they retired to their rooms. Only Phil was slightly drunk. Richard had matched Tan's two drinks but Phil had returned several times to the bar to replenish his glass. He was soon fast asleep. Tan invited Richard into his room for coffee and the two men stayed there till the early hours discussing all the previous events, ideas and plans for future campaigns. At 3.30 Richard left to return to his own room but before he did he turned and said quietly to Tan.

"You were right to kill Sarah. Next time, to prove I am with you one hundred percent, let me do the next one."

Tan smiled as he eyed him intently gazing at him in silence for a moment. He placed his hand on his shoulder and whispered. "I will!"

CHAPTER SEVEN

Professor Edward Willis had just finished his tenth and last post mortem of the day. He and his team of pathologists had removed the brains and organs of one hundred and twenty nine souls whose deaths had been attributed to ricin. He was tired and drained after several sleepless nights and this once easy going, mild mannered man had been destroyed and broken by the events of the last few days. He'd accepted full responsibility for the loss of the poison; his one lapse in a long and distinguished career. Headlines in one of the national daily papers had called for his immediate dismissal, accusing him of being senile and negligent when it came to matters of security and safety. He walked down the row of recent victims who'd just been disembowelled on the mortuary tables. He stopped and checked the label fastened to the big toe of a once beautiful girl and checked the name on the tag. He lifted a report laid across a blood stained sheet and began to read, 'Sarah Anne Harrison, white caucasion, female, Age 27. Cause of death, Heart Attack due to Acute Heroin overdose.' He approached the sheet covering her head and lifted it clear and he stood staring at the grey face with blood matted hair hiding the crude couple of catgut stitches that held the top of her skull to the rest of her head, ready for the undertaker to beautify her once again for the final inspection by her family. He checked the needle impregnated arms that confirmed regular use of the addict's needle and the newspaper report flooded back into his brain. Senile, negligent.

Paddy, his loyal assistant had been watching the professor for the last few minutes, and worried by the look of his boss, came over and stood by his side.

"Why don't you go home now Ted," he said quietly. The Professor looked around slowly and gazed at Paddy. His eyes were bloodshot and glazed, he hadn't bothered to shave for the last few days and his beard was spiked with ginger hairs as they peered through a mass of stiff grey whiskers.

"Do you know Paddy," he said half smiling trying to ease the worried look in his friend's face, "I am tired, I think I'll go have a lay down in the office."

"Good idea, it's finished now, you shouldn't blame yourself." Paddy began to lead the Professor to his office.

"Is it though Paddy, how many more will he kill before he's caught?"

"Oh they'll catch him soon enough, don't you worry. There'll be no more killing that's for sure." Paddy opened the door and led the Professor to the couch especially installed for catnaps during the long hours often spent in the lab.

"Thanks Paddy," said the Prof as he eased himself down onto the couch. "Leave me now and tell everyone I don't want to be disturbed."

"All right Prof," replied Paddy as he checked the Prof was comfy before he left him to sleep.

As soon as the door closed the Professor eased himself up and he walked across to his desk. Opening a locked drawer he picked a ready filled syringe. He placed a letter he had written earlier, addressed to his wife, on the blotter pad. He fingered a large folder containing two year's research into various toxins and he picked it up and dropped it into the waste bin. He walked back over to the couch and sat down. His mind was totally blank and he seemed to be in a dream-like state. He didn't feel tired anymore and a burden seemed to lift from him as he pushed the needle into the top of his thigh and felt a stiffness in his leg as the cyanide flowed into his bloodstream. He felt it rise into his mouth as his lungs fought against the poison and he began to breath rapidly. His throat began to burn and the burning rose into his brain as his eyes lost all vision and in less than twenty seconds he was dead.

In London on Fleet Street the crime editor of the Daily Chronicle, James Delany, was holding a crisis meeting on the ricin murders. He was disgruntled with his team of reporters who'd been ordered back from Yorkshire due to the lack of information or any further developments.

"God Damn It," he cursed, to a group of eight men

assembled in his office. "The biggest story ever to hit and we've run out of steam!" A small wavy haired reporter who sat chain smoking under the window responded.

"Ah come on Chief, give us a break, we've been working our tails off on this one."

"Yeah," agreed another. "We've already milked it dry." A chorus of mumbled moans filled the room till Delany quietened them.

"All right lads calm down, calm down." The group of journalists quiet once again, he continued. "Now that's better children. He lit a King Edward from a box on top of his littered desk and blew a train of blue smoke upwards into the air before he continued.

"What about we print an open letter to this Heyes weirdo?"

"And say what, ask him what he's going to do next?" Delany responded quickly.

"Precisely, let's ask him nicely why he did it, what he intends to do next, what colour his fucking socks are!"

"Balls," chipped in the wavy haired journalist. "God! He's a mass murderer, a terrorist, God he's fucking killed more people in one breath than the IRA have in three years. Who do you think he is-Fanny Craddock offering readers the recipe for slaughter parties!" A chuckle of laughter rang round the room.

"Yes," retorted Delany. "But he may also be an egotist, who knows? Didn't he leave the police an easy trail to follow? God, they'd still be running round in circles these stupid sods up in Yorkshire."

"Aye, probably still looking for a man with a geordie accent," referring to the Yorkshire Ripper, quipped the curly haired man amidst a room of laughter. Delany waited for the laughter to die.

"No, serious now lads. I've got a feeling about this. Our man's no yobbo like those pratts at Wapping, he's no brick thrower or agitator. He's the elite and ex-fighter pilot with a grudge. God they don't spend a million pounds to train a pilot without first finding out he's a nutter or not." A serious silence fell as the gathered men began to realise that James Delany was talking sense.

"Why do you think the government slapped a D Notice on any reference to his air force career?" James Delany knew, if he could force some sort of response from Anthony Heyes he could sell every paper they could print as well as open a line of contact for the police to track. A door burst open suddenly at the back of the room as a reporter burst in.

"Professor Willis has been found dead. Chopped himself in his office," he blurted our excitedly.

"Don't just stand there lad, get the rest of the story." The young reporter stood staring back for a moment.

"You mean I get to.write it?"

"Course you fucking do, now get on with it." Delany clapped his hands and surveyed his small team. "Right lads, let's see if we can tempt our man outa the woodpile."

David Galbraith was shocked to hear the news of Professor Willis's death. He'd liked the old man as did most people who'd known him. The other victims were all strangers but he'd taken the Prof's death very personally, after all he'd worked on many a case with him especially over the last two years. He'd even slept in the Prof's office while he'd waited for the result of a post mortem and once whilst the Prof spent three hours stabbing a dead pig to verify the shape and depth of cuts in a murder victim. Now he would work every waking hour, every minute every day to catch this evil man once and for all. He'd spent most of that day at RAF Finningley near Doncaster trying to piece together a profile on Anthony Heyes from his days as a pilot there. He'd located two of his former colleagues but all they'd say about him was that he was just a regular sort of chap. The MI5 had removed all their records of his dismissal proceedings, and in all David felt he'd had a wasted day. He knew his only chance of catching Heyes was to locate the jet, he knew he had it somewhere, otherwise why would MI5 be involved chasing round removing records from files. But where? Where could one hide a jet without suspicion. 'Maybe he did destroy it years ago.' Doubts began to enter into his head as he delved deeper and deeper. He couldn't think where anyone could secrete a jet away without someone eventually stumbling across it sooner or later or even its discarded remains. He knew probably the only chance of catching Heyes and his accomplices was to locate the hiding place of the jet, especially now with every crank in Britain reporting sightings of him in every town and city one could imagine. 'Damn those fools for offering that stupid reward.' David stopped the car and checked the map once more. He'd turned off the A628 on his way back from the RAF base and was now heading towards the small village of Saddleworth just outside Oldham. He didn't have to check the house number as he drove onto a small neat council street, a crowd of reporters were camped outside a red brick semi, its curtains completely drawn. David's heart sunk. A police constable guarded the small gate and a plain clothed officer sat in a Vauxhall reading a paper as David pulled slowly to a stop behind a row of vans and cars. David approached the detective in the car, although he'd never seen him before he recognised a fellow police officer when he saw one.

"Evening," he said as a thin faced detective looked up at him.

"You come to relieve me?" he replied mistaking David for his relief.

"Sorry chum," replied David flashing his Special Branch warrant card under his nose. "She in?"

"Only if you've got a written order, and then the old bag will probably tell you to piss off."

David ignored the officer's request for an interview document and turned and proceeded arrogantly towards the constable on the gate. Without recourse the constable, recognising a higher ranking officer when he saw one, saluted politely and opened the gate. The detective in the car watched David for a moment before he returned to reading his paper.

"Try the back door, Sir," said the constable.

"Thanks," replied David as he strode past rounding the side of the house he was glad to be out of view of the prying eyes of the reporters. He knocked hard on the half glass door and he saw the curtain move slightly at the rear of the window and then a woman's voice came from behind the door.

"What do you want?"

David cleared his throat before replying in a soft warm voice.

"Mrs. Heyes, I'm David Galbraith, I'd like a word about your son."

"You the police?" replied Anthony's mother in a rich Oldham accent.

"Yes I am but..." She cut him off in mid sentence.

"Piss off, I'm not talking to any police."

"You don't understand, I'm a friend of Tony's. I was in the air force with him," lied David. He waited a moment till a clatter of bottles signalled the door was about to open. A head of hair with a mixture of colours, brown, blonde with a touch of red through the many shades it had been dyed over the years, peered round the door.

"Well," she said as David stared at a pleasant rounded face heavily made up with mascara with thick face powder hiding the lines and deep red lipstick on large protruding lips.

"I can see you're Tony's mother, you've got his kind eyes," lied David again knowing one wrong word would find the door closed again.

"What's your name again?""she asked still reluctant to let him in.

He repeated his name adding, "We trained together at Cranwell." Her eyes screwed up scrutinising him closely.

"You said you were a copper."

"I am but I'm here as Tony's friend. I could have lied but I didn't." This did the trick. The door opened fully and she nodded signalling him to enter. He followed her into a neat room. An old but well looked after suite dominated the room. An old radiogram and a tiled fireplace remainded him of a house of the sixties. A picture of Tan in a cheap gold frame rested in the middle of an old sideboard, another in his full RAF uniform hung from a wall at the back of the room.

"Sit down." She offered David a seat on a chair in the dimly lit room. David obliged and took the incentive quickly.

"I don't think Tony's done what the papers say." She stared back at him hard without responding.

"I mean, that's not the man I knew, a mass murderer."

"Why not him?" she retorted, still eyeing him suspiciously.

"He's a quiet reserved deep thinking man, who cared about people."

"Nonsense," she shouted harshly. David's heart sank as he

thought his visit had just ended.

"That was all front." She smiled a sweet sort of smile at him and suddenly David felt she was coming onto him a little as she re-arranged the thin cotton housecoat she was wearing to reveal a large cleavage and for the first time he noticed her large round breasts being pushed proudly outwards straining against the housecoat. She lit a cigarette and sucked on it seductively and crossed over her legs to reveal the underside of a fat rippled thigh.

"You know if we ever had any visitors, even my own sister's kids, his cousins, our Tony would go and hide under the bed. Did you know that?"

"Not Tony," replied David, "he was always life and soul in the mess."

"Don't know about that, but our Tony was a strange lad, perhaps he changed when he got older."

"You mean to say you hardly saw him when he left home?"

"I never hardly saw him before he left home, always over the moor, he spent more time on them hills than ever in here." She suddenly stood up and picked up an envelope from behind a clock on the mantlepiece and handed it to David.

"Read that," she said. He slipped the paper from out of its resting place and began to read. It was headed 'The Daily Echo Fleet Street London'.

"Dear Mrs. Heyes, I am pleased to inform you of our offer of £50,000 for the story of your son's upbringing." David stopped reading and handed the letter back. "You should accept it." He meant it, what harm could it do?

"Oh, I already have." She came close to him and sat on the arm of the chair opposite, her legs wide apart. He caught sight of a pair of white lace panties, and he felt a little ashamed of himself as he became aroused by the older woman. Maybe it was the semi darkness of the room, or maybe because of the smell of cheap perfume that breezed around when she moved or the sordidness of the situation. She lowered her head till their faces were almost touching and he smelt the whisky on her breath.

"You don't know our Tan at all do you?" she said softly looking straight into his eyes. "That's his nickname, he only tells close people his nickname." She kissed him gently on his forehead and lifted his chin upwards. "I haven't had a real man in a long time," she said as she kissed him softly full on his unprotesting lips.

"You come upstairs with me sonny an I'll tell you everything you want to know." She lifted his hand and pushed it down the cleavage till it found a resting place round her large breast. He lifted it clear, surprised at its firmness and size. As he kissed her saucer sized nipple his trousers grew tight as his penis became erect and she led him up the stairs like a temptress she was, as if taking a young boy to bed for the very first time, his eagerness spread unashamedly across his face.

It was the early hours of the next day as David closed the back door behind him and sauntered casually down the garden path. A different constable than before had been half sitting half leaning on the gate and he jumped to his feet as David surprised him. He checked his watch and made an entry in his note book and gave David a shy look.

"Good morning Sir," he said sarcastically as he pushed past. A sleepy reporter's face appeared at one of the van windows and stared for a moment, before disappearing out of sight. There were two detectives in the Vauxhall now, one was asleep and the other one jumped out of the car and hurried by towards him.

"Get in touch with your office at once," he blurted out. David just nodded as he strolled past. 'Fucking pratt,' he thought. He knew they'd do a run down on his registration plates on the XR3 and report in with the details. He started the car and revved the engine particularly hard till the engine screamed. Several more curious but disgruntled faces appeared at the other car and van windows, one mouthed the word 'Bastard'. David just smiled. He jammed the car into reverse and sped up the street backwards. He slammed on the brakes and pulled the steering wheel over onto full lock. The car front came right round to where the rear end had been and he thrust the car into first and with blue smoke bellowing out from the spinning rear wheels he screamed down the small road touching seventy before braking to meet the road junction. His six weeks advanced vehicle driving course had been put to use for the first time if only to deliberately wake the vultures who waited outside for their scraps of news. He drove at a steady fifty now; the roads were completely free of traffic and he pushed himself back into his seat, a smug self satisfied feeling about him. He'd delved every detail of Tan Heyes past life, from her and he'd enjoyed one of the best fucks he'd ever had, one thing David had learned a long time ago you can never know the contents of a package by its wrapping. He picked up the radio phone from its resting place and plunged the red button into life. A woman's voice came from the earpiece.

"That you David?"

"But of course my cheri," he replied in a mocking tone.

"You drunk?" The woman's voice sounded cross.

"Oh piss off, narky knickers, where's the old man?"

Inspector Forrest had been waiting for David's check in call and had come out of his office on hearing the radio conversation. He snatched the handset from the young woman operator just in time to hear the end of David's message.

"This is the old man, you cocky young sod. What the hell have you been doing all the time in Mrs. Heyes' house? I've had the Chief bloody Constable of Lancashire giving me an ear bashing every bloody fifteen minutes."

"Fucking," interrupted David.

"What was that?"

"You asked what I was doing and I said, fucking."

"Who were you fucking?" Alan Forrest was suddenly aware of the young woman constable sat by his elbow and he blushed as their eyes met. David's voice came back on the air.

"I was interviewing Mrs. Heyes, what do you think I was doing? "

Well why don't you ask permission if only out of courtesy?" Alan Forrest's curiosity had kept him at his desk all night. He'd known exactly what time David had entered Mrs. Heyes' house by the ear bashing about diplomacy from a high ranking officer in the Lancashire force. But he now wanted to know what information the young detective had gained. Knowing the rest of the enquiry team hadn't even got through the door.

"Well what have you got?"

"Oh just the usual stuff."

"Don't be reticent with me you young pillock, I'll have you back in uniform."

"Sorry Sir, but we are on air."

The Inspector knew David was correct.

"Get your foot down lad and be in my office within half an hour," he retorted sternly and then as calm as you like he said, "Bacon and eggs all right?"

"Do nicely." He hung up. David turned onto the A672 and hit the throttle hard driving through the small villages as if he was on the RAC rally. Five minutes later he turned onto the M62 motorway and he had the car cruising at 120 mph, and inside twenty minutes he pulled to a stop outside the Special Branch offices in Leeds.

Inspector Forrest was sitting at his desk when David strolled in.

"Well, give us the SP" he asked impatiently. David sat down in a chair by the desk.

"I figured she might be able to tell us something too," he said half apologising.

"You mean you were in there a few hours and you got nothing?" David smiled.

"Well nothing new! Seems she hardly saw him once he left home."

"You mean I've waited up half the frigging night for nothing?"

"Seems so."

"You pratt." The Inspector pulled his jacket from over the chair and folded it over his arm. He leaned over the intercom and pressed the button.

"Oh Janice," he said, "cancel that breakfast."

Tan was joined by Phil and Richard as he sat in the Novotel dining room eating his breakfast.

"God, pass me the coffee. I'm parched," said Richard as he sat down.

"My mouth feels like the bottom of a budgie's birdcage," added Phil. Tan smiled at them.

"It's that bottled beer makes you dehydrate more rapidly. You should have drunk the draught." A waitress came and took the late arrival's order. Tan threw the newspaper onto the table in the direction of Richard and said, "Read that." Richard lifted the paper and began to read. The headlines read:

'An open letter to Mr. Heyes.

Dear Mr. Heyes,

Whether you are aware or not you have most of the population of Britain quite terrified. We as a newspaper would like to know why you assassinated those innocent people. We know from our research of your past you are a caring man. Why else would you work for no recompense for five years for the Greenpeace Organisation? We refer to the bombing of the Rainbow Warrior. Is this a vendetta because of that or are you just another freaked out junkie who did it for kicks?

What are your intentions for the immediate future? We as a representative of the British public invite you to reply to our questions. The front page will be reserved for your reply. Please give the relatives of those people who died the satisfaction of knowing why their loved ones died. Or are you just another back street bomber without conscience or reason? We dare you, Mr. Heyes, to reply!

The letter finished 'yours faithfully, James Delany- Editor.'

"Wow," said Phil as he'd been reading the paper over Richard's shoulder.

"Very cleverly written," added Richard noticing they'd not used words like 'mad' or 'murderer'. Tan nodded in agreement.

"Will you respond?" asked Richard.

"What would you do?" he asked.

"I'd reply," said Richard.

"Yea, man," agreed Phil, "tell them for why."

Tan had already decided to reply, he'd intended writing to the papers anyway to explain his views to the public.

"Okay, I'll reply," he said, "but not today, we'll let them sweat a day or so."

Tan felt safe for another night at the Novotel, nobody took much notice of them, after all hotels were always full of strangers. That night he stayed in his room and worked on his reply to the paper, for early the next day he had decided to try and extricate the jet from the tunnel. Richard and Phil had been back down to the bar for a drink and as they returned to their room Richard stopped off to pay Tan a visit.

"How's the letter going?" he asked as Tan let him into the room.

"Oh I finished that hours ago," replied Tan as he walked over and switched off the TV he'd been watching.

"Where you going to post it from?" asked Richard sitting down in an easy chair.

"I thought you and Phil could take a train to London for the day and post it there;"

"You mean direct at the news office?"

"Oh no, don't do that, they'll no doubt be watching and filming the outside of the building hoping that we will turn up in person. No, with a London post mark it will distract them from this area for a bit." Tan plugged the kettle in and offered Richard a coffee. When it was ready Tan sat on the edge of the bed sipping the fresh brew.

"Besides you could take Phil and get him some shit while you're there." Tan referring to Phil's love of cannabis resin.

"Listen Tan," said Richard as if he'd been plucking up courage to speak.

"I have an idea for the poison." Tan smiled. His thoughts lately had all been on the Harrier and he had forgotten about the poison for a while.

"Well let's have it."

Richard shifted to the front of his seat and leaned forward slightly. "About three years ago I worked in the meal packing area at Heathrow airport." Richard lit a cigarette while Tan waited for him to continue.

"You know these pathetic meals they give you in tin foil boxes on the plane."

"Do you mean poison the food?" interrupted Tan.

"No better than that, but let me finish first. It's the water, they take large pans of water onto the jets to make the tea and coffee from." Tan smiled, his brain warming to the idea.

"Give me all the details," he said.

"Well it's simple really. Near Terminal One is the processing area, you know, they have all these women chopping up cheese and tomatoes and bits of pie and packing them in the food trays.

Do you know how many they do in a day? Ten thousand."

"Ten thousand" repeated Tan.

"Oh sometimes more. It's not a lot really when you consider a jumbo jet can carry 400 people and there's one landing and taking off every 60 seconds. Well not just Jumbos you know."

"Tell me more." Tan was becoming more and more interested.

"Well, at the back of Terminal One is the water shed. Where they fill, clean and preheat the water pans. All you need is a smear of ricin in each drum and you could easily wipe out thousands. Make Pontefract look petty."

"You could get in alright?" asked Tan.

"Easy. The shed's not even in the main building and airport porters come and go all day bringing empties, taking refills, you know the gen, no-one takes a bit of notice."

Tan's mind became excited at the thought.

"You'd have no qualms?"

"None. I'm as dedicated as you. Your ideals are now my ideals. I think it is necessary. If we had to kill all the population and start again from scratch it wouldn't bother me. At least the air would be clean to breath and we could get back to basics and began to worry about the real things in life like three good meals a day, keeping warm and dry and healthy. People have detracted from the real things and when people start dropping like flies they will being to realise just being alive is more important than anything else in the world. They'll not take their existence for granted.

Tan sat, quite stunned by Richard's short speech. He was impressed.

"Quite the Philosopher, I should have let you write the letter," he said patting Richard on the knee. "Oh, I'm sure you'd have done us proud."

"But don't you see Tan, this is bigger than all of us. It is up to us, the three of us, to bring some sanity back to the world"

"What about Heathrow! Shall we do it?" Richard was eager to prove himself worthy of Tan's trust.

"Can you get in and out okay?"

Richard removed a yellow card from his wallet and

handed it to Tan. Tan looked at a small photo of Richard with his name embolished on the plastic card. At the top the words 'Heathrow Security Pass, Auxillary Worker'.

"But surely this is out of date?" enquired Tan.

"There is no date stamp just a yearly colour code. Last year blue, year before red. Guess what's this year's colour? They are back to yellow. They have a magnetic swipe but nobody swipes them."

The next couple of hours the two men worked out a plan of action. Phil would stay behind and help Tan locate a new place to stay. Richard would first drive to Leeds and collect the ricin from its hiding place in Becket Street Cemetery. Tan explained he'd hidden the container in the top soil of a steeple jack's grave, "You can't miss it," he'd said. "The headstone is shaped like a miniature mill chimney. In the box it's burried in are two eardrop dispensers. Use one to take a file full and take the other to dispense the ricin into the pans. Use only the minutest drop per pan. Take only what you need, leave the rest for another mission."

The next morning the three men checked out of the hotel quite early. Richard was to take the Cortina to Leeds, pick up the poison then catch the 7 o'clock train to London. That should give him time to join the lunch time workers going back into Heathrow. Tan handed him the letter in the foyer of the hotel.

"Don't forget what I told you, do it on the train journey, you'll have plenty of time. Get some writing paper from the stationers at the station, be very careful with the ricin. Use the rubber gloves, don't breathe in when you unscrew the lid, but if you can't hold your breath keep the container as far away from your face as you can. Tan shook Richard by the hand. Meet you lunch time tomorrow in the Old Boar, Market Street, Huddersfield." Richard waved at Phil who had been reading the various papers on the news stand. As he opened the glass door to exit the foyer a police patrol constable came pushing past. Richard smiled politely.

"Thanks mate," said the policeman. Tan had joined Phil at the news stand. The policeman came over and selected a couple of papers from the rack and paid the night porter the exact amount. Tan selected his papers and stood directly next to the constable as he handed the porter a pound note.

"What's the weather going to do today?" he said deliberately distracting the constable from his reading. The policeman looked up at Tan and stared as if examining closely. Phil panicked a bit and moved slowly towards the exit.

"Oh, grey and cloudy as usual, bloody depressing, I hate this country, the two W's, Tan looked bemused.

"The two W's, what's that?" he asked.

"The weather and the wogs, gone to the dogs."

Tan smiled, "Never heard that before," said Tan patronisingly, "I'll remember that. Good one." 'Prick,' thought Tan. He nodded a sort of cheerio before joining Phil who was waiting in the Landrover.

"Jesus!" exclaimed Phil. "I know you look different with the bald head an all but you didn't half put the wind up me. I mean, what if he'd sussed you? What then?"

"I'd have had to shoot him wouldn't I," smiled Tan, as he eased the Luger out of his pocket and placed it under the seat. Phil started the engine.

"Where to now, boss?" he asked.

"Huddersfield. Let's find a nice cottage to rent, somewhere in the countryside up in the hills. Let's breath some."

Richard arrived in London Kings Cross at 10 o'clock. He bought some stamps from a machine and posted the letter. He then crossed the road to the coach station where he boarded a bus to Heathrow. By 11 o'clock he'd arrived. He walked back round the terminal and into the Continental lounge where he could watch the security gate to check the pass colour. If the colour had been changed again he would have to slip through from the transit side. He knew it wouldn't be easy, not now they had tightened security after several terrorist attacks on the airport lounges throughout Europe. Richard eyed a machine gun clad policeman and smiled to himself as he thought that by the time the policeman had thought whether or not to pull the trigger in an attack he would probably be dead. A man with a gun must be prepared to shoot first and ask questions later. His father's voice reminding him of when he was sixteen and his father took him to a gun club for the first time. 'A gun has only one purpose, and that is to kill. If you have any doubts about using a gun don't bother to pick one up. Shooting at paper targets is only to learn to handle the gun, to aim and feel its recoil. If you ever point it at a man for whatever reason you must be prepared to use it.' Richard's father had fought throughout the second world war till he'd been wounded at Monte Casino. The war had scarred him deeply and had hardly ever left his thoughts even now some forty years on. Richard's eighteenth birthday present had been a Berreta automatic pistol which he'd learned to use with some dexterity. He smiled again to himself as he thought of his father. He'd be the only father in Britain who'd probably be proud if he found out his son was an armed terrorist.

Richard decided to enter the watershed at lunchtime, hopefully only a few people there. He watched as a worker strolled through the security gate and waved a pass in the air. He sighed with relief. It was yellow. He made for the door pushing past people coming out onto the sidewalk. He walked along the side of the building at the end, it joined a high wire fence topped with barbed wire. The gate through was thirty yards away and Richard's stomach rumbled slightly as he approached. The security guard sat on a large stool in the doorway of the small security hut. Richard held the pass high in the air as he walked through the gate. The guard hardly bothered to look. He walked on for about fifty yards till he came to a small building. He entered a door he knew was the cloakroom. Rows of lockers and hooks with coats and personal belongings filled the place. Sounds of coughing came from the toilet area indicating he was not alone. Richard acted quickly and took off his jacket and lifted a grubby blue overall off it's hook. He placed the bottle of ricin in the pocket of the overall and pushed the rubber gloves in his trouser pocket along with the dispenser. The toilet flushed and Richard bent, pretending to tie his shoe laces as an old man emerged from one of the toilets. Still coughing and spluttering, a cigarette hung from his mouth. Richard went into one of the toilets and locked the door, it was 12.32. In 28 minutes it would be lunch time and he could seek out the watershed to complete his task.

Richard dozed off slightly tired from his early start. A hustle and bustle of doors banging and people flooding into the cloakroom woke him, signalling it was the first shift lunch break.

He left the toilet and kept his eyes to the ground on the off chance someone he'd worked with previously might recognise him, although he'd only worked here six weeks to get enough money to go touring around France, some three years ago. He came out of the cloakroom and turned left down the side of No.1 departure lounge and strolled the hundred yards until he turned right onto the airport apron itself. Two 727's were standing on the edge of the departure gate's long extending covered gangways which stretched from the terminal building right to the door of the planes, doing away completely with the passenger stairs. One of the planes was being unloaded. A large scream of engine thrust as a Boeing 747 had just come into land, its four Rolls Royce engines screamed as the pilot reversed thrust to slow the plane to one hundred miles per hour landing speed. Row upon row of planes lined the apron. Richard eyed the huge beasts of the air with the fascination of a child. He could never comprehend how something so huge could lift into the sky. He noticed the different insignias painted on the fuselage, Air France, Lufthansa, Quantas, Pan Am and many more. Standing magnificent in its own bay was a plane, smaller than the rest, Concorde with its sleekness of shape and the famous drooping pointed nose. A horn sounded distracting him as he moved to allow a small tow truck pulling two small cages packed with cases and it stopped by the open belly of a British Airways Jumbo jet. Richard was quietly enjoying himself he wasn't afraid or nervous. In fact, he felt quite the opposite, excited and elated with what he was about to do. He came to the middle of the terminal building about a half mile's walk from the cloakroom and there on his right a large door with the word 'water' written in white letters was open wide. Trollies lined with stainless steel containers waiting to be rinsed and filled, waited to be tended. A man in a white boiler suit climbed onto an already filled trolley and drove the wagon directly past Richard, giving him a small wave as he passed. Richard walked straight into the water shed. His heart began to beat hard against his chest and his mouth became dry as he realised he was well inside the shed and totally alone. Hose pipes were left abandoned on the floor and he quickly found two trollies stacked and loaded with full water containers. He wanted to drop the poison into newly rinsed containers, he didn't want to waste time removing lids and replacing them. At the far side of the large shed he noticed a steam cleaner and quickly deduced that a fresh stack of the square shaped containers had just been rinsed. He checked around him, he was still alone. He lifted a small phial of ricin from the overall and placed it carefully on top of a container. He then removed the rubber gloves and placed them awkwardly on his hand in his eagerness to complete his task. He lifted the eardrop dispenser from his trouser pocket and was just about to unscrew the ricin container when a small man in a blue boiler suit came in whistling through another door that led from the main building.

"Watcha mate," he said in cockney slang. Richard responded quickly.

"Alright-mate," he replied as the man walked over to a tap and turning it on, he drank straight from the nozzle allowing the water to fall directly onto the grating on the floor. "Thirsty work unloading that bloody luggage," he said cheerfully as he strolled back, still whistling, the way he had come.

Richard didn't waste another moment. He rested the file on a small wooden stool and slowly unscrewed the lid. He turned his head as far away as he could and held his breath just as Tan had instructed. He lowered the eardrop dispenser into the small amount of fluid and squeezed the small rubber top, then released it until the dropper had filled with the fluid. Still holding his breath he dropped the empty file into a long drainage grate that ran the length of the floor. He placed the dropper down on the stool and walked away several paces before allowing his lungs to empty. Then with a giant lung full of air he strode back to the dropper and proceeded to drop a small droplet of ricin into as many containers he could until finally he was done.

Leaving the airport was just as easy as entering. After recovering his jacket, after first dumping the overalls in case the owner was on the lookout for them, he just sauntered through the gate without even bothering to show his pass. He knew the security staff were there to stop unauthorised people entering and didn't really bother with people who came out. He boarded a bus outside the main entrance and sitting back he grinned to himself as he realised that he'd just planted the biggest time bomb any terrorist could ever have imagined.

Tan's letter had been collected from the post box in Kings Cross, taken to the main sorting house and delivered across the city with the lunchtime post at two o'clock.

James Delany was beginning to wish he'd never invited a reply from Anthony Heyes, his office was stacked with letters from cranks reckoning to be the Pontefract Poisoner. A small team had been designated the task of opening and reading the letters, as well as a Special Branch man who stood in readiness to act on receipt of the genuine reply.

Ginger Watson, a long serving crime journalist was just about to read his seventy-second letter of the day when suddenly he stood to his feet, a large grin, a look of excitement on his face as he shouted.

"I've got it, I've got it!" James Delany rushed from the back of the room, scrambling his way past two young women nearly sending them sprawling, he reached out and pulled the letter from Ginger Watson's hand.

"Get the envelope!" he shouted.

The small team pushed and bustled in the middle of the letter filled room, all eager to see the letter Tan had written.

"All right, get back," shouted Delany.

"I'll read it out, but shut that door, this is hot news."

The detective from the Special Branch had been inspecting the envelope. He held it in rubber clad gloves.

"Hell," he shouted, interrupting Delany, who was just about to begin. "He's here in London, this letter was franked 11.15, Kings Cross, today."

"Can I continue now?" said Delany sarcastically as he angrily eyed the detective who held the letter by the corner for him to read. He looked down at Tan's hand written letter and began to read out loud.

'Dear Mr. Editor,

I thank you for the chance to air my views through your paper to the people of Britain. No doubt, it will increase your volume of sales. However, regardless of the motives, I do need publicly to explain my actions.

Firstly, I would like to offer my condolences to the relatives of those people of Pontefract who died recently. Those people were martyrs, but by the time I am finished I hope my toll to be more in the tens of thousands than in the hundreds.

Why did I kill those people? I assassinated those people purely and simply in the way one would cull the seal or deer population. My aim is to rid the world of as many people as I can before either I myself am killed or captured, neither I fear.

My reasons for this grave act are solely to protect the very environment we all live in. I have been disgusted by the way we all abuse the very thing that sustains us. Our forests are dying through chemicals poured into the atmosphere from industry. As you will know, trees are the main source of oxygen on our planet. Brazil has just deliberately burned down an area three times the size of Britain so man can settle and produce more destruction.

Money and greed are society's ideals these days. What price? Cheap electricity! If one of our nuclear power stations explodes, making half the country uninhabitable, the surviving people will be dodging the radiation clouds that remain in the atmosphere for years to come.

However I could go on and on, seas polluted by nuclear and industrial waste, seals and dolphins dying in their thousands but forget about all this, this is mere trivia compared to what I am about to reveal. As you know the ozone layer is breaking down. A hole the size of Australia is hanging over the north pole. What you may not know is that radiation from the sun bounces off the ozone layer and out into space. In 1902 a proton event on the surface of the sun produced a massive explosion on its surface sending 160,000 tons of radio active solar particles bombarding into the ozone layer. Scientists believe the radiation count was 10,000 rems. Without the ozone layer half the planet would have been destroyed. Again in 1957 another proton event occurred which was monitored and is recorded at the Solar Scope unit in Sun City Boulder Colorado. However, at this moment in time a huge gathering of sun spots over sixty times the size of our earth is building up on the surface of the sun. This is being watched closely by the sun scope people in Colorado. They expect the proton event to happen at any time. Flames from the sun will climb over 50 million miles into space bringing our sun 43 million miles nearer to our earth.

Without an ozone layer what chance do we have. Oh, you may think this is all science fiction but I assure you this is fact. We had the evidence on the Rainbow Warrior but now you know why the French Government sank us.

But I warn you most of the governments of the world are aware of the facts but if you consult them before you go to print they will censor you forthwith. Yes, I am an angry young man but because I have the strength of my beliefs people, millions of people, fear me because I threaten their existence. Now they will listen to what I have to say. Perhaps if we all listened we could save our planet then the killing could stop and we could build a better world.

Signed Yours Faithfully,
Anthony Heyes (Greenpeace)

P.S. I have already instigated my next phase. Nothing anyone could do would stop its inevitable outcome. I will inform you first before the outcome only if you print my letter in full.

Also another tit bit for your paper. We have targeted a prominent politician for assassination. After his assassination the world will be a better place.

James Delany lifted his eyes from the letter and surveyed the gathering surrounding him. A look of terror fixed on all of their faces. Delany's eyes fixed on a wiry thin faced man, a huge pair of glasses seemed to cover his face.

"Fixby," he called the editor's name. "What you make of this?"

Fixby removed his glasses making his face shrink. "Incredible but feasible," he replied. "Now this stuff, not many people know about. The sun scope in Colorado watches the sun day and night! I doubt they'd tell you anything. You couldn't print any of that stuff, it would cause a world panic!"

All eyes were fixed on the boney faced man. "But as is common knowledge sunspots or proton reactions can easily build up and disperse without so much as a whisper, any sun watcher knows that it would flare up tomorrow and melt our planet, within seconds, this threat has always existed and will always be there till the end of time. A huge sigh of relief rang around the listeners and smiles returned to their faces.

"I can't print it, more's the pity," cried Delany, "well the bit about the sun, he knew I wouldn't, too many people would sympathise with him and you know how gullible and naive the public at large are, God they'd stop going to work, society would fall apart, crime would increase, murder, rape, Jesus," he stopped to think for a moment, "I'll dilute this letter a bit and see how Heyes responds. Let's make this our front page story tomorrow."

CHAPTER EIGHT

Tan and Phil had tramped round the estate agents in the centre of Huddersfield till finally they found a small isolated cottage for rent just on the edge of the Pennine Hills near Melton. It was ideal. The Harrier was only 20 miles or so away up in the hills.

Tan paid a month's rent explaining to the assistant in the estate agents shop that they were on holiday and needed a house to live in while they explored the countryside. She gave them a key and a small map explaining the directions and three quarters of an hour later Tan and Phil turned up a lonely winding lane. A small wooden sign read 'Ambleside cottage'. A mile further up the hill they came to an old weaver's cottage half snuggled into the stone covered hillside. Sheep were grazing in the garden and they scattered as the Landrover approached.

"Man this looks great!" said Phil as he leapt from the Landrover and walked to the small door in the front of the cottage. "People must have been small in the old days, he said. Tan slipped the key into the lock and it turned easily. He entered a small hallway and began to check out every oom one by one. It only had one bedroom, an old style bathroom, a front parlour and an equally large kitchen with an electric cooker. A large pine table stood in the middle. The front room had a neat cottage suite with green upholstery, a small bookcase with three books and several rugs hiding the bare threads of a worn carpet. It was sparcely furnished but it was clean and tidy and Tan felt at home immediately.

"How long will we be here," asked Phil as he realised he was destined to sleep on the couch again.

"A week or so," replied Tan as he gazed out of the window and down into the valley below. He couldn't have picked a better spot than this away from prying eyes, the nearest cottage must have been a mile or so back down the hill. Yes, he thought, this will do nicely.

David Galbraith had been ordered by George Redburn to interview some of the crank reported sightings of Anthony Heyes. He'd protested vigourously till George had threatened to take him off his team and send him back to his department.

"Ordinary police work, laddie, that's how we'll get the bastard," said George as David walked out the office door cursing. An hour later he was summoned back into the office, a copy of Tan's letter had arrived on Redburn's desk. A team of detectives had been trying to analyse its contents.

"Well Wonder Boy, what do you make of it?" asked George after David had been scrutinising the letter for several minutes.

"Nothing!" exclaimed David in reply.

"Nothing?" repeated George, surprised. "I thought they said you were some sort of genius or something."

David grinned and explained his reply.

"All he does is winge about why he's a terrorist. He hasn't left his address or told us anything of what he is going to do next apart from the threat to kill someone."

Redburn looked stunned. "I'm bloody flabbergasted Wonder Boy, what about the sun stuff, what do you make of that?"

David smiled, "Oh that, I didn't see what relevance the sun had to this case."

Redburn's face grew redder than usual, he could see David was chastising him but he refrained from using profanities and politely requested David's views on the matter.

"Utter nonsense," he replied, "I once saw a T.V. programme by the astronomer Patrick Moore who was talking about the sun. He predicted the life of the sun at 500 million years. He also stated that some scientists believe the sun could burn for eight million years but he also stated that there's nothing to stop the Sun disintegrating tomorrow. So much for science."

David pondered a moment before he continued. "I can see probably how it maybe sparked Heyes into action but they always have excuses don't they. When the IRA have a united Ireland they'll find another reason to blow people up, these people always do!"

The Chief Superintendant was one of the people who when reading Heyes' letter in full had panicked a little. He was pleased now Galbraith had reassured him.

"Just exactly what I thought too," lied George, glad he'd reacted the same way he had to Galbraith's smugness, especially in the crowded room. "What about this prominent person bit?"

"Yes, I've been thinking on that."

David read the letter over again. A sea of heads gazed back at him and he got the feeling Redburn was trying to make him look foolish.

"Prominent person, but then he writes, 'after his assassination.' That rules out the Prime Minister because she's a woman. So he's got a grudge against someone prominent. Could be old Cecil at the Department of the Environment." David disliked the minister for some reason he wasn't sure about, that's probably why he'd thought of him as a target. But like him, only Heyes would know who his hated politician was. Although he'd only stated 'a prominent person' in his letter, he knew it had to be a high ranking minister.

It always was, but then a thought came into his head. He pondered for a while, a sudden glare of wonderment appeared on his face. "Emile Gerand," he spluttered out.

"The President of France," said George his eyes wide in surprise. "Why him?"

"Greenpeace. Heyes was on the Rainbow Warrior, it was the French who blew it up."

"The Common Market Conference is next week in London. He's there already, the post mark on Heyes' letter."

"Not necessarily," replied David. "We know he has at least two helpers, and may have more for all we know."

Redburn lit a cigar and leaned back in his chair pretending to ponder the situation.

"What course of action would you take say if Gerand was the target?" David smiled smugly. He knew whatever he said next, George Redburn would act accordingly. But Redburn spoke first.

"We could use him as bait. But then say if he uses the poison somewhere along the way Heyes would be long gone before we even knew Gerand had been got to."

Galbraith gave Redburn a look of exasperation, a look of such distaste that even the older man for once noticed, but before he could speak one of George's minions leapt into the fray.

"I think this whole business of including the French President in this matter is utter conjecture without any foundation whatsoever."

Galbraith became suddenly agitated. He glared at the detective and took on his challenge.

"You empty heads!" he spoke calmly.

"It's under your nose but you do not see it, do you?"

Blank faces stared back.

"Answer me this," he challenged them, "why have MI5 been on the scene? Why has there been a D notice banning any reference to Heyes' Court Martial and the crash of the jet? I'll tell you exactly why, Heyes has got the jet stashed away."

One or two sniggers came from the gathering but Galbraith ignored them as he pulled a file of papers from his brief case. He began to read aloud the RAF's report on the crash of the jet Heyes had flown. He pointed out that not one witness had been found to corroborate Heyes' story, no explosion was heard. An immediate search followed, no sign of wreckage, no sign of Heyes, not until eighteen hours later did they find Heyes. Eighteen hours in which he'd softly landed the jet, secreted it and returned to the crash site to be rescued. A submarine searched for two months and found nothing. Galbraith smiled. But the best clue of all that confirms Heyes has the jet. He opened his note book and read his notes on his Strangeways visit to Raymond Seymour. 'Look up to the sky when you hear a noise like a jet going over and then you'll hear a big bang and the whole building will come down on you.'

"He's got the Harrier, where, how?"

"He's got it"

All eyes stared back, there were no more sniggers. Redburn relit the cigar that was hanging from his mouth.

"Surely if he has got the jet it won't be in flying condition," said the Superintendant blowing the foul smelling smoke at David who leaned back as far as he could to avoid the fumes.

"Perhaps Sir, but then again if it's been stored correctly and kept at a steady temperature there's no reason why it couldn't fly."

"Do you think we should take expert advice on this?"

"Already have Sir, you've just had it. The Harrier is quite simple. It has one jet engine encased in the main fuselage. The flaps and rudder are all controlled by steel rods. All it needs to fly is power and guidance, it would need very little maintenance at all." David's trip to RAF Finningley had not been totally useless.

"But if he had it, why hasn't he used it before now?"

"Who knows. Perhaps he is waiting for Gerand." David smiled.

"But then it could be our own Prime Minister, we are only guessing after all. Then it could have been the money. We know he's changed some or Bradbury's £100,000 allover Bradford. Perhaps he needed the money to get the jet in the air."

Later that evening a meeting was held between all the various branches of the police force who had been ordered to pool their efforts and information. The order had come straight from the Home Secretary himself. Over two hundred high ranking officers had converged into the main council chamber at Leeds City Hall. The briefing room at Milgarth proved to be too small to hold such a gathering. George Redburn chaired the meeting and he insisted that David joined him on the top table overlooking the select gathering. Chief Superintendant Redburn opened the meeting by reading a directorate from the Home Secretary. It instructed the different forces across the country to forget all inter-department rivalries and work together as a complete unit to track down this mad man at large. The meeting had begun at 5.30 p.m. and as David stared at his watch it was now 3.15 a.m. He yawned. The various heads of forces came forward and had voiced their ideas and theories of what should be done. Nothing new was suggested till at 4.05 George Redburn stood up in front of some of the most intelligent police brains in Britain and began to offer his ideas. He began by stating that in his opinion and that of his colleagues, Anthony Heyes had successfully stolen a Harrier jet. The gathering mumbled and some sniggered, especially those who knew George. But George Redburn had been reborn, his zest for his work had returned and his once befuddled brain had been sparked into life. The whisky bottle locked away now for several days, George Redburn, once the most highly regarded policeman in the region, was back in business.

"You can snigger and laugh," he continued, "but I've heard nothing constructive whatsoever. I want this man caught and put away soon. I'd eat a bucket of worms if it would tell me where to find him." Some of the more tired policemen in the gathering forced themselves up in their seats as George's booming voice continued his oratory. He read out all the facts from Galbraith's report. "Let us assume he has the Harrier secreted away. Where is it? Has he abandoned it, or has he been maintaining it for a purpose?" George pulled a large map down that had been hanging in wait from a tripod. A specially constructed map of Yorkshire and Humberside stretching down to Lincolnshire and Norfolk. George pointed at the map with a snooker cue. "Let us go back to when Heyes stole the jet." He pointed the stick of ash at a spot in the middle of the Wash. "The last contact with the flight lieutenant's jet was here at 0600 hours. No contact with Heyes was established till nearly eighteen hours later when he was found floating at this point." George pointed to a spot ten miles east of his last known position about five miles off the coast near Wolferton. "If he had gone into the sea as he reported, his emergency rescue signal would have started immediately, but it wasn't picked up till 0132 a.m. the next day!" A tired impatient chief constable from Manchester rudely interrupted George.

"But we all know this George, what's the point?"

"Bear with me Cedric, old boy," he retorted glaring at his colleague with a phoney smile spread on his face but his eyes couldn't disguise his contempt. George continued, he was enjoying every minute, never had there been such a meeting of the elite in the history of the force and he wanted his full ten bob's worth.

"We've all seen the letter Heyes has written practically declaring war on society. Even if he has destroyed the jet he probably still has four rapier missiles at his disposal. But personally myself and my team are convinced he still has the jet and he is going to use it." George looked at David and David smiled confidently back at George who turned and carried on.

"Whether you like it or not it's the only lead we've got to go on. We must find its hiding place, it's got to be in this area somewhere," he pointed out Yorkshire and East Lancashire. "We must pool our men and lift every blade of grass." George sipped a glass of water on the desk and looked at the men directly in front. "It is now over two weeks since the Pontefract affair and what have we got. Bloody nothing!"

"Don't be stupid George, we know a hell of a lot," came a voice from the middle of the room.

"We only know what Heyes wants us to know," shouted George.

"God, he's told us everything, he's leading us a bloody tango all over the place. We've never had as much evidence in a case in all my years on the force.

"I will finish in a moment but first I would like to suggest we take the following steps. Firstly we must publish the facts behind the Harrier business and ask for the public's help and vigilance in finding its whereabouts." George realized he'd have to appeal to the Home Secretary to suspend the 'D' notice issued on this matter blocking all publicity. "And secondly we must scour every lockup building, every abandoned warehouse, every hole in the ground, anywhere the jet could be hidden." Redburn returned to his seat. A superintendant from the Metropolitan Police Force made a brief opposition but was soon shouted down and all in agreement to an all out search for the Harrier, the meeting ended.

It was 7.05 when David came out of the town hall into the bright sunshine of a new day. He was tired and hungry as he strolled over to a news stand at the side of the building and bought a Daily Echo. He smiled at the headlines, 'Heyes declares war on society'. George Redburn was coming out of the entrance surrounded by his colleagues and a large group of reporters who'd been barred from the meeting eager to learn the latest. He saw David reading the paper.

"Excuse me gents, I'll be back in a moment," pushing his way past. He came to where David stood.

"I hope you're right about this jet business because if this business doesn't work out, Galbraith, I'll have your guts on the table." And with that Redburn turned to the reporters to wallow in his momentary triumph. David stood pretending to read his paper but was still pondering his superior's words. He was just beginning to like him too.

Richard was already sitting at the bar in the Old Boar when Tan and Phil came in. Tan ordered a round of drinks before they retired to a quiet table. Although it was midday the once busy pub was empty apart from the three men. Richard's smiling face told Tan he had accomplished his mission and quickly filled them in on all the details. Then Richard handed Tan a copy of the Echo he'd brought with him from London that morning. Tan read it slowly and smiled at Richard.

"You copied the letter exactly as I told you."

"Of course," Richard gave Tan a sympathetic smile.

"Told you they'd not print a word about sun spots, it's as if nobody cares!"

"Ah well," replied Tan, 'almost expected that, at least they printed the rest and we now have a voice in a national daily paper!"

At Heathrow airport twelve planes had been loaded with the contaminated water. Their destinations varied from Singapore to Los Angeles, Australia, Paris, Rome, Cyprus, the Arab Emirates, Pakistan, Bahrain and included a group of two hundred invalids and terminally ill people making a pilgrimage to Lourdes. Most of these planes had taken off either the night before or early that day. Three empty contaminated jets stood on the tarmac but were not needed till later that evening and the other was to take off to the Caribbean early the following day. The first plane to touch down was a 747 Jumbo jet. It had left Heathrow at 5p.m. the previous evening and had arrived in Calcutta in the early hours of the next day at 4.45 a.m. GMT. Nearly all the passengers had taken either tea or coffee throughout the twelve hour flight including all of the crew. In all, 347 people were in different stages of the toxin's absorption depending on how much of the liquid they had drunk. One man who had drunk nothing but spirits in the first class section was not contaminated and there was a three month old baby girl whose only liquid content was supplied by her mother's breast.

As they sat drinking in the Old Boar, Tan eyed his two accomplices and he was pleased. Pleased with himself in his choice of the two men as his conspirators and pleased with the way Richard and Phil were conducting themselves in the advancement of their ideals. Richard interrupted Tan's thoughts.

"Don't you think it would be wise to inform the Echo of our latest escapade? It could be days before anyone connects the dead people with the aeroplanes." Tan smiled.

"I was already thinking on those lines, it would have been nice to have a death or two confirmed first." Tan took a sip of his bottled beer and pondered for a moment.

"You sure you got the poison in the right tanks?" he asked again, Richard smiled confidently.

"Two hundred per cent sure, I could have done more if I'd had more stuff."

"Right, I'll ring the Echo and inform them of our latest attack, but after the pub shuts at 3.00." Tan looked across at Phil and said, "I think Richard deserves a small celebration for his brilliant idea and masterful execution of his plan don't you?"

"Right on man," replied Phil, "let's have a bottle of champers for a change."

"Inn Keeper," shouted Tan at the depressed looking barman reading another magazine to relieve the boredom in the empty pub, "a bottle of your finest champagne."

James Delany had been in conference when Tan's message came through and a note from the news desk had been ferried to him. Delany read the note and his eyes narrowed, his mouth became rigid and he lifted the 'phone and screamed angrily down the line.

"News desk and quick." A woman's voice answered.

"Who the fuck took this message, why wasn't it passed through to my office?" The woman at the other end of the 'phone began to shake with fear at the anger extended towards her.

"Was it you, woman?" he screamed again. The woman responded, her voice wobbled.

"Yes, Sir, but..."

"Never mind fucking buts, get your coat and fuck off, you're fired." He slammed down the 'phone and cursed as he pondered on the missed opportunity to actually speak to the most wanted man in the world. His journalist eyes stared at the paper in his hand. The headlines were already beginning to form in his brain as he read, 'Heyes poisons a fleet of jets bound for every corner of the globe.' Then the immenseness of the tragedy overwhelmed him and he picked up the 'phone again.

"Get me Commissioner Roberts at New Scotland Yard and for Christs sake hurry." A telephone call later by the Commissioner to the police office inside Heathrow relating to Tan's message instigated the sending of a telex to all crews who had landed and were sleeping over in various parts of the world. The response was immediate. Two stewardesses were sweating profusely and had taken to their beds in the Sheraton Town House Hotel in Los Angeles. Three crew members were taken ill in Karachi and inside the hour several more passengers and crew from various flights had also been confirmed to be ill. Heathrow airport was immediately closed down. All incoming flights were diverted to other airports and all outgoing flights were grounded indefinitely. A small riot began in the Inter Continental Lounge as tired and frustrated passengers were told all flights had been cancelled. Then a panic ensued as rumour of the poison began to spread amongst the two thousand or so people waiting in various departure lounges. By six thirty that evening Heathrow airport was empty bar two hundred & fifty soldiers who had been called in to vacate the place. two hundred policemen were drafted to question all the ground ancillary workers and a team of forensic scientists in their protective white suits began to search through the water shed looking for clues. A small group of men who worked in the sheds were questioned vigorously, their interrogations were recorded on video film just in case they too had been contaminated by the toxin and would not survive the next few hours. A look of fear shone from their eyes as they were badgered and bullied and even refused permission to go home to see their loved ones for what maybe the last time. By 9.30 that night the first death was reported. A sixty three year old man suffering from arthritis and on the trip to Lourdes had begun with the symptoms at only five o'clock that same afternoon. In the VIP lounge a co-ordination headquarters was set up to trace all passengers and planes that had been loaded with the poisoned water. By twelve o'clock that night six hundred & ten people had died and 3872 people had been confirmed as terminally ill.

Tan smiled as he watched the scene broadcast live from Heathrow on a newly acquired portable television. He smiled as the Prime Minister was interviewed in an empty transit lounge at the airport.

"This man must be caught whatever the cost," Tears trickled down her cheeks as she spoke. "Why would any sane person want to do such a thing? It's barbaric." Richard sat on the settee next to Tan.

"How dare she say that," he said as he swigged beer straight from the bottle, a little drunk. Several empty bottles littered the floor.

"Her hands are covered in the blood of men who died in the Falklands."

"Yea, right on man," agreed Phil who was sitting on the floor enjoying every bit of the scene on television.

"Wait till we hit the bastards with the jet," he shouted at the T.V. Richard looked across at Tan.

"What is the target going to be for the jet?" he asked knowing now that he had proved himself Tan could not refuse him an answer.

"I am going to shoot down the French President when he crosses the Channel to attend the Conference next week," Tan replied without hesitation.

"Be a waste of a missile," replied Richard.

"No way, man," interrupted Phil, "that bastard sank the Rainbow Warrior. He thinks he's nice and safe, protected by his bodyguards giving out orders. Now it's going to be his turn. He'll shit his fucking pants when he sees Tan come flyin alongside." Richard and Tan smiled at one another.

"I wish there was another seat in that jet. Wow." Phil's face lit up at the thought of what he'd just said.

"Hey, Tan,can I paint your plane for you?"

"What you going to paint on it?" asked Richard.

"Why, I'm gonna paint the words 'Rainbow Warrior II' all along both sides, hey Tan?"

Tan's face lit up. "Why not, I think the French President will crap himself when he sees that."

"Yeah man," quipped Phil again.

"I've never been as happy in all my life as I am now it's all happening." He held a clenched fist up in the air.

News of the Heathrow affair had stopped dead in its tracks George Redburn's plans to locate the Harrier. The teams of searchers were called off by another directorate from the Home Office. They'd decided in London that Heyes didn't have the jet. They reasoned he would have used it before now. The plan was to check out every person in Britain with a house to house search. The biggest ever man hunt operation was to be carried out by the police force and assisted by every man and woman available from the armed services.

George Redburn was seething with anger. He'd been hitting the whisky again. 'If only I had waited a little,' he thought. 'If only I hadn't listened to bloody Wonder Boy.' He knew he'd be a laughing stock throughout the police force after spending half the night convincing them that Heyes had the jet. 'How could I have been so stupid,' he thought. 'It all seems so ridiculous now, why the hell did I let that young cock-end talk me into it.'

All the fears and the mistakes came flooding back once more from six years ago when he'd been second in command on the Ripper enquiry. His guts moved, it seemed to be hollow up to his chin. He reached into his desk drawer and lifted out a brand new bottle of Teachers whisky. Pouring himself a large tumbler full he threw it to the back of his throat and swallowed it without tasting. As with all insecure people Redburn's earlier elation had suddenly deflated to an all time low.

David Galbraith had unplugged his telephone for the day and retired to bed. Only his emergency bleeper was left switched on and at 6.20 in the evening its bleeping tones aroused him from a deep sleep. He replugged the 'phone and dialled the number of his office. Inspector Forrest answered the call.

"Turn on the television quickly," he barked, his voice in a high pitch of excitement. David was still half asleep as he "walked into the next room of his small flat and turned on the seldom used T.V. A news reporter was standing on a roof somwhere. Rows of aeroplanes stood on the tarmac over his shoulder. The camera zoomed down onto a group of men going in and out of a doorway at the tarmac level. David recognised the white space-like suits immediately and he turned up the sound to listen to the commentary.

"How many people have been poisoned is not yet known but we think it's more likely to be thousands rather than hundreds. The Prime Minister has ordered a full cabinet meeting for 11.00 tonight and they will no doubt sit throughout the night in an effort to find a solution to end the freedom of this mad man, Anthony Heyes. David turned up the volume. He moved into the kitchen to make a sandwich and a cup of tea. The bleeper sounded again and he dialled in while chewing on his sandwich.

"Did you catch that report?" asked Forrest.

"Yes, I saw it, was it in the water."

"Yes, we don't know how many planes they got to."

"Least it proves the Pontefract business was just a trial run."

"Listen, stay away from Redburn, he's been on the blower asking your whereabouts, he's after your blood says something about stuffing a Harrier up your arse. I think he's going to be taken off the case anyway. He's becoming more unstable than ever."

"Listen boss," said David, "do you need me in the office?"

"What's the problem?"

"I need a couple of days off."

"You onto something?"

"No, I'm tired. I need a rest I've hardly slept in the last two weeks." A short silence followed.

"Don't see why not, the Yard will take over now."

"Okay."

"See you in a couple of days."

David turned off the television and sat down in the easy chair by the fireplace. For the first time in his life his mind was muddled and confused. Moutains of words and voices crashed in and out of his brain, he couldn't rescue the right formula to piece them together. He was tense and still tired although he'd just awoken from nearly ten hours sleep. He lay down on the sheepskin rug and was asleep again in seconds. The scream of a high powered motor bike some way off in the distance brought him back to his senses. The street lamp outside the room window shone onto the stone fireplace illuminating the reproduction Georgian clock resting on the mantlepiece. David focused onto the finely embossed hands. It was 2.30 a.m. He lay there for quite a while unmoving. He felt safe and secure as if he'd become part of the room although his mental and physical strength had been replenished by the sleep. His mind began to churn over all the facts it had absorbed about Tan Heyes. There was something in there he needed to find and as he lay there his mind ticked in time with the Georgian clock. His thoughts went back to the very first day he'd discovered the missing poison from the path lab. His retentive brain relived every, action every word spoken and every cup of coffee he'd drunk, nothing escaped. Once seen not forgotten. Then his mind wondered for a moment and an old school teacher's face stood in front of him and his eyes focused on a picture of a cow on the wall of the classroom. "You're not listening Galbraith." The teacher's voice came through as if he was still there chastising him. He could see his face clear as a bell, the false teeth that moved away from the gums as he spoke.

"We all know of your brilliant memory, Galbraith, but that doesn't mean you are intelligent, boy. A parrot can remember and repeat words but it doesn't understand one iota." David smiled at the words of wisdom of the teacher's voice as it faded away. He pushed himself from the floor as if breaking the spell he'd been under and flicked on a small table lamp. The brightness blinded him for a moment. Perhaps he'd relied too much on his powers of recall. Perhaps his mind had been damaged under the strain of all the garbage it had amassed in the years gone by. He picked up a large notepad from on top of the small bookcase filled mostly with biographies of famous people. A pen resting on the mantle piece was gathered up. He sat back in the easy chair and for the first time in his life he began to separate the thoughts from his brain and transport them onto the paper in front of him. He wrote on the first line.

Question: Likely whereabouts of Heyes. Answer: Yorkshire, Lincolnshire, possibly Norfolk. Knows the areas well, likes the hills and countryside. Jet somewhere in these regions. David had tried to force the jet from his thoughts but it wouldn't be pushed away. He carried onto the next line.

Question: How to trace whereabouts. Answer: Relatives

and friends. David drew a long line through the answer illuminating it. Accomplices: Two known, of no reliable descriptions.

Question: Where would he live? Answer: Bedsitland. Logic: Past abode. Where plot was hatched: Irrelevant. David crossed out the answer. That was before Heyes had money. He listed hotels, boarding houses rented accommodation.

Question: Aliases? Answer: Anything - possibly David's mind returned to his lovemaking with Tan's mother as she'd told him the many answers to his questions. He thought of Tan's father's name, Rodis. 'Yes", he thought, 'why not?' He knew Tan liked to leave clues knowing he was always one step ahead.

Question: Appearance? Obviously a complete change. Beard, glasses, moustache, change of clothes (style). Logic: Picture of Tan broadcast throughout Britain no sightings. He ignored the crank sighting. Complete change from student garb. Opposite - suits, ties etc. David's mind was working hard covering every angle, every little scrap of knowledge he'd had stored about Tan had been thoroughly analysed and examined. The dawn began to break as David rested the pad on the coffee table. He checked the time and went into the bathroom and began to run the water into the bath. He returned to the room and turned on the radio. A Strauss waltz blurted out as he entered the bathroom. He stared at himself in the mirror. He rubbed the dark lines under his eyes as if trying to wipe them away. A few grey hairs were dotted here and there amidst the unshaven stubble on his chin and the youthful good looks that had opened many a door in the past were on the decline. He smiled and a row of well kept teeth smiled back and the image changed completely. 'That's it,' he thought, 'you'll have to smile a bit more.' His scutiny of his face was suddenly interrupted by a well groomed voice announcing the five o'clock news. He hurried back into the room and sat almost on top of the small Sony radio.

"The latest figure of the death toll from the Heathrow poisonings now stands at 4,339. Several more are expected to die throughout the next few hours. Police still have no clue as to the whereabouts of Anthony Heyes who is believed to be responsible for this latest outrage."

David switched off the radio and returned to the bathroom. He lay in the soothing warm water thinking about the people Tan had killed and as he did he suddenly realised that somehow he hadn't cared. He was sorry for what had happened to them but he was immune to the grief that he should feel. 'Am I so cold and unfeeling?' he began to question his emotions. He tried to remember the last time he had laughed. He couldn't remember. He tried to blame his job, after all he worked long unsociable hours often in the cold outdoors. How could anyone be cheerful doing this sort of work. Then he thought about friends. He had none, only the odd crony at the golf club who was more interested in winning his money, shallow empty people. As he lay soaking in the warm water reflecting and self analysing himself, he began to realise all he'd ever done in the last five years was work. Even when he wasn't working he was thinking about it. Had he succeeded in brainwashing himself or was he just a robot? No, he had enjoyed his work, but not for a couple of years now. But then why was this feeling inside of him so strong? The wanting to be the one to catch Heyes so badly. Does it matter as long as he is put away. Do I want him because he kills people or for the glory and the acclaim that would be plied on his captor. Then he began to see himself for what he really was, as if a door had suddenly opened and he could see himself clearly. 'God, am I a supercilious fool?' He cringed for the first time at the thought of himself. Playing things close to his chest, never sharing his info till the last possible minute. How they must have hated him. No wonder he'd no friends. Was it so hard to ask for advice and help and show one's feelings. After all he was human and wanted to be liked by his fellow man. He thought of George Redburn, he knew he was approaching retirement and wanted to leave in a blaze of glory. But he'd made him look a fool. All right he'd given him good advice and information but he'd gone about it the wrong way. By not advising George to play things close to his chest he'd allowed him to throw himself into the cess pit and now he was half way down the drain. A flutter of pity passed through him; the first human spark to be rekindled inside him for a long time.

Saturday 26th July six a.m. Tan had the Landrover loaded and ready to go. Phil and Richard came out of the cottage both still feeding themselves with the remains of the breakfast they'd hurriedly devoured. It had been three days now since the Heathrow poisonings and it was another three days before the European summit in London. Tan knew he had two days to extrocate the jet from its tomb in the moutainside. Phil drove his beloved Landrover to within two miles of the tunnel and loaded with gear the three men trudged the remaining distance on foot. It was going to be a hot pleasant day, but till the sun began to rise the early morning mist hung low over the Pennines. It was 7.40 when they reached the entrance to the tunnel. Tan instantly checked the welds and padlocks for tamper but the flakey rust eleviated any fears. This time though they were to open the wicket gate in the metal grid. The padlocks cut quite easily with the large bolt cutters but the welds took nearly an hour to chisel free. They removed all evidence of their entry twenty yards inside the tunnel and Tan clipped a new padlock locking the gate behind them. Tan had dipped the new padlock in dark stain before rolling it in the dirt in the garden of the cottage. At first glance it looked old and rusted. It was half an hour before they reached the jet; on the way they had stopped to clear bricks and other debris that had fallen from the roof of the tunnel. As Tan approached the jet he felt an excitement flow over him and he hurriedly pulled the larger canvas sheets off the fuselage and stood staring in awe as the three men merged their powerful torches on it, illuminating it like the star of some Broadway show.

"I never realised they were so small," said Phil breaking the silence.

"You won't say that when we've dragged it the seven hundred yards out of this hole," replied Richard, not a great advocate for manual work.

"Ah, but man, if she flies, man, this will be the icing on the cake. They'll be begging us to give ourselves up."

"I can hardly see Maggy appealing to our better natures offering us a Greek Island to live on if we'll just go away and leave them alone," said Phil. Tan ruffled his hair in a jocular fashion. "You never know what they'll do in Westminster thanks to

Richard's brain child." Tan didn't miss the chance to praise him for his great contribution to the cause.

"When you going to see if it'll start?" asked Richard as if he was referring to some old car.

"Soon as we can get her to the outside, maybe when it's dark tonight."

"Well what the fuck are we waiting for, let's get going."

Tan lowered the rucksack to the floor and took out a small hydraulic foot pump. He gave it to Phil who proceeded to pump vigourously on the front tyre which was half flat. Tan and Richard removed the rest of the loose tarpaulins and folded them onto one of the wings. A flashlight was taped with electrical tape onto the end of each wing, so they could see the clearance on each side when they began to push the jet out. Another torch was fastened to one of the rear wheels illuminating the sleepers and any other obstacle they may have missed. Tan wasn't sure the three of them would be able to move the jet with nothing but brute force. But he'd seen just two men of the ground crew move one quite easily. But that was on smooth Tarmac and not uneven gravel and old wooden sleepers. Not to mention the plane was the wrong way round. Richard finished blowing up the tyres and came round to the front where the other two stood waiting.

"How much does this thing weigh?" he asked.

"Oh about 14,000 lbs with the missiles included I should think," replied Tan who noticed a doubting look on Richard's face.

"But it's so well balanced once we get it rolling a little it shouldn't take too much effort."

"Well let's get going," said Phil eagerly as he shoved his shoulder into the hydraulic suspension arm of the rear wheel.

"Okay, but not too fast, watch for the wing tips against the wall." Tan tied a rope round his shoulders and then fastened it to one of the rear wheels. This way he hoped he could help steer it a little. Richard bent down on the opposite wheel to Phil's and on Tan's command they all heaved together. The jet stuck rigid, the wheels had seized slightly but as they pulled and pushed rocking the plane backwards and forwards suddenly it broke free and began to move. Every few yards the plane had to be straightened to stop it scraping into the wall, but apart from that it went quite smoothly, and after just an hour they'd managed to move the jet nearly one hundred yards. By 3 o'clock they were just 50 yards from the grid covered entrance. Tan strung a piece of rope across the entrance about 40 yards into the tunnel and draped the canvas covers to act as a screen from the rope hiding the jet. Per chance an unsuspecting rambler might appear and glance into the dark void. They decided to leave the last few yards till it got dark and Richard and Tan got to work cutting through the portculis shaped grid while Phil got out his paint and brush and under the carefully placed lights began to signwrite on the side of the jet. The motorised tungsten cutter that Tan had used eight years ago would not start and it took till 8.30 to saw through nearly thirty bars till at last the grid hung by just two small ropes strategically placed to hold the grid in place. A quick tug on the longer length of rope would release the knot sending the heavy steel grid crashing to the ground. Richard had enquired how the blazes Tan had managed on his own to replace the huge grid.

"Well it was easier than you think," he replied explaining how with a single wooden pully he'd roped to the top of the grid still fastened to the roof of the entrance. Then he'd tied a piece of rope to the grid on the ground. He then fastened the end of the rope to his motorbike and drove away pulling the grid back into place. Then he'd used a thick piece of wood and a car jack to level the bars up before fastening them in place with more rope, and then welding them back with a portable welding torch. Tired and exhausted Richard and Tan sat in the gloom of dusk outside the entrance of the tunnel. They ate hungrily some of the sandwiches Tan had prepared earlier that morning. Phil had been summoned to join them but refused, totally absorbed in his painting.

Richard gave Tan a worried look. He'd grown to like his mentor, a form of hero worship like a child whose hero is a great footballer or popstar. He admired Tan for his determination and single mindedness; in his eyes a quality only found in great people. But now he was worried. The poison was easy to distribute, despatched wherever, normally unseen, unchecked and by the time the first reaction is felt the perpetrator is often miles away. But this jet business, this was different; he would be exposed, traceable and Richard needed Tan to look up to more than Tan needed him. But he knew nothing he could say would deter Tan from his goals.

"What will you do with the jet if the mission is successful?" he asked interrupting Tan who had been watching the sun disappear over the far hills. Tan smiled.

"It's sad but it can only be used the once. Once they know for sure we've got it they'll scour the land. Anyway there is fuel and it needs servicing. It'll probably leak hydraulic fluid all over the place. I just hope it functions long enough for me to blow Monsieur Le Premier out of the sky. "

"What will you do if it malfunctions?"

"Eject of course, if I'm high enough and that will only be when I'm going into the attack."

"But the jet, you're not going to bring it back here?"

"Glad you asked that. How do you like Wales?"

"You mean Welsh Wales?" Tan laughed.

"Of course. That's where I'm going to dump the jet. Just off the coast into the sea near Abbenfrow in Angelsey." Tan went on to explain.

"There's no coast road there and no high land to overlook the sea. I want you to buy a motor powered dinghy and pick me up about five miles out to sea. Must be a high powered engine, something like a Johnson and Johnson 250 horse-power. We'll need some power in case we're spotted."

"Will Phil be with me?"

"No, he's off to Paris for the weekend." Just then Phil came carefully through the wicker door interrupting the conversation.

"Finished. Looks fucking superb if I do say so."

"Oh good, come and sit down and have a sandwich. I want to explain the plan for Monday." Tan briefed the two men roughly on their tasks, they'd work out the finer points later. It was now 9.30 and quite dark although a half moon kept appearing between a break in the spasmodic cloud. Phil replenished, they set about the final stages of removing the Harrier from the tunnel. The canvas screen was moved onto the grid. Tan thought it best not to show any lights after all. Just after ten o'clock the Harrier stood just ten yards or so from the grid and, all lights extinguished Tan squeezed through the wicket door and standing well back released the two knots holding the grid in place. It dropped easily to the floor with a thud. Tan smiled at the sight of the rear of the jet just feet away from leaving its tomb. Ten minutes later the nose began to crawl through the exit and they stood gawping like three proud parents who'd just given birth for the first time. The jet stood in the half light of the moon like a praying mantis. Its shape and contours not that unlike a giant fly with its swept back wings and large dome shaped cockpit. Phil summed up the awe inspiring sight with a single word, "Wow!"

Tan wasn't sure if he was admiring the jet or Phil's handywork. Directly under the cockpit Phil had painted in yellow paint the words 'Rainbow Warrior II'. Above the words he'd painted a flying white dove, the symbol for peace. Under the words he'd painted a small rainbow. The work was very professionally done, had it not been Tan would have painted it out. But only when Phil had set off for Paris.

"I only had time to do the one side,"said Phil admiring the art work.

"Ah! You'll have to attack from the left side then," replied Richard smiling.

"Port, you ignorant junkie." Richard's smile disappeared for a second and then returned. Richard knew Phil was right although he'd been off the hard drugs for nearly a year now, the word junkie still hurt and he knew it was Phil's way of reminding him of that fact.

"Well then start her up," said Phil suddenly in a dominent tone.

Tan and Richard looked at each other and smiled.

"Hang on a mo," replied Tan. "I've got to connect the new batteries in first." Tan had no trouble locating two 12 volt batteries, in fact he'd found that the batteries were exactly the same as those used in an MGB sports car, specially designed to fit under the small rear seat. They'd brought them up in the rucksacks. Tan began inserting them into the mounting brackets under the rear fuselage. A buzz of excitement flooded through him as he connected the last wire. A small click sounded as the power flooded through the system. Tan shuddered excitedly at the thought of flying this powerful beast once again. He fastened on the convering plate before ducking under the wing and coming round to where Phil and Richard were waiting impatiently. He then climbed up onto the wing and walked on top of the fuselage till he came to the portside air intake opening. He lifted up the dome shaped cockpit canopy and pushed his foot into one of the retractable steps in the side of the fuselage. He reached down into the rudder pedal crevase and pulled out a helmet and flying suit he had stolen before he'd quit the RAF.

The green cotton overall smelt a little foisty and was badly creased but Tan climbed into it just the same. He felt the hard paper filled knee pocket bang against his leg and he removed the slip of card from its resting place and stared at an old flight plan of eight years ago, and proceeded to finish fastening the suit. Phil and Richard stood in awe. Impressed by the lettering on Tan's flying suit which read 'Flight Lietenant Heyes' with the wings of the RAF above, confirmed to them any doubts they may have had, if any, about Tan's ability to fly the Harrier. Tan pulled the crash helmet over his head and then climbed into the jet. His heart was thumping in his chest as the adrenalin flowed like an electric current through his body. All his pre-flight checks came back as if it was only yesterday. He leaned over the side and instructed Phil to place a brick against the front wheel when he landed again.

"But stay clear of the jets on the side, they'll boil you." He ushered the two watchers to stand further away to avoid the down blast as the jet hit the ground. The moment of truth had now arrived. Tan flicked down the power switch. The instruments immediately responded and came to life illuminating the cockpit. Tan pulled down the shoulder straps of the seat harness and locked them together. He pulled down the bullet-proof cockpit cover and locked it into position. A deep anxious hollow feeling welled in his chest as he fingered the turbo start button and then he plunged down hard with his thumb. For a split second nothing happened, and then he heard the whir of the starter as it thrust round the large titanium fans inside the jet engine itself. Tan could feel the engine turning behind him quicker and quicker till it reached a high pitched whistle indicating the jet was now running itself allowing Tan to release the starter button. He checked the throttle on his left hand and also the position lever of the four jet nozzles. Tan let the engine run for five minutes and then he looked across at his two accomplices who were standing transfixed with their mouths gawping wide. He signalled he was to take her up by pointing his thumb upwards. He checked all the instruments once more and then he pushed the throttle forward making the engine scream, bits of grass and dust started to rise and were sent threashing in all directions. The two onlookers had to hide their faces as they were pelted by the swirling stinging debris. The noise reached a deafening pitch and then suddenly the plane began to lift. Tan's heart rose to his mouth and a tear of joy slid into the corner of his eye. At thirty feet he eased back the throttle slowly till the plane stopped rising and just hung there. He then pressed the left rudder pedal and the jet turned slowly till he could see the two men who were jumping up and down below. Tan then pulled the jet nozzle lever back till it slotted against the stop. He increased the throttle slightly and the jet responded by flying backwards. Tan felt an overwhelming urge to scream down the hillside but he restrained himself and brought the jet back round to its starting point and gently let it settle back onto the ground. He knew the verticle take off used a lot of fuel and he needed to preserve as much as he could. He pulled back the throttle and as the Rolls Royce engine began to die he quickly cut all the electrical power by flicking the ignition switch off. Phil eagerly came round the front and jammed a brick under the front wheel. Tan lifted the glass dome and climbed down the side dropping the last five foot or so as he moved away from the still noisy but dying jet engine.

"Fucking wow," screamed Phil using his favourite word.

"Man, that was incredible."

Richard came over and patted his leader on the back. He was lost for words, but his admiration for Tan, if possible, had just been increased ten fold. An hour later three exhausted men, having pushed the jet a few yards back into the tunnel, pulled the large steel grid temporarily back into place. The large canvas screen was hung against the inside hiding the jet once more from view and the three men crawled into the sleeping bags just inside the entrance and were soon asleep.

The next day the sun shone in a clear blue sky. Tan woke the others quickly, it was after ten and they still had a lot to do.

Phil and Richard were despatched off quickly on their various tasks while Tan made himself comfortable just outside the tunnel entrance. He would stay there now till he flew the jet on Monday, he wouldn't risk leaving the jet at all, not for one moment. Armed with the Luger he would shoot any persistent busy body who came near. It wasn't until six o' clock that night that Richard returned, a cold Chinese meal under his arm.He smiled as he approached.

"Got everything you wanted?" quizzed Tan.

"No trouble with the dinghy?"

"None," replied Richard who'd followed up an advertisement in the Exchange and Mart, aquiring a dinghy complete with Johnson outboard.

"You got a good radio?" Richard removed two small two-way radios from his rucksack.

"Sanyo. Got a range of thirty miles." Tan nodded.

"Phil get off alright?"

"Sure, got the twelve thirty train to Dover from Manchester Central. Saw him right onto the train. Got the telephone numbers from the boxes in the village, everything's perfect." Richard sat down next to Tan who was removing the lid from the foil container before scooping a finger full of chicken and rice into his mouth.

"Mm, not bad at all."

He handed Tan a bundle of rolled up newspapers and Tan spread them on the grass eyeing the headlines as he ate. The words 'Murderers' and Cowards' shouted out from them as he munched unconcerned taking in the smallest details.

"They still don't understand us do they," said Richard as he threw down a paper with the headlines 'Murderous Bastards'.

"I doubt they ever will," replied Tan.

"Someone does though," smiled Richard. "I saw some graffiti in Manchester. Someone had painted across a large billboard in red letters. 'Thank God for Anthony Heyes, the sanest man in the world.'

Tan stopped eating and looked up. His eyes shone excitedly.

"You see, we're not alone," Richard smiled.

"I know, Tan, I know."

Richard spent the night sleeping in the entrance to the

tunnel to keep Tan company. Although Tan had told him to go back to the cottage Richard had refused. The next day Sunday was a little cooler and the two men spent most of the day talking and making plans for future campaigns. At two o'clock Richard went down to the village ten miles away and waited for the pre-arranged 'phone call from Phil who was now residing in the airport hotel at Orly Airport in Paris.

"It's bloody great here," screamed Phil excitedly down the 'phone. "I even had caviar for my breakfast."

"How was the crossing?" asked Richard.

"Straight forward although no-one was using the bars or restaurants on the ferry. We've got them scared shitless."

Richard cut short the call just in case an unsuspecting operator was listening to Phil's last remark. He finished with the words, "Tomorrow, don't forget." Then he hung up. He wondered how long the five hundred pounds that Phil had taken with him would last.

Earlier that Sunday David Galbraith, feeling refreshed and in a good mood returned to his office. It was nine o'clock when he sauntered along the empty corridor and into the office of his boss, Alan Forrest.

"You well rested?" asked the tired Inspector who had been at his desk for most of the night.

"Yes thanks," replied David slightly apologetically. "I needed to clear my brain."

"Did you come up with anything?"

David handed him the three pages of notes he'd been working on.

"Well, well!" exclaimed the Inspector, "we have been busy."

"Just ideas that's all." David sat down while the Inspector read the notes.

"Mm not bad, but we've got most of this stuff sorted already. But this, this is something." He pointed at the paper.

"The name Rodis, not common, his father's name. It's worth a go. Janice!" A tired young WPC came into the office.

"I want a check on every hotel in Leeds and Bradford for

the name Rodis, anytime during the last three weeks." Inspector Forrest saw the look of dismay on the young woman's face.

"I don't mean you personally Janice, get it down to Milgarth, let them use it." A look of relief spread across her face. "Then get off home," added the Inspector wishing he could do the same. Down at Milgarth another WPC brought the request of a computer search direct into the office of another tired officer.

George Redburn was sitting at his desk, cigar in hand, with his usual glass half filled with whisky on his desk. He was staring at a piece of paper direct from the Cabinet Room in 10 Downing Street,one of the several that had been bombarding his office from Westminster these last two days.

'Re:- Anthony Heyes.

We thank you for drawing our attention to the fact that the French President may be a target of his vengeance. We have instructed the French Security Services who in turn have requested we send over a liaison man, someone who can brief them on all the details of the case and accompany them on their journey back across the channel. However no mention of the Harrier must be made. We do not think Heyes has the jet and we do not want to alarm the French President unduly.'

The letter was signed by Lord Strong, the Home Secretary. George Redburn cursed himself. Every time he heard the mention of the name Harrier he cringed. Even MI5 had kept a low profile on their suspicions of whether Heyes had the jet and for the umpteenth time in the last few days he cursed himself for listening to David Galbraith. The WPC handed Inspector Forrest's letter to her boss who had just downed the last of the whisky.

"What's this?" snarled Redburn as he snatched the letter from the nervous girl.

"Memo from Special Branch, Sir." George cursed to himself. He read the letter instructing him to check for the name Rodis. He picked up the 'phone and asked for Special Branch.

"Ah, morning Alan," he said in a friendly tone when finally connected.

"See you've got my memo," replied Inspector Forrest who nodded across at David who was drinking coffee sitting on the D.I.'s desk.

"Who's your source?" asked Redburn straight back to business after the Inspector had not returned his greeting.

"Sorry, privileged info, but it's good. It's worth a try and I know you and your team of part-timers are bogged down." Inspector Forrest smiled and winked at David. A small silence followed before George responded, his tone now quite angry.

"If you're referring to my rumoured departure as head of the investigation, Forrest, you can forget it. Obviously the Home Office has no confidence in any other senior officers to take my place. Anyway it's one of your men who's made me look a bloody fool." The Inspector grinned and mouthed the words George was saying to David. David smiled back. He could half hear what George was saying as he shouted down the 'phone.

"Speaking of your men, where is that wonder boy of yours?" George calmed a little as a thought suddenly crossed his mind.

"He's in the office."

"Well you tell him to get over here at once, I've a little job for him to do that I think he'll enjoy. Oh, and Alan, don't you think it's time you went home. You might just be in time to catch the young P.C. who's been fucking your wife all night." Before Forrest had time to respond George slammed down the 'phone and rubbed his hands like a naughty school boy. An evil chuckle emerged from his mouth. 'I got the old windbag that time.' The thought cheered him for the first time that day.

Forrest was seething at the last remark and his face glared angrily. "Did you hear what he said about my Susie?" David looked across, the colour drained slightly from his face as he thought of the time several weeks back when he'd taken advantage of his boss's young wife. Well it was the other way round really, he'd called with some flowers from Alan after he'd forgotten their second wedding anniversary and she'd practically ripped off David's clothes as he came through the door.

"Don't worry about your Susie, Sir," replied David sympathetically. "She's a one-man-woman, you know that." He smiled to himself as he thought, a different one every day.

"Yes but all the same, time I was off home," replied the Inspector putting on his jacket. "Janice," he screamed, "get my car round at the door at once." He glared across at the D.S., "and you better get over there and face his wrath, he wants to see you."

David drove the half mile down the Headrow and into the car park of Milgarth Police Headquarters. The brand new building with all the modern facilities had been opened five years previously. David likened the red brick building to an old victorian wash house. George Redburn was still in his office reading one of the numerous reports on the Heyes sightings.

"Oh, Wonder Boy returns," he said sarcastically, "so you were in Forrest's office after all. I bet the old bald headed eagle was off home like a bat out of hell eh."

David smiled. "Yes Sir, you put the wind up him alright."

"Good," sniggered Redburn, "now it's your fucking turn."

David didn't like the sound of his voice. "You still convinced Heyes has the Harrier?" George Redburn stared a hard cold stare into David's eyes.

"Yes Sir, I - do." The Superintendant handed him a letter. David stared at the blue lettering heading which read, 'The Prime Minister's Office, 10 Downing Street.'

He began to read. It was addressed to Chief Superintendant Redburn, Leeds CID.

> *'Due to the irrational behaviour and ridiculous inference on the part of yourself with reference to the unfounded reports of the suspect ricin killer, one Anthony Heyes, having a stolen RAF Harrier in his possession, the French President has refused to attend the all important summit on Monday the 30th August, unless he can be reassured and afforded full protection on the day of his visit. The protection of course will be handled by the London Special Branch. However, the President requires a full up-to-date briefing on all aspects of this case. The P.M. has instructed me to have a man sent to Paris to deal with this in the utmost urgency. Please single out this man to carry out our instructions which are: Anthony Heyes, the suspect in the recent poison attacks, does not have or never has had access to a fully armed jet of any kind. The President must attend the Conference at all costs.'*

A keen reporter for the Figaro had reported George Redburn's briefing about the Harrier's possible whereabouts and the paper was the first to publish the connection between the French Government's involvement with the Rainbow Warrior incident and the fact that if Heyes did have the jet the President was surely a number one target. Also one hundred and ninety four French people had already died through the Heathrow poisonings and the French Security Service had demanded to be updated and told the truth on this matter of whether or not Heyes had the jet.

David finished reading the letter and placed it gently on George's desk. George smiled an evil cold glare at David's emotionless face. David read George's mind and before he had time to speak David began.

"You want me on the President's plane, don't you?" Redburn's face never changed.

"But of course. How can you reassure the President if you are not prepared even to fly back to Britain with him. "

"You've read the letter. Even the P.M doesn't think he's got the jet."

"What does she know about such things, it's not her job to shift through piles of evidence and..."

"Now, now," interrupted George, "that's our leader you're talking about. Our top intelligence men were advising and helping the cabinet on this matter. Who the fuck are you!" David glared at Redburn.

"Yes, Sir, I agree but they are ignoring the one per cent possibility that he may have the jet." David's frustration showed on his face.

"That's enough," shouted George as he stood up and came round the desk to where David stood and stared insanely, directly into David's eyes.

"You fly from Leeds Bradford Airport at one o'clock tomorrow and catch the three o'clock flight to Paris from Gatwick. Now piss off."

David walked out of the room into the corridor. George Redburn's secretary came out of her office where she'd been waiting for David. She handed him a small envelope.

"Your tickets and £100 expenses," she said smiling

sympathetically, "you look like he's just bitten you."

"He has. I only hope he's not got rabes," replied David smiling lustfully at the pretty secretary. His thoughts were distracted momentarily. David wasn't the least bit upset by George's condescending manner towards him. He'd expected that. He was upset by the fact that nobody took any notice of the fact that Heyes did have the jet and now he had been ordered to accompany the President on his journey to England. An air of impending doom surrounded him as he made his way out of the building and back to his car. He drove out through the city centre and on towards the Otley road where a half hour later he found himself overlooking the beautiful view across the valley that was Otley Chevin. He searched through his mind trying to think of a reason why he shouldn't go. But he knew it was a direct challenge from George Redburn. It was nearly lunchtime when David came to a decision. He would take up Redburn's challenge and go, but deep down he knew it was wrong. The hollow empty feeling he had in his stomach all morning would not leave him. But then once the decision had been reached David accepted it completely and now his thoughts turned to his survival. He started the car and drove back onto the main Leeds Harrogate road. He turned towards Leeds and three miles down the road just past the Leeds Bradford Airport he turned into a small roadway. A sign at the end read 'Bradford Aero Club,' and underneath a small sign read 'The Blue Eagle's Free Fall Team.' He drove on for half a mile. Two light aircraft stood outside a large hanger. David recognised the Cessna belonging to the free-fall club. He drove to the rear of the hanger till he came to a large hut. Several cars were parked outside, mainly Jaguars and Porsches and a couple of sports saloons which indicated to him a lesson was in progress. This was an expensive sport. A sport David had himself enjoyed until his finances became punctured in its pursuance. He'd made some excuse about hurting his back and withdrew his membership. In fact he'd made nearly a hundred free fall descents before he gave in to sanity and his bank manager. He leapt the three wooden steps and opened the half glass door. In the middle of a large sparse hall a young man of about twenty was suspended from a harness fastened to the ceiling. He hung parallel to the floor, but about five feet above and he was counting out loud. His arms and legs were spread in the stranded stall position of the free-fall parrachutist.

"One thousand, two thousand, pull." He simulated the pulling of his ripcord and a large framed man suddenly came from the middle of the onlookers who were surrounding the suspended student.

"No! No! No! Eric, you pillock. You didn't bring your right hand in to compensate for your left hand. The drag would have forced you into a spin and at two thousand you'd not have time to recover."

"Sorry Frank," replied the swinging youth.

David pulled the door, it closed hard behind him making a loud bang. All eyes turned in his direction. The big instructor recognised David and came over to greet him.

"David, me lad, where the hell have you been hiding?"

"Hello Frank," replied David shaking his much admired old instructor warmly by the hand. Frank ordered a minion to carry on the class while he took David over to a small make shift bar in the corner of the room. Frank took a can of beer from a badly made shelf.

"Sorry David, got no juice, you'll have to...."

David cut him short, "A beer will do nicely."

Frank passed him his already opened can and plucked another from the shelf.

"When did you start on the soup?" asked Frank, a surprised look on his face.

"Just now!"

Frank could see something was bothering David and although he'd not seen him for some time David had always been one of his favourite pupils. Frank Jackson was a kindly man of about sixty. He was a much liked and well respected man who'd been a paratrooper during the war. He had been taken prisoner in the battle for Anheim where he lost his right leg from the knee down. But even with this handicap he had made over five thousand free-fall descents.

"You working on this nutter case?" asked Frank swigging back his beer.

David nodded. "Is this why you need a drink?"

"No not really, I just wondered what it tastes like."

"What do you think?"

"Tastes like it smells. Not bad though! I think I could get used to it."

David smiled, then his face became serious once again. "If I told you I thought this nutter Heyes had a jet stashed away somewhere already armed and ready to fly, what would you say?"

Frank stared at David unsure whether he was going to crack a joke. But then the constant look on his face told him otherwise.

"I'd say tell me where he is so I can stay in my air raid shelter." The two men stared expressionless at each other till Frank spoke again.

"You're serious."

"Yes, he's had one stashed away since he stole it from the RAF some years ago."

"Jesus Christ."

"And what's more he's going to use it on Monday."

"On what?"

"On me and the French President somewhere over the Channel in a fucking 747 or something."

"If you know this, why don't you have the jet intercepted or bring the President over another way."

"Because no-one believes me."

"Why are you so sure?"

David smiled and shrugged his shoulders.

"Because Anthony Heyes' mother told me when I was fucking her."

Frank burst out into a fit of laughter, a huge belly laugh that distracted the students momentarily.

"You take the biscuit you do David. You mean you actually fucked this nutter's mother," said Frank trying his best to compose himself.

"Well I had to do. She wouldn't tell me anything unless I went to bed with her. She wouldn't even let the Chief Constable of Manchester into her house to question her. Can you imagine that. Her son's the biggest mass murderer since Genghis Khan and when the full might of the whole Metropolitan Police Force knocks on her door to question her she tells them to piss off." The two men burst into simultaneous laughter.

"When you were giving her one did she just come out and say, 'Oh by the way he'd got a jet stashed away'?" Frank smiled again.

"Well not just like that, a bit more subtle. I did a six month course in interrogation, every form, violent, polite, pretending to be friends and believe it or not interrogating people in the process of lovemaking. I asked her the same question but in several different contexts and the answers all came out the same. His mother thinks he'd got the jet. I think he'd got the jet, but no-one else does." David's voice became loud and excited.

"Well you've convinced me."

"Thanks Frank. I never doubted you wouldn't believe me," said David relaxing a little.

"But that's not why I'm here. I need a parachute."

Frank smiled again. "Won't do you much good if he blows the plane to smithereens with a missile."

"No, but he may take it with a cannon fire, and that way I may have a chance."

"But surely you can't sit on a plane with a fucking great parachute harnessed to your back. You'll put the wind up everyone." Frank smiled at the thought.

"I've thought about that. What if I stripped the covering off the actual chute and just wrapped it round my chest under a zipper jacket? How would that work?"

"I don't see why not. You could always use one of the smaller reserve chutes and fasten it to a training harness. Let's have a look in the packing room." Frank led David into the rear of the hut where the spare parachutes were packed and stored. He pulled the cord on a small reserve chute and carefully lifted the thin nylon canopy clear.

"This should do." Then he lifted a shoulder harness that was hanging from a hook. He unclipped the stainless steel ring that held all the canopy string to the reserve chute bundle and then he clipped them to the loose harness.

"There you are, let's give it a tryout."

David looked surprised but he knew Frank meant every word.

"Here." Frank handed the opened parachute to David.

"I'll get you a jacket." A minute later he returned. David was struggling to wrap the loose material round his body.

"No! No! That won't do." shouted Frank as if back to work on a student. "It would be better to fold it against your back then hold it in place with your pullover. Then you can take off the jacket, reach over with your hand and pull out the small drag chute from under the pullover." It took five minutes for Frank to help David pack the chute under his pullover. The harness straps ran between David's legs as on a normal chute but they could be shortened later. A borrowed blue and white zipper jacket covered the whole thing except for the leg straps. Frank strapped a reserve chute over the front of David's lower abdomen and complete with helmet and goggles the two men set off to join the waiting prepared pilot who'd been warming up the Cessna. The small plane was used solely for parachuting, all the seats had been stripped out and the door had been removed completely. Only the pilot's seat remained making it look like the inside of a scrap car.

"Thanks Carl," said Frank acknowledging the favour of the pilot for taking them up at short notice.

Ten minutes later after a short delay whilst clearance was given by the control tower, the small plane was thrashing down the runway at sixty knots. David felt the old excitement as the plane lifted quickly into the air. It banked quickly to the left and Carl waved at a familiar face in the control tower as they passed over it and began the long climb up to ten thousand feet. David's fingers began to feel the cold and he began to rub his hands together to keep them warm. He checked the altimeter that was fastened on top of the reserve chute and he watched as the hand began to edge nearer the dropping height. Frank screamed into David's ear, with the wind propeller noise it was difficult to speak.

"You go first and I'll follow you down. If you can't get the canopy open at two thousand use the reserve." David nodded in agreement. Carl turned and signalled the thumbs up sign. That was David's signal to climb out of the door and balance on the long wheel strut to give him room to clear the aeroplane. Carl cut the engine and banked the plane over to allow David to drop away. He pushed himself clear and immediately he went into the stall position to slow his descent. The quietness and sense of peace absorbed David as he thundered down towards the earth at one thousand feet per second. All the excitement returned and as he fell he was elated. His mind returned quickly to the task at hand. He brought both hands in together under his chin leaving his elbows sticking out the sides still causing enough drag to slow him but keeping him stable and stopping him going into a spin. He pulled down the zipper together with both hands. The jacket thrashed and flopped against his face as the rush of air forced it into a knot about his head. He glared at the altimetre, five thousand feet. He'd three seconds to rid the jacket from his arms and as he tried to pull one arm clear of the jacket with his other hand, he went into a frenzied spin. The ground seemed to spin below him as he glanced down once more at the altimetre, two thousand five hundred. He'd half a second to act. He reached his hand over his shoulder and, ignoring the still flapping jacket, he reached down into the rear of the pullover and pulled at the folded canopy inside. He felt it come clear as the updraft shot up into the space in the pullover where the canopy had been. He waited for the tell tale jolt that told the falling man his canopy was open. He checked the altimeter, just over a thousand, it was now or never. He reached for the ring pull on his reverse chute when finally the jolt he'd been waiting for came. The upward sensation as the air trapped inside the open canopy reassured him everything was all right. He checked his altimeter and gasped as the needle read under five hundred feet. He knew he'd hit hard as he wouldn't have slowed enough, but at least his chute was open and the elation still flowed as only one who has laughed in death's face knows. Then he was down. The ground seemed to rise up and hit him hard, and for a moment he blacked out. Frank had followed David's descent helplessly but his knotted gut had eased as he guided his sports chute almost in on top of David, who was now sitting slightly doubled over taking deep lungfulls of air.

"You alright?" he enquired as he unclipped the harness and bundled his chute quickly and expertly under his arm.

"Just," replied David still gasping but doing his best to

smile. "It was the jacket. Too hard to take off against the updraft."

"Thought it would be," said Frank as he checked David's legs for broken bones. "Ah you're alright nothing broken."

"What do you mean, you thought it would be?" said David, a puzzled look on his face. Frank smiled.

"Well if you can take a jacket off, especially a tight fitting bomber jacket, under ten thousand feet you can do almost anything." David pushed himself to his feet a surge of pain shot up his spine. He pulled the tangled mass of blue and white nylon that was still hanging from his back.

"You mean this," he said holding out a piece of material.

"Oh good lad," replied Frank a huge grin on his face. "I thought you'd lost it."

Sunday evening Tan let Richard relieve him from guarding the jet. Tired and grubby he returned to the cottage and was glad to bathe and change his clothes. He made himself a meal of sausage with tinned potatoes and he sat to eat his meal in front of the television. At nine o'clock the BBC news programme was once again about him. Where is he,what would be his next move and then suddenly Tan was distracted from his meal as the newscaster reported on the French Newspaper, Le Figaro's story on whether the French President would be attacked in any way on his visit to London the next day. The newscaster made no mention whatsoever about the jet, although his French counterparts had spoken of nothing else. Tan was relieved. His biggest fear was that the President would be escorted across the Channel by a squadron of Mirages. But he discarded the idea as quickly as it had entered his head. Although he had wondered if the President may use a scheduled flight but if so Phil would spot him board the plane and pre-warn him. Exhausted through lack of sleep Tan retired to bed. The clean crisp sheets and soft mattress soothed his tired body and he was soon asleep. At six a.m. the small travel clock sounded its alarm. Tan was already awake. The excitement of what was ahead had been flooding round in his brain since he'd woken an hour ago. He looked out of the window to check the weather. It was a dull grey cloudy morning and he smiled to himself. Twenty minutes later he was behind the wheel of the Landrover, the dinghy attached to the roof rack and the powerful outboard almost filling the rear of the jeep. At seven thirty he drove up the hillside and pulled the vehicle to a stop right outside the tunnel entrance. Panic overwhelmed him till the wicket door opened and the sleepy head of Richard came through. The Luger hung loosely from his hand.

"God you frightened me half to death," he said as he came up to greet Tan who'd just stepped from the jeep.

"You'd better get down to the phone box just in case he's early," replied Tan eager to get on.

"Check the radio when you get there and don't forget to place the Out of Order sign on the door." Tan watched as the rear of the jeep bounced and bumped down the hillside till it was a mere speck in the valley below. The early greyness was fast giving way to a brighter clearer day and Tan felt relaxed and relieved as he sat down on the grass and lit a cigarette, the radio by his side waiting for the call to scramble.

Phil had just devoured his fourth croissant in a row and was washing them down with a large bowl of thick french coffee he belched as the taste of red wine came back into his mouth. His head was unsympathetic to his previous night's over indulgences in the seedy bars and cafes of the Paris backstreets where he'd squandered most of the five hundred pounds.

He left the airport cafeteria and strolled across to a bookshelf where he stood in front of a rack filled with international newspapers. He smiled as he picked out the word Heyes on almost every headline. A two day old copy of the Daily Mirror was pushed in amongst them and he paid the seven francs for it and left the book shop. He seated himself near the busy entrance doors to the airport terminal building. Phil wasn't at all sure what he was doing there. He knew his orders were to locate the President when he arrived, and then find out which flight he would take. But even Phil knew the President would be secured in the VIP lounge. He could enter the airport at any entrance, if he didn't use this airport he might even be flying from Charles De Gaulle and not Orly as Tan had insisted. But then as he sobered slightly, Tan's words came back to him. Remember only Orly airport; the President's DC10 is garaged there so he always flies from there. But also keep an eye from the terminal and viewing terrace; he may go straight onto the tarmac and board a scheduled flight. Watch out for a convoy of black Citroen limousines with the Tricolour of the Republic and possibly several outriders on motorcycles. Phil checked his watch, it was seven fifty. He made his way outside onto the roof terrace and found a seat where he could see the tarmac and approach road for passengers to the terminal building.

David Galbraith had arrived in Paris at four thirty the previous day. He was met at the airport by an officer from the Guarda Republic who would translate for him. He was located in a middle class hotel just off the Champs Elysée before the translator, Jean Mouson, took him to the Elysée Palace where he was interviewed by the President's Chief Security Officer. David refused point blank to reveal any information by stressing he was an ambassador directly from the Prime Minister in London and his message was for the ears of the President only. An hour later he was led into a giant marble room where, seated behind a great walnut desk, sat the President himself. An hour and a half after a long and satisfying discussion David left the Elysée Palace well pleased with himself. He'd found the President an intelligent well informed man, who'd listened patiently to David's information and had accepted his explanations without challenge. At ten thirty p.m. after a light meal David was collected from his hotel by Jean Mouson who'd arranged an evening's entertainment at the Les Folies Bergére. He was returned to his Hotel at 2.45 a.m. a little wobbly after allowing himself to partake a little of the local pastis. He slept well, had a large English breakfast in the restaurant before returning to his room to collect his luggage. He lifted the parachute out of the holdall and lay it on the bed. He stripped off all his clothes except his underpants and socks. He then began to fold the small parachute into a flat square shape, holding it with loosely applied masking tape. He pulled off about a yard of the tape and fastened it onto the middle of the chute with about a foot of tape hanging over each side. He carefully eased on the heavy harness strap, taking care not to disturb the bundle of nylon cloth held gently folded by the tape. He'd already cut out the heavy metal release clasp that held the shoulder straps and the leg straps together in the middle of his chest. He'd completely cut away the lower straps that came up on the inside of his legs by his crutch. He'd replaced those with the strong nylon ribbon used by climbers to bond ropes together and to make a temporary but strong harness with. He brought the two pieces of ribbon up between his legs and threaded them through the two shoulder straps and then he tied them together like the chest strap in a pair of lederhosen to stop the shoulder straps falling off over his shoulders under stress. He then slowly pulled on an extra large thin wool polo necked sweater taking care to pull the two pieces of loose rope round the front of his chest pulling the folded parachute even closer to his back. He then pulled on a large pair of loosely fitting slacks he'd bought back in England and as he checked himself in the full length mirror on the wardrobe he was pleased with the result. Only a slight bump appeared on his back but as he put on a larger sized checked sports jacket he could hardly see any bulges at all. He folded over the collar of the sweater neatly amidst its folds. He checked for easy reach to locate the handkerchief sized igniter chute, that when pulled free would catch the up rush of air and withdraw the main chute from its resting place. David felt a little stupid as he trundled down into the reception to meet Jean who was waiting to collect him for the return trip. He gave David a quizzical stare as he approached in his obviously huge oversized jacket. David passed off the jacket explaining he'd had to replace his corset that held his bad back in place and the jacket was the only thing loose enough for him to tolerate. Jean just nodded. David still felt like a clown. It was nine fifteen a.m. on Monday morning the thirtieth of August when the two men left the Hotel and returned once more to the Elysée Palace. After a brief cup of coffee David was invited to sit in the rear car of a convoy of three black Citroen limousines waiting below the wide stairway on the gravel drive. David was aware the cars were bullet proof by the inch thick windows on the door as he climbed in. Four plain clothed security men carrying FN machine pistols got in. There was one either side of him, one in the front passenger seat and the other unfolded a small backward travelling seat so he could view the rear window in easy comfort. A mass of other security men placed themselves in the other two cars and with four police outriders, two in front, two in the rear, the convoy set off towards the airport. David saw the grey hairs on the President's head in the middle car as they drove along, and his heart sunk down into his stomach. The nightmare he'd been thinking about the last few days had begun.

Phil was standing on the terrace looking down at the planes parked below. Some of the large jets parked near the London departure gate had the long telescopic loading corridors that ran straight to the jet's passenger doors, directly from the departure gate. Apart from a small window they were completely covered and he could only just see through into the platform. A small panic overcame him and he was just about to rush down again to the main entrance when a distant siren distracted him and he turned to see the cavalcade of the President's entourage heading down towards a perimeter gate. People stopped and applauded as their President drove past and Phil watched as the guard lifted the steel barrier then stood back to attention as the cars drove straight through and round onto the tarmac till they finally pulled to a stop almost directly where he stood. He watched in amazement as doors were flung open and the heavily armed men clambered out surveying every point and angle of a possible assassin. Then amidst the men he caught sight of the familiar grey-silver hair of the President. He strained his head over a guard rail as the men pushed through a door directly into the departure area. Phil became flushed with excitement and he watched half leaning over the rail till he saw the entourage pass the window of the boarding platform onto a white 747 with the words 'Air France' painted on the fuselage. Ten minutes later the portable corridor was retracted and the plane was pulled clear by a small truck. Phil shot to the stairs and almost fell down the three flights. He darted to an empty phone box quickly inserted five ten franc coins. He pulled out a small note book from his pocket and dialled the first number listed above another. He waited a few seconds but the line just hummed. He dialled the number again and listened carefully as each number clicked down the line. His heart beat furiously against his chest for what seemed ages and suddenly the ringing tone began to sound. Another few seconds passed, then a click came as the receiver was lifted, a familiar voice said,

"Hello."

"Rocket to base," Phil gave the password. Richard responded.

"Mike Mercury here, go ahead." Using the names of characters from a sixties T.V. puppet show.

"747 Air France colour white, taxi-ing, now 11.02."

"Gotcha, Rocket. See you soon."

Richard dived into the open door of the Landrover and picked up the small Sony handset.

"Mike Mercury to Brains over." The line crackled and Tan's voice answered.

"Brains here."

"747 Air France take off now 11.03."

Tan threw the radio to the floor. He'd already dropped the huge grill to the ground and he nearly tripped on it as he sprinted over into the tunnel. He clambered up onto the wing and swung into the cockpit. He put on his helmet and plugged into the oxygen socket and lifted the mouth cover over his face. He locked the cockpit, flicked down the ignition switch, checked for low throttle before his thumb hit the red turbo starter. The jet whistled and then began to scream as the Rolls Royce engine drank the pre-heated fuel. Tan eased forward on the throttle allowing the jet to move slowly forward a foot at a time till it came once more out of it's tomb. As soon as it was clear of the entrance he moved all four jet ducts into the down position then he eased the throttle more and more forward till it began to scream. The plane broke free of the earth's gravity and slowly began to lift. At twenty feet from the ground Tan eased the jet nozzles slowly backwards and the screaming jet began to move slowly forwards. A few seconds later he was beginning to pick up speed and he retracted the landing gear before he eased the throttle lever another inch forward. The jet responded immediately as the surge of power took Tan up to two hundred knots and the 'G force' pinned him back into the seat. He checked his instruments before bringing the compass on a south westerly course.

A sudden beeping noise told him he had penetrated into ground control's radar beacon and he pushed the stick forward as the jet's nose dropped and the beeping stopped. He was now down past Manchester and flying about two hundred feet off the ground. Ground hopping it's called in the RAF, a common practice where the jet follows the contours of the ground too low for the ever watchful eye of the ground controller's radar. He turned west to avoid the airport at Manchester and checked his watch. It was eleven thirteen. He eased back slightly on the throttle slowing the jet. He was ahead of his schedule by more than a minute, and the slower speed gave him more time to spot the land hopper's nightmare, electricity pylons. Tan was pleased with himself. His reactions were as quick as ever and the adrenalin flowed to his brain heightening his already ecstatic awareness. The feeling of being in control of such a magnificent machine was one of a high sexual well being without the erection. A mental self indulgence of high gratification only the privileged people who had piloted the beast would understand. He felt saddened as the sudden thought that after this flight he would never ever again feel the thrill of a jet fighter under his body, and then he cheered as he thought he'd savour every minute, every second and he smiled as he thought of his unsuspecting prey getting nearer and nearer. He caught sight of the River Severn and he turned further west and dropped down to follow its path. The great Severn road bridge came quickly upon him as he soared between the hundred feet or so betwixt the river and the underside of the road. He followed down the river and passed the great power station on Barry Island and then he was out over the widest part of the estuary of the Bristol Channel. The sun came shining through into a near clear sky as he left the spasmodic wisps of cloud behind. Tan eased down on the stick and turned the plane south east. He was flying by both compass and ground sight heading for east of Portsmouth where the flight path of all Paris London planes began their descent. Tan checked the fuel; supersonic jets were highly inaccurate due to the placing of several fuel tanks throughout the aircraft, but he'd worked out a safe strike range of two hundred and fifty miles. Tan flicked on the radio and began to listen to various take off and landing instructions from Bristol airport control tower. His radar warning receiver was still silent although he was not unduly worried about being picked up on their screens. They'd probably just take him for a military plane on low flying exercise. Tan checked the airspeed indicator; he was just under three hundred and seventy five knots, about half the full speed of the jet. The sky was clear blue now and hardly a sign of cloud. He dipped down over Torquay and screamed out low into the bay turning due east about two miles out from the coast line. He checked his watch, it was eleven thirty one. It had taken him a mere eighteen minutes to reach the Channel. He pulled back on the throttle and turned on the radio once again. Various air crew were chatting away asking instructions on what height to fly or what course to take. Unlike military planes most civil airlines did not have on-board radar and are totally dependant on the ground controller to keep them clear of other aircraft. The Harrier was now coming up on the Isle of White and this was Tan's marker to climb up to twenty thousand feet. He pushed the throttle full forward and pulled slowly back on the stick as the Harrier's nose lifted and it soared up sweetly and screamed up into the blue heaven. Tan's enjoyment was interrupted by the RWC as it started to bleep. The air traffic controller's voice came from the radio.

"Unidentified aircraft over Portsmouth airspace, please identify."

Tan just smiled. He checked his radar screen. It registered four bleeps all within the fifteen mile radius above. The voice became more agitated.

"Unidentified aircraft, I repeat identify."

The controller waited a few seconds for an answer. Then the voice became excited. Britannia Airlines 749 please turn on a course heading one four seven and climb to twenty eight thousand feet.."

"Roger, Wilco," came the reply. Tan watched the blip make its turn on his radar screen.

"Lufthansa flight 1570 please alter course to a heading one hundred and twenty degrees and drop to twenty thousand feet." Tan watched the blip move away. He could see the traffic controller trying to make a wide corridor for him. Tan eased back on the throttle and levelled the jet at twenty thousand feet. The voice pleaded for identification once more.

Ignored again it began to clear another corridor. Then suddenly Tan heard the words he'd been waiting to hear.

"Air France 747 please take evasive course we have unidentified aircraft in your air space. Stay at the same height and turn to one hundred and thirty degrees." Tan's heart thumped as he heard the plane's captain respond. He watched the blip slowly turn and he was pleased with his calculations of interception. The 747 was almost directly above. Tan looked upwards for the tell tale sign of white slipstream. There it was turning eastwards. Tan eased forward on the throttle and lifted the nose of the jet. He screamed upwards at over four hundred knots till he could see the sun reflecting off the brilliant white paintwork gaining fast on the huge unsuspecting 747. He could see distant faces peering out through the fuselage windows. The controller's voice came franticly over the airwaves again.

"Air France 747. Unidentified plane approaching fast on course 120, can you see him, over?" The captain could not see the Harrier as he was flying above and away from it. The captain replied.

"No, we have no contact." The controller's voice screamed out at Tan.

"Whoever you are please identify!" Tan levelled off the jet at thirty thousand feet. The 747 was about one thousand yards away on his starboard wing still flying away from him. The controller's voice screamed again.

"Air France747 you must see him now, he is almost on top of you, on the port wing." The big Jumbo banked over and altered course to give them a chance to see the Harrier. Tan flew nearer but at such an angle making it impossible for the Jumbo's crew to spot him.

"Jesus, fucking hell," screamed the controller on the verge of a breakdown.

"He's going to hit. Dive. Take immediate action. Collision imminent." Tan smiled as he came up under and slightly behind the tail of the large jet still undetected by the Jumbo's crew. It responded to the air controller's demands and suddenly began to descend. So quickly, in fact, that some of the women passengers who'd been standing fell crashing into the isles tumbling into other seated passengers.

The plane levelled out at twenty five thousand feet. Tan came up from below and eased slowly alongside the starboard wing of the giant jet. Hundreds of faces peered out in amazement and Tan waved in a jocular fashion as he cruised slowly alongside then he drew level with the flight deck. The captain's attention to the jet's presence was drawn to him by the second officer and he leaned round his co-pilot to see Tan waving back at him. The panic stricken voice of the controller barked out again.

"What's happening up there? Do you have contact?"

The captain replied, obviously relieved. "We have visual contact with an RAF Harrier but no radio contact. I will try to speak with him."

Tan smiled as he listened to the conversation. The captain spoke directly to Tan.

"747 to Harrier do you read? Over." Tan pressed the transmit button.

"Bonjour Mon Capitaine," he said in fluent French, "how are you today?"

The ground controller interrupted. "Please identify yourself and speak English."

"Oh very well if you insist," replied Tan in a nonchalant manner enjoying his moment of revenge.

"Oh good, now will you please identify." Tan cut the traffic controller short.

"Now you listen carefully to what I have to say and keep quiet." He waited listening for a response. None came.

"That's better. Now then you frog eaters I have come to right a wrong for a dear departed friend of mine. But first I would like to speak to your President." Tan waited a moment.

"I am sorry Monsieur. You wish us to make a call to the President for you?" replied the captain.

Tan's excitement turned immediately to anger.

"In sixty seconds I am going to blow you from the sky. So it is irrelevant if you lie. I know the President is on board."

"Please switch your radio into the passenger communication system; I want to speak to them," demanded Tan.

"I am sorry Monsieur, I cannot have you alarm my passengers." Tan's smile immediately disappeared from his face and he barked angrily down into the microphone inside his oxygen mask.

"I know he's onboard you lying French turd. Now you bring him to the blower." Tan watched as the captain's alarmed face peered back at him through the side window of the flight deck.

"Please Monsieur I give you my solemn oath, the President is not aboard." The captain began to sweat a little; he didn't like the sound of Tan's voice, the angered tones and the extreme nearness of the fully armed jet. Tan smiled to himself again under the oxygen mask, what did it matter he thought, if he was on board he would be listening to the conversation anyway and if he wasn't, no doubt the ground controller would be recording the full content of his transmissions for the inquiry that always followed violation of airspace. He'd wasted enough time already.

"Now listen carefully you sub-human excuse for a dog shit. My name is Anthony Heyes. Up to date I have killed quite a few people." Tan was enjoying his moment but he knew he couldn't hang about too long. He realised full well the RAF would launch a flight of Tornados almost at once if they hadn't been launched already. "No doubt you have read of my exploits." Tan waited a second for a reply but none came."One thing you probably don't know is that I was on board the Greenpeace Ship that was sunk by your government in New Zealand. I have come to repay that atrocity."

David Galbraith was just behind the flight deck in the upper cocktail lounge. His pure white face was pinned against the window as he glared at the painted words Phil had written on the side of the jet. He stared hopelessly at the man who sat only fifty feet away. He felt he was about to die. Tan spoke to the captain again.

"Do you understand why you who are innocent of any crime must die?" The captain's brain had gone into a panic, he'd just realised who Tan was and he knew there would be no reprieve. He searched for the right words that might save all their lives but none came.

"Au revoir," said Tan. He turned to bank away in order to give him room to fire a missile. As he did he noticed three blips coming up fast from behind. They were three French Mirage jets that had been fuelled and ready for such a crisis and had been in the air the minute Tan had made contact. They were now only about thirty five miles away and closing fast. He eased the throttle into the full position and the jet leapt forward and left the Jumbo in its slipstream. Tan kept his eye on the radar, as his speed hit five hundred knots he suddenly decreased his speed by rotating the four jet nozzles coming round immediately to face the oncoming jets. He flicked a switch to arm all four missiles. The yellow indicator lights ignited at once. He was speeding back towards the Jumbo and he waited until the three blips converged almost into the blip of the Jumbo. Then he fired. He sent all four rockets screaming off towards the merging targets. He threw the stick forward. The jet responded immediately and went into a vertical dive at about six hundred miles an hour, ever increasing. Tan heard the chirping sound of the heat seeking missiles as they locked onto their targets. He knew the French fighter pilots could not launch an attack on him because he'd kept the 747 between him and them but now he was vulnerable and he began to sweat profusely as he glared at the radar, for any weapons that had locked onto him. It took only three seconds from launching to impact of Tan's rapier missiles. The first two hit the leading Mirage blowing it into a thousand pieces in a huge ball of flames as the high octane fuel fed by the explosion roasted every piece of twisted and gnarled alloy as the inferno fell from the sky. Another missile hit the Jumbo's starboard wing outer engine and the whole wing disintegrated. The explosion ripped the wing clean away from the fuselage leaving a gaping hole in its side. Passengers who were sitting in the immediate vicinity of the wing were either killed by the explosion or sucked out of the plane still fastened to their seats as the air depressurised, sucking luggage, magazines and people out into the great void, many still alive as they plummeted to their deaths. As David Galbraith had stared at the Harrier before the attack his initial thoughts were of his impending demise and one of his own stupidity for allowing himself to be on the plane, especially after he'd talked the

President into not taking the flight but to travel by ferry earlier that day. Who in the blazes was he out to impress? The drunken face of George Redburn flashed momentarily into his mind. Then his immediate boss Alan Forrest's face appeared with the ridiculous ill-fitting toupée perched on his head. His mother's face spoke to him as it appeared.

"Look out for yourself, not all people like policemen and you remember that." She'd spoken these words as he'd passed out from the police college and he was proud as could be marching up and down as his widowed mother stood watching in the crowd. That's when he felt the tear squeeze from his eye. The thought of his old mother who'd brought him up on her own after his father had been killed helping a neighbour repair the underside of a car which fell on him crushing him to death. He'd hardly seen her for over a year now and suddenly he missed her as the guilt of his neglect overcame him. Then the Harrier accelerated away and as it did, something snapped inside. I'm not ready to die, he thought. Suddenly his brain was alert, as the fear merged with his will to survive spurred him into action. His first thought was to open a door and leap out relying on the parachute for his safety. But then what if Heyes didn't attack, the depressurised effects of the plane once he'd opened the door could be just as drastic. No, he thought, Heyes, if he was going to attack would do so from the front. That was the direction David assumed as he'd not banked away but sped ahead. He climbed down the small spiral staircase down onto the passenger deck. He walked briskly but calmly towards the rear of the half filled plane. A stewardess stopped him in the middle section and asked him to strap himself in as ordered by the captain. He smiled at her as he passed but said nothing. She followed him protesting till he reached the rear of the 747. The toilet catch read vacant. David opened the door. The stewardess protested even louder.

"Monsieur you cannot go in there whilst..." David grabbed her and pulled her with him into the toilet, she screamed and fought as he pushed the door to, locking it behind. The stewardess screamed even louder and David slapped her hard across the face as best he could in the small space. A passenger came to her rescue and started banging the door. The girl stunned by the blow stopped screaming, a look of sheer terror in her eyes. David stared back unsmiling, not speaking. His face dripped with sweat and his heart seemed to beat in time with the pounding on the door. The stewardess secure, aware she was not going to be harmed, shouted at the banging man who'd been joined by another, to return to their seats. She recognised the look of sheer terror in the eyes of her captor, a look she'd seen in a cow's eyes as it was led off to slaughter when in her childhood days on her father's farm, she could never understand how they knew. "What is it Monsieur?" she asked kindly. David just stared at her waiting for the impact that could end his life. It had seemed like they'd been in the toilet for hours bit it was only seconds when the impact came. The plane seemed to stop in mid air and then shudder a few times before it started to twist and spiral down with its starboard wing completely gone. It twisted and spun like a single winged sycamore seed. David and the girl were thrown together; they fell over and over as the plane twisted and began to disintegrate. Paper towels tried to fight their way under the door as the suction of decompression caused them to fly round the small room. Screams filled David's ears as he turned upside down and round and round the girl clung desperately to him. He was alive, David gave the cabin pressure time to equalise with the outside air before he made his move. It took him longer than he thought to undo the catch on the door as he couldn't co-ordinate himself due to the spinning of the plane.

He tumbled upwards and then down and round till the door fell open. As the air frame twisted he and the stewardess spewed out into what was left of the revolving plane. David was horror struck as he caught sight of the hole in the side. Rows of seats had completely vanished and luggage from the cargo hold spilled out through a great hole in the floor every time the plane spun a full circle. People to the rear of the plane were still fastened in their seats, an old grey haired man stared at David for a split second as if he was a fellow passenger on a bus journey, and then he was gone. The huge plane broke into two across the gaping hole and the front disappeared from sight. David was helpless, the gravity of the spinning increased pinning him to the floor as if on a roller coaster. He saw sky and then sea and the patch of land through the open end of the fuselage. Something heavy was pushing against him and he could hardly breathe. Suddenly the rear door of the aircraft disappeared. The force of the spin contorting the air frame allowed it to depart it's hinges. On the next spin David was thrown out of the hole. The noises that had been about him had now gone. All was peaceful apart from the familiar rush of air he'd felt on many a parachute drop. His senses suddenly returned as he realised where he was and he tumbled out of control towards the earth. The heavyness had moved to around his waist and suddenly he realised the stewardess in her terror was holding onto him. He locked his legs around her armpits and gripped her as best he could. Their descent steadied a little and David could see the white breakers on the clear blue sea, a piece of the tail and small pieces of fuselage fell below him; twisting and tumbling they followed them downward. He reached up his right hand for the drag chute tucked under the polo neck of his sweater. He felt a great relief and he clasped it tight and he screamed out loud as he threw it up into his own slipstream. He felt the pull on the nylon string attached to the main chute resting under his jumper and as the chute fought to free itself from the rear of his pullover he screamed aloud. He felt the main chute pull away from his back, and still gazing upwards he watched it flap and blow till the rush of air finally forced it open and it hung there like a small red mushroom, lowering the two people gently down towards the sea.

Tan was diving fast away from the impact of his missiles. His eyes were fixed firmly onto the radar screen and as he watched the result of his attack, he saw the lead plane flown by the squad commander disintegrate and disappear from the screen. He saw the 747 break and fall from the sky, but his eyes were scanning for the two Mirages that had escaped the attack. As they broke away, full afterburners ignited at the supersonic speed to avoid the incoming missiles. One of the missiles' guidance systems had failed allowing it to drive itself harmlessly into the sea. Tan came down to a thousand feet and levelled the jet. He turned north east to try and make a run to where Richard would be waiting in Anglesey. He was pleased with himself. He didn't care if the President had been on the jet liner or not. He knew every word spoken would have been recorded. He was satisfied he'd made his point. He'd seen the great jet fall from the sky, it was revenge enough for the sunken ship. He was pleased with the way he'd handled the jet, as if it was only yesterday he'd flown it. It wasn't the flying of the jet that was difficult, he knew as did most pilots, that a ten year old could fly a jet. It was the ability to think and react with only a split second to make a decision. Then his self glorification thoughts were interrupted. As he saw a blip on the radar screen turn onto his course as one of the French pilots angered by the death of his leader, had decided to seek his revenge on the Harrier. The other Mirage pilot had been nearest to the exploding jet and the shock of the impact had sent hundreds of small fragments of steel into the underside of the jet, crippling it. The young lieutenant was glad to be away from what was likely to be his first ever fully unprovoked attack. The second pilot had searched the sky with his radar till he finally saw the blip of the Harrier racing away to the east. Tan was about twenty miles in front of the superentendant and twenty thousand feet below. The coastline suddenly shot underneath him and he dropped down to hug the land. The blip of the superentendant disappeared and Tan breathed a sigh of relief. The French pilot had been well trained and all his experience told him to stay high in the thinner air allowing him to gain distance on the Harrier. Although he'd lost radar contact he knew its direction; unless the Harrier did a complete 'U' turn he'd got him. Tan's eyes kept returning to the small radar screen. He flew about three hundred feet from the ground, and all his concentration was required as he strained into the distance looking for the low hill or chimney that could end his flight once and for all. It was a few minutes now since he'd seen the blip of the superintendant on the small screen. He relaxed his grip slightly on the stick and his shoulders loosened and he slid back into the seat. He flicked on his radio to hear all the requests for help in the area as the controller gave the co-ordinates and kept reporting. "We have a 747 down in the sea." Tan smiled to himself as the pent up rage he'd felt after he'd learned the French government were responsible for the sinking of his beloved ship seemed to leave him, and he felt as if a burden had been lifted from his shoulders. His thoughts were suddenly interrupted by the bleep bleep of the radar warning receiver as it told him he was being tracked by another aircraft. Tan checked the screen and his heart missed a beat as he saw the blip of the French jet about ten miles behind.

Tan knew he was in range of the French pilot's missiles, although he wasn't sure whether or not the pilot had the metal to fire them. But then his questions were quickly answered as two blips emerged from the larger blip and two laser guided missiles were launched simultaneously. The tell tale bleep on his control console told him they'd locked onto him. Tan knew he had about ten seconds to act. He reached over his head and pulled the steel handle that hung ready for such an occasion. The next instant the glass domed cockpit cover blew up into the air as the explosive charge around its rim blew it clear of the already lifting seat. The rockets under the seat fired a fraction of a second behind the exploding glass dome as Tan was propelled with enormous thrust upwards and the jet screamed away underneath. Two blurs followed by the flame from the rocket's tail fire flashed past him and in another fraction of a second they caught the Harrier, enveloping it in a cloud of flame as it exploded disintegrating in an almighty thunderous clap that almost deafened Tan. The parachute opened and he began to drift down the three hundred or so feet to the sea. The Mirage jet came thrashing past about a hundred yards in front of Tan and the slip stream made the parachute collapse in on itself momentarily before it reopened and held him still fastened into the pilot's seat. Tan looked down below him as the brown thrashing water came up to meet him.

He hit the water and sat on top of a swell for an instant, still fastened to the seat. Then the parachute came down on his right hand side and its soggy weight made the seat roll and in an instant Tan was under the water. The seat had air trapped inside it and it floated and bobbed with Tan still strapped to it but he was upside down. All he could see was murky brown all around with a lighter area that was the surface above him. He fought with the quick release button, it held fast, the force of the ejecting seat had thrown his weight against the straps and somehow it had jammed. He began to panic as some sea water came up into his nostrils and went down his throat forcing his mouth open he swallowed some more. He tore at the shoulder straps with his hands trying to force himself downwards out of the seat. Suddenly he noticed the light was fading. It was as if in a dream. The seat had lost the air that had kept it on the surface and was now slowly sinking. His lungs were bursting and his brain was screaming. He suddenly stopped his thrashing as if accepting his fate. Although his mind still functioned and for some silly reason he wondered how deep the sea was at this point. The light had gone now and it was only darkness. It was serene and peaceful and he began to descend deeper and deeper the floating parachute with air trapped in its folds stopped his descent and he hung under it like a giant jelly fish. Scenes of his life long ago flashed into his brain. He was on the hills aged thirteen gazing at the sky and wondering where its infinite eternity ended. His mother kissed him as she had done on his seventh birthday because he'd not complained there was no present for him and he heard her say to Uncle Donald, her lover of the moment, "he's different our Tan, more mature than other kids, it's like living with an adult not a seven year old." The next instant he was standing on an ice flow in the Antarctic watching hundreds of penguins hopping into the icy water. A man called to him a camera held in front of his face. He lowered the camera and the face of the murdered photographer from the Rainbow Warrior was gesticulating for him to come with him, his lips were moving but Tan couldn't hear a sound. A darkness suddenly descended and as the sun disappeared forever and his mind emptied, he was still.

David and the stewardess plunged into the cold sea. The salty water forced into his mouth and throat by the weight of the girl who still clung to him in a severe state of shock. Coughing and spluttering he kicked and thrashed till he broke free of her and clawed his way upwards, finally breaking through the surface. The taste of the salt water burned the back of his throat, but the euphoria he felt at being alive overcame all the discomfort. A mop of jet black hair bobbed through the water in front of him as the girl gasped and coughed clearing her lungs of the foul tasting water. David reached out and grabbed the collar of her uniform jacket and pulled her towards him so she faced him. Her eyes were staring and wild as he held her tight as if subconsciously he'd thought we've made it out of the blown up jet, we'll make it the rest of the way. Then she blinked several times and although the black mascara had run down across her cheeks David couldn't help but notice how remarkably beautiful she was. Her lips quivered slightly and she spoke.

"Bonjour Monsieur." David smiled and nodded as if being introduced for the first time at some pleasant social function. It all seemed unreal. David lifted his head clear of the water but could see nothing in the swell. Occasionally they bobbed up on a crest of a small wave but his vision was obscured by the ocean as it swirled and lifted around them. But then he heard the distant but unmistakable sound of the rotor blades of an approaching helicopter and he began to wave and scream. The pilot of the Wessex Helicopter had already spotted the red parachute that still floated attached to David's back and was homing in to take a better look.

"God," he shouted into the microphone, "there's someone down there."

David's relief was distracted momentarily as the thunderous roar of three RAf Tornado jets screamed low out to his left. "Go get him, the bastard," he cried after them. The fear he'd felt only minutes earlier had disappeared through anger and a slight sadness for the other poor souls whose lives had ended that day. He could still see faces of people who had been alive only minutes before, faces whom he knew now would be floating expressionless and still.

The helicopter came slowly above them. Its rotor blades sent a cold down-draft that turned the white froth of the sea into thousands of small ripples. A diver clad in a rubber suit leapt out of the open side of the helicopter and crashed into the water a few feet away.

"You're alright now, we've got you," he shouted in a reassuring and commanding tone. A canvas sling was quickly lowered from the helicopter and the diver hooked it over the still shocked girl and signalled the winchman to hoist her up. The diver pulled a knife from its sheath attached to his leg and began to cut through the guide ropes still attached to the harness on David's back. He eyed David suspiciously as he cut away chute with his knife.

"You come out of the Air France job?" he asked.

David nodded. He knew the diver was puzzling over the parachute but then the winch was lowered and the diver hooked the strap under David's arm and wrapping his legs round him he signalled the winchman to begin the lift and they both came out of the water together. In the helicopter the girl was quickly wrapped in blankets and laid on a stretcher. She was shaking uncontrollably through the cold and shock. David saw her as he came in through the doorway.

"How is she?" he shouted at the winchman through the deafening noise of the engine and thrashing blades.

"Not too good," came the reply as he draped a large woollen blanket over David's shoulders. Ten minutes later the helicopter touched down at Sandown on the Isle of White. An ambulance was waiting on the tarmac and the two survivors were transferred quickly into the rear of the vehicle. A police car led the way, sirens blaring loud as the two vehicles sped the four miles to the nearby hospital.

The weight on his back and a voice in a dulcet Somerset dialect enquiring if he was alright, brought Tan quickly to his senses. A trickle of sickly tasting sea water ran from his mouth and he coughed and spluttered as the pressure was released from his back once more.

"He'll be okay," another voice said. Tan felt nauseous and groggy as he pushed himself up on one elbow and stared at his surroundings. He was on a boat. What was he doing there, his mind began to track back to that morning and then he saw the pilot's seat and the parachute in a tangled mess near the small storage house on the old fishing boat. An old man, well into his sixties appeared in front of him. His heavily wrinkled eyes stared at him for a moment before the face full of grey whiskers parted and the voice he first heard only seconds ago spoke.

"You're in good hands, squadron leader. We will soon have you on dry land." The old man and his grandson had been fishing a mile or so away from where Tan's parachute had landed in the sea. They quickly abandoned their labours and raced to the spot where the parachute lay partly on and under the water. They'd dragged on the chute with their boat hooks and hauled the unconscious man into the small fishing boat. The seriousness of Tan's predicament forced him into a sitting position.

"Where are we?" he spluttered coughing water still from his lungs. The smell of fish guts filled his nostrils.

"Oh we'll be in the harbour inside a few minutes," replied the younger fisherman.

"What harbour?" asked Tan, knowing had to act quickly if he was to escape capture.

"Minehead," came the reply.

A thunderous roar distracted all three men as they simultaneously looked skywards. The three low flying Tornados screamed overhead scanning the area for any sign of Tan's wreckage. The two fishermen waved their arms franticly in the air and the younger man waved the soaking parachute aloft screaming.

"He's here, we've got him."

Tan reached inside his flying suit and pulled the Luger from his belt.

"Stop that fucking noise," he bellowed as both men stopped at once and gazed down at the still prostrate man. Tan eased himself to a half standing position supporting his back against the small wheelhouse. The two men stood on either side of him, a look of utter amazement spread across their weatherbeaten faces.

"You," ordered Tan as he thrust the Luger nearer the younger man's head, "get back in the wheelhouse and get this thing into the harbour and quick." The small harbour was only about two hundred yards away by now as the fisherman did as he was ordered. He removed a small rope from the brass wheel that had been holding it in place. The tone of the old diesel engine increased slightly as he slipped the throttle onto full. One of the jets soared over again only a hundred feet or so above Tan's head. Tan could easily see the pilot as he craned his neck through the domed cockpit glass. He saw the chute and recognised the flying kit of the man still attached to the seatbelts of the descended Harrier seat.

Tan waved the Luger at him.

"That's alright," he shouted aloud, "I'm still alive." He knew the pilot would be relaying his finding straight to his superiors and he realised he'd have to act quickly.

The small boat chugged slowly past the old stone wall of the outer harbour. It had been less than twenty minutes now since Tan had gone into the water and he knew he still had a small chance to make his escape.

"You got a car?" he snapped angrily at the old man. The man glared back hard at Tan. A mixture of disobedience and aggression shone from his eyes.

"Don't be stupid old man," cried Tan, "I could easily kill you both now." The old man still glared his anger, but responded quite readily.

"Jamie's got a car."

Tan tapped the Luger on the wheelhouse window.

The young man turned his head and handed Tan small key ring with just one key. He snatched the key and inspected it carefully.

"What make of car is it?" he asked as the man steered the boat up to a small berth against the harbour wall.

"Cortina," answered the man nervously. Tan threw the key onto the wheelhouse floor. He knew Cortina's ignition keys were double sided keys and not single sided keys as he'd been given. He cocked the Luger in one swift movement and held the gun against the white cheeks of the fisherman.

"I'll ask only once more." His tone was menacing. Before Tan could continue the young man held a bunch of well used keys for Tan who scrutinised them. He recognised the type of key as that of a Cortina.

"Where's it parked?"

"Over by the pub," the man pointed as he pushed the throttle into the idle position and the boat hit the side of the harbour wall with a thud.

"Colour?" demanded Tan.

"Red, you can't miss it, got a hub cap missing off the right hand rear wheel." Tan noticed one or two people were beginning to congregate along the walkway above where the boat had now docked.

The old man threw a line to a man who'd come to greet them. Tan suddenly leapt onto the walkway and sped along its length pushing people out of the way as he went. Two hundred yards down towards the main road he caught sight of the Ford parked alone on the edge of the small car park. It started first time and Tan spun the wheels on the loose gravel in his eagerness to get away. He turned left into the small main road that led through the village and within two minutes he was out of the clutter of buildings and speeding along a narrow country lane surrounded by fields and high sided hedgerows. The salt tasted strong in his mouth, his throat stung from the sea water he'd swallowed but the tightness in his stomach eased a little the further he left the coast behind. Five miles inland a police helicopter flew over in the opposite direction heading to the harbour to pick up Tan's trail. Tan switched on the dated Motorola radio in the dashboard of the car. He located a national channel and listened intently to a report of the destruction of the Jumbo.

"Two hundred and twenty seven people were believed to be on board the airliner, we believe there are two survivors. The details of this tragedy are not yet clear and as soon as we have any more information we..." Tan turned off the switch. 'Bastards are keeping quiet for the moment,' he thought. He knew they'd know by now roughly where he was. They'd have questioned the fishermen and they'd be setting up road blocks all over the county. A small wooded glade caught his eye as he sped past. He slammed on the brakes and reversed back. Turning off the road he came to a stop well hidden from the road by the foliage of the trees. He searched through the car for a map on anything that would be of use to him in his escape but found nothing. He sat there a few moments trying to gather his wits. His brain searched for a solution to help him in his predicament but he knew it was hopeless. He was weak from his ordeal and his spirits were low.
He switched on the radio once again but all he could get was music from a local station. He switched it off again. He sat listening to the leaves rustling in the warm summer breeze. He watched a small group of young sparrows fighting and frollicking on the wing in the first summer of their lives. A distant siren distracted his peace, till it was joined by another then another. Tan

smiled to himself as he imagined the hoards of police cars zooming in to block off every road and lane. He imagined how a lamb felt as it bleated in fear when used as bait to tempt the tiger to the trap. 'Should I cheat the hunter?' he thought as he fondled the cold steel of the Luger. He did not fear death for he realised it was inevitable, everything that lived and breathed must die. He became suddenly angry with himself, he wasn't fulfilled, his dreams had only just begun and now it was to end, but he decided not to give in to the Luger, not until there was no alternative. He shoved it back into his belt and patted it affectionately like an old friend.

"Not yet," he said out loud, "not just yet."

The strong antiseptic aroma that lingered in the air of the hospital ward reminded David of the hours he'd spent waiting in similar buildings in pursuance of his work. He'd been asleep for some time but he'd been awake now for an hour or so reminiscing over the day's events. The small room was dimly lit by a small wall light and alone in the room David felt secure. The happy serenity of someone who'd cheated the reaper elated him. His mouth still burned and the acrid taste of salt rose from his stomach. He reached and pressed the buzzer on the end of the cord. The door sprung open and the rustle of starched cotton announced the arrival of a middle aged nurse.

"Ah, you've slept for quite a while," she said as she leaned over and tucked in the corner of the sheet near David's head.

"There's quite a queue of people waiting to see you, you're quite a hero."

"What time is it?"

"It's ten p.m." David smiled.

"How's the girl?"

"She's fine, she's asleep still under sedation."

David reached for the water jug standing on the bedside cabinet. The nurse intercepted his hand pouring him a glass. The relief was immense as it trickled soothingly down his throat, the water had never tasted so good. The door opened again and in came a stockily well built man dressed in a white coat.

"I'm Doctor Walker. How are we feeling?" he said as he

came and sat on the end of the bed.

"I'm fine thanks," replied David. "Can I get up now?"

"Certainly. There's a shower in that room and one of your colleagues has brought you a change of clothes, you'll find them hanging behind the door."

"Thanks," replied David as he slid his feet out from under the sheets resting them on the floor.

"There's about 300 people out there waiting to speak to you, you feeling up to it? Oh, and your Chief Inspector insists on seeing you as soon as he can. Shall I send him in?" The doctor stood and walked towards the door.

"Yes send him in, I want to see him also."

Two minutes later the swing door burst open and the large frame and red round face of George Redburn came bustling in. " How's my boy," he said , a large grin on his face. He sat on the bed and placed his hand on David's shoulder.

"We showed 'em eh! We knew he had the frigging jet."

He somehow seemed delighted. David stared at him, an amazed expression on his face. He went into a verbal attack.

"You make me sick," he said wiping the smile off the DSI's face.

"You're a shallow insensitive old burk."

"What?" George sat open mouthed before composing himself.

"Now see here Sergeant, remember who you're talking to."

David glared at him in silence and rang the bell for the nurse.

"Get me a pen and paper please, nurse," he asked as she came back into the room. She removed a pad from a drawer by a table in the private room and handed him the pen from her uniform breast pocket. David began to write on the paper and then handed it to the waiting man.

"As required by the police authority, there is written notice of my resignation. I quit. You stupid drunken half brained microbe."

The nurse came out of a nearby room where she was waiting for her pen.

"Is he on drugs or something?" the bemused man asked. The nurse shook her head. "No, Sir, he's had no medication at all."

George stared at him undecided whether to speak. David rose from sitting on the bed, went into the shower room and turned on the taps. George followed. Something inside David had snapped on seeing the man who sent him on his errand of death. He'd been a fool, he knew, to go but he had been conditioned without really knowing it himself to follow orders. He was still thinking as he stood under the warm jet of water and he let some trickle down his throat washing away the faint taste of salt. His mind was clearer now. It wasn't Redburn he was mad at but himself. He knew he would have ended up another booze sodden wreck sooner or later if he hadn't quit as he had just done. He'd begun to enjoy the release found through the bottle, but why should he need release? He was a young man with no family worries, no it was the Force. It was the living, breathing and now nearly dying for his profession. He came out of the shower and began to dry himself on a large towel. Redburn was sitting like a scalded child on a chair by the doorway. David stared at him. He looked pathetic and he pitied him. Was it because he saw himself in him? He began to compare himself. George had been dedicated to his work and had obviously been good at his job sometime or other to reach the high rank he had attained. David looked at the ruddy well worn face and could see that he too had been a good looking young man in his day. George broke his thoughts.

"I'm sorry David. I apologise for whatever I've done, I realise what you've been through. It was very insensitive of me."

"Cut the crap George." He called him by his first name instead of Sir for the first time. "You're full of wind. You should retire and let someone else come through." His voice softened slightly as he could see the man's resolve was crumbling.

"I agree with you." David looked surprised. "I should have let go twenty years ago. But it was my life you see. I had position, respect in the community and I was a good copper."

"Perhaps you were George, but you've lost all your feelings. You're cold hard and lonely and you just don't care about anything or anybody except good old George Redburn. Do you know how I know all that George?" David stood in front of him and stared down at him. George stared back. "Because I am just the same as you. An empty worthless being, oh, but what a bloody good copper I was." David finished drying himself and walked back into the room. George came out slowly and rested himself against the bed. He put his hand in his rear trouser pocket and pulled out the silver hip flask and took a long swig.

"No need to hide it from you, you seem to know all about me."

David looked in the cupboard and pulled out a shirt hanging there. He looked at George.

"You brought these?" George nodded.

"Hope they're what you wanted and I'm not going to get another bollocking."

"Thanks," replied David. "How did you get in my flat?"

"One of the lads broke a window. Don't worry though we had a glazier waiting to repair it. It came in the helicopter with me. Got to get the star his wardrobe. You're main line news, Davy boy, you and that young bird you saved. The whole world's out there waiting to hear your story." David had forgotten about the Harrier.

"What about Heyes, did he get away?" George filled him in on the details.

"He's trapped somewhere in the countryside round Minehead. It's sealed completely. A mouse couldn't squeeze through."

"That's good," replied David, "but it's allover now anyway." George looked puzzled.

"How's that?"

David began to pull on his socks and then lifted his portable shaver from his toilet bag and began to shave.

"The Harrier's gone. He'll have used most if not all the poison, what more of a threat is he?"

George finished the dregs from the hip flask. David gave him a worried glance.

"Is that wise?" he asked.

"Too late, much too late. Doctors only given me a year maybe a bit longer."

"Sorry."

"Me too, but I've had a good innings. You know sommat, though."

"What's that?"

"I've never been happier than I am now. I love all this fucking attention."

David was unsure Redburn was telling the truth about his illness. Although he'd heard rumours he'd decided to ignore it for the moment. He smiled and finished shaving. He'd softened to the old man again. George Redburn the old pro had worked his subtle magic on him and he hadn't known. He needed Detective Sergeant Galbraith badly. George held David's resignation note in the air.

"I respect you, you know, for getting out. I should have done the same. But would you do an old man a favour or two?" David eyed George suspiciously.

"Would you just hold off with the resignation for a day or two. I'll keep the letter and give it to Alan when we return to Leeds or if you change your mind I'll just tear it up. I need you to face the press and then we could nip down to Somerset and face this madman when he's caught. What do you say?"

David knew the answer straight away but he pretended to think about it for a moment.

"Alright George, I'll see it through but I'm still adamant about finishing."

"Fine, Davy boy, fine." George's red face looked genuinely pleased. "Just one thing though, Davy lad. Don't call me George in public, do you mind." David just smiled.

After he'd dressed the two men left the room. David had thanked the nurse for her care she smiled and kissed him on the cheek. They walked down a corridor and through a rubber flap door. The flash of cameras and bustle of bodies surprised David as the waiting press pushed and jostled to get near to him.

"Don't say anything yet," said George as the swarm enveloped them. "We'll hold a press conference after you've been debriefed." A microphone was thrust under his nose. Various voices all tried to ask questions at the same time.

"Did you see the Harrier?"

"Did you jump before the missile hit or after?"

"Where did you get the chute?"

"Is it true you forewarned the President not to travel?"

Two large police constables fought their way through the crowd and encircled David. "This way Sir," one said.

They'd been on station waiting to escort him to the special reserved room for the debriefing. He was pushed into a lift along with George who nearly got left behind as the doors closed. They emerged on the fifth floor to an empty corridor and the two men were led into a large room with several empty beds pushed into one corner. About thirty men were waiting in the room, some were in police uniform, some were not, but it was obvious they were all the hierarchy of the country's police. George introduced the five or six top men; a commander from Scotland Yard, the head of Special Branch, the Chief Constable of the Met. David knew of them by name. He was sitting at a table already prepared and, handed a much needed pot of tea, was asked to tell his story from receiving his orders to travel in Leeds. George had already briefed them on his side of the story and was praying David would give him as much credit as he had awarded himself. David began his story. His recollection of the events was completely accurate and precise. He left nothing out. He started off from when he was called into DSI Redburn's office and read the directorate from the Home Office. A copy of the directorate had been handed around the room. David got the feeling it was an enquiry not a debriefing. Sir Kenneth Doring, the Police Commissioner, asked David what his instructions had been from DSI Redburn. David glanced at George who twitched slightly.

"I was told to try and make the President take an alternative form of transport across the channel."

"But surely," said Sir Kenneth, "the directorate from the Home Secretary was to apologise for the actions of DSI Redburn's outspoken suggestions relating to the stolen Harrier?"

David grasped the situation quickly. It appeared to him that all these men in front of him were on the rack. It was probably these men sat staring back at him that had quashed all knowledge of the jet.

"I certainly did as instructed but towards the end of my conversation the President asked me for my own opinion and I gave it." David realised he could see now they were trying to save their skins.

"What was that opinion?" asked the Commissioner.

"I told him it was highly improbable that Heyes had the jet but then again it was also highly probable he had not."

"That was quite a contrary statement," commented Sir Kenneth. "Is that why you took the precaution of taking along a parachute?"

"Oh that was the DSI's idea," lied David. "He was absolutely convinced Heyes had the jet and would use it to seek revenge on the head of the French Secret Service, the President."

Sir Kenneth's eyes narrowed slightly; he could see David was nobody's fool. David glanced again at George who sat on a chair near the wall. His face tried to look unconcerned but a glow of satisfaction shone from it as he tried his best to look modest.

Sir Kenneth continued. "But surely the directorate was for the Superintendent himself to go to France and escort the President on his journey, and to assist in security?"

David caught George's eye and he looked a trifle squirmish. "You mean why did he send a lowly detective sergeant on what was obviously an important task?"

"Precisely."

"Quite simple. The Superintendent is an ill man and the journey would do his health no good at all. Secondly," David paused, "this is just my opinion, Sir, I think that there was some sort of internal politics involved."

"I don't understand," said Sir Kenneth, "explain yourself."

"It seems someone was out to discredit the Superintendent Sir. After all he was the only officer to broadcast his opinion that Heyes could possibly have a jet hidden away, even though for some reason a 'D' notice had been placed on any reference to the jet. I think Superintendent Redburn was trying to save lives, he probably knew he was putting his career on the line."

David couldn't help glorifying George in front of the squirming hierarchy before him. George was beaming away by the wall like the cheshire cat.

"Anyway, Superintendent Redburn suggested the French Security Service would probably take no notice of anyone who went, even the Foreign Secretary himself."

A small titter rang round the room, the arrogance of the

french was well known here. David was becoming frustrated with the questioning and much to the surprise of the audience he carried on with the rest of the events. He wasn't interrupted again. He'd reasoned those responsible for the cover up would have to face up to it and take whatever punishment was due to them. The inquest on the victims of the 747 would see to that and once David was placed on the stand all hell would freeze over.

David was instructed on what he could and could not say to the press. He could not mention his meeting with the President and his reason for being on the plane was as a public relations officer. He had to say he always wore the parachute due to a fear of flying. The whole meeting had taken just over an hour and after some more tea he was taken to a room below where the long awaited press conference began. George sat proudly on David's right. Questions began to flow and disregarding his superior's orders David was determined to answer them all truthfully.

"Why were you on the plane?" he was asked.

"I was directed by the Home Office to accompany the President apparently because a report in a French Newspaper suggested Heyes the mad poisoner had stolen a jet and was going to use it on the President when he crossed the Channel.

"Why the parachute?"

"Insurance just in case." David explained it was hidden under his jumper. One bright reporter detracted from the crash and turned to Heyes.

"You were obviously working closely on this case, what do you think of this madman Heyes?"

"I think of him as a man who needs to be brought to justice."

"Do you hate him for what he's doing." David thought for a moment. He was going to answer yes but he changed his mind.

"No, I don't hate him, I pity him and despise him for what he has done. I just think he's a mixed up environmentalist at the end of his tether." George Redburn cringed. He stood up and quickly brought the interview to an end.

"Just one last question," insisted the bright reporter. George was trying to pull David through a rear door.

"Do you think he's insane?" David smiled.

"Of course he's insane, but aren't we all!"

CHAPTER NINE

Philip Sellers had returned to England via Calais and Dover. Travelling on the car ferry he'd spent most of the two hour trip sat on the deck smoking several small joints of cannabis and, by the time he arrived in the custom building on the main land he was high and giggling uncontrollably at anything and everybody. He sauntered through the crowd, rattling and clinking several bottles in a plastic carrier bag as he went. A tired and bored customs officer who particularly hated the masses of drunken yobs who passed through his domain made a point of singling him out for a spot check. Philip took one look at the gold braid on the man's navy style peaked cap and burst into another fit of laughter.

The customs man, one of that special breed of humourless beings, stood glaring down, his face contorted as he fought hard to hold back his rage. Philip sat on the low slung inspection desk, his face nearer to the narked customs man and a whiff of sweet acrid smelling breath hit the official's nostrils. The man's face changed immediately. A sadistic glee filled him and he smiled as he recognised the sweet scented smell of cannabis resin. After being escorted to a room where he was stripped and searched, a small bundle wrapped in silver paper was found in the toe of Philip's right shoe. Still laughing as he was cautioned, Philip was led away in handcuffs to Dover police station where he was locked in the police cells till his case could be read and tried in the morning's magistrates court.

Richard Normans had waited about five miles out to sea off the coast of Anglesey as Tan had ordered. He'd waited in vain till about four o'clock in the afternoon but deep down he knew something drastic had happened. He'd been listening to the radio and had heard a report about the 747 going down but no explanation or any further information was forthcoming. Desolate and dejected he returned to the Landrover and decided to spend the night in the back of the vehicle, monitoring the radio till more news of what had happened to Tan came through.

At precisely eleven o'clock that night the first true facts of what had taken place after a news blackout were broadcast on the news. Richard's gut turned over as the broadcaster said, "Anthony Heyes is believed to be somewhere within a fifty mile radius of Minehead. All roads are sealed in around the last sighting of the world's most wanted terrorist. The Prime Minister has ordered ten thousand troops to enter the area and turn every blade of grass. This man must not escape. No-one is to approach this man. He is believed to be armed and extremely dangerous. People in the area are warned to lock and bolt all doors and not to venture out unless it is absolutely necessary."

Richard knew there was nothing he could do. A feeling of utter dejection filled him. Even if he knew where Tan was he wouldn't get past the road blocks. But he cheered a little. At least he's still on the run, he may still have a chance of breaking out. He may already have got through the cordon. Richard's mind churned the newscaster's words over and over till finally he gave in to the hopelessness of the situation, and overcome by exhaustion, fell into a deep sleep.

Earlier that day Tan had camouflaged the Ford Cortina by hiding it under a mass of broken branches. It would be hard to spot under the fresh green foliage. He knew it would be too early for the police to cover all the surrounding countryside. He'd seen one or two helicopters go over in the distance and to cover him from view he took a large broken twig from a horse chestnut tree and tied it to his back with his belt. That way if he was caught out in the open countryside he could drop face down to the ground and hopefully the large leaves would be enough to protect him from view from the air. He'd decided to head south east down into Exmoor and was quickly striding out, his long lean legs breaking into a steady jog to put as much distance between himself and the abandoned car as he could. In a way he was lucky the surrounding countryside was sparsely inhabited. Small country lanes dissected the countless fields. High sided hedgerows ran along each side of these roads and Tan kept as close as he could to the field side of the hedge, his eyes and ears alert for any signs that he'd been spotted as he ran waist high in the long grasses that had missed the harvester's blade. He always kept to the low ground taking himself miles out of his way to avoid the hills that rose up on the edge of Exmoor. He knew he'd be easy to spot if he left the safety of the low country. Several times he'd crash to the ground as he heard the large Chinook helicopters, scouring the countryside. He was glad they didn't land nearby. He knew each 'copter could carry as many as a hundred men. Battered and bleeding, cut by the many thorn hedges he had crossed and crawled through, he lay panting inside a small sheep shelter that lay on the edge of the great moor. Tan checked his watch, it was seven p.m. The sun still shone brightly in a cloudless sky although it was sinking away in the west nearing the end of its day. It would be two hours or more yet before the darkness would hide the fugitive in its velvet blackness. Tan lay still thinking of which course to take. His lips were dry and parched, the salt taste still lingered, but this he could bare. His first instincts were to head up into the two hundred and fifty square miles of Exmoor. But its sparseness of grass and vegetation would make it difficult for him to hide from the ever increasing attentions from the sky. He decided to cut away towards the west and the coast; he knew his only hope was to keep on the move even if it meant him running round in circles for a few days. Hopefully they might think he'd slipped out through the cordon. Although he didn't feel under pressure, he'd hardly seen any of the vast forces that were being massed to search him out and in his tiredness, a tiredness which lulled him into a false sense of security, he decided to sleep for a short while. He closed his eyes and was quickly asleep.

Tan woke suddenly with a start. He listened intently to the noise that had disturbed him. It continued as he listened but he sighed as his faculties returned to him and he peeked around the doorway to see a large cow slowly munching on the cud she had just regurgitated. It was dark now. He checked the time, ten minutes after ten. He'd overslept. He cursed out loud. He felt his gut churn as the fear of what was to come caught him momentarily off guard. He quickly composed himself, his control instant. The self discipline and confidence in his judgement which he had learned as a trained professional were fully in command. He came out of the stone sheep shelter and stretched his back, swinging his arms to restore the circulation. His eyes strained through the still of the darkness that shrouded him: nothing but silhouettes of the trees. He listened. Apart from the cows munching, it was still. The sickly hollow sensation in his stomach lifted as' the nerves relaxed their hold on his intestines. He was safe for now. He knew he must be on his way again but his mouth was dry and dehydrated. He approached the old dairy cow and gently but slowly he felt along her side before he crouched and pulled on the nearest large teat. The warm jet of milk crashed onto his nose before he found his mouth, and he drank for a full five minutes till he'd taken his fill. He thanked the old cow and slapped her warmly on the rump. She turned and gazed at him with big comforting brown eyes; she stopped chewing for a moment and then carried on totally unperturbed by his presence. Tan stood admiring the simple beast for a moment, his brain hard at work. The bits of jigsaw were suddenly joined and he was about to turn and make off up the hill when suddenly the cow's tail lifted and the old cow began to urinate practically on his feet. Tan smiled to himself and he quickly sat on the ground, took off his shoes and socks and held his bare feet and legs under the steaming waterfall. The last piece of the jigsaw was now complete. His only chance of escape was to avoid contact with any other person. Once they knew within five miles where he was he'd had it. He realised they would have found the car by now though he reckoned he'd come some twenty miles since he had abandoned it. He'd also left his old flying suit inside. They'd have dogs on his scent by now, the cow's urine on his feet would leave no trace of him on the ground, the fields were full of animal dung and urine stench and every time he came across a cow pat he deliberately walked in it. Tan made his way up the hill to the higher ground. A large boulder stood some twenty feet into the side of the hill and Tan crawled up along one of the sloping sides. As his head came over the top of the huge rock he peered back down the way he had travelled earlier. The knot in his stomach returned. Fear filled his entire body as he gazed at the incredible sight that lay before him. About ten miles away masses of small lights flickered and moved. Thousands of them all in a straight line as far as he could see. Bigger much larger lights at intervals seemed to back them up. Larger searchlights fastened to vehicles, thought Tan as he gazed mesmerised by the sheer number of lights. He lept down from the rock and raced the last half mile to the top of the hill and his worst fears were confirmed as he saw the continuance of the lights, only broken by some distant hill or dimmed as the search rounded a large tree. He turned and could see a small glow spread over the higher terrain towards the south. Tan's heart began to beat loudly against his chest, rising to his ears as he stood listening to the thud thud of his own heart. He cursed out loud, "The bastards have got me surrounded." His hand fingered the Luger once more; his thumb rubbed backwards over the serrated edges of the rolled cocking hammer. But once again he refused to use it, 'Not yet,' he thought, 'I've a few hours yet. You never know Tan old lad you just might get lucky.'

He took off at a run down the far side of the hill. The adrenaline of fear filled him with endless stamina and he ran and ran without stopping for hour upon hour towards the furthest point south where the oncoming lights were dimmest. He skirted round several farms and roads, searching for somewhere he could hide, a cave, a hole in the ground, his mind ever looking for an answer as he ran on, feet blooded, cut, swollen and blistered. He tried to put his shoes back on but his feet were too badly swollen so he placed them back round his neck. Hanging from the tied laces they beat against his chest as he ran. He would have discarded them but for fear of them leaving a trace. It was the early throws of dawn before he finally stopped. Tan screamed and fell in agony. The small toe on his right foot had been severed by a small piece of flint sticking out of the ground. The state of trance that had held him and kept him immune from the pain lifted with the shock of his fall. His feet screamed in agony, blood poured from around a piece of jagged bone that was all that remained of his toe. His lungs burned as they gasped and heaved lifting his chest up and down as if trying to leave his body forever. Sweat soaked him to the skin, his eyes burned where the salty fluid had run constantly into them. He lay, his eyes staring wide and glazed up at the dim half lit sky. Steam rose from every part of his body like a race horse who'd just been ridden to its limits. He lay where he fell; his agony was almost unbearable but the immense pain fired more adrenaline into his brain. A brain which still searched for a way out, its own self survival, that is the secret of life itself. He rose to his feet and pulled both his socks over the damaged right foot. Subconsciously it felt better as does a cut when a sticking plaster is taped against it. He stumbled forward just as the first sun burst broke through, announcing the arrival of the day. A reflection caught his eye and he noticed a lake about a mile away to the east. He set off willing his now stiffened legs to move. It was mostly downhill to the lake as Tan's legs fell one in front of the other wobbling and buckling as he went. But not once did he fall, even though the path he followed was hard and his feet screamed for him to stop. Arriving at the lake Tan's legs finally gave in and he tumbled and crashed head first into the shallows at the edge of the lake. The water cooled him immediately and for a few seconds as he lay resting his hands on the bottom he felt refreshed. He drank his fill, probably three pints or more to replace the fluid he had lost on the night's marathon run. He sat upright waist deep in the water and stared at the hills that surrounded the lake. He noticed a stone wall that ran along one end of the waterside and then a small sturdy stone building almost in the middle of the wall, a large pipe jutting from it. Tan suddenly felt vulnerable again. The daylight was fast approaching and he scoured the surrounding hills searching for any movement with hawk like eyes. He knew the searchers would soon be upon him. He stared once again at the small stone building that lay about one hundred yards to his right.

Then, growing even nearer and louder he heard the vish vish whirring of helicopter rotor blades coming the way he'd just come. He jumped quickly to his feet and struggled to the edge of the bank. A small clump of grass grew from a small overhang where the water had eroded the soil. Tan lay gently against the foot high soil bank taking care not to make too many ripples on the still water. He pressed his face hard into the clay like soil of the bank as the noise grew and grew till it came down almost directly the way he'd come, but then it soared out to the middle of the reservoir and up over the edge of the far hill. Tan lifted his head to follow the pulsating beat as it subsided and was gone. He breathed a sigh of relief as he pushed himself to his feet. His injured foot throbbed with pain as he grabbed a broken branch which had been floating at the edge of the water in order to support himself. He stumbled and ran the hundred yards to the stone shed at the edge of the reservoir. As he neared he could see a large pipe emerge from the rear, disappearing into the ground about fifty yards further down the hill. It was a small pumping station used only in the case of drought to fill other reservoirs further down towards the coast. Tan circled the building slowly, his hand dragging against the large blocks of moorland stone that were of equal size and shape moulded firmly onto black lime cement. It was about six feet long by five feet wide. A small sloping stone slabbed roof reached about eight feet in the middle as it fell away at each side to the gutter five feet from the ground. Tan stopped by the only door; a full steel door held firmly in place by two large hasps and staples. Tan recognised the two impregnable Chubb Battleship padlocks that hung there defiantly. He'd inspected them when purchasing some padlocks to replace the ones he was to cut off the tunnel entrance before he'd stolen the Harrier. The hardware salesman had shown him one. These padlocks have a five-lever mechanism, totally unpickable. They are also drill resistant, saw resistant and made from case hardened quarter inch thick steel. The salesman's words rang round Tan's mind as he stared at the thumb thick locking bars. He tried to push the door with his shoulder, but he winced in pain as it did not budge a fraction. 'Good,' he whispered to himself as his eyes lifted to the roof, 'this should do.'

The police helicopter swooped low over the Exmoor hills. David sat next to the pilot. George Redburn sat in the rear smoking cigarette after cigarette, his fear of flying subdued only by the fear of losing the younger man sitting in front of him, his head pinned to the glass dome scouring the heather and ground some fifty feet below. David turned to the pilot and enquired how much longer they could stay in the air. He checked his watch, it was eight am.

"About twenty minutes, no more," replied the pilot.

"Okay, take us down to the search coordinator's caravan at Dunstar," replied David, much to the relief of the white faced superintendent. The helicopter turned smoothly as the pilot eased the stick over gently to the left. They flew back over the lake they'd passed some ten minutes earlier, frightening a lone mallard into flight as the pilot came low over the water before skimming the roof of the small shed and then down into the valley at the north end of the lake. David signalled the pilot to take them higher, he twisted the grip of the control stick altering the angle of the rotor blades. The helicopter responded immediately and they were soon cruising at one thousand feet. About five miles from the lake and sweeping up the valley, a huge line of people spread as far as the eye could see. David turned and pointed out the spectacle to his superior in the rear. George nodded; a half smile spread on his face as he tried to hide the fear he felt inside.

"We'll soon have him under lock and key," said George, "Ordinary search-and-find police work, he'll not get through the trap we've got him in." David was not so sure. It seemed a vast area to search. They flew over the heads of the searchers, below some of the soldiers waved at them. He knew this was no ordinary man they were chasing. This man with the brain of a fanatic David suspected would have been trained in survival by the RAF. He opened the folder that had been resting on his knee and removed a photograph of Anthony Heyes. Only this time the hair had been removed and a bald dome had been transferred by a photographic technician. This description was given by the two fishermen who'd saved him from certain death. 'Very cleaver,' thought David as he hardly recognised the younger man whose face had been transfixed on his mind these last few weeks. The shaved head with hair at the sides made him look twenty years older. 'Yes, Mr Heyes, you are something special. I hope we can meet face to face before too long.'

They landed in a field alongside several other helicopters near to the field headquarters of the various police, army and media caravans. The lanes and fields were crammed with cars and lorries and it reminded David of some large fete as he walked through the various tents and makeshift buildings till they reached the clearly marked control caravan. A T.V. camera team were waiting outside and recognised David as he approached trying in vain to waylay him on the steps of the caravan. A young constable saluted and opened the door for him without question. He entered, closely followed by George Redburn. The van was about thirty feet long by about ten feet wide, a large table in the middle held a one inch to a mile scale of the whole of Exmoor. Several men were gathered round shading in areas as the searchers progressed.

A fattish man with sunken eyes wearing a tweed reefer jacket came forward recognising David from the T.V. He introduced himself as Mervin Trevellion, the Chief Constable of Somerset. By his unshaven appearance it was obvious he'd been in attendance throughout the night. David shook hands with him as well as two colonels and several other police officers before he eagerly got down to the matter in hand.

"Has Heyes been spotted yet?" he asked.

"Not as such," replied Trevellion. "We've found the car he abandoned and we tracked across country for several miles but then his trail just went cold."

"How do you mean you tracked him?" asked Redburn who leaned over the map peering at the red line that marked the trail.

"Dogs got his scent from his flying suit, tracked him to the edge of this field, but then the dogs lost the trail."

"Could he have got out, a helicopter perhaps?" asked Redburn eager for some reason to impress himself on the gathering. He'd noticed that most of them treated David as if he was in command. David on the other hand had been unaware at the scale of the media attention given to him on his miraculous escape and without any doubt he was the man of the moment.

"No chance," interrupted one of the army officers who wore a grey beret, the winged dagger insignia embroidered on the front." We dropped over thirty men out there last night, we have every piece of high ground covered. We expect Heyes only to move at night, but all the men are armed with night-sights. If he moves we'll spot him." David leaned across to examine the large map.

"May I?" he asked politely.

"Certainly", replied Trevellion, "We have been ordered from the very top to proffer every courtesy towards you." He smiled a warm smile at his VIP guest. "And any suggestions you may have would be very welcome, we know you were working closely on this case." David returned the man's smile before he began to study the map carefully.

"As you can see," began the SAS Captain, "We've got the whole area completely cut off. Some three hundred and fifty square miles are sealed by over one hundred and fifty thousand volunteers, soldiers, police, the fire service, you name it, we've got it." He pointed to a black line that surrounded the whole of the moor. "As you can see, as they progress we add a thin red line."

"What's these crosses here?" asked David.

"They are search-and-seal tactics. Every building is searched by the army. Every male person between the ages of eighteen and sixty is to be questioned and identified. Any doubt about a person's identity then the man has to be detained. We have over two hundred unidentified people in a school here at Porlock. Someone soon comes along and identifies them and we let them go." David stared at blue dots on various buildings on the map.

"What's these?"

"Houses already searched and guarded. A man is left to watch over every dwelling house or group of buildings. His orders are to inspect the building every half hour or so. We intend to check every farm house, factory, dog kennel anywhere he may try and hole up. We have helicopters with infra red cameras searching the moors in case he's dug in anywhere, but as you can see the main search is from the closing outer ring. We should have him by the end of the day." David walked over to where George Redburn was pouring himself a coffee from a percolator.

"Looks like they've got every angle covered, eh," he said as David held out an empty cup.

"Just about," agreed David, "but what about all these civilian searchers, couldn't he slip amongst them, there must be thousands?"

"That's been taken care of," George smiled, "Every volunteer has been stamped with a local library rubber date stamp on the inside of his left forearm, we used the libraries for coordinating and also vetting the volunteers. But I agree, David, there is a possibility that he could slip through, there's always a possibility." David smiled at George Redburn, it was the first time he'd used his full first name without shouting it. George had warmed to David, his attitude had changed dramatically towards him since the 747 was shot down, not just because he'd survived, but because he knew David was a superior policeman in every sense. He realised he was an old fashioned copper, himself. No he'd decided to tag along for whatever glory would come his way but when all this was over it was retirement for him. He'd made up his mind to enjoy his last days away from the force. David sat on an empty chair near a half open window, the sun shone brightly now as it began its climb across the morning sky. A pile of morning newspapers were scattered across a small desk, torn and crinkled after being read by the occupants of the caravan some two hours earlier. David picked up one of the nearest tabloids. A large picture of his own face spread across the front page under the headlines, 'Man falls from sky clutching an angel.'

David threw the paper back amongst the rest and blew a sigh of exasperation. Superintendent Redburn noticed the crumpled discarded paper and came over and sat next to David.

"Don't take much notice of the press, they always enjoy distorting facts," he smiled a consoling fatherly smile through his nicotine stained teeth. He stared hard at David as if trying to find the words.

"Listen," he said after a long silence, "what really happened up there?" David's eyes narrowed, a puzzled look spread across his face.

"You heard my report."

"No, I mean what did you feel when you saw the Harrier?"

David gazed straight ahead for a few moments recollecting his thoughts. He turned and stared at the pinky red face of his superior. "I felt fear, panic, a kind of disgust with myself for being on the plane in the first place, and then I remember running down the middle of the isle the fear totally in control. I just hid in the toilet shaking with fear."

"The girl, what about the girl?" asked George.

David smiled, "She thought I was a raving loony, she came to the door and tried to restrain me, I just grabbed her and locked us both in the toilet. The next thing we were tumbling together through space."

"Did you see Heyes in the jet?"

"Yes I saw him quite clearly. He just looked like any regular jet fighter pilot, full helmet, oxygen mask. But the jet, it looked immaculate." David's photographic memory held the picture again in his mind. He focused on the rainbow and then the painted sign. But all this he'd reported earlier and he didn't feel the need to explain any further. He shivered slightly at the thought of what had happened and then quickly put it out of his mind.

CHAPTER TEN

Tan awoke from his sleep, his head stiff and aching from where it had rested against the large rusty pipe. He checked his watch by a small ray of light that entered the dark building through a lockless keyhole on the steel door. It was four thirty. He'd slept for some ten hours solid. He tried to ease himself into a more comfortable position and pushed himself into a sitting position with his back against the rear wall. His legs ached and protested as he forced them to move. They had stiffened up completely during his sleep. The shattered toe still throbbed but it had eased slightly. He reached down and felt both his swollen ankles with a hand on each. He cringed slightly at their feel as more pain responded to the touch. His lips and throat were dry and he eased himself down to where he could hear a faint drip of water till his hand made contact with a small puddle, a mixture of condensation and a slight leak from the large stop tap that the small building protected. He lowered his lips and sipped at the rusty tasting water from the cold stone floor. It felt good as it passed down his parched throat and it revived him slightly. His eyes began to become accustomed to the dark and he checked around him. Inside the small building it was completely bare, apart from the Victorian iron pipe that rose two feet out of the ground just by the front door. A large iron wheel rose another foot on top of the pipe and when turned it would release the water from the lake down into the reservoir further down the moor. At each side of the twelve inch diameter pipe was about two foot of space; Tan sat on the left hand side. He lifted his head to stare at the roof about five foot above him. He checked the stone slate at the corner for any signs of light that might shine through. He smiled to himself as he recalled the times when as a boy he used to enter a building near his home by lifting the corner tile of the roof and easing himself through the small gap that led into a loft above the the women's changing rooms of the local swimming baths. He remembered how he and Eddie Spungen had giggled as they watched a portly middle aged lady squeezing herself painfully into a girdle. Then one time they had been caught as Eddie had lost his footing on the joists and his foot had crushed through the plaster sending a cascade of debris onto a half naked woman below. After being taken to the pool manager's office in complete fear of what might happen to them the two boys sat speechless through two hours of interrogation by the local constable of how they'd managed to enter the loft. The only trap door was located in the ceiling in the middle of the roof. Eventually after a stern ticking off and with a promise to let the boys go home Eddie had told the puzzled policeman how they'd climbed in. Tan fondled the small stick he'd used to hold open the gap in the large stone slate, a gap of only nine inches but wide enough for a lithe man such as he was to squeeze through without leaving any sign of his entry. He felt quite safe locked inside the small shed.

Sergeant Bryan Gibson had lain on top of the hill for most of the day. It was a warm sunny day with a few wisps of cloud here and there dotted throughout the sky. The lake below looked peaceful as he lay on his stomach, it reminded him of two years ago when he lay on a similar hill on an island in the South Atlantic surveying the landing beaches on San Carlos water in the Falklands. Even though he knew the surrounding hills were not filled with enemy soldiers he had hardly moved a muscle from six fifteen a.m. that marning when he'd been dropped there by helicopter. His only movement was of his head as he scanned the lake and its surroundings through non reflective binoculars. He'd seen nothing all day. His eyes scanned the stone building about eight hundred yards to his left and through his powerful binoculars he could see clearly the two untouched Chubb padlocks holding fast the rusty plate door. He lay down the glasses for a moment and was distracted by a small ladybird that was crawling up the webbing on the barrel of his Galil assault rifle that lay beside him in the heather. He brushed the insect off his beloved weapon. Although an Israeli made rifle, not one of the normal issue for the British Army SAS NCO's were allowed to choose any make of rifle, he preferred this weapon most for its lightness and with the folding butt could be made quite small and easy to conceal or carry. Also, as well as a most deadly sniper's weapon it could easily be converted to a tripod resting machine gun in less than two seconds.

A small click on the short wave radio which rested against a tuft of dry grass was followed by a brief message.

"Onlooker seven, over."

Gibbo flicked the transmit button down on the small radio.

"Seven, over," he answered.

"Any sign, over?"

"Negative control, over."

"Can you see the sweep, over?" the command voice referring to the oncoming search party which Gibbo had been watching for some time coming up the valley some two and a half miles away.

"See them clearly. ETA two hours. Get them to check out small building to the south of lake, looks okay from this side but needs a close inspection."

"Over."

It was eight thirty p.m. when the first of the search party reached the south end of the lake; Some two hundred and fifty soldiers, a mixture of Royal Engineers from Aldershot Barracks and a smaller group of territorial paratroopers based in Taunton. In command of the troops was 2nd Lieutenant Simon Napier, a new recruit to the professionals, having failed to find a position in civvy street after gaining an economics degree from the LSE. Napier's troops were glad to reach the lake. They'd been on their feet since nine o'clock that morning and had covered over thirteen slow miles since then. Many of the men on reaching the lake began to discard their heavy boots and waded into the cool water. Napier soon reprimanded them and ordered his men back to form a picket line extending across the south edge of the lake and up into the hillsides, fearful in case Heyes could pass through the line during the night. On the way to the lake Gibbo's instructions to search the stone building had been relayed to Napier and once he had organised the pickets for the night he returned with his two NCO's corporals to inspect the shed more closely.

Tan was listening intently behind the steel door, his ear pressed against the cold rust. Although exhausted and weak his brain was still alert and sharp as ever. The picket line stretched across the front of the small building. The voices of the soldiers consisted of the usual moans and groans of their day's trials. Then Tan heard the uppercrust accent for the first time. "Stand easy men," followed by fast approaching footsteps that stopped outside the steel door. Tan jumped back with a start as the officer fruitlessly rattled the heavy padlocks one after the other, his ears deafened momentarily as the clanking caught him by surprise. Tan's heartbeat seemed to step up a gear and it beat so loudly in his chest that he thought they might hear it outside. He heard the officer speak again.

"Get these things off corporal." The corporal replied abruptly.

"Sorry Sir, I don't have the key."

Tan heard a few sniggers from the encamped soldiers in the picket line.

"Not you personally you stupid oaf, get some of the bloody engineer chappies up here, that's what they do best don't they, idiot?"

Tan began to sweat profusely, the word engineer hit a nerve, he knew they would be able to cut off the padlocks at a stroke. Tan's sweaty palm closed tightly round the Luger as he pulled it clear from his jacket. A bead of sweat dripped from his forehead onto the tip of his nose and he instinctively scratched it with the barrel up to his eyeball, 'It's over anyway, you didn't do too badly did you. The whole world knows your name, you've done all you can.' He lowered the Luger slowly and smiled, 'I'll take as many with me as I can, the last bullet, that's mine.' His mood was verging on the hysterical through lack of food and his claustrophobic environment. He slid down the wall onto his haunches and started to laugh, his fist jammed into his mouth staunched the noise. He bit on his fingers till the blood began to flow, he wanted to scream out. 'I'm here you stupid bastards. I'm here.' But he just bit harder as he shook from his innards, totally and utterly hysterical.

David sat staring at the anxious faces that surrounded him

in the caravan. It had been too long, the net was tightening and still no sign of Heyes. The SAS captain came in through the caravan door opposite where David was sitting. He came across and sat next to him.

"Good show that parachute lark, could do with you in our mob, fancy a go?" he said smiling.

"No, definitely not, I'm not the superman type," replied David who couldn't help but notice the worried look on the soldier's face.

"He's flown hasn't he?" The captain's head nodded slowly. "Perhaps."

"But then he's no mug, this Heyes character, he's bloody good. Always the worst are fanatics. He's out there somewhere but if he's dug in we'll not find him." A police constable came round with a tray of tea and the two men gratefully accepted a cup. The captain sipped his loudly before resting the cup on a pile of newspapers on the table.

"Do you remember that chappie from your neck of the woods?" he paused for a moment while he thought of the name. "The Black Panther, that's what the press named him, robbed several post offices, killed one or two postmasters and kidnapped that young heiress." David's brain flashed back to 1976 and he quickly interrupted the captain.

"You mean Donald Neilson, and the heiress's name was Leslie Whittle."

"Of course," replied the captain.

David just nodded; he hadn't been in the police then, he'd read the report just out of interest some years later.

"Well that guy buried himself in a wood somewhere, for three days he lay there," continued the captain.

"I mean, would a normal man do that sort of thing?" David's mind was still flashing through the report. The wood was in Harrogate and the length of time Neilson buried himself to avoid capture was two days not three. He did not correct the captain, he just nodded his head in agreement.

"No, he wouldn't." The captain finished his tea and stood up. He leaned forward so no-one else could hear.

"I'm afraid if we don't get him by tonight, it's possible he's got through." He strolled across to the middle of the van and stared out the window leaving David still seated. David stood up and strolled to the end of the caravan. George Redburn had been chatting to a young constable who manned the radio.

" Could I have a word, Sir? " he said as George saw him approach. David returned to the privacy of the far end of the van. George followed two minutes later.

"What is it, Davy Boyl" he asked, a half smoked cigarette hanging from the corner of his mouth.

"Nothing really George, I'm just curious about our SAS friend." Both men turned and stared at the captain who was leaning over the map table surveying the ever closing red line. George read his thoughts.

"You mean why the need for his mob when there's all the regulars and police out there?" David nodded.

George smiled, he'd thought the young detective had known and it gladdened him to be the one to explain. He checked over his shoulder to make sure no-one listened. He continued, his voice quieter.

"Shoot to kill policy. The beaters and the hare." He could see David was still puzzled. He spoke in plain language.

"The SAS boys are positioned on all the high ground throughout the moor, right." David nodded again and his eyes widened.

"You mean he's to be shot on sight?"

"Got it," snapped back George.

"Brought most of these chaps in early this morning from Northern Ireland. The powers that be want him dispatched at the earliest." George pointed a finger skywards.

CHAPTER ELEVEN

Earlier that morning Philip Sellars had been taken from his cell to a large waiting room that contained several other felons who were waiting to stand before the bench. The talk of the cell had been about the mad man, Heyes, shooting down the 747 and his escape across Exmoor. Phil was pleased. He'd sobered somewhat and was a little disappointed with himself for letting the side down but he'd keep quiet, plead guilty to the offence and take his punishment and hopefully rejoin his comrades at a later date. He reckoned on three months if they were generous. At ten o'clock he was led into the court. His eyes scanned the small wood panelled room with its empty public gallery and high wooden bench that ran almost the lengh of the far wall opposite him from where he stood in the dock. A thought occurred to him on how all court rooms seemed to look the same. But then his eyes caught the glare of a small man sitting at the long bench; his head and shoulders only just cleared the top. He'd been reading the charges levelled at the man in front of him. A large plump clerk sat in front of the desk and as he collected the charge sheet from the magistrate he began to read out loud. His mouth opened and then closed and he turned to the bench again.

"Er, there's no name written in here Sir," he said perplexed by the absence of a name for the prisoner. A constable who was presenting the case for the prosecution with a police lawyer stood up and interrupted.

"Excuse me, Your Worship, but the prisoner will not proliferate any identification.

" The magistrate eyed Philip again and a look of disgust etched onto his face.

"Do you not have a name?" he asked indignantly. Phil took his hands from out of his jeans pockets and began to pick his nose.

"I have no name, I am a free spirit, man." The magistrate looked at the constable who just shrugged his shoulders, he then returned his glare to Phil. He hated these worthless louts who would not conform to society's rules and regulations and was quickly making up his mind how many months this lout was to spend behind bars.

"We must have a name before we can continue with this case." Phil was staring at something hanging from the end of his finger.

"Why not call me Bogey," he said smiling. A few titters ran through the sparsely populated room. He then flicked his namesake out into the court.

When Phil had been arrested at the dock he had no form of identification on him having travelled on the ferry without a passport. It was quite common to do this on a day trip return. He'd done it several times before in the past. He was reluctant to give his real name in case they tied him in with Tan. Although he knew it was unlikely they had anything on him he didn't want to take the risk.

He'd been in court several times before; the various offences to do with his picket line forays but each time he'd been fined and released.

The fat, portly clerk stood up and began to read out the charges.

"Er, Mr. Bogey." The titters began again. "Er, Mr. Bogey, you are charged with being in possession of an illegal substance, namely cannabis resin. Also illegally transporting the drug through Her Majesty's Customs and with vagrancy. How do you plead?" The vagrancy charge was levelled at Phil because he'd only ten pounds of the five hundred pounds he'd set off with and he would not offer any address of residence. Phil was beginning to enjoy himself, he enjoyed pitting himself against the bourgeois.
"Guilty ma Lord, but with grounds of diminished responsibility."

"I'm not a 'Lord' but a mere 'magistrate'. On what grounds do you base your diminished responsibility?"

"Insanity Sir," replied Phil. The clerk smiled at him, after two drunks and a flasher he needed cheering.

"Temporary or permanent insanity?"
Phil waved his finger in the air. "Ah," he insisted, "Mr. Bogey, my name's Bogey, remember." Phil thought he saw a twitch come from the corner of the magistrate's mouth. He wasn't sure whether it

was an attempt to smile or he was angered.

"You don't seem to realise the seriousness of your position young man," replied the magistrate, deliberately not using the name Mr. Bogey.

"Oh but I do, Your Worship, nothing I can say will avoid me being incarcerated in one of Her Majesty's hotels. What you got in store for me, one year, two years? I bet you've decided already." Phil had hit a nerve with the magistrate.

"Look young man, I'll give you one last chance to be sensible." said the judge unsure of how to handle this scruffy red eyed young man.

"No man, you be sensible. Sensible's too heavy for me. I prefer not to be sensible. No you just go ahead and send me off to prison. Prison won't bother me. I don't work, never will. I have nowhere to live, and you know I like it that way. I'll just put prison down to a new experience, I'll still smoke grass whenever I get the chance, I hear you can even get a joint in prison now and again. No man, I'll never be sensible you just do your stuff, whatever you suggest is alright with Mr. Bogey." The magistrate smiled as the titters rang round the room again. He composed himself. He'd begun to feel a little warmth towards this weirdo as his granddaughter would have called Phil. For some reason his easy going laid-back attitude had awoken something in him and for a few moments life's burdens were lifted.

"Do you wish me to pass sentence on you or would you prefer to be tried by a higher court? I see from the customs and police reports you have come clean and completely admitted your guilt." Phil smiled at the magistrate.

"No, I like you man, you go ahead an' do the business, whatever you do is alright by me." The laughter erupted once again and the judge now warmed towards the prisoner he was about to sentence.

"Well, Mr. Bogey," said the judge. He waited to continue while the laughter died. "Mr. Bogey, I sentence you to six months in prison with three months suspended." Phil was led away after a quick wave towards the bench, a huge grin spread across his face. 'Not bad,' he thought as he was led to the cells, three months. I think I handled that quite well.'

Richard Normans had returned to the cottage hoping Phil

would return soon. He wouldn't know for some time what had happened to his friend but he felt quite safe for now. He had been listening to the radio on the trip back from Anglesey and he knew Tan was still on the loose. He turned on the seven o'clock evening news on the portable television and the programme began with a view of the scene on Bodmin Moor. His heart sank as the pictures from the scene brought home the enormity of the operation. The camera zoomed in on a reporter holding a microphone in the middle of the mobile search headquarters.

He began, "the man known as Anthony Heyes is still on the loose tonight somewhere out there in one of the most desolate spots in Britain. I was speaking to one of the police spokesmen earlier who assured me that Heyes would soon be flushed out, probably before morning." Richard felt totally helpless. He sat there for some time contemplating what action he should or could take till suddenly a thought struck him and he jumped up from the chair as though an electric current had run through him.

"Right you bastards," he snarled at the T.V. set, "you just watch me go."

Lieutenant Napier was resting his feet in the lake when the corporal returned with a stocky sergeant from the Royal Engineers.

"Ah, Sergeant," Napier said pulling his feet from the water, "can you oblige those padlocks." Napier pointed his head towards the steel door. The sergeant walked up and inspected the padlocks. Napier came up behind, still shoeless.

"Could do yes, Sir," said the sergeant in a warm geordie accent, "if I had some gear with us, but we're on search duties. No gear, Sir."

Tan heard the sergeant come up to the door and he rested his back against the forewall, Luger held out in front pointing towards the door, his eyes squinting to the cracks of light that shone through each side of the door.

The Lieutenant had shown his lack of experience in front of his lowly NCO and was now very agitated.

"Well," he exclaimed in his supercilious Oxford tone, "I'll just have to open it myself." He removed his Browning automatic from its holster and marched up towards the door.

Tan trembled from head to foot and he nearly laughed out loud in terror as he'd heard every word spoken from the other side of the door. He had been ready for them to open it, he was committed wholly to his fate, his brain was screaming for them to open it. He was on the verge of losing control.

The corporal and the sergeant gave each other a hopeless glance.

"Excuse me Sir," said the sergeant just as the lieutenant was taking aim at the top padlock. The lieutenant lowered the gun and turned towards the sergeant.

"What is it man?"

"Could I have Sir's permission to remove myself and the men to a safe distance?"

Napier gave the sergeant an inquisitive glance. He could see the NCO was an experienced soldier. "Safe distance Sergeant?" he repeated. "I can handle this pistol you know," his tone indignant.

"I've no doubt you can, Sir, but that door's a quarter inch steel plate, and those padlocks are made from armoured steel, you're more likely to shoot yourself from the ricochet than open those locks with that peashooter."

Lieutenant Napier's face turned crimson as he realised the sergeant was right.

The sergeant decided to let the naive officer off the hook. "Look, Sir, as far as I can see there's no one in that shed, those padlocks haven't been opened for some time and he certainly couldn't lock himself in from the inside could he?"

Napier composed himself a little.

"My orders are to search every building, Sergeant, without question."

Tan was shaking from head to foot. He trembled, psyched up ready for them and had come to terms with his own end. He wanted to scream at them, 'I'm here you pricks. Open that fucking door.' He was near breaking point now but something held him in control as he stood in the darkness of the small room, the Luger shaking vigorously in his hand. Then he heard the geordie accent of the sergeant.

"Tell you what, Sir, just to put your mind at ease we could always smoke it." A few sniggers rang round the standing men and the lieutenant had had enough for one day.

"No, Sergeant, leave it be. There's no one in there, just forget it, go back to your section." The lieutenant picked up his shoes and hurried off away from anymore embarrassment. One of the watching squaddies whistled the tune 'The Lonesome Cowboy' as he went.

Tan was laughing again inside the shed. Tears streamed down his cheeks as he held his fist firmly in his mouth, the Luger still pointing at the door. He stood transfixed for several minutes before he fell to the floor.

Sergeant Gibson had watched the scene with interest from his vantage point a half mile away up the hill. He placed the non reflective binoculars down on the ground and felt in his pocket for another everlasting soldier pill. He popped the amphetamine tablet into his mouth and swallowed it in one. As well as keeping him awake the pill intensified his concentration and they also made him feel quite happy. He'd taken about one hundred or more in just over a week when on sniping duty above Port Stanley in the Falklands war. He'd never been happier in all his life as he sent several young Argentinian conscripts into oblivion, although when he came down from Mount Langdon he had slept for three days solid and he'd lost twenty eight pounds in weight. He'd made up his mind that when the squaddies came past his surveillance point tomorrow he'd go down and blow those locks off the shed door with the two ounce of plastic explosive he had in his tunic. Not that he thought there was anyone in there; he just fancied blowing the door to bits.

At one a.m. the next day Tan who'd been asleep for some four hours had decided to make his move. He had to escape this darkened tomb, he wouldn't be able to keep control if he stayed there another minute. He knew the troops were encamped to the front of him. It would be impossible for them to camp behind the shed due to the steep gradient that sloped away down the valley, whereas the ground by the lake was quite flat. He'd also reasoned there'd be watchers scanning the countryside with nightsights which made their vision almost as good as daylight. He just couldn't stand his confinement another moment longer. He needed to breathe the fresh outside air and feel the breeze on his face. It was time to go. He'd been listening at the door for a while till it was quiet out front. The swelling in his feet had subsided and he was able to put his shoes back on. The severed toe still hurt and pinched up badly in the shoe but he could stand. His legs were completely stiff and it would take him a couple of miles to loosen them off if he made it that far. He eased his head up against the stone slate and pushed it up a couple of inches. He could see dying embers of various fires and silhouettes of some of the soldiers on watch. If he was quiet he had a chance. He re-lowered the stone slate and felt on the ground for the small stick he'd used to wedge the slate open on his way in. He found it where he'd left it. He pushed open the slate again very slowly till it was about ten inches from its resting place. He could see clearly now. There was no moon and apart from the odd flicker of flame from the peat fuelled camp fires it was black as sin. He raised his hands and clasped the wooden joist that supported the slates and pulled himself upwards swinging his feet till his heels rested in the open space where the tile had been. His arms were weak but the thought of release from the tomb gave them strength. His heart raced as he pulled himself down the small beam, his legs half dangling out into the open. He was expecting a shout of discovery any second but none came. His back and shoulders came through and he twisted round so his face grazed the top of the wall. He released his grip on the beam and gravity did the rest. He fell the last foot onto the soft ground. He lay still for a moment. Someone coughed nearby just as he was about to stand, he froze. He slowly turned his head towards the silhouetted groups of sleeping men. There was no movement. Tan reached up and withdrew the wedged stick, lowering the slate back to its original resting place. He ducked down and slid silently over the crest of the gradient and rolled to his feet. He was laughing again inwardly. A nervous excited feeling swept over him as he realised he'd escaped once more. He was still weak but he was mobile and the gradient helped him along as he half stumbled and fell downwards away into the valley below.

Regina Peters pulled back the thin cotton curtains on the

bedroom window of the small cottage. She gazed at the twisted fingers as she struggled to grip the thin cloth thinking of the time many years ago when they were smooth and straight before the arthritis had turned them clawlike. She smiled as she saw the sun coming up in a clear blue sky, amidst spasmodic scatterings of cloud announcing another fine day. It had been a good summer so far. She put on an old worn cardigan with holes through the elbows and struggled to fasten the three buttons that remained. She pulled on a pair of men's trousers that she'd taken to wearing on the death of her husband some ten years ago. She didn't wash, there was no need. No-one came to visit anymore and apart from the soldier's visit a day and a half ago she'd not seen another human being for some months. She hated men in uniforms, it reminded her of the war, although these uniforms were brown, the same as her husband had worn and not the dreaded field grey of the hated Boche. She lowered her feet into the old pair of men's laceless boots and began to shuffle towards the bedroom door. A cock crowed out in the yard. The front room was as sparse as the rest of the cottage, just the essentials, apart from three framed photographs. There were two chairs, an old well worn pine table and an ancient half bald rug made from bits of old cloth which lay in front of the Victorian fire grate. She blew the ash off the few half burned embers and a small glow told her that the fire was still lit. A few hen feathers and dried leaves ignited into flame and she placed a few broken sticks and a dried cow pat onto the flaming leaves. Her entrance into the front room had disturbed an old hen who'd been roosting under the table. The fat bird fluttered up onto the backrest of the wooden chair and began its clucking. She checked under the table and removed a solitary egg from inside the old slipper that lay there and she placed the egg in a small pocket of the woollen cardigan. Opening the front door she shuffled out into the yard where other hens had congregated waiting for their first feed of the day. She went into the large barn that was twice the size of the cottage and filled a steel bucket with seed from a sack that lay in the corner. She squeezed past an old Minor Thousand pickup truck that was used only once in a while for fetching supplies to the small farm. Although practically self sufficient the old woman sometimes had to venture out to buy bales of straw or extra seed for the long winter months and the salt and flour she needed to bake the bread that was part of her staple diet. She peered out of a small window at the rear of the barn checking to see if the old cow was all right. It was munching away at the long grass at the bottom of the field. She expected to find the cow dead one of these days as she'd had it so long and she reckoned it was about twenty five years old. Its milk had long since dried up but she had a goat for that. She kept the cow because it was no trouble to look after and she used the pats to supplement her cooking fuel. Besides, she was fond of the old thing and felt an affinity towards her for reaching her grand age, the same as she had done. She emerged from the barn where the twenty hens had been waiting by the door and she began to scatter the seed out onto the ground. They began to feed furiously as if they hadn't been fed ever before. She dropped the bucket onto the floor and walked over to a small stone built shed across the yard. She pushed open the remaining two planks that was all that was left of the door and proceeded to place the egg she'd had in her pocket into an egg tray resting on the window sill of the shed.

She stared at the half empty tray for a moment and then she caught a faint smell, a smell she'd not tasted for some years but she knew immediately what the smell was. She shuffled back towards the cottage and took a loaf of yesterday's baked bread from the cupboard. She cut off several slices on the table in the front room, her eyes glanced from her task towards the shed door which she could see easily through the window. She hung a filled kettle over the flames from a hook that came from the back of the grate. She checked the shed once more. The kettle began to boil as she shuffled out of the cottage and approached the shed. She stood in the open doorway staring into the small cluttered room and said, "I've made you some breakfast if you would please join me." She stood for a moment before returning back to the cottage. Tan had watched her through the crack of the open door of the old wardrobe he'd been hiding behind. He'd seen her enter the barn and feed the hens. He'd watched the cottage for any sign of anyone else inside but he knew she was alone. He eased himself up from his hideaway and sent an old watering can flying as he stumbled towards the door. His legs were stiff and lifeless and the poison in his severed toe had spread up into his ankle making him limp as he came out into the yard. He flicked the safety off the Luger and pulled the flap of his grubby shirt over his belt to hide it from view. The smell of toast hit his nostrils as he approached the cottage door; although he'd eaten eight of the old woman's eggs in the shed he was still hungry. He rested against the door frame and peered inside. The door led straight into the small room, the old woman sat on a chair toasting bread speared at the end of a long wire fork held up to the flames of the fire. She glanced at him as if she knew him and then gazed back towards the fire.

"Come, " she said pointing at the only other chair in the room with the long fork, "there's dockleaf tea in the pot. "Tan smiled at the thought of the herbal brew as he limped over to sit opposite her. He watched as she carried the toast to him on an old chipped enamel plate. He gazed at the twisted fingers with dirty nails and then he held his gaze on the wrinkled well worn face. He noticed that nearly all her hair had gone, just long matted twists of grey hung down lifelessly onto her neck. Their eyes met, examining one another, and though the rest of the old woman's physical appearance was decrepit and unpleasant to behold, her eyes shone with intelligence and strength.

"Thank you," he said, as he accepted the plate and began to eat the half burnt bread. She poured a steaming brew of the green liquid into a grubby tin mug and offered him the handle. He drank the putrid tasting liquid, the warmth of it felt good as it passed down into his stomach.

"You him they search for?" she said as she returned to the chair.

Tan nodded. He detected a slight foreign accent in her voice.

"Française?" he asked. She smiled at him showing teeth that were brown and crooked.

"Oui, parlez vous Français?"

"Oui, I speak excellent French," replied Tan in the language she hadn't heard for forty years.

"Where do you come from, Paris?" he guessed.

"Non, I come from Thepviel,"

Tan nodded. He'd noticed the two photographs on the mantlepiece. One of a middle aged man in officer's uniform and the other of a pretty young girl dressed in outdated clothes sitting on an old square shaped car indicated the period of the thirties. A row of medals hung from ribbons in a small glass fronted box in the middle. He pointed to the soldier.

"Your husband?"

"Yes, my husband." Tan assumed the medals had been his. Another picture hung from a string at the end of the fireplace. It was much older and browner that the others. Tan recognised the uniform of the Poulou, the French First World War uniform. It was a picture of her father before he'd been killed at Paccendale. Tan noticed the old Bush radio on the floor by her chair. He pointed at it.

"Does it work?"

She nodded. She knew all about him, what he'd done, and now he was here in her house trying to be pleasant to her, making small talk as if nothing had happened. She stared at him and as he ate, underneath the filth and grime she saw a handsome unlined face, the face of a child. But the eyes, she'd seen those eyes before, wide and staring as if not enough light were passing through. They were cold, hard, calculating, always working, examining, thinking eyes, mean and hungry; eyes she'd seen many times before; eyes smiling as they stood in front of the chair, her arms strapped to its sides, eyes that smiled as the nail plyers removed her toe nails one by one; eyes that narrowed, angered because she wouldn't talk.

"We know who you are Mademoiselle Noire. We know you have transported hundreds of men over the Channel to England. We know you have killed many of our comrades. Her mind went back to the side street cafés of Paris frequented by the grey uniformed men; the face of a young man, the words, "dance?" and then a smile from the face as it enquired, "Do you live alone?" Then the walk of death down the cobbled side street checking that the van was following slowly, unseen. Then the deafening explosion as the pistol exploded as they embraced. Her senses stunned for an instance till the warm sweet tasting blood ran down her face and bits of brain and bone stuck to her lips as she tried to spit away the blood. Then her comrades in the van sped up and dragged the lifeless form into the rear. She followed, the small Walther smoking in her hand. The body was stripped of its uniform and pistol before being thrown out into the road like a discarded doll as they sped away from the scene. She'd done this so many times she could not remember. She had been nineteen the first time and twenty two that last night. She'd left the club with a half drunk young oberleutenant; they'd walked for over twenty minutes before she'd found a killing place. The van had followed. It was quiet, no-one to be seen. But then the explosion. Her pistol was still in her handbag. Another explosion and another, the van began to speed away, the bullets ripping it open as it swerved on and on. Then the night sky erupted into day as the van leapt into the air the flash of flaming gasoline leaping higher, lightening the darkness as it burst from the exploding vehicle. The man smiling down at her ripped the bag from her hand removing the small automatic and then striking her three, four times till she fell onto the cold ground. The rush of feet sounded like thunder as the jackboots crashed against the cobblestones, men appearing from buildings and vehicles. Then she was back in the room fastened to the chair. They bandaged what was left of her feet and treated them with antiseptic. They cleaned up the urine from underneath her naked behind where in fear and agony she'd pissed herself. They gave her a drink of water till she'd recovered slightly then they began again. She sat naked, her arms and legs tethered to the torture chair. Wire was placed tight around each nipple on her breasts. One man pulled the wire so one of her breasts pointed out, her nipple on the verge of being torn away. The SS major then circled a piece of cheese wire around the flesh and severed each breast from her body one after the other. She did not talk; she was not brave. She wanted to talk but there was nothing to tell. She knew all the safe houses would be moved. The airmen would still be transported through to Spain. Only the innocent would suffer. Unsuspecting landlords who'd rented their rooms to the Resistance would be dragged away pleading innocence before the Mauser silenced them forever.

She'd wanted to die. She'd pleaded with her torturers to kill her. She'd begged them. They knew their business well.

Everyone talked, some sooner, some later but they all talked. They'd been surprised she didn't talk after the dog mounted her, the specially trained Alsatian that would mount from the rear as she'd been fastened naked to a table specially built for that purpose. Several men had crowded the room to watch her degradation. She'd screamed continuously as its paws had gripped her stomach and began its expertly trained task. She'd shaken uncontrollably as it had licked her behind, licking away its own sperm that ran down her leg. The onlookers stood and laughed. But she did not talk. Then her mind returned to the day the black shirted man came no more and a smiling English major entered the stinking dungeon that had been her home for several months. The major was a doctor, the man who would nurse her back to health for two whole years. The man who married her despite her deformities, the man who'd brought her to this new place where nothing ever again would remind her of her past. Nothing that is till now. The eyes she'd been staring at were that of her torturer, the eyes had come for her once again.

Tan had noticed the woman staring at him whilst he'd been eating. He thought perhaps it was his filthy appearance but then thought better. She wasn't much cleaner herself, although it wasn't a scruffy lazy unkemptness rather that she liked it that way. The room was the same, sparse of anything but the essentials, but functional and quite comfortable. Perhaps he would stay. The woman would do as he ordered, he wouldn't have to harm her, just frighten her a little, she seemed to him to be half senile anyway.

"You lived here a long time?" he asked questioning her to find her state of mind.

"thirty five years," she replied. Tan tried again.

"You live a very meagre existence madam, you have no luxuries."

"I have everything I need," she replied still staring, her face hard and expressionless. She functioned reasonably, he thought now he would intimidate her.

"You know I am a killer of many people?" He watched her expression closely. It didn't alter. "Do you know why I kill?" He was making a statement but stopped as her face changed to a half grin and then nodded as if in agreement

"Oh," he exclaimed, "you do know why I killed so many!"

"Oui Monsieur, I know why you kill," she paused, her eyes narrowed. "You kill, Monsieur, because you are weak." Tan smiled at her. "You kill because you are a failure and want to be a success. You kill because the man next door has a beautiful wife and you do not, you kill because you are right and everyone else is wrong. You kill to draw attention to yourself. Look at me, see me, fear me. I've seen you, Monsieur, many many many times."

Tan smiled at her but she glared back. For some reason he felt he had to justify himself to her.

"No, Madam, you are wrong. I seek revenge against what is going on out there in the real world." He pointed at the window and then waved his hand in exasperation. "Ah, how would you know about what's going on out there?" He touched a nerve.

"Is it so different out there, Monsieur, than it was when I was young? I listened to your reasons on the news programmes, they are good reasons, you have a good cause Monsieur, but you have a bad mind." Tan laughed forcefully. This angered her. "You!" she shouted pointing her finger at him, "you think you can take over where the madman Hitler left off, eh?"

For some reason Tan had brushed aside the shirt flap and he subconsciously pulled the Luger from his belt. Her eyes glared wildly as she recognised the sidearm used by the hated Bache.

"You going to shoot me now because I disagree with you, the same as the madman?"

He smiled as he realised he was waving the pistol in the air. He hadn't shot anyone yet, he began to wonder what it would be like. Perhaps he should shoot the old hag after all. The old woman stood up and began to walk towards the kitchen. He watched her shuffling along, her short steps comic like. He laughed.

"Where you going?" She did not turn but responded.

"I am going to get you some water, Monsieur. You smell worse than my goat." She returned a few moments later struggling with a large steel bucket filled with water and placed it on the hook above the flames. He'd noticed the strength needed to carry the heavy bucket. It was the silly gait that made her look frail. He realised she must be impaired.

"What's wrong with your legs Madam?" he asked politely.

"I have arthritis in my knees," she lied. He stared at the laceless boots and as she returned to the seat opposite him she glared at him again watching like a hawk, hardly blinking as if waiting for the right moment to swoop and clutch him in her talons. He stared back again and this time he saw the cold inhuman glare in her eyes and for a moment he shivered.

"I know you," he said smiling. Her facial expression changed to a look of interest, she had been famous several years ago. Did he know?

"You're a fucking old witch, that's what you are, a smelly old witch." Tan thought he was being humorous but he found it difficult. She was relieved. He didn't know who she was. She stood and went to the corner of the room by the fire. Several dried logs and bits of wood were thrown against the wall. She picked up an old rusty axe and began to splinter some of the wood. Although her hands were twisted with arthritis she could still grip the thick handle of the axe quite easily. She shuffled back and threw the wood onto the fire. The flames shot up the soot riddled chimney almost at once and in two minutes the bucket began to steam.

"I have some of my husband's clothes, I'll get them," she said. "You go wash in the sink." She pointed to the half open door of the kitchen. She shuffled across the room.

"And a razor?" asked Tan feeling the rough stubble on his chin. He pushed the Luger back in his belt and picked up the bucket from the flames. The handle nearly burnt his hand and he almost dropped it as he fought the pain before resting it on the floor. He looked round for a rag. An old lace curtain rested on the edge of the mantle piece and he picked it up. The photograph of her husband struck him again and he stared at it closely. He stared at the middle aged man dressed in his officer's uniform. A smart obviously educated man with a small pencil line moustache. He noticed the just visible badge of the RAMC and then his gaze rounded onto the neat row of medals protected by the small glass box. He noticed that all the medals bar one were French. He could see the markings clearly. The Medaille Militaire, the Croise de Gure, and the DCM. He returned to his task and carried the water into the small kitchen where he lifted the bucket and stood it in the stone sink. He stripped off his clothes and kicked them over to the far side of the small room. A small piece of grimy soap rested on a shelf and he began to splash and soap himself allover. He washed the matted hair till his hands felt no more grease and he scrubbed his legs before dipping his injured foot into the now mucky water. He washed off the scabs of dried blood before inspecting the severed toe. A half severed bone stuck out white as snow from the blue swollen flesh that crept back towards the ankle. He wouldn't get far on that. The door suddenly opened and the old woman stood there eyeing his naked body. She stared long and hard. He did nothing to hide his modesty but just stood and watched her watching him. 'Was she aroused, did she feel anything at all stir inside that decrepit exterior?' he wondered. She lowered a bundle of clothes onto a chair, her eyes nearing his genitals as she moved downwards. "Thanks for the clothes," he said. He distracted her and she turned and hobbled slowly out of the room. She pulled the door to slowly leaving it open about an inch.

He had stirred something in her only for a moment but it had stirred. A picture of his white penis hanging against a mass of pubic hair was still imprinted across her mind. It had been a long time. She felt the breasts that were no longer there and the ugliness she'd felt inside for all these years became unbearable again. The reason she'd hidden herself away from society seemed to flood into her whole body. She limped over to the fireplace on the stubs that had been her legacy for helping hundreds of nameless men. She stared at the rusty axe as it lay against the pile of sticks. Another feeling passed through her body, another feeling she'd not felt for some forty odd years; a feeling only one who can kill as easily as making a cup of tea. She collected the axe and gripped the shaft tightly. Her arms were strong and her hands gripped firmly on the axe. She returned to the kitchen door and peered through a crack between the dried out planks. She'd placed the clothes on the chair so he had his back to the door as he retrieved each garment. Tan had just climbed into some outsize trousers, his belt would hold them fast. He picked up the clean white collarless shirt and paused for a moment. He was feeling better mentally than for the last few days; something had been released from within, the greyness and hate that he carried like a weight on his head.

She waited till he picked up the shirt. It was buttonless till the top three and he had to lift his arms high in the air to slip it over his head. The tail slid down his back and he struggled momentarily to find the entrance to the sleeves. She eased the door open slowly. It began to groan from the hinges but he ignored the noise as the shirt slipped further down till a stubble of mousey coloured hair protruded from the top. She turned the axe to the blunt edge purposely to avoid any chance of the sharpened end striking a glancing blow. She knew she'd have only one attempt. She knew all the killing points and, although crude, this was always the best way to kill, a way favoured by most of the soldiers in the trenches in the First World War. They soon realised a shot or stabbed man could quite easily fight on till he either bled to death or his heart stopped, but a man whose brain was crushed even though he did not always die immediately was nothing more than a cabbage. The shirt came down further exposing most of his cranium and she swung the axe through the air with all her strength. It clipped the underside of the top of the door frame as it descended down onto his head, deflecting it slightly. She felt the skull casing collapse as the heavy axe entered his brain before the force of the thud made it fly from her grasp and it crashed into the far wall. Tan fell without a murmur. His body twisted as it fell and landed at her feet. His eyes were rolling and his eyelids fluttered. Blood pumped from the open skull indicating he was still alive. A feeling rose from the pit of her stomach, a warm gay feeling that spread up into her brain. His eyes began to flutter wildly and his body began to twitch. She saw the Luger where he'd placed it on a shelf between the old pans. She lifted the gun clear of the shelf. The feeling was now complete. The power of life and death that had existed in her all those years ago. She felt the orgasm about to arrive, a feeling she thought had gone forever. She quickly lowered the gun towards the fluttering eye, she struggled against the trigger as it held rigid and would not retract. The burning ecstasy was leaving her brain heading towards her stomach. She remembered the safety catch on the side of the pistol and reached across and clicked it upwards just as the ecstasy was changing down deep into her thighs. The gun was resting on the eyeball itself as she squeezed the hair trigger and the explosion once again emerged into her orgasm and she threw herself down onto the warm lifeless body writhing on top and mumbling, "Yes, oh yes. Thank you, thank you." She lay still as the warm urine passed down between her thighs and her mind was a mixture of present and past and she thought once more of the puzzled look on the oberleutenant's face as she submitted to every torture imaginable. It had never occurred to him for one minute that she'd been enjoying every little moment.

CHAPTER TWELVE

Chantille Orgina had dressed behind a screen while her parents waited impatiently, occasionally giving one another worried looks.

"You should come back to Lyon with us my dear you need rest and relaxation after your ordeal." Chantille's mother followed her daughter as she came round from behind the screen, her eyes hung heavy as she gazed hound-like at the daughter she thought she'd lost.

"Look Mama, I will come home when I've found him and thanked him for saving my life." Chantille was becoming impatient by her parents' overbearing attitude to the whole affair. "Please father," she pleaded, "take mother home and I'll come when I've done what I have to do." Maurice Orgina walked over and kissed his daughter on both cheeks.

"Of course, my dear, I'll take her home, but promise us you will return as soon as you can." Monsieur Orgina still could not believe his daughter was there, walking, talking in front of his very eyes. For over 24 hours he too had believed she had died in the 747, and he wanted to hold her and smother her till her sudden reappearance could sink in. Chantille kissed her mother goodbye.

She knew if she let them they'd smother her with love and kindness the way they had when she'd been a girl. Being an only child sometimes could be difficult especially now that she had broken free from the protection of her parents, knowing that all they wanted to do was shower her in love and affection. She was relieved as they left. She pulled on the navy cotton jacket that had been hanging over the screen. She collected the hundreds of telegrams and left them on the base of the bed. She had a last quick glance at all the flowers that were placed on every available surface throughout the room and then she turned to leave. The nursing sister who'd looked after her was waiting by the door. Chantille kissed her and thanked her for all she'd done and waved at the staff nurses who'd come to bid her goodbye. The sister walked with her to the end of the corridor where the driver from the French Embassy was waiting to collect her.

"Bonjour mademoiselle," He said as he politely took the small vanity case from her grasp. They entered the waiting elevator and as the doors closed he said to her, "There's half the world's press waiting for you in the main reception, if you like I will..." She interrupted him.

"No, that's alright, they have a right to see me, but only this once."

When the lift doors opened in the reception area she wished she'd left through one of the smaller satellite entrances. For no sooner had the doors half opened than a stampede of human beings rushed towards them. A thousand lights began to illuminate the area as the flash bulbs burst and died as if the sun had burst through the ceiling and was growing brighter by the second.

"Bon ami," she gasped as she tried to push her way from the lift in amongst the throng of reporters.

"Make way s'il vous plait," pleaded the driver as he tried to push and fight his way through. Several microphones were thrust towards her as she had only made a yard from the lift.

"What's it like to be alive?" asked one.

"Did you see the Harrier?"

"What were your thoughts as you tumbled through space?"

"What are your plans now? We hear several thousand pounds have been offered for your exclusive story, is this true?"

Her brain was still thinking over the first question as they reached the black Citroën bearing the CD plates waiting at the door. A gang of cameramen ran alongside the car till it gathered speed and left them behind. Many of the reporters followed in a fleet of cars and vans till finally the Citroën drove through the iron gates of the French Embassy. The ambassador greeted her warmly to a cavalcade of applause by the other diplomats and staff as she entered the building. Shouts of 'Bravo' echoed round the large building as Chantille blushed profusely at the warmness of her countrymen.

The ambassador, a well groomed man in his fifties bowed

gently and offered his hand in greeting. "I am ordered, Mademoiselle, by the President himself to put myself and the whole embassy at your disposal. Anything you require you must only ask."

Chantille smiled at the ambassador who had been studying her closely for the last few moments. He was enchanted by her, she wasn't exactly beautiful but she had something one could not define. She was small and slightly overweight which suited her; her jet black hair shone with health and her small rounded face always seemed to radiate a warm smile. He had fallen under her spell and secretly inside wished he'd been twenty years younger.

"There is something you could do for me if you don't mind, Sir?" she asked in reply. Her lips parted and she smiled displaying a near perfect set of white teeth. The ambassador sighed to himself. His virile french mind was thinking of her intimate parts. "Anything Mademoiselle, anything."

CHAPTER THIRTEEN

David had woken up stiff that morning. He folded the blanket that had been handed to him earlier. George Redburn saw him as he began to wake and came over from the front of the caravan where he'd been talking to one of the other superintendents.

"Ah, David ma boy, good news." David sat up immediately.

"We've got him?" he asked in anticipation.

"Well, no, it's not that. We've found the Harrier's hidy hole." George explained that some walker had found the debris left by the men at the entrance to the tunnel and informed the police.

"Of course," replied David, "why the hell didn't we think to look there?"

"Oh it's easy after the event to know the answers," stated George, "and another thing, we've found a cottage nearby. The lab boys are up there now dusting and cleaning, looks as if it was them living there alright."

"You have been busy," said David as he stood up and looked about for the sign of any coffee on the go.

"Can't let you have all the glory," said George pleased with himself.

"So it was our boys who found the place I presume and not the Met?" David already knew the answer by George's smugness. George just smiled.

"Like to go and take a look? We could use the 'copter and be back if anything happens here."

"I thought you didn't like the thing," said David.

"Nonsense," snapped back George, offended.

David realised that he'd spoken out of turn. He'd seen the look of fear on George's face when they'd arrived by the helicopter but George had never mentioned anything about his fears.

"Sorry boss," said David apologetically, "I think it must have been Inspector Forrest that mentioned he didn't like helicopters."

"That old woman, he gets dizzy going up the stairs.

George walked across to where Mervin Trevellion, the Chief Constable, sat dozing in the chair. He nudged him gently.

"Excuse me, Sir, could I borrow the 'copter for an hour or so?" Trevellion sat up slowly. He was grumpy when first awake.

"What you want it for?"

"Take a trip up the Pennines to see what's happening at the rented cottage," George hating having to ask but this was Trevellion's mannor and he was totally in charge.

"Sorry, but no. What if a call comes through that Heyes has been found?" How will we get up to the moor?" The tiredness and the tension of the waiting was beginning to tell.

"But there are three helicopters out there," moaned George.

"Well ask the army for one of theirs, I'm sure they'll oblige." Trevellion raised himself from his feet and left the caravan. The depression by not being able to locate Heyes had spread throughout the whole mobile search centre.

"Pillock," shouted George out of earshot of the superior officer but so everyone else in the top end of the van could hear. This was George Redburn's one and only way of covering his embarrassment. He turned and decided on a change of venue.

"What time is it?" he asked, although he was wearing a watch. A large electric clock hung from the wall above the radio controller. David glanced upward.

"eleven ten," he replied.

"What time the pubs open down this neck of the woods Johny?" asked Redburn to the radio operator. He called everyone Johny whose name he didn't know.

"Open now, Sir, eleven am," came the reply in a broad Somerset drawl.

"Fancy a scrumpy?" asked George imitating the drinking of a pint by lifting his empty hand up to his mouth.

"Why not," agreed David. Anything to ease the boredom. George tapped the side of his nose and nodded his head towards the constable who sat at the radio desk.

"Excuse me, Johny, but do you have a vehicle we can borrow?" The man threw George a leather key tag with one key hanging from it.

"White Chevette patrol car parked at the very end of the

row near the shit tent." George caught the key and winked and then smiled at David.

"You don't think he's trying to tell us something do you Davy boy?"

"I didn't hear him address me, Sir," replied David smiling. David had seen a change in George Redburn, whether it was the success of investigations so far; the head man always gets the credit, or whether he'd just decided to loosen up a bit, David didn't know although David's immediate boss back at Special Branch headquarters in Leeds had warned him, "When George is sober he's one of the nicest chaps in the world, but when he's had a drink or two he's one hell of a bastard." David thought perhaps this wasn't such a good idea as they trudged across the field that served as a car park.

Sergeant Gibson had been watching the helicopter grow nearer as the pilot, enjoying himself, swept low over the moorland before lifting over the crest of the hills and, turning in its own circumference, dropped and landed about thirty feet from where the sergeant stood. A young slim built soldier leapt out of the open doorway of the Gazelle and turned to reach in for his gear. The sergeant gave the pilot a quick hand signal indicating he was not flying back down the hill with him. The young SAS man came running to where the sergeant stood and smiled.

"Whatcha, Gibbo, how's it been?" The sergeant gave the pilot a wiring hand gesture indicating both men were clear of the rotor blades. The pilot signalled with a thumbs up before he twisted the grip on the joystick and the angle of the rotor blades changed lifting the 'copter quickly away. The sergeant turned to face the young NCO who looked back at him.

"What's up, Gibbo, you like it so much you're gonna stay an' hold me hand eh?"

"Piss off, Parsons, and less of the 'Gibbo'. Just 'Sergeant' to you."

Private Parsons was a newcomer to the regiment and had only just finished his basic training. Sergeant Gibson had been instrumental in most of Parson's instruction and had decided to put him to the test. As the young soldier bent down to pick up his gear from the ground, Gibson quickly plucked the young man's beret from its resting place on the NCO's head. The young man turned just in time to see the sergeant stuffing the fawn coloured cloth into his tunic. In training all new recruits were warned that squadies from other regiments, would go to any lengths to steal an SAS soldier's beret, a prized trophy among other regiments jealous of the elitist tag that was the highest pinnacle any true professional fighting man could attain. To return without one's beret would open the soldier to ridicule from his comrades. Many had been taken but none kept. Parsons eyed the sergeant menacingly. He knew it was an open challenge.

"I'm warning you, Gibbo, you give that back." The sergeant smiled confidently. He stood, feet astride, his weight slightly forward balancing only on his toes ready for the attack that was to follow.

"Take it, you ugly spotty get," said Gibbo taunting him. He knew the youngster was good, after all he'd trained him. The youngster suddenly aimed the sole of his boot directly down onto Gibbo's left knee. The sergeant had anticipated it and removed his leg, just in time The blow, had it connected, would have broken his leg.

"Good, very good," said Gibbo. "Is that your best shot?" Gibbo aimed a right hand at the youngster's throat, Parsons saw it coming and went to block with the palm of his left hand. Gibbo's blow came over the top of Parson's left hand and smashed him in the middle of his forehead with the palm of his hand. Normally it would have been a fist, but the palm was enough to ground the young man.

"Bloody hell, Gibbo!" enthused Parsons as he flipped to his feet in one movement. "You'll have to show me that one, that was bloody brilliant." The sergeant was the best there was, and he knew it. He flung his cap to the youngster who caught it and placed it back on his head.

"One day," he said smiling, "I'll take you."

"I've no doubt about that, son one day you will."

Sergeant Gibson left the young man and marched off down the hill towards the lake. He was glad to be on the move, that's the reason he didn't ride the 'copter back to the search headquarters; after two days, he needed the walk. Besides something had been irritating him about that small shed at the end of the lake. As he strolled down the hill he thought of the searchers that had come up the hill to where the sergeant lay. Several young territorials had nearly wet themselves when they came practically on top of the camouflaged soldier who had leapt to his feet and shouted. "Bang, bang, you're all dead." He was still smiling to himself as the memory of their shocked faces as he came up to the small shed. He removed a small flat strip of what looked like yellow plasticine and broke it in half. He moulded the pliable explosive into the movable part of the hasp on the padlock. He repeated the process on the second padlock then pushed the small bullet like detonators into the plastic till they held fast. After removing the safety cap he pressed the small red buttons simultaneously on top of the detonators and began counting. He rounded the side of the shed and stood close to the wall. He only got to four when the explosion blew the padlocks into a thousand small pieces, the force blowing the door half open till it stuck fast on the stone floor. Gibbo waited a few moments for the smoke to clear before coming round to the front of the shed and rushing into the small room.

The small pub, some eight miles and three road blocks from the search headquarters, was empty apart from the two Yorkshire policemen. The landlord was surprised to see them as they walked through the door, the mere presence of Anthony Heyes in the county had emptied nearly all the pubs of customers, fearful he may somehow have poisoned the beer. The innkeeper, pleased at least to have some company, insisted on buying most of the drinks and a small party soon developed.

Chief Superintendent Redburn had half emptied a full bottle of Teachers whisky while David had been hitting the local cider, unaware of its potency till his legs began to feel a little unsteady. George began to reminisce about the old days when he was a constable on the beat in his native Barnsley.

"Used to be a lovely place old Barnsley, Davy Boy, before the reds got onto the council and that twassack, Arthur Scargill, came on the scene." The two men laughed as George likened

Scargill to a demented parrot with a shredded wheat on his head. David couldn't help but notice George's insatiable appetite as he constantly threw back double after double till the last drop in the bottle had gone. Although he'd drunk a whole bottle in just over an hour he didn't appear to David to be one iota drunk. the landlord retired to the rear to make a plate of sandwiches and David decided to question George on his intake.

"You know, George, you'll kill yourself drinking all that." George shrieked with laughter and nearly choked on his last mouthful, coughing and laughing at the same time. David began thumping his back to help relieve the congestion.

"What's the joke?" George settled a bit and still smiling replied.

"You are." His faced turned serious.

"You've seen a doctor then, I take it." George stared at the younger man,

"You don't miss much do you?"

"What's the diagnosis?"

George pondered his answer for a moment. "Acute alcoholism, advanced cirrhosis of the liver, if I stop drinking I might last a year or so, and if..." he paused in mid sentence and looked down at his empty glass.

"Why don't you pack it in and..."

"go lie on a beach somewhere," George finished the sentence.

"What with, Davy boy, this old copper's skint." David was wondering how he could be broke. George answered his question for him.

"An ex-wife to keep, two daughters in private schools, not much change outa my salary."

"But you'll get a good pension when you finish," said David.

"Aye, but it'll all go the same way as the rest."

The landlord returned from the rear of the pub and placed a pile of cheese sandwiches on the bar.

"On the house gents, tuck in."

David reached across and helped himself to a large crusty sandwich. "Thanks," he said before taking a large bite. It was obvious the superintendent didn't really want to eat but he took one out of politeness and took a small courtesy bite. The landlord returned to the rear after refilling the men's glasses. George looked across at the young man who was obviously enjoying his food.

"You're a good copper, Davy lad," he said. He pulled out David's letter of resignation from inside his jacket and waved it in the air. "Do you really want to go through with this?" David eyed the letter, his mind was made up. As far as he was concerned he was through.

"Yes, I just want to see this man caught and to look into his face, and then I'll be off to fields anew."

"It's funny that," said George. "When you hunt a man for a while you always feel the urge to meet face on. It's a sort of trophy, the gazing at one's victim if you like. They're nearly always a disappointment as well."

David lifted the cider to his lips and washed down the last mouthful of bread. He'd been thinking about his resignation again, rechecking his reasons to himself, and then another thought struck him, something that had not occurred to him till now. He'd lost his dedication, it had just vanished, the urge to be the best policeman in the world, his whole existence was geared to that end. Somehow it didn't matter what he was any more. He looked at the red face of the old man standing next to him and watched how his hand trembled slightly as he held the whisky glass up to his lips. He could see himself standing there in twenty years time. he realised it had been George's dedication that had destroyed his life. He'd heard tales in the past how Superintendent Redburn was one of the best detectives on the force. And then David thought of the long hours spent in pursuance of a perpetrator of a crime; the broken marriage because he'd never come home, the drink, manditory throughout the force, and now his very life. George Redburn would soon pay with his life for his dedication to his job. David knew finally and without doubt he would not be a policeman this time next week. His thoughts were interrupted by the creaking door of the pub as it began to open slowly. The two policemen turned and stared at the opening door. The old woman entered nervously into the room and stood just inside the door. George eyed the scruffy woman from top to toe; the oversized torn man's jacket held close with string; the baggy trousers tucked into manure stained old boots minus the laces; the hard weather beaten skin on the hands and face; the thin unwashed matted hair. George likened her to a pig farmer he'd once known back in Wakefield.

"Could you tell me where is the policeman?" she pointed through the doorway to the white patrol car the two men had borrowed. The door sprung closed behind the woman. George winked at David.

"Go tell her it's broken down and the bobby's gone for help. We don't want to get bogged down in local crime."

"Ah she'll only want a direction or something. I'll see what she wants." David walked across to where she stood and said, "Can I help, I'm a policeman?"

"You don't look like a policeman." David produced his warrant card and she held it close to her nose, examining it thoroughly. A strong smell" emerged from the direction of the woman and David opened the door and asked if she'd mind talking outside. He grinned to himself as the old woman shuffled out after him.

"Now what can I do for you?"

"It says on your card that you are from Leeds. You look for that man no?" He noted the strong foreign accent to her speech.

"Yes, I seek him," he replied.

"I know where he is. I have him." David's eyes narrowed and he stared unbelievingly at the old woman.

She could see the young policeman doubted her so she shuffled back towards an old Morris 1000 and lifted an old rag from the passenger seat. She came back and gave the bundle to David. It felt heavy as he slowly lifted away the soiled cloth to reveal the German made pistol. He walked quickly towards the pub door and pushed it open.

"George," he shouted, "you'd better get out here quick."

George downed the dregs of whisky in one go and reluctantly left the stool he'd been perched on and walked out of the pub. David was standing next to the police car examining the Luger as he approached. He held out the gun with his little finger hooked through the trigger protector and George bent down and stared at it as if he was examining an unfamiliar breed at Crufts.

"It's a Luger," said David.

George lifted his eyes up away from the gun and gazed at the old lady for a second before returning his gaze to the pistol. Then he straightened and looked at David and said, "It's a Luger, Heyes threatened the fisherman with a Luger."

David was glad George's brain worked and wasn't too befuddled with his wet lunch. George turned his red face towards Madam Peter and glared unblinking at the rag clad old woman.

"She says she's got Heyes," said David half unsure whether it was some sort of joke, stage managed as a leg pull. The cider made him grin.

George erupted into a huge belly laugh and rested his hands on his knees to stop him rolling over. The contagious roar infected David and soon the two men were doubled over in an unstoppable inebriated bellow that brought tears to their eyes. The sight of Madam Peters as she shuffled Charlie Chaplin like back towards the old car in disgust, waving her arms in the air cursing aloud in French only made the men roar louder. It was only when the engine of the Morris began to turn over that David managed to compose himself and begged the old woman's indulgence.

"Please, we're sorry, please," David opened the door and gently drew the old woman from behind the wheel and led her to the rear of the pickup. George was leaning over the bonnet of the Chevettes till in raptures. It was only then that David saw the small hen feathers matted into the white strands of hair on the old lady's head, and he almost lost control of himself once again.

"Please," he said trying not to look at the woman's hair in case he began to laugh again. "You say you have him where?" Madam Peters stood silently for a few moments, her wrinkled face spread with anger. She thought the two men were fools and had decided to say no more, but then perhaps it was fools that she needed.

"You follow me in your police car. I show you where." She began to shuffle off towards the open door of the Morris. The large laceless boots scraped and flapped along the gravel road and made George lift his head to look once more at the wreck of humanity that came towards him. His red face had turned beetroot as if every bloodvessel in his head had converged there and were about to burst. He erupted once more into his bellowing roar and fell back down across the bonnet of the car. David asked the woman if he could accompany her in the passenger seat and he opened the rusty door and climbed in without waiting for an answer. He shouted at George to follow, but he just looked up and waved his hand as if to say no, but then the old lady proceeded to do an eight point turn across the narrow roadway and David saw him climb into the patrol car and begin to follow. The woman drove at a constant fifteen mph jerking whenever a gear was changed with rattling of the untimed tappets. The pickup was filled with white feathers and stunk of decay and hen droppings. He regretted his decision to ride shotgun. He turned every once in a while to check that the superintendent was following, only to see the red face still beaming through the windscreen of the Chevette. George Redburn wasn't going to miss the encore. He hadn't laughed so much in years.

Sergeant Gibson stood in the middle of the small shed, his hand resting on the large steel pipe that led to the rear wall. He'd barely been in the shed for a second before his nose told him someone else had been inside also. The smell of urine and human excrement hung in the still air. The sunlight filtered through a small gap in the corner of the room and the SAS man pushed upwards with the barrel of his rifle lifting the slate that Tan had used to climb out about a foot or so upwards. 'So the bastard was here all the time, he thought. A flush of excitement filling his body. He searched the shed till he found a small pile of excrement up near the wall. He felt it with his fingers. It was still soft and pliable indicating it had not been there too long. He rinsed his fingers in a small puddle by the dripping pipe and cursed himself for not inspecting the shed sooner. He came out of the shed and walked to its rear. He knew no one besides the searchers had passed up the hillside where he'd kept vigil. He removed his binoculars from his pack and began to scan the valley below, back and forth checking every field, anything that could indicate a man had passed. He could see for miles nearly down to the coast some twenty five miles away, but not with any clarity he knew his man could easily be ten or more miles in front of him by now. He lifted the small handset radio to his lips and was just about to flip down the transmit button when suddenly he changed his mind. He could see the tracks made through the flattened heather and decided to follow them down. If there was the slightest chance of getting a shot at the fugitive he would relish the chance. After all the order was to kill and the Sergeant like most normal people hated the likes of Heyes; terrorists who could kill in cold blood without caring about who was the target; women; children; old people; anybody who stood in their way or just happened to be at the preordained scene of the ambush. He gazed down at the countryside below. It reminded him of Crossmaglen, the border country where IRA snipers lay in wait for the Brit patrols as they swept the field checking for mines. But this time he wouldn't have to crouch as he progressed or have his rear protected by a comrade. No, this time he would run and travel free of the fear of the sniper's fire. He set off down the glen following the easy track made by the man he hated, running as fast as he could go, leaping over the large clumps of heather which turned into the pasture grass in the lower fields. He found it harder and harder to find any sign as he rested on a stone wall and raised his binoculars. A small crop of buildings layoff to his right about 4 miles across the fields. They looked almost deserted and derelict, but the small stream of smoke from the chimney stack indicated a presence. He set out at a slow walk towards the direction of the smoke. About two miles from the smoke he saw two cars emerge down the side of a small hill not far from the cluster of farm buildings. Perching on a large boulder still on the higher ground overlooking the scene he focused in on the cars as they came nearer and nearer towards the buildings. They'd been only flashes of colour as they had snaked through the hedgerowed sunken roads, but now as they turned onto a long rough surfaced track he could see the red coloured pickup and the following police patrol car quite clearly. He watched till they came to a stop and as the two men converged outside the front door of the cottage, their attitude was casual and jocular as they stood waiting for the old lady who was taking her time leaving the old Morris. The small radio suddenly crackled and a voice came over the airways.

"Seven, over." He dropped the binoculars and slid off the

rock till he was sitting with his back against the huge stone.

"Seven here, over." he said as he held the radio up to his mouth.

"Command here." It was the captain's code name. He'd had a report from Parsons, Gibbo's relief on the lake top, about him half blowing up the water shed and taking off down the valley like a racehorse.

"Been poppin' too many soldiers," remarked Parsons referring to the amphetamine tablets they all used.

"What was in the shed, over?" asked Command. Gibson thought for a moment before replying.

"Target, Sir, over." A short silence followed as Command absorbed the message.

"You have contact, over?"

"Negative, Command. Target had been in shed at some stage, urine and a couple of turds inside, but it was difficult to say how old, could have been there from two days ago, quite humid in the shed, over."

"Where are you now, over?"

"Bottom of the moor, followed a track, but along with the search party mess it became difficult to follow. Target probably still in the trap, over." The sergeant referred to the encircling sweep which was now near on closing.

"Do you need a backup helicopter, over?" Gibbo thought for a moment.

"No thanks, Command. If he's out here I'll find him, helicopter will only make him go to ground. I'm coming in from the higher ground. If I spot anything, will inform. Over and out." The sergeant knew an experienced ex-service man like the target would easily hear the rotors of an oncoming helicopter long before they'd any chance to spot him, and with the correct camouflage even at fifty feet he'd be difficult to spot from the air. After all, if he had got through the sweep Gibbo knew he could be anywhere by now. But out there on the moor the sergeant was quite happy. He knew that as soon as this war was over it was back to the squalor of a bedsit in east Belfast, and you never know, he just might get a shot yet.

David eyed the clump of buildings that surrounded him. As far as he could make out from the old apple crushing stones it was an old cider farm. It had obviously seen better days and was in need of a great many repairs. George had composed himself now on the fifteen minute journey to the farm and was standing next to David as the old woman came shuffling towards them followed by several hens who always associated her with food. "Chicken," said George imitating an American southern accent.

"That's enough," replied David who'd been trying to reason where the woman had got the gun from as he'd sat next to her in the pickup. He had thought maybe she'd found it or it wasn't the same gun, but as they'd come up the lane something had sobered in him, and he decided to take the old woman seriously.

"Where is he?" he asked. The old woman pointed to the small front door.

"He's in the kitchen. But I assure you he is quite dead." David lifted the old rusty sneck on the flaking painted door and slowly pushed it open. George, seeing how serious the younger man was, sobered as he followed David into the small front room. The smell hit David first; just a faint smell of gun oil and cordite hung in the air, a smell he'd smelt several times before on the police shooting range after the discharge of his weapon. There was only one other door leading from the room and he made straight for it. He paused a moment outside before he pushed it slowly open about a foot or so. It stopped opening as it wedged against something on the floor. A mass of bluebottles which had been feeding on the blood splattered room all took off at the same time protesting at the intrusion. They began buzzing round and round between slits of deflecting sunlight that shone through the back kitchen window. David pushed his head into the gap and stared down at the motionless body on the floor. He squeezed through the half open door and bent down to examine it. At first glance he could see it was Heyes alright. He bent closer to the eyeless corpse just as a large fly that had crawled into the empty socket came buzzing out in its alarm. In unnerved him for a moment and he moved upwards crashing into the superintendent who had come up from behind him.

"What a bloody mess," said George as he stared at the floor where the back of Heyes' head had disintegrated and exploded in all directions, bits of blood splattered brain hung from the walls mixed with fragments of bone. The sight of the body composed George, the giddiness gone, his policeman's brain began to function again.

"I don't know how you do it, Wonder Boy."

"What's that?" asked David as he inspected the old clothes that Heyes had discarded.

"You must lead a charmed life, falling out of aeroplanes and now this! I mean what were the odds that we chose that particular pub and the old woman stopping there? Do you see? You've got the Midas touch, Davy Boy." 'The Midas Touch!'

"Do you think she did it?" asked David as he examined the blood stained boot marks that led out of the kitchen and over to the fireplace. The small shuffling walk had turned into long slurrs of blood as the old woman's soles hardly left the floor.

"What?" replied George who'd not been listening but thinking very deeply about something.

"Do you think she did it, could she be protecting someone?"

"Ah, yes, someone else," repeated George still far away. "Better check the house." George entered the bedroom, and looking out of the window through the grimy old lace curtains, he smiled to himself as he saw the old woman milking the goat as if nothing at all had happened. After checking the room he walked out of the bedroom and back into the front room where David stood holding the small case of medals in his hand examining them closely. He then picked up the photograph of the young woman leaning on the car. He suddenly looked up at George with a stunned expression on his face.

"I know who she is!"

"What's that?" asked George.

"I know who she is!" repeated David.

"Well!" exclaimed George, "who the bloody hell is she?"

"She's Mademoiselle Noire, the most decorated woman of all time." David returned the photograph to its position on the shelf and then pointed to the row of medals in the case. See that one in the middle, that's the Croise de Guir, the highest medal award for gallantry. That medal was awarded by De Gaulle himself." David went on to explain about what the Gestapo had done to her career in the Resistance.

"How do you know all this?" asked George, impressed.

"I read a book about her some five years ago. In fact, there were several books written about her, glorifying her as some sort of wonder woman." David eyed the photograph of the woman and the car again. That picture was on the front cover of the book I read, only this time the author, Tim Sebastian, didn't glorify her but branded her a malicious and sadistic killer."

"Ah, yes," said George, "I recollect one of the national dailies did a serialisation of the book, I read some of it." George pondered on some of the blood curdling facts he could remember.

"Jesus!" he exclaimed, "but are you sure that's her?"

"Absolutely positive," said David who was staring at the photograph once again. A cloud had blotted out the sun and as it emerged from behind, a burst of sunlight came through the rear window of the room and struck the photograph. David saw the reflection of the old woman who was standing in the doorway and had been listening to every word. He turned quickly as did George and the woman stood, tears dripping from the bottom of her chin. George rushed over to her and led her to the wooden chair by the fire and sat her down. He caught the look of anguish on David's face as he stared at the utterly pathetic sight of the crippled woman whose world was beginning to crumble before her very eyes. If she'd had the Luger in her hands at that moment she would have used it on herself. When would the nightmare end? Once again she would be in the newspapers, once again her self imposed exile would be threatened. She remembered the small cottage she and her husband had shared in Cornwall after the war. They'd been happy until the book brought their existence to the public eye. The intrusion of sightseers who would peer through the windows forced them to move away, only for them to be found and then to move once again. This was the only place she'd found sanctuary; for years she'd had peace and now it was to end. George had filled an old cup with water and brought it to the distraught woman. She calmed herself.

"You must take him away from here," she said in a croaky voice. "I have done your dirty work for you, now you must take him away." George couldn't believe what he was hearing, neither could David but for different reasons than his colleague, David replied.

"Yes, Madam, we will take him away as soon as the lab men are through and we've..." she cut him short.

"No! I mean now, take him. I cannot be involved."

"But why not, Madam? No-one will hurt you. In fact, you will be rewarded," said David referring to the money. George's face was smiling till David had mentioned the reward and his expression changed to a worried frown.

"I want no reward." George's expression returned. "Don't you see, I live like this to keep people away, I like my solitude. If I am exposed as the executioner of that man my world will end." The tears still ran down her cheeks, although she didn't sob and was completely in control. George nodded his head, gesturing for a private word. David followed him out of the front door and the two men faced each other in the yard.

"I've just had an idea, Davy Boy." David saw a glint of excitement in George's eyes. He eyed him contemptuously.

"What idea?"

"The reward. We could have the reward. It probably stands at about five million pounds by now. Just think, Davy Boy, we could be millionaires!"

"Bollocks," replied David a look of annoyance on his face. "You're off your rocker, you know policemen can't claim that reward."

"No, I can't but you can!" George reached into his pocket and held David's resignation letter up in the air. By all intents and purposes you resigned two days ago."

"You're drunk," said David.

"Oh no, I'm not. As your immediate superior officer I accepted your resignation two days ago and that is final.

" David decided to call his bluff. "Okay, so I'm not a policeman anymore, but you still can't make me take that reward or even apply for it." George wasn't too worried about that for the minute as the immediate thing was to remove the body from the cottage.

"You're right of course," he said pretending he was no longer interested in the reward.

"It was just a thought."

David returned to the front room where the woman sat, still weeping.

"Listen, Madam Noire," he unconsciously used her maiden name and she looked up startled. "Listen, there is a reward, a great deal of money offered for the capture of that man, no-one will hold it against you for shooting him either. You could start off anew back in your native France perhaps," he smiled at her compassionately.

"I'm too old to move, and what would I want with money, money I already have?" She pointed to an old biscuit tin resting on a shelf in the corner. George reached over and lifted it down.

"Please look in there," she said. George forced open the lid expecting to find a bundle of fivers but instead there was a mass of papers. He looked through them. There were several title deeds to properties and an old bank statement dated 1972 showing a last balance of £320,427. There were stocks and bonds, a title deed for a vineyard in Bordeaux and several more items George did not bother to read.

"God, she's a millionairess already," said George astounded. She reached over and gripped David tightly by the hand. Her eyes pleaded.

"Please Monsieur, all I have, all I want is my farm and my animals. You take everything in the box and the man in the kitchen away. I have not long left on this earth." David stared back long and hard at the pathetic sight in front of him. Her eyes still pleaded and her lips trembled, and he thought of what the world had done to her already. The mental scars she carried around with her, the squalor she lived in. He wondered if she was punishing herself for all that had happened in the past. George could see David was fighting with his conscience and slowly nodded his head as if to say, 'Do as she says.' David blew a sigh of exasperation.

"George, outside a moment." George obliged leaving the two alone. David knelt down in front of the woman and looked into the tear stained eyes.

"Madam, we don't want your money, but I will take away

the body only if you will put me straight on the details of how you killed him and what Heyes had to say to you before he died." She nodded and quickly began to tell David of all that had happened that day. She said it was the sight of the Luger that made her kill him, it reminded her of the weapon carried by the other enemy long ago. When she had finished he made her promise not to breath a word of Heyes' visit to anyone.

"No, Monsieur, I keep my word, not even the Gestapo can make me talk." She spat on the floor at the mention of the name Gestapo. George had been listening outside the half open door. David came out to join him. He was frustrated and angry at the young man's attitude towards money.

"You prick," he said, "we could have helped ourselves to a fortune in there, what bloody good is it to that old bag." The two men squared up to each other and David glared back angrily at the older man.

"Money, money, what the hell's got into you? Didn't they used to call you 'Honest George'?"

"Pah," George waved his arm in the air, "I'll tell you what's got into me. Suddenly just when my life's nearly over all this money seems to be waving about under my nose. The old bag doesn't want it, you don't want it, but what about me, "Honest George?" He leaned across and prodded himself in the chest, his red face had turned almost crimson in his anger.

"You know what hurts the most?" he said calming down a little, "I will not even live long enough to spend my pension, that really pisses me off." David wasn't sure all this talk of George dying was the truth or not, but he was not to be moved on his stance against taking any for himself. It was bad enough moving the body, but obtaining money by deception, that just wasn't his style, but he could see by George's expression that he wasn't going to give in easily.

"What about the body?" asked David eager to change the subject.

"Let's move the body away to a field somewhere and say we just saw it lying there. The boffins will presume he's shot himself." George had already thought that one out.

"What about the lack of blood and bits of flesh at the scene?"

"Oh, that's no problem, you see whenever a body is left out in the open its like a gift of fresh meat to all the animal population. Carrion crows will eat the flesh, bones, brain, anything. Dogs, cats, foxes, badgers will take their fill, small rodents. It's obvious he's been dead for some time now. Anyway who's gonna care as long as he's dead. The SAS captain practically said he was to be shot on sight. No, they'll be glad he's found, that's all." George's manner had calmed a little.

"Sounds easy."

"Course it's easy."

"Sounds like you've done this sort of thing before."

George smiled, "You'd be surprised what I've had to do Davy Boy. You'd be bloody well surprised." George smiled a wicked sort of grin. David thought he was thinking of the times in the past when he'd pulled a fast one or two. In fact George was grinning to himself because he knew once David had helped him move the body he'd be open to blackmail. Then George would get his hands on the money and it was as good as his. He would sort the young smug bastard out later.

"Just one thing," said David, "I'm moving the body for one reason only and that's to spare that old lady in there, without her help Heyes would have slipped through the net, I think she deserves to be left alone."

"Agreed," replied George.

"Now let's get that stiff into the back of Madam Peters old van before the rigor mortis sets in or we'll never get him in."

George had been right what he'd said about scrutiny of the death scene. They'd found a small wooded area that led onto an old quarry just off the roadside. There, they'd sat the body down and let if fall naturally onto its side leaving the open skull to the sun and elements. George had placed the gun in Heyes' hand and fired the trigger. The bullet embedded itself harmlessly into the old slag pile at the bottom of the quarry. He knew if they did a paraffin test on Heyes' hand it would show he'd fired the gun. thirty minutes later George had returned the old pickup back to the farm and David had radiod in with the finding of the corpse. The first helicopter carrying the Chief Constable and two of his superintendents swooped down and landed in a nearby field. A swarm of cars and the inevitable press corps followed suit and amidst much hand shaking and back slapping it was more like a carnival than the scene of a suspicious death.

"You're sure it's him?" asked Trevellion, the Chief Constable.

"One hundred and twenty per cent sure, Sir," replied George who was enjoying himself again in his moment of glory.

"What were you doing out here anyway?" asked Trevellion, his policeman's brain collecting all the knowledge for the inevitable press conference that would follow.

"Been out to lunch, Sir. One of your men here kindly lent us his patrol car and recommended a nice hostelry just up the road. Absolute co-incidence, I just saw a flash of white as we drove past and stopped to investigate and there he was dead as a dodo." Trevellion stared down at the body.

"Rather clean, don't you think Redburn."

"What's that, Sir?" George pretended not to hear.

"A bit clean, clothes and all, for a man on the run across open country," repeated the Chief Constable.

"Perhaps he stopped off for a wash and brush up," said George smiling. Trevellion pretended to laugh.

"No, it looks as though he's had a change of clothes and a wash somewhere, but that doesn't matter. Main thing is he's here, and we've got him." He paused for a moment and took an old pipe from his pocket and placed it between his lips.

"I tell you what though... George, isn't it?" Trevellion paused and seemed to change his mind on what he was about to say.

"Yes, Sir."

"I was getting more than a bit worried that he'd slipped through the net, I can tell you." David had been standing behind George listening to every word. He was experienced enough to let one man do the talking. That way there'd be no contradictions.

"Now you two," said Trevellion as he turned to face the two heroes, leaving the police camera team photographing the remains. "I want a full report as quick as possible, every detail from leaving the search headquarters. Got that?"

"Just one small detail," George said. The Chief Constable waited for him to continue. "Mr. Galbraith here, Sir, is no longer in the force, he will have to write a statement not a report." Trevellion eyed the two men suspiciously. 'What's he up to?' thought David.

"Oh, when did all this occur?" asked the Chief Constable. George withdrew the letter and held it out for Trevellion to inspect.

"Oh I see." George folded the letter and put it back in his suit pocket. David was cursing the sly old bastard under his breath when the Chief Constable turned towards him and said rather uncaringly.

"Oh sorry to lose you, but then you've been through quite a bit recently. Anyway, well done. Good man!" He shook David by the hand and trotted off to enjoy the rest of the carnival.

"You bastard, " said David as soon as they were back in the car.

"Petulance, dear boy," smiled George. "Haven't you been warned what a bastard I am already? Tut, tut. You've a lot to learn about life, Wonder Boy, a fucking hell of a lot."

One hour after the reported discovery of Heyes' body a press conference was held in the roadway just fifty yards from the canvas cover frame where Tan lay. Wynn Trevellion acting on instructions direct from 10 Downing Street, stood against the thorn hedgerow surrounded by over a hundred pressmen and television crews. He relayed the brief knowledge he had. A body believed to be that of Anthony Heyes had been found by two officers who'd been travelling along the roadway. He had apparently shot himself. He was about to conclude the brief conference when a television reporter standing at the front thrust a microphone under his nose.

"Tell me Chief Constable, who were the officers who found the body?" Trevellion swallowed hard and thought about whether or not to reveal further details. He'd felt embarrassed enough that Heyes had slipped through the cordon and to say he was perplexed by the whole situation was an understatement. He cleared his throat and pretended to read from a clipboard he had under his arm. A thought had been niggling away in his brain, something about Redburn and Galbraith, something was not right. And then in a flash he had it. He realised what had been bothering him. His thoughts were distracted by the reporter repeating his previous questions and he said as if surprised.

"Ah yes, the two policemen were Superintendent Redburn and Detective Sergeant Galbraith." A murmur of surprise ran round the gathering. Trevellion thanked the reporters politely and tried to push his way through the mass of men and equipment. A barrage of questions was thrown at him. He just ignored them pushing and shoving his way back to the taped cordon across the road. He cringed as he heard a remark passed by one of the gathering.

"Bit of a co-incidence that it was Galbraith who found the body."

'If only they knew he'd resigned as well,' thought the Chief Constable. He knew the hounds of the press were quick to smell a rat, the same way he'd smelt one when Redburn had thrust Galbraith's resignation under his nose. He knew they were after the reward, what else could it be. They wouldn't get a single bloody penny, he vowed to himself as he ducked under the plastic tape, relieved to be clear of the claustrophobic gathering. He looked around for any sign of Galbraith and Redburn but they had already left the scene. 'Bastards, I'll have them for this if that's their game,' he thought, 'I'll bloody well have them.'

Richard Normans was sitting in front of the television in the neat one bedroomed apartment he'd rented in a suburb on the edge of Manchester. No more tacky bedsits for him. He'd collected all their gear from the rented cottage near the Pennines as well as the several thousand pounds from the Bradbury affair, and had decided to lie low for a while. He'd already watched the scene earlier that day as the police had found the cottage and he knew they'd surely have his fingerprints by now. A police spokesman filmed outside the cottage had already stated they were seeking two other men, at least so he thought they'd not picked Phil up either. He was puzzled where he'd got to and was annoyed they'd not made a contingency plan to regroup somewhere. He was not unduly worried about Phil although he wished he'd had someone to talk to about what was happening to Tan and if they could do anything to help him if at all. But then suddenly some of his questions were answered as the poker thin face of Wynn Trevellion filled the television screen in front of him. He sat stunned as the announcement of Tan's death was broadcast live and he listenend intently. The word 'suicide' kept repeating in his brain long after the news bulletin had finished and a Bugs Bunny cartoon blared back at him from the TV set. Somehow he'd had visions of Tan being taken alive. He'd had dreams of his rescuing him and forming an even more fanatical team than ever before. But the more he thought, the more he realised that Tan would never have been taken alive; no lengthy show trial for him; no stage for Tan to speak to the world. He knew Tan must have known this too. That's why he must have shot himself; no soldier's bullet for him, he'd shown them he was not afraid to die. A lump came to his throat as he thought of the genius in the man he'd grown to love and respect. But then, after a moment of sadness, his mood suddenly changed. His nostrils flared and he jumped from the chair, kicking the television screen so voilently with his foot that it exploded into several pieces. Sparks and flames jumped into the air and a ring of smoke hung over the broken remains.

"Don't worry, Tan," he said out loud as if he were there with him in the room. "I'm still here, I'll make them pay. They'll not forget Tan Heyes' name for a long time. You watch me, Tan, wherever you are." He stared as the flames from the TV died away. His anger had died with them. He was calm again. He suddenly remembered Tan's words which explained to him about the temperament needed to be a fighter pilot and one's strategy to consider all alternatives and then and only then should one act. He decided at that moment what he needed to do. His last course of action would be to carefully check and recheck all the facts and details, only then would he act. He would keep a low profile at all times. He would not even risk a parking ticket, from that moment until he acted he would be Mr. Clean. He slid back into the comfy chair and lit a cigarette from the packet resting on the unmarked coffee table, and for the first time in his life he suddenly felt confident, confident that he, like Tan, could work alone, could live alone and could act alone. It was as if Tan had not died but had joined in body and mind with him, as if they were one. It was as if the shroud that had clouded and confused his life had suddenly vanished, had been lifted and for the first time he could see the way. Suddenly he felt an inner deep joy within as if he'd found the very secret of life itself. He was alive and free and had a purpose, a great purpose to fulfil which would only end when his life's breath had been extinguished. He stared at the half smoked cigarette and smiled to himself before he extinguished it, screwing it round and round in the porcelain ashtray on the table. He would waste no more time before he would act. Let them rejoice in Tan's death, let them feel confident to go out into the streets without fear. That would be when he would strike. He walked over to the window and looked down onto the street, a floor below. People were going about their business unconcerned and unafraid. He whispered to himself as he stood smiling, 'Watch out you screwed up bastards, Tan Heyes is still out to get you, he's still here you simple sods.'

A newspaper vendor some distance away on the corner was waving a paper in the air. Richard opened the catch on the window and leaned out to watch the scene more clearly as people hurried towards the newspaper seller to read the latest bulletin of the affair. They seemed insect like and insignificant and he suddenly realised why, after all these years, he'd been anti social, non-conformist; a person who rebelled against society. He hated his fellow men. He despised them all.

David collected his car from the long stay car park at Leeds Bradford airport where he'd left it nearly a week ago. He had returned alone from Taunton that morning by train after collaborating on a statement with George Redburn, whom he hoped he would never have to see again. It felt good to be home as he rounded the corner that led into the cul-de-sac where his flat was located, the ground floor of a semi at the end. He cursed under his breath at the sight of the collection of press vehicles parked outside. He pulled to a stop at the end of the long line of vans and cars and was immediately besieged by the twenty or so press who'd been waiting patiently for him to return. David was tired and ill-tempered, it had all been a strain these last days and as with a lot of the cases he'd worked on, this one had ended half up in the air.

Heyes' sudden death was an anti-climax and left many questions unanswered. But those questions did not concern him anymore, he had a new life to built for himself and most of all his thoughts that morning had been working on a solution to his problem. He was thirty one years old. He had approximately two thousand pounds in the bank and he owed ten thousand on the mortgage for the flat. He realised the next few months would not be easy. He pushed his way through the ever persistent reporters as a multitude of questions were bombarded at him. He remained silent until he reached the front door where he turned and held his hands in the air, gesticulating silence. The response was immediate.

"Thank you gentlemen." He paused a moment as the reporters readied their equipment and waited impatiently for him to begin. "I have no comments to make whatsoever. I will, however, make a short statement on my own personal status. I have resigned from the Force. My resignation was immediate and accepted from the morning I left the hospital ward where I had been treated after the plane crash. My resignation was due to my personal displeasure with my job and it was a decision I'd been thinking of for some time. I have no wish, nor will I ever issue a claim for the reward in the capture of Anthony Heyes. Nor will I sell my story to any paper whatever the amount offered as, no doubt, you are all instructed to do." He fumbled for the keys in his jacket as the men gazed on. "Now," he said with a note of displeasure in his voice, "will you all go and leave me alone."

It was just starting to get dark when he opened his eyes. He'd slept the whole afternoon. It had felt good to sleep in his own bed again. In fact he'd felt quite different about everything for some time since the crash. Things he'd taken for granted which had not seemed all that important now seemed to be of great value. He'd taken his very existence for granted, but now he'd begun to realise that life alone was a very special thing to feel, to touch, to see, to smell, all these things he'd just accepted. He'd seen trees and animals from the train window as if for the first time on his journey north that same day and marvelled at nature's incredulity to provide such things. He'd wondered for a time with this new awareness whether he'd found God. Does a born again Christian suddenly feel this way? He'd soon discounted this, he was no bible basher. In fact, he was more of an athiest than a Christian. No, he realised he was taking joy in things he had not been meant to see; he'd survived the destruction of the 747; he'd been given a second chance in life and he'd vowed to himself he would look on every day from then on, as a bonus and live it to the full.

He checked his watch; it was still early. He wondered whether he should ring his boss, Inspector Forrest, and brief him on what had happened. He stared at the unplugged telephone for a moment before deciding against it. He'd ring later. He was about to drop into the soft chair by the window and watch television when the blur of a black car drew to a stop outside. He peered out as the driver's door of a large Citroën opened, and a uniformed chauffeur climbed out and opened the rear door. The two stalwart photographers who'd remained after the others had left, reaped their reward and began to flash away with their cameras.

He recognised her straight away as she stood on the pavement and inspected the building from top to bottom, the way a prospective purchaser would look for faults. The chauffeur opened the garden gate and she strutted through confidently towards the front door. A gentle knock sounded as she rapped against the outside door. David's heartbeat increased and began to race in his chest. He hesitated a moment, smoothing down his ruffled hair and checking his clothing before he opened the door.

"Hello!" she said, her hand across her chest as if relieved to find he was there.

He gazed back open mouthed. For a moment they stood in silence staring at each other, she trembled slightly at the corner of her mouth as the embarrassment of her unannounced arrival made her fearful of his reaction. He saw her uneasiness and quickly responded by gently gripping her elbow and led her into his small flat like a blind person.

"Oh, please, let me take your coat." She slipped it off and handed it to him. Its feel was sharp and heavy and he hung the expensive garment carefully on a hanger and turned to face her.

"I hope you don't mind I've come to visit you," she said.

"No," he replied still surprised by her presence and unsure of what to say. He held out his hand, gesticulating for her to enter the front room, which she did. He followed in her wake. The sweet, exclusive fragrance of her perfume struck him immediately and he quickly composed himself and held the chair by the fireplace as she sat herself, perching on the edge of the cushions, her back straight and dignified. He gazed at her in awe. She could feel his uneasiness in her presence and her training of dealing with nervous people took control.

"Could I have a coffee please, it's been a long drive up from London today."

"Certainly, but I've only instant."

"That's fine," she smiled with perfect white teeth as he removed himself to the kitchen and began to make the drink, his mind still etched with her beauty. He could see the crystal blue eyes as he had done once before but this time they were warm and smiling and not frightened and fearful as he'd seen them before. He hurried his task eager to rejoin her, but he'd no need to because as he poured the boiling water into the cups she came into the kitchen and stood blocking the doorway, a deep frown spread upon her face.

"I'm angry with you," she said.

"Oh," he replied, surprised at her formal attitude.

"You did not call in to see me before you left the hospital." He smiled.

"I enquired after you and was told you were sedated, but I had work to do." Her frown disappeared and she smiled again.

"I shall forgive you then." He loved her strong French accent.

Chantille Orgina had been no ordinary air hostess, she was from a very wealthy background educated at the Sorbonne in Paris and later at a finishing school in Geneva. She owned shares in the family vineyard left to her by her grandmother as well as a small fortune in cash. Her father was extremely disappointed when Chantille explained to him she wanted to work in the real world and he could not dissuade his stubborn only daughter when she insisted on joining Air France as a cabin crew hostess. That had been four years ago when she was twenty two. She'd enjoyed her independance, travelling the world being free of the shackles that her parents had placed on her. She had had three lovers in the time she'd worked for the airline, all had been air crew. The latest was the second pilot of the 747, a married man whom she'd met wherever and whenever she could during the last six months since the affair began. He was now dead along with twenty other air crew that were both friends and colleagues. Her grief was immense, but somehow she'd kept it inside, deep inside, so outwardly there was no sign. This is why she'd needed to see the man who'd saved her life; somehow she knew he could share in her grief and help her to survive the great loss and sadness she felt inside. Just being here had made her begin to feel better already. She'd thought over and over the events that led up to the crash and of the strange man who'd locked her with him in the toilet as she fought with all her might to escape his clutches. She'd remembered tumbling down through space as his strong thighs gripped her tightly round the waist and the jolt of the parachute as it slowed their descent. The face in the water that had held her from slipping under, the smile, the warm brown eyes and the concerned voice enquiring after her as she was lifted into the ambulance. She'd followed his story in the press as she lay recovering from her ordeal, she'd read the facts, his past life, his present life and now she wanted to see the man. She was glad when she'd read that he was unmarried, not that she had any preconceptions in that direction but it would have been awkward to get to him, to speak to him with a grief stricken wife, relieved at her husband's survival, clinging to him in her joy and love. But somehow as their eyes met she felt as if she knew him already, as though they were not strangers. David's thoughts were unsure of why she'd come to see him but as they returned to the lounge to drink the coffee his policeman's brain had reasoned that she'd come for an explanation of the events of the plane crash.

"Listen," he said suddenly as the frown returned on her face. He fought for the right words. "Do you understand what happened up there?" She nodded.

"Oui, I read what is said in the papers, yes."

"No, I mean when you followed me to the toilet before the missile hit."

"Oui, yes I remember."

"Then you remember that it was just circumstance,

nothing but sheer luck that we came out of the aircraft alive." She stared at him, her eyes began to glaze slightly as if she felt a sudden rejection. He saw the expression and it reminded him of a little girl just about to burst into tears. He smiled and began to rephrase his last sentence. "What I meant to say is that I didn't deliberately intend to save your life, it just sort of happened." She quelled the tears and he felt a strong urge to place his arms around her to comfort her. She forced a polite smile.

"I understand that, but whether intended or not you did save my life and I wanted to thank you personally for that." She felt he wanted her to leave but somehow she stayed rooted to the seat and she was relieved when he offered her more coffee. David, in fact was completely overawed by the sheer beauty and presence of his guest and, as with most women of upbringing and class, he felt completely out of his depth. But suddenly as if his eyes had opened, he could see what it was that was troubling her.

"Chantille," her eyes widened at the sound, it had been the first time he'd called her by name. "Listen, I know what you feel." She gazed back, an interested innocence written on her face. She waited for him to continue. "you feel guilty that you are alive when so many have died." She looked surprised.

"You feel it too?"

David laughed. "To be honest no, no I don't."

"But you know how I feel."

"Apparently it's quite common to feel that way after one's survived against the odds."

She smiled, "Are you a philosopher, no?" David laughed again.

"No, I'm just a simple policeman." The smile suddenly disappeared as he remembered he was no longer in the Force. He told Chantille of his resignation. She seemed concerned and looked disappointed.

"But why resign?" He smiled again.

"Look around you, what do you see?" She glanced round the small room. It was neat and tidy, no ornaments, nothing that wasn't functional, the curtains were badly fitted and much too long. She wasn't sure what he meant but she decided to risk a guess.

"It looks alright to me although it could use a woman's touch."

David threw himself back into the chair and began to laugh. There was something about her that made him smile all the time. He was beginning to like what he saw more and more. He composed himself.

"You're perfectly right, of course. It could use a woman's touch. No, I meant this is all I have to show for eleven years of being a policeman. No children to greet me, no dog to wag its tail when I come home." he purposely left out 'wife'. Chantille smiled at him.

"But you are young and carefree, why do you think of such things, you have plenty of time for a wife and family later." She was right, of course. He'd been making excuses to her for his reasons but he felt he'd not known her long enough to bore her with all the politics of his reasoning. He also found he'd been making excuses for the dull surroundings in which he lived. Chantille, he realised was not the impressionable type, but earthy and with simple tastes. The expensive coat and the chauffer driven car had thrown him off guard for a moment, but as he casually strolled to the window and scrutinised the Citroën he had seen the CD plates clearly on the boot lid. He quizzed her about the car and she smiled as she explained that the French Ambassador insisted she came to see him in it.

"It was he who tracked you down for me, I was waiting for you to return home." David blushed, slightly flattered by her statement and he suddenly thought of the promise to his mother that he would collect her and take her for dinner at seven thirty. He'd phoned her from the airport when collecting his car. He checked his watch it was now five thirty and he panicked at the thought of her leaving so soon.

"Listen, are you staying overnight in Leeds?" She smiled, and a warm affectionate expression spread across her face.

"Oui, I am registered into the Queen's Hotel."

"Good," he replied, "then I insist you accompany me to dinner this evening."

"I would be delighted Monsieur Galbraith." David laughed again.

"Please, David," she returned his smile and the chemistry of his presence was beginning to work on her and she wondered just for an instant what sort of lover he would be.

David explained that unfortunately he would also have to bring his mother along and she replied politely that she would be honoured to meet the mother of the man who'd saved her life.

"I want no more mention of that business," insisted David. "The past is past and now we will begin to enjoy the precious time we have been given." He escorted her to the waiting car as the two photographers snapped away again from every angle. He felt an electric buzz of excitement inside as he stood waving as the car drew away. He couldn't wait to see her again.

Back in the lounge David re-plugged the telephone and dialed his mother in Harrogate. After confirming the dinner appointment he then dialed Inspector Forrest's number at the Special Branch offices. The familiar deep tone of his former boss's voice droned at him down the wire.

"So you've decided to let me be the last to know what's been going on." His tone was irate and as he spoke he looked through the file on his desk till he found the ex-detective sergeant's resignation note.

"You'll be coming in to clear your desk, I take it"

"Yes," replied David not liking the sound of the inspector's voice, "in about twenty minutes if that's alright." Forrest smiled to himself.

"Oh, that'll do just fine. See you later then."

Thirty minutes later David entered the Special Branch building and rode the elevator to the fifth floor. He stood outside the steel plated door and pressed the buzzer for admission. He smiled at the overhead camera as he'd done on a thousand occasions till a click announced the door was open and he entered. As he strolled down the corridor he caught sight of numerous faces glaring at him without speaking. Although he nodded politely he could feel the animosity towards him as he neared the Inspector's closed door. He knocked hard and confidently on the glass door.

"Come," said the deep voice of the Inspector.

David entered and stood in front of the desk where the Inspector sat head bowed, writing vigorously. He carried on for a while as David stood staring once again at the ridiculous jet black toupée that seemed to have landed on the man's head by accident.

Eventually he lifted his head and threw the pen he had been writing with on top of the paper. His eyes glared with hatred as he stared evilly unblinking at the erect man. David waited for what the man had to say, it was plain to see something was bothering him quite badly and he thought it better to let him spit it out. Forrest stood and began to walk round the desk.

"So you honour us with your presence, your highness." 'So that's it.' thought David, 'He's bleeding jealous of all the media attention that I've been given.' David just shrugged his shoulders and stood silently. Forrest became more aggressive. He raised his voice an octave.

"Would it have been so much trouble to pick up the phone and let your fucking department in on what the fuck's being going on down there?"

David thought about his reply.

"You got my resignation, I take it?" The Inspector reached for the paper and held it up for David to see.

"Did you take note of the date on the draft?" Forrest checked the date.

"So?" His tone was defensive.

"You realise I resigned the day I recovered in hospital? You'll see that it's written on hospital headed notepaper."

Forrest could see what he was getting at. He went back on the attack. "Is it not a common courtesy to inform one's superior officer of one's decision?" David smiled.

"But I did, Sir. George Redburn, if you remember I was assigned to regional crime, the Chief Super's branch for the duration."

"You smart arse pillock," snapped back Forrest as he came up and pushed his nose about an inch from David's who could smell the stale cigarette smoke on his breath and it nauseated him. He'd had enough.

"Look, Forrest, what's bothering you?" The Inspector's face reddened and he backed off from David and pushed the glass door to with an almighty crash. He returned to the nose to nose position, his eyes glaring wildly into the younger man's face.

"You dirty, filthy bastard, you know what's bothering me." David realised what the man was getting at. He knew that he'd slept with the Inspector's younger wife. In fact, due to the media and press coverage David had been getting, Allison Forrest had for some strange reason told her husband that she'd been having an affair with David and that when he returned from Somerset, they were going away together and he'd been waiting for his moment to sort the matter out. David had slept with Allison Forrest, and although only the once, it was not altogether his fault. He'd been asked to collect some papers from the Inspector's home and when he rang the door bell Allison Forrest answered dressed in a completely transparent negligée. Once inside the hall she'd stepped out of the garment and lay on the stairway legs apart offering herself to the detective sergeant. Like most hot blooded males David had found this extreme temptation too much and quickly succumbed to the woman's charms, although he had stayed well clear of the house since, even after several pleading phone calls from the Inspector's wife. He couldn't blame the man for his attitude towards him. David felt the man was going to strike him any time and had decided that should he do so, he would not retaliate, even though he was bigger and stronger than the older man.

"I take it you know I slept with your wife." He wondered whether or not to add that he'd not been the only one but decided not to hurt the man any more than he had to. Forrest seemed to relax a little as if pleased he'd had a confession.

"You admit you fucked my wife." he emphasised the word 'fucked'.

"Where?"

"I made love to your wife on one occasion only. I regretted it immediately and I have had no contact whatsoever with her since." David felt he was giving evidence in some murder trial again. Forrest barked again.

"Where?"

David told him the complete story, only adding that it was more his seduction than Allison's, although Forrest was too good a policeman to believe him he thought it worth a try. Suddenly when he'd finished, the Inspector lunged at David aiming a blow towards his face. The blow struck him on the side of the cheek leaving David with a small burning sensation. He discounted it as a gesture of Forrest's frustration more then intention to hurt and he stood his ground. The sudden thrust of the Inspector's blow had dislodged his toupée and it had gone flying across the room landing on the floor. The two men stared at the small mass of black hair crumpled on the floor. David wanted to snigger but somehow he quelled the urge and stood, teeth gritted, pretending the blow had hurt him. Alan Forrest strolled over to the wig and slowly retrieved it from the floor. He looked at it slowly for a moment before he dropped it, never to be worn again, into the rubbish bin. He turned to David, calmer but still an anger was flaring inside him. His mouth twitched and spit came from his mouth as he shouted angrily at David.

"I've got your resignation. Go clean your desk, hand in your warrant card, hand in your weapon and then piss off! I never want to see your scheming face again." At that moment, whatever regrets David had about leaving the Force were gone forever, he had made the right decision.

David was subdued a little by the time he went to meet Chantille, but as he watched her emerge from the elevator in the lobby of the Queen's Hotel, her radiant smile immediately dislodged all the thoughts of his meeting with Forrest. Any misconceptions he'd had about her welfare were destroyed by the ink blue chiffon Pierre Cardin evening dress that hung provocatively from her sun tanned bare shoulders. Her short black hair had been swept slightly backwards away from her face, a neat row of pearls hung round her neck and the way she walked confidently through the crowded room under the gaze of approving by-standers told David she'd done it a thousand times before. She hurried towards him and pushed her hand through his arm and clutched it gently. At that moment his chest filled with such pride. He knew he was the envy of every other man in the room.

"Bonsoir," she said in greeting, an enormous radiant smile etched onto her face. "Bonsoir, Mademoiselle, you look stunning." He leaned across and kissed her softly on the cheek as if it had been the most natural thing to do. His insides turned a somersault as he caught the sweet fragrance of her perfume, he knew at that moment he was besotted. He would feel all eyes burning into the back of his head as he led her towards the door and out across the pavement to the waiting Citroën. The chauffeur stood holding open the rear door. A photographer who'd followed her earlier that day appeared and began to flash away much to the amazement of passers by. David laughed to himself as though he couldn't believe what was happening. He felt a little like Cinderella, only his fairy godmother turned out to be the most stunning woman he'd ever seen.

She entered the ambassador's car first and seated herself in the middle making sure he had to sit as close to her as he could. She had a warm loving feeling towards him although she wasn't sure why. She'd thought about him every moment since the hospital, she'd longed to be by his side. She'd carried the vision of his wet face and slicked back hair as they'd bobbed amongst the waves, and a smile that said, 'Don't worry I've got you, we're safe now.' The strong hands that had gripped her and held her rested on his knees as the chauffeur closed the door. She reached across and gently rested her hand on his and suddenly she felt safe again. A lump came to her throat as the joy she'd been feeling since he'd not rejected her that afternoon overwhelmed her, and without a word she kissed his cheek and whispered softly into his ear.

"Thank you."

The drive to Harrogate took fifteen minutes and a bemused stare from behind the lace curtains from David's mother made the young girl laugh. David explained that although he'd forewarned his mother he'd not be alone, the large black car he'd not mentioned. Several other faces appeared at the windows surrounding David's mother's house, all curious to see the man whose exploits they'd been following in the national dailies. David left Chantille in the car while he brought his old mother from the seldom left sanctuary of her bungalow. Chantille waited curious of what to expect till the two emerged from the front door and the old woman waved cheerfully at Chantille as she strode boldly down the path. The ice had been broken in that one small gesture and David sat in silence as the two women exchanged niceties on each other's outfits, Mrs. Galbraith embarrassing David slightly by suggesting how it was that a woman as beautiful as Chantille would dare venture out with an ugly duckling like her son. David had to explain to Chantille that unless one had hair cropped short and parted down the middle and an Errol Flynn moustache, mother considered any man ugly. The whole evening that followed was a complete success. The French chauffeur, Louie, joined them in the small restaurant they'd patronised out in the countryside of the East Riding. Chantille showed herself to be a caring and unimpressionable person by insisting on Louie's presence, much to the delight of Mrs. Galbraith and David who by now would agree willingly to everything Chantille suggested. It was the early hours of the next day that a totally drunk old woman stood in the floodlit doorway, smiling as she waved at the young couple who waved back at her from the disappearing car.

"Your mother's wonderful," stated Chantille as she leaned her head on David's shoulder as the car sped along the short journey to Leeds.

"I know, " agreed David who vowed to himself to pay her more visits now was free of the long hours of police work. The next moment the car drew to a halt outside the old but majestic building of the Queen's Hotel. David saddened that the night had gone all too fast, escorted Chantille up to her room on the second floor. He opened the door for her and stood outside handing her the key. She smiled cheekily as she gently lifted the key with her finger and thumb from his grasp and walked slowly into the room. She turned slowly and stared at David who, being on his best behaviour, was gentlemanly waiting for his invitation to enter the room. Chantille, a seductive smile spread across her face, slowly closed the door, leaving David staring at the number 201 on the green paintwork. Suddenly, while he was still undecided what to do the door flew open again and Chantille leapt at him and half dragged him into the room. She slammed the door and pushed him backwards so his back rested against the closed door. Then she fell against him pinning herself as hard as she could against him. But this time there was no spinning over and over, no screams and creaks or groans as the airframe twisted and broke. She looked upwards at his face. It was smiling and unafraid, no wild look of fear and pain. Had it all been a dream? The wine had impaired her thoughts and she felt a sudden urge to sleep. She felt her legs come free of the floor as he lifted her gently and carried her over towards the bed. He lowered her. Her arms clung round his neck as he tried to break free, but he quickly realised it was a gesture. She was begging him to lay with her, not to leave, and he lowered his body gently down beside her. She opened her eyes and smiled at him before closing them again and turning towards him. She held him tight.

He watched her, admiring her, as she fell into a sombre peaceful sleep, her head wrapped in his arms. His thoughts were of her only. How long would she stay, was she with him out of confusion or just to thank him for her life? He too was confused, for the first time in his adult life he lay on a bed with a beautiful girl draped in his arms, and there was no lust in his thoughts. Just being with her was pleasure enough. It was as though life had opened a door and shown him a secret room. He'd entered the room to find it filled with a marvellous happy sensation that clung to him, passing on the contagion even when he'd walked out of the room. The happiness was still there and as he watched her the air in her lungs parted her small lips with every exhalation and he wondered what power could a woman have to do this to a man, what magnificent power?

It wasn't until dawn broke that they finally made love. Chantille awoke to find David in a deep sleep still dressed in his jacket and trousers. She began to remove his clothes to make him more comfortable and the inevitable happened. It wasn't earth shattering, it was more of a necessity, for to know someone, really know someone, all inhibitions that can stand in the way must be dispensed with. They both realised this and now they had been intimate the final obstacle had been removed.

The next two weeks found the young lovers inseparable. They walked the hills of the Peak District, rowed across the width of Windermere, staying several days in a small guest house overlooking the great lake. They lost the last of the following reporters and finally life returned to normal. On the last night in the guest house they lay huddled together in the small room. The rain lashed hard against the bedroom window lit by a half moon, the lovers content in every way watched the droplets cascading down the window pane till Chantille broke the silence as she suddenly broke free from his grasp and turned to face him, a worried expression on her face.

"What are you going to do to earn your living from now on, Cherie?" David was relieved, he thought she was going to spring something more disastrous on him. He smiled. "Trust a woman, back to practicalities, eh."

"I'm serious, Cherie. How can I marry a man with no prospects. What can I tell my father?" David was stunned for a moment.

"You would marry me?" he asked as he pushed himself up and stared unbelievingly into her smiling face. She laughed and pushed him playfully.

"But of course, Cherie, I'm never going to leave you ever again. You are my life." She spoke the words with such sincerity and warmth that David reached across and pulled her closer towards him, holding her as tight as he could.

"I accept your proposal," he whispered into her ear as he kissed her temple. She pulled gently away and looked straight into his eyes.

"I have money, Cherie, we could go away anywhere and buy a business." David stopped her by putting his finger against her lips. He knew she had money; he'd read all about her as he waited in the surveillance caravan in Somerset for news of Heyes' capture.

"Ssh," he said. She stared painfully for a moment waiting for him to speak. He began.

"If you marry me, you do so on my terms. I'm the breadwinner, I'll make the money and we live on that and that alone. Agreed?" She smiled.

"Oh, anything you say, Mon Capitaine." She saluted mockingly and he leapt on her playfully, forcing her to fall out of the bed on the the floor with a thud. She cursed him momentarily in her native tongue before she leapt to her feet and dragged him by his foot from the warm comfort of the duvet to join her on the floor. They lay on the crumpled carpet panting with their exertion and the words David had been longing to say to her just flowed without prior thought from his lips.

"I love you, Chantille." She beamed at him radiantly. The very last obstacle had just been removed and now she was the happiest person in the world.

"My Cherie," she replied, "I love you too."

George Redburn had remained behind in Taunton till after the inquest on Tan's death. The coroner followed the evidence of the pathologist's report which had decided that due to lack of human tissue at the scene where Tan's body had been found, it would be recorded that Heyes had been killed by person or persons unknown.

This increased Trevellion's suspicions about the two Leeds detectives.West Yorkshire CID would still head the search in the North whilst the Met and Scotland Yard would continue their inquiries in the South. Trevellion decided to have one last chat with Chief Superintendent Redburn before he returned north later that day. He stood by the window in his office re-reading the letter of congratulations from the Prime Minister's office on his handling of the whole affair. He was pondering on the almost certain knighthood to add to his CBE that would be bestowed on him sooner or later when a knock came on the door. He seated himself behind the huge oak desk and gently placed the letter into a top drawer intending to have it framed and hung on the wall of his office.

"Enter," he shouted as he sat stern faced, his hands clasped in front of him like a disgruntled school teacher. George Redburn closed the large door behind him and walked confidently up to the desk. Trevellion gestured for him to sit on the soft high backed chair at one side of the desk.

"Ah, George," he said as he stood, "may I be so bold as to. . ."

"Please do, all my friends call me George," replied the Superintendent who although half cut from his lunchtime quota was still more of a policeman than any ten Trevellions. The Chief Constable continued.

"You'll be off back to Leeds I take it today?"

George smiled, "That's right, Lawrence old chap, off back to the real grind of police work. Shame to leave such a nice quiet spot as this. You must get quite bored at times."

Trevellion's neck turned red as the blood pressure rose into it, swelling it into his collar. He forced a smile denying George any outward sign of anger.

"Anyway George, I just wanted to congratulate you on a damn good bit of police work. Bloody well done." George was just about to reply when the Chief Constable turned his back on him and walked back to his seat at the desk. George scrutinised him as he sat and began to rustle papers in the right hand drawer is if searching for something inside. He was younger than George, clear soft skin tones for a man of about fifty, obviously tea total, no nicotine stains on the fingers. 'I bet he's the type that washes his hands when he has a piss,' he thought. 'Supercillious bastard.'

"Ah, here it is," said Trevellion handing George the Prime Minister's letter. George glanced through it briefly. Some years ago he might have been impressed, but now it was patronising garbage. Trevellion sat with a sanctimonious grin on his face as George handed the letter back crinkling it deliberately. He had Trevellion sussed.

"You met the PM?" George asked casually.

"No, not yet. Have you?"

"Oh yes, several times, very nice lady, got a lovely little bum." George nearly erupted into hysterics at his own humour but just grew a deeper red as his face quelled the urge. Trevellion began to realise that the more experienced detective was toying with him and decided to get right to the point.

"Look, George, before you go have you any other thoughts on this Heyes affair, something that we could get our teeth into?" Although he didn't like anything about the man sat in front of him Trevellion was a giant in the groveller's league. George smiled inwardly. 'So that's his game, wants to pick your brains to see what comes out.He pondered a moment before replying.

"What do you mean, Wyn?" George began to tease the man. Trevellion swallowed hard.

"You know, George, one copper to another." He winked pathetically.

"How do you mean 'one copper to another'?" George was enjoying it now. "Give me a clue."

"Well," Trevellion coughed and cleared his throat, "the body."

"Go on," said George who crossed his arms and sat back in the chair pretending to look interested.

"We all know the body didn't get to the spot where it was found on its own and I wanted to know what your thoughts were on who put it there." George lit a cigarette much to the disdain of Trevellion."

"Oh, is that all?" George took a deep draw and blew the largest chain of smoke he could towards Trevellion. "Is this off the record, Wyn? I mean, can I trust you on this one?" The Chief Constable's eyes shone in expectation. He nodded in agreement.

"Off the record."

George blew another chain of smoke into the room and then perched himself forward a little on the edge of the chair. "I know who put the body there." Trevellion waited impatiently. George sat silent, enjoying himself and determined not to reply till Trevellion asked the question.

"Who put it there?" George prodded himself in the chest with his thumb.

"I did."

"You did!"

"I did."

"But where, how?"

"Hold on a moment." George took another drag and checked the look of sheer misunderstanding on Trevellion's face. "Well, you see," he paused a moment, "this is confidential between you and me isn't it, Wyn? It is alright if I call you Wyn, isn't it?" George said sarcastically.

"Yes, yes, go on."

"You won't believe me."

"Go on."

"Well, when me and my colleague, Detective Galbraith, were in the pub. This little old lady comes rushing into the pub, she'd seen the squad car outside you see."

"Go on."

"Well, she says, I've got that chap you've been looking for, shot the bastard right in the eye I have. So you better come and get him. 'The Chief Constable gave George a disbelieving stare. "Anyway, I just laughed till she pulls out this Luger and to cut a long story short, there he is outside the pub, dead as a Brontosaurus sat in an old wheelbarrow. Anyway I gave her ten bob for the remains and two quid for the wheelbarrow."

"You bastard," shouted Trevellion, unamused and angry.

"Now, now, Wyn."

"Get out, shove off back to Leeds where you belong." George stood up and dropped his stub onto the carpet, treading it in deliberately. "You bastard, you filthy disgusting bastard. Get out." Trevellion's voice was high pitched and he was beginning to lose all self control. George strolled casually towards the door and opened it slowly. He turned to stare at the irate man.

"Well, I can see it's the Chief Constable's funny half hour so I'll be off now. Ta ta." He strolled from the room into the corridor leaving the door open. Trevellion raced across the room and closed the door crashing it behind him with the sole of his shoe. The whole corridor shook as people peered out of doorways to see what all the commotion was about. A young woman constable gave George a puzzled look.

"Doesn't he like old women or something?" he said as he strolled past.

"Must have been sommat he ate."

At three thirty that afternoon the unmarked police car waited outside the Pig and Whistle public house just off the main street in Taunton. The driver was becoming impatient as he could see himself not returning home till later that night. George Redburn as usual was the last to leave the pub. The doors were bolted and locked behind him as he stood on the pavement and his brain was searching for a solution as to what his next move would be when he saw the agitated face of the police driver and the jig-saw pieces came together. He lit up before climbing into the rear of the car.

"Home, James, and don't spare the horses," he said laughing to himself as the driver revved the car, accelerating away as fast as he could, forcing George to slide off the seat onto the floor. The next thing George knew a hand was shaking him and a voice in his ear was pleading for him to wake up.

"Where are we?" he asked, smacking his lips together forcing saliva back between the dry skin.

"Milgarth, Sir. You're home."

"I don't fucking live here you prick."

"My orders were..."

George interrupted. "Joking, dear boy. This will do fine."

The humourless driver dived back into the car and was a blurr in the distance as George made the first step into the building. Harold Swain, the Chief Constable of the West Yorkshire Constabulary, had been waiting for the Chief Superintendent to return to this office all afternoon. He'd had an angry Wyn Trevellion wittering down the 'phone about Redburn's conduct suggesting in no few words that he was nothing more than an inebriated drunk. The duty sergeant bleeped the Chief as soon as George staggered through the door.

"Send him straight up, and I mean now," came the reply.

George knocked and walked straight into Swain's office and without invitation plonked himself down in the chair opposite the desk where Harry Swain sat.

"What's up, Harry?" asked George as he peered at his immediate boss through dreary blood shot eyes. Harry Swain was about the only person in the whole Force who liked George, or maybe he pitied him, he wasn't sure, but he did care.

"Good work on the Heyes case, George."

"Luck, sheer bloody luck." George lit his first fag for three hours. The only time he didn't smoke was when he was asleep or he'd run out of matches.

"How you feeling George?" Swain got right to the point. He was one of only a handful of men who knew of George's illness.

"You mean, how's the old liver standing up?"

"If you like."

"Oh, it's just the same, pickled beyond recognition." George began to come round slightly and he eyed Swain suspiciously.

"What's up, Harry, you look worried about something?" Swain opened a folder on his desk and lifted out several sheets of paper. He handed the top copy to George.

"When you have read it, sign at the bottom and I'll let you have this." He held a smaller piece of paper in his hand. George scanned his medical discharge notice briefly and signed it without hesitation.

"When's this effective from?"

"As from now," replied Swain relieved it had all gone so smoothly. The two men were old colleagues and he knew how bad George could be if he was in the mood. He handed him the cheque.

"twenty thousand, what's this for?"

"Gratuity, on top of your fifteen thousand pension, of course. I'm sorry George but your illness is self-inflicted. If you'd been injured through the job, well..." George laughed out loud.

"You know I won't last six bloody months, what good will fifteen thousand a year be to a dead man?" Harry Swain was an old hand at dealing with George; he knew just how to handle him.

"Don't give me all that self-pity crap. I'm too long in the tooth. We're all going to die sooner or later, it's just that you've been given prior notice." George smiled at the older face.

"Always said you were a smart old bird Harry, got the gift of the smozzel. Always knew you'd go to the top." Harry Swain smiled.

"You forget all about me, the Force, go off on and get yourself a dolly bird and live it up."

George stood up, he knew that last remark was the end of Harry Swain's interview. He turned without a word, without a shake of the hand and walked silently out of the room.

Harry Swain shouted, "Good luck," after him as the door closed. He felt a lump come into his throat. He hated his job sometimes.

George walked down the empty corridor and switched on the light in his empty office. He picked up the old brown leather briefcase from next to the filing cabinet and began to tip the contents of his desk drawer into it. When all the drawers were empty he clipped the strap on the case closed and dropped the full case into the empty waste bin by his desk. An old coat hung on the back of the door and he unhooked it and threw it over his arm. He opened the door and the sign that hung in front of his eyes screamed back at him. 'Chief Superintendent Redburn'. He ripped it from the veneered door and threw it towards the briefcase in the bin. He walked slowly along the corridor and descended the two flights of stairs into the reception area where the duty sergeant was inspecting some documents presented to him by a Pakistani bus driver. A tear escaped from the corner of his right eye and hung momentarily from the bulge of his cheek before falling to the floor. Had it been thirty five years since he'd walked into Barnsley Police Station, proud as punch in his brand new uniform? It seemed like only a week ago. The tears were fallling fast and furious by the time he reached the outer door. A smattering of rain had begun to fall and the grey dusk was drawing in. He walked up the Headrow amidst the early evening revellers just starting out on the inevitable pub crawl around the city centre. He wanted to call someone, a friend, or a lover to share in his sorrow, but there was no-one. A red light caught his eye and he glared up at the sign. A huntsman's head in a black riding hat and red jacket stared down at him. Underneath the sign read 'Tetley's Ales'. He knew in the warm surroundings of the pub he'd find someone to share his sorrow, he knew only too well that most pubs were full of the loneliest people in the world.

Sergeant Gibson had just sat down to eat his cooked breakfast. It was now eleven fifteen on Monday morning. He'd arrived home at four pm the previous day and had slept solidly for sixteen hours. His young wife fussed over him, glad to have him back after four weeks away. He'd told her he'd been on a course in Scotland but the truth was he'd been squatting in a bedroom of a catholic sympathiser's house in the Davis Street Flats just off Shankill Road in West Belfast. He was exhausted. She'd seen the weight loss immediately he'd come through the front door, but the pale grey complexion due to many sleepless nights peering through binoculars and the lack of fresh air and exercise had shocked her. As far as Sandra Gibson knew her husband was a sergeant in the Parachute Regiment and like most wives of SAS operatives she hadn't a clue about his real work. She kissed him gently on the cheek before refilling his cup with a fresh brew of tea.

"Like some more sausages?" she asked as the hungry man devoured the last thick sausage.

"Love some," he replied. Two things he always looked

forward to after an op. Sandra's cooking was one of them.

She tipped the three extra sausages she had prepared onto his plate. He fondled her buttocks tenderly before she giggled and broke away. Although her need was as great as his she could wait for him to finish his meal.

"How do you fancy a nice week in Spain?" he asked as she began to clear the table.

"Spain! How can we afford Spain what with the mortgage and the kids' clothes, not to mention..."

"Alright, point taken. Just a thought," interrupted Gibbo as he gulped down the last sausage.

"Now if you'd found that Heyes chap, we could have had the twelve million pounds reward like they are going to give that young copper." Gibbo stared at his wife in disbelief.

"What's that you're on about?"

She picked up the morning paper and handed it to her husband. "There on the front page." Gibbo stared at the headlines.

'Former Detective Sergeant David Galbraith will probably receive Heyes reward.' He read on. 'Retiring head of Leeds CID, Superintendent George Redburn, has written to the trust holding the twelve million pounds reward fund for the capture of Anthony Heyes, asking that the money should go to the young detective. Redburn explains that the detective had already resigned from the Force when the two men found Heyes' corpse and being a civilian should receive the reward. A spokesman for the trust has suggested that the money could well be paid out to the detective as he is the only justifiable claimant.'

Gibbo followed the story over to the next page where pictures of David Galbraith and George Redburn were framed at the top of the page.

"The bastards," exclaimed Gibbo as Sandra turned, shocked to hear him use such language.

"I beg your..." She was cut short in mid sentence as Gibbo, still clutching the paper, brushed past her and made for the telephone in the hallway.' He dialled a number.

"Fitzgerald please." Two seconds later a voice returned. "Fitzgerald here."

"It's Gibbo, Sir, Ive got some info. I'm coming straight in."

Earlier that same morning Chantille brought David a cup of coffee and handed it to him as he propped himself up in the bed.

"You'd better hurry and dress, Cherie, those people will be here to see the flat in half an hour." The flat had been up for sale for the last two weeks and David was considering two definite offers. He stood to make at least twenty thousand on completion, which he would use to help him buy a small business. He was in the shower when the 'phone rang.

"David," said Chantille holding back the shower curtain, "there's a George Redburn on the 'phone." He emerged still dripping with water and wrapped a towel round his waist. To say he was curious about Redburn's call was an understatement.

"Ah, Wonder Boy," came the familiar voice down the line, "seen the papers this morning?"

"No, I haven't." David covered the microphone on the receiver and beckoned to Chantille to fetch the paper from the mat behind the front door. She returned promptly handing it to him. He couldn't miss the bold headline. He read through it quickly.

"You bastard," he cursed down the 'phone.

"Now, now. I only want half, give the rest away if you like," replied George.

"You'll not get a cent because I'll refuse to take the reward." David was angrier than ever and he was just about to slam down the 'phone when George's tone changed from being forthright to almost pleading.

"Look, Davy Boy, you're a young man with all your life in front of you, a pretty girl to share it with." He'd seen the photos of him and Chantille in the papers. "I'm a dying man with only months to live. I've no job just my pension. Please Davy Boy, you could make my last days very happy." David felt sorry for George, but knew if he took one penny of the reward he would lose his self respect.

"I'm sorry, George, even if I was dying myself I still wouldn't take it." George's attitude changed again and he started to rant.

"You'll take the money and be damned because if you

don't I'll tell the world about how we moved the body and how you shot Heyes in cold blood. I'll fucking destroy you." David did not reply as he considered Redburn's threats. "Do you savy, Wonder Boy?" screamed George impatient for an answer. David was angry but deliberately kept his voice calm as he replied.

"You'd better hang up and get on with telling the world your lies then, George, 'cause there'll be no money no matter what you do."

"I'll see you in hell, or better still I'll see you rot in prison you scum bag." The line went dead as the caller slammed the receiver down hard.

Chantille had been listening to half the conversation and she had never seen David so upset and angry. He filled her in on the rest of the conversation, also explaining about Madam Peters and moving the body from her farm.

"Oh you big soft thing," she said warmly as she hugged him round the neck, "you did all that for a little old lady."

David told her of Madam Peters' past. Her face turned to a look of horror.

"You did the right thing Cherie, that poor woman. But what about Redburn, his threats? "David thought for a moment.

"We will just have to see what line he takes."

"You know this man well?" She asked wondering what sort of man Redburn was.

"Well enough," he replied.

"Will he carry out his threats."

"Probably, after all he's a dying man. What's he got to lose?" Chantille knelt in front of David and gazed up lovingly into his eyes.

"Cherie, I have money, let me pay him." David stood up quickly, his face became contorted with anger.

"No! We give him nothing I'd rather go to prison than pay that old drunk a brass farthing." Her face stared up at him and as he saw the look of fear in her eyes he realised how tactless he'd just been.

"I'm sorry for shouting at you, Chantille,and I am truly grateful that you would do such a thing for me, but this is much more than any amount of money. It's all about dignity and respect and people's lives. Anyway, perhaps he's only bluffing," he said to cheer her but deep down he knew George Redburn would carry out his threat. He could see now in retrospect that Redburn had planned it this way from the time Madam Peters had taken them to the body. He knew also that Redburn was desperate and cunning and to sort this mess out would take a lot of careful thought and planning. The door bell rang distracting his thoughts and Chantille said with a panic in her voice.

"Oh no, those people, the house buyers, they are here.

The brown coloured Ford with army number plates ground to a stop outside the main entrance of Taunton police station. Sergeant Gibson and his commanding officer, Captain Fitzgerald, climbed from the rear of the car and briskly and businesslike entered the building. Wyn Trevellion had been waiting with impatience since the Captain's 'phone call earlier that day and without any further ado the three men were quickly ensconced in the Chief Constable's office. It was five pm when a beaming Trevellion escorted the two soldiers back to the waiting car. He shook their hands vigorously and stood waving as the car disappeared into a side street. He rubbed his hands together with excitement as a shiver ran down his spine at the mere thought of what he was about to do. 'Lawrence, my boy, this will be the making of you. This is it. 'He leapt the four stairs in one jump and came bounding back into the building. Crashing through the double doors leaving them thrashing in his rear he almost ran to the duty sergeant's office.

"Get me everyone who's in the building from the A. team in my office Pronto! Oh, and get me an officer who knows the local farmers on the west side of Exmoor."

At ten o'clock that night two warrants had been issued for the arrest of George Redburn and David Galbraith by the Somerset Constabulary. At five past ten three cars left the front entrance of Taunton Police Station; two carried the warrants off towards Yorkshire and one was sent to bring in Madam Peters for questioning. It was one am when the unmarked police car found the driveway that led to the isolated farm house where the old woman lived. She'd retired early that night and was sleeping quite soundly when the headlights of the car illuminated the room where she slept. Still half asleep she propped herself up on her elbows and stared at the bright lights that shone through the window. Several car doors slammed shut and she heard footsteps across the yard. Her heart began to beat louder in her chest, sweat began to pour from her brow. One of the detectives began hammering with his fist on the door and began shouting the woman's name.

"Madam Peters, will you open the door please, it's the police." A surge of fear ran through the old woman's tired body. 'They've come for me,' she thought, 'I knew they would come one day.' Her mind was confused. It was 1942 again and the Gestapo were once more coming to take her away. The impatient young detective kicked at the old door with the sole of his shoe and the rotten framework gave way easily the door hanging open on the last remaining rusty hinge. The old woman stood in the bedroom doorway, the car lights illuminating her trembling outline. The detective was startled for a moment.

"Madam Peters, I wonder if you..." He stopped in mid sentence as the old woman shuffled towards him and he followed her as she walked past him, still dressed in a long tatty nightgown and the laceless old boots, out into the yard. "Would you get your coat please," he asked as he followed her out of the building. She did not respond but kept on shuffling across the yard towards a small wooden building. One of the other young constables began to snigger at the old woman's gait. She reached the hut and opened the door. The detectives followed behind bemused by her actions.

"It's only the toilet," said the older of the three detectives, "leave her, she'll be out in a mo." The waiting men handed round the cigarettes and leaning on the car smoking, they waited for the old woman to re-appear. Inside the toilet the old woman, tears streaming across her cheeks, felt for the ball of bailing twine that rested on top of the old water closet high on the back wall. She tied a rough knot on the old rusty bracket that held the cistern to the wall then looped it through the main wooden spa that supported the tin roof of the hut. She tied a slip knot high up near the beam and climbing up onto the toilet lid she stuck her head through the empty loop. She leaned against the door with her hands as she slowly eased her feet off the toilet and the thin twine easily took the weight of her frail body. Her last thoughts as the noose tightened around her throat were of her beloved animals and who would take care of them till the blackness entered her brain and at last the torment and pain she'd carried with her every day for the last forty years died with her.

At about the same time the other two cars arrived at Milgarth Police Station in the centre of Leeds. A local constable was assigned to each car specially to direct the strangers to the residence of the wanted men. The first car arrived outside George Redburn's grubby ground floor flat only to find several rows of full milk bottles, and after battering down the front door with a sledgehammer it was clear the former Chief Superintendent had flown the coup.

David Galbraith was listening intently to every car that turned up King Lane till the one he'd been expecting stopped outside his front door. He reached over and shook Chantille gently by her shoulder.

"They're here," he whispered. Her eyes opened and she clutched him lightly. "Now, now, I'll sort this lot out. Don't worry."

The policemen were at the front door now as David opened it after the first knock.

"You David Galbraith?" a thick set detective enquired, his manner curt and direct.

"I'll get my coat." The detectives cautioned David as he followed him to where his jacket lay on the back of the chair.

"Where you taking me?"

"Taunton."

Chantille had dressed and entered the room. All eyes turned towards her.

"They are taking me to Taunton." David touched her arm and kissed her gently on the cheek. "You know what to do."

"Of course, Cherie, I know." She wanted to shed a tear but she smiled bravely, oozing confidence. David returned the smile and then he was led away.

The next morning Chantille rang the French embassy in

London and asked to speak to the ambassador. He was pleased to hear her voice but a little distressed. He could tell she was upset. She'd already written to him some weeks earlier explaining where she was and what she had been doing but mainly thanking him for helping her. He in turn had replied and congratulated her on her happiness and added that anything he could do to help her he would. She explained David's arrest and what had happened and asked if he knew a top criminal lawyer who would help. He told her to stay by the 'phone and ten minutes later he rang her back. He had found her just the man, Sir Isaac Goldstein the best criminal lawyer in London.

"I've just had a quick chat with him on the phone and he's asked you to ring him straight away." Chantille thanked the ambassador and after ringing off she dialled the London number he'd given her. After a short wait while he finished another call the deep tones of a cheerful voice came on the 'phone.

"Goldstein here, who am I addressing?"

Chantille introduced herself and told him the story of what had happened. Sir Isaac seemed sympathetic and agreed to take the case without further ado. Chantille felt a little better and marvelled at the power of her new found friend, the ambassador, who in turn had assured Goldstein of Chantille's unquestionable credentials and wealthy background. Goldstein certainly wasn't cheap.

Back at the Somerset Constabulary Headquarters David had been locked up in a cell for more than four hours. No-one had been near him or answered his request to use a telephone. He knew from experience this was the being left to sweat and contemplate period. He wasn't unduly alarmed but more worried for Chantille and what she would think of him. The cell itself was of the modern type; a neatly plastered room with a bed and a fitted toilet but no flush control, that was done by the officers from the outside. Many a cell had been flooded with the old system after some drunk, given half the chance had decided to wreak havoc on all his surroundings. Excrement on the walls was bad enough. A small but thickly glazed window let in the dying rays of the sunshine. There was a small plastic mattress under the bed which he lifted up and placed on the wooden bed. Keys rattled in the lock and the door suddenly opened. David was led away to the charge desk where a 'phone was resting off the hook. The constable nodded and he picked it up half expecting to hear Chantille's accented voice, but instead it was the deep comanding voice of Isaac Goldstein.

"Listen to every word I say my boy," he said after introducing himself. "Tomorrow you will appear in the Taunton Criminal Court. I will be there to meet you ten minutes before we go in. There may be a chance for bail also, so keep your pecker up. You've not been formally charged yet I take it?"

"No, " replied David. "I'm not sure what it's all about. "

"We'll sort that out tomorrow. Just keep stum. I've just spoken to the Chief Constable and he has assured me you will be charged tonight. Say nothing, got that, nothing."

"Yes Sir."

"Oh and your wife sends her love."

He hung up and David felt as if he'd just been talking to a whirlwind, the man had spoken so quickly and directly. As he was led back to his cell he smiled as he recalled how Goldstein had said 'your wife'. He vowed then and there that the next time he saw Chantille he would fix the day.

The next day Sir Isaac arrived in Taunton in his chauffeur driven Rolls Silver Ghost. Chantille met him as arranged outside the door of the law court buildings. They were taken to a room where thirty minutes later the door opened and David was led in wearing handcuffs. The constable with him stood impassively by the door while David and Chantille hugged each other as best they could. Sir Isaac coughed; he had work to do.

"There'll be plenty of time for that when I get you out of here," he said confidently. He meant it too. Sir Isaac was rarely beaten in court. Not only because he was the best, but simply because he never took hopeless cases. He just hoped doing a favour for the French Ambassador wasn't going to add to his failures list. He'd been up most of the night doing his homework, and through the old boys' network had practically sorted out the police case against David. He now had to know his version. David was precise and direct and told him everything from the first meeting with Madam Peters to removing the body. At this point

Sir Isaac tut tutted and nodded his head disapprovingly. Then he covered the implication of George Redburn and his insistence that David should collect the reward, which David denied he'd ever wanted or would ever receive.

"Good, good," said Sir Isaac as he took notes of everything David had said. He produced a typed letter from his briefcase and handed it to David.

"Have you ever seen this before? It was a photocopy of a letter sent to the trust handling the reward money and David flushed with embarrassment as he read.

'Dear Sir,

I would like to lodge my name as claimant for the monies offered for the capture of one Anthony Heyes. I was the only civilian present when, together with Detective Chief Superintendent G. Redburn, I stumbled across Heyes' corpse. I would, therefore, like to have this claim placed on record and hope to hear from you soon.

Yours sincerely,
David I Galbraith.'

"I didn't write this," protested David as he handed the letter back to Goldstein who looked at David over the top of a small pair of cut away reading glasses.

"Superintendent Redburn I presume?" he said. David nodded. "Not to worry, it's not the main issue," added Sir Isaac.

David reared a little. "But surely it's very important."

"Tut, tut," interrupted Sir Isaac, 'I didn't say it wasn't important but if we can establish the fact that you are innocent of the charge of perverting the course of justice, because this one charge alone, if found guilty automatically proves the other charge, i.e. you moved the body purely for monetary gain. But on the other hand, if we can prove that you are innocent of perverting the course of justice, the other charge of fraudulent deception will not exist, because as a private citizen you would be entitled to the reward."

"But..." David tried to interrupt but Sir Isaac held up his hand to silence him.

"Just trust me, ma boy, I feel sure we can beat both

charges." He leaned forward out of ear shot of the waiting policeman, a cheeky grin on his face. "After all," he whispered, " we're only up against a bunch of country bumpkins." A knock came on the door and a head popped round telling them the court was ready.

The court was a very small room, but that David knew this was only a legal requirement; a person cannot be held in custody for more than twenty four hours without a court appearance. A local JP sat in attendance and was obviously totally in awe of the presence of Sir Isaac Goldstein whose impeccable reputation was known throughout the world of the legal profession.

Chief Constable Trevellion stood alongside the out-classed police barrister who was no doubt relieved that this was not the place to do battle. Several journalists packed into the small public gallery writing eagerly as the preliminaries began. David was read the charges against him, asked how he pleaded and remanded to the custody of the police, after being refused bail. The local JP announced that owing to the severity of the charges and because it of national interest the police prosecutor was asked if the trial could be heard in the main criminal court of the land. Goldstein smiled before nodding his head.

"Agreed."

Chantille who was sitting to the right of Sir Isaac leaned over and asked, "What does that mean?"

"It means, dear girl, that we've frightened the pants off the Chief Constable over there, he wants to hand the case over to be tried by a Peer of the Realm in the Old Bailey."

The whole proceedings had taken just three minutes, but just before His Worship dismissed the court Goldstein appealed to the bench.

"Could I just say a few words directed to my learned friends the police prosecutor?" The man nodded in agreement. Sir Isaac lowered his glasses.

"I am very distressed that you feel fit to bring such ridiculous charges against this young man of impeccable repute, and I will, when this matter is settled in the high court, seek recompense of the utmost damages against Mr. Trevellion and the Somerset Constabulary." Sir Isaac had gone into the offensive from the word go. He knew his every word would be repeated in the tabloids of the land before the day was out. He knew also that some would-be juror would read his statement and that alone could influence his final judgement. He smiled to himself as he loaded his briefcase. He knew he was the best.

George Redburn was sitting by a poolside in St. Thomas in the Virgin Islands staring at the turquoise crystal waters of the Caribbean Sea. A dusky attractive girl of sixteen sat on the stool next to him dressed in a pink flowered dress and matching pink shoes, only the second pair she'd ever owned, having prostituted herself for these paltry material possessions. George had been there for two weeks having spent one week in Miami and another week in Barbados. He'd been picking up various English papers on his travels and he knew there was a warrant out for his arrest. He downed his fourteenth double vodka of the day and it was only three o'clock in the afternoon. His skin had turned to a grey yellowy colour, but the sun's tanning rays had disguised his exposed flesh so his head, arms and legs didn't look too bad. He'd also been passing blood through his urine for two days now and the poison from his disintegrating liver was beginning to spread throughout his system. At five fifteen, still sitting at the poolside bar of the Palm Court Beach Hotel he ordered his seventeenth double vodka of the day. He took a sip and leaned over to grope under the skirts of the giggling girl when his eyes began to roll. A gurgling sound came from his throat and before he fell off the stool dead he vomited a mixture of blood and the vodka that he had been pouring into his stomach all day all over the pink flowered dress of his young companion.

Wyn Trevellion had just read the letter with the heading '10 Downing Street, London W1'. His face was contorted with anger. It was only the second letter he'd ever had from the Prime Minister and unlike the first this was a total and absolute rebuke. His knighthood had just gone out of the window. She stated that he'd demeaned the whole police force in Britain in his ridiculous crusade. For what end? To bring once again to the public's attention all this business of the Heyes affair, not to mention the part he had directly played in the suicide of one of the great heroines of our time. If any misdemeanurs had taken place they should have been handled discreetly and without any prosecutions. She was appalled how a professional man in such a prominent position could handle this matter in school boy fashion. She'd chosen her words carefully stating no names that could incriminate her or show her to be taking sides in this matter, although it was obvious what side she favoured and the personal attack on Trevellion himself by calling him a school boy.

The letter ended with a rebuke referring to Trevellion's lack of intelligence in disregarding orders direct from the PM's office, the words plainly in brackets stood out in block capitals, (TARGET TO BE ILLIMINATED) followed by a footnote of no questions to be asked. The PM finished with a reference to a baboon in charge of a highly delicate matter.

He cursed and threw the letter into the rubbish bin, better still he took it out and burned it in the ash tray on top of the desk. If anyone read that he would be the laughing stock of the police force. He wished to God he'd never clapped eyes on Captain bloody Fitzgerald and listened to his NCO. His whole case had fallen apart. His main witness, Madam Peters was dead. George Redburn had disappeared off the face of the earth, his whole case against Detective Galbraith was in tatters. His whole career now depended on the outcome of the trial.

CHAPTER FOURTEEN

The police had spared no expense in their bitter campaign to see one of its former detectives behind bars. A top barrister, Peregrine Gilbert, had been recruited for a fee of forty five thousand out of Somerset rate payers' money. Gilbert had been slightly apprehensive about taking on such a high powered QC as Isaac Goldstein, but if on the off-chance he did win the case for the police it would do no harm to his already distinguished career. The judge who was to preside over the hearing was Lord Clover, a master of the rolls. Although well into his eighties he had a great mind and intellect, though it was known that he had tended to favour the police a little in previous close fought campaigns.

The public gallery was once again packed out with reporters and the odd goul who'd had to queue all night for the privilege of his seat in the country's main criminal courtroom. David stood high in the dock guarded on each side by a police constable. Chantille sat in the upstairs gallery where she could see David quite easily. Her mother and father sat on each side of her as David thought, 'What an introduction to see her parents for the first time!' The two lawyers sat across from each other on each side of the main aisle; frocked in their dark cloaks and bewigged in Georgian headgear they made an imposing spectacle. More so Sir Isaac with his large rounded face and huge Jewish nose on which rested his half cut reading glasses. He was supported by a small team of associates who sat on his left along the long wooden seat. The jury had been selected without any rejection; eight men and four women and at twelve o'clock on the seventh November, after the charges had been read and David had pleaded not guilty, Peregrine Gilbert began his opening speech to the jury.

"My Lord, good citizens of the jury, we have two specific charges to deal with pertaining to the guilt of the defendant, the former policeman Detective Sergeant David I. Galbraith. The first charge is related to the perversion of justice, to pervert the course of justice. I will show beyond all reasonable doubt the man you see before you in the dock, did absolutely and unquestionably pervert and mismanage the scene of a crime, in this case a murder." He added the latter as an after thought. "The second charge of fraudulent intentions would or could be more difficult to prove. But I will show that the whole purpose of the defendant's mismanagement of a murder was undoubtedly and solely to gain access to this incredible amount of money that was just sitting there waiting to be collected." Gilbert sat down and glared at the jury. David's stomach churned. The words he'd just heard made him feel less confident than before he'd entered the courtroom. Peregrine's manner had been tight-lipped, direct and without a hint of a smile. Isaac Goldstein stood up and strolled over to stand in front of the jurors. He directed himself first at the bench then turned and greeted the jurors as individuals by smiling and nodding to each one as he began his opening remarks.

"My Lord, ladies and gentlemen of the jury and my fellow learned friend. Today we are in for a rare treat." He paused before continuing. "A treat you might say. Yes, a rare treat. We are going to be blessed by the presence of a great hero in this room today and we are going to hear a tale about a great heroine. The man I speak of, my client in the dock there." He pointed towards David. "The former Detective Sergeant David Galbraith, as my learned friend introduced him, is not guilty of any crime, and before we come to the end of this trial, you will see that man come out of that dock and walk down those steps and out that door a free man, his reputation intact." David's stomach stopped churning. "That I promise you." He walked over to his seat and sat down. Chantille wanted to applaud out loud. If the opening speeches had been a tennis match Goldstein had just won the first set.

Peregrine was up on his feet in seconds, a younger man than Goldstein had not yet learned the art of patience. He spoke.

"I call as my first witness Christopher Gibson."

Sergeant Gibson was led through the courtroom by the usher and sworn in.

"Now then Mr. Gibson, please state your name and profession!"

Gibson stated he was an NCO in the 6th Parachute

Regiment.

"Could you explain in your own words where you were on the day of the capture and demise of one Anthony Heyes."

The Sergeant began to tell his story, starting when he found Heyes' hidy hole and followed his tracks down the hillside. He told how as he came to the farm he saw the marked police car from across the field. He saw the two officers loading something like a body into the Minor 1000 pickup truck. He described George Redburn in unmistakable detail and he'd pointed to D.S. Galbraith as the other man in the farm yard.

"What was your assumption of the scene," asked Gilbert.

"None Sir," he replied, "after the police car and pickup had gone, I followed Heyes tracks right up to an outbuilding. I found where he'd spent some time there and some empty egg shells he'd obviously been eating."

"Then what?" asked the Q.C.

"The old lady went out the back to the cow in the field and I slipped into the farm house. " He paused for a moment as he caught a glimpse of the ever alert eyes of Isaac Goldstein peering over his rimless glasses. He continued. "I was immediately struck by the smell of cordite indicating a gun had been fired sometime earlier. I'd say, two hours previous."

"Go on," insisted Gilbert.

"The whole house consisted of four rooms; two up, two down." He swallowed hard and stared at David. "I entered a small kitchen area where I found a recently washed area, a few blue bottles were feeding amidst the water on the floor. I bent down and around where the flies had been feeding and I dislodged a spent bullet from a hole in the stone floor. The bullet was a nine millimetre as used by a small handgun, probably a Luger."

Wyn Trevellion was sitting just behind the prosecutions' seat, he smiled smugly to himself. 'Justice is being done,' he thought.

"How could you be sure it was a Luger?" asked Gilbert.

"Because I found the shell case and the markings were quite clearly German and the Luger was the only nine millimetre automatic pistol ever made by the Germans." Gilbert turned to the jury holding up the shell casing stating that the shell came from the gun that was found on Heyes' corpse. The used bullet was entered as exhibit 'A'. He also stated that tests on the cartridge case and fragments of skull removed from the farm house floor did belong to Heyes. He would be offering evidence later from the Somerset Police Forensic Department.

"What were your assumptions at the farm house when you found all this evidence?" Gilbert asked smugly, beginning to think the case was his.

Gibson brushed back the short cut bristles on the side of his lean face and just before answering he caught sight again of the eagle eyes of Goldstein, who seemed to be examining him for top to bottom. "That bastard Heyes, had just been terminated," came the reply.

Sir Isaac smiled a reassuring smile at David who by now was sweating profusely.

"He's just given himself away!" whispered Goldstein. "We may have him now."

David tried to enquire what he meant but the Q.C. shushed him as he still peered at the Sergeant, who was still speaking.

"I radioed in and was told to come in as Heyes had been found."

"Why did you leave it for more than six weeks before you came forward?" Gilbert enquired.

"Been overseas Sir, didn't piece it all together till I came back and realised that that's why he moved Heyes' remains so the old lady couldn't claim a penny."

Goldstein noticed a few disdainful glances from the jury towards David's direction but just at that moment, Gilbert Q.C. stamped over to his seat and sat down, a smug expression spread across his long thin face. "Your witness."

"No questions." David looked surprised but Sir Isaac gave him a glance as if to say don't worry I know what I'm doing. The court recessed for lunch at one o'clock. Chantille and her parents lunched with Sir Isaac at a small restaurant round the corner from the courtroom. Chantille was worried and suggested the case was going badly. Sir Isaac, infuriated, his mouth full of asparagus, protested.

"On the contrary, dear girl, it's going bloody marvellously." She was confused but still managed a smile. The court resumed at two thirty and Gilbert continued his attack. He produced the leading detective who'd been sent to Madam Peters' house on the day she died and between them they both blamed David for her death.

"Whatever happened in that small cottage that day was enough to drive that woman to suicide." When offered his chance to question the detective, again Sir Isaac declined.

The next thing Gilbert did was to produce the signed letter asking for the reward money. He produced a hand writing specialist who swore the signature was that of David Galbraith, no questions about it. Sir Isaac cross-examined. The handwriting specialist was a middle aged woman who wore her hair long, her face wrinkled and worn did not match the youthful hair she seemed to carry proudly. Her dress was also of the gay sixties garb, bright red flowered colours. Sir Isaac hated people who tried to prolong their youth and couldn't understand why they couldn't grow old with grace and dignity. He went for the jugular.

"How long have you been a handwriting specialist Miss Beavers?"

She corrected him, "Mzz," she said.

"Sorry, for me to mispronounce something so important, Mzz Beavers." She flushed. He turned to the jury and pretended to push his front teeth back in. Only they saw him do this and most of them smiled. He was working on them.

"Fifteen years," replied Ms. Beavers.

"Where did you train? No, let me rephrase that, we don't want to be here all day wasting your valuable time..."

"Objection!" shouted Gilbert standing up, "that's a deliberate and personal attack on the witness."

"Sustained," agreed his Lordship. Unperturbed, Sir Isaac continued.

"Am I correct in saying there is no formal training of any kind, university, technical college, etc?"

"Yes," she replied.

"So, you are self taught I take it? Good, good, now we've

dispensed with your qualifications we can continue." A contagious giggle rang round the court; Goldstein's eyes watched the jury's reaction. They all smiled except one woman. 'Oh, God,' he thought, 'another feminist,' He continued.

"Am I correct when I say one never actually writes the same word, or letter for that matter, exactly the same twice; similar probably but not exact?" She stared at him her face still flushed with embarrassment.

"That is correct." He had such an overpowering effect on her that she found herself chosing her words carefully. Goldstein turned to the bench and begged the court's indulgence.

"If you will allow me just ten minutes, Your Lordship, I can show without any doubt once and for all that my client did not write this letter." A projector screen was brought into the court and a slide of the signature was projected in enlarged form onto the large screen. Goldstein explained that this was the signature on the letter. 'David I. Galbraith'. He smiled at Ms. Beavers and she looked a little relieved.

"Now then, Mzz Beavers, confirm that is the signature on the letter in front of you." She inspected both signatures for some minutes, careful in case some trickery wss involved.

"Definitely, the one on this letter is the one on the screen." Then Sir Isaac produced David's note of resignation that had been given to George Redburn.

"Next I would like you to check the signature on this letter." Ms. Beavers studied it for several minutes.

"It's the same. It's exactly the same."

"Good, good. In laymen's terms, my good lady, you mean both signatures on two different letters are exactly the same, every line every squiggle, in fact, in duplicate?"

"But, of course," she replied.

"This, as we talked about earlier, is an impossibility," added Sir Isaac. "Just to confirm Mzz Beaver's findings I have another slide of the signature on the resignation note." He signalled one of his aids who placed the second slide in front of the first and twiddled about with them till both signatures were alligned. "They matched exactly!"

Sir Isaac went on to explain that the resignation letter was signed some four months previously and therefore the second signature was a duplicate, copied by some person out to discredit his client. Also, having excused the witness, he went on to explain how David had been offered thousands of pounds for his own personal story of the whole Heyes affair, but he had refused point blank. A man of high moral standards. Goldstein described him and went on to add, "Is it probable that a man who is preparing to receive millions of pounds, sweats and toils to open up a small greengrocer's shop? To find him guilty on this charge would be a travesty of justice."

The case was adjourned shortly afterwards till ten o'clock the following day. David was led away quietly confident that he would be freed very soon. He felt all had gone well.

The next day the court resumed. Gilbert called to the stand two officers who had attended the presumed spot where Heyes body was taken to. Sir Isaac appealed to the judge.

"Your Lordship, with my learned friend's permission I would like to call back to the stand Sergeant Gibson." Gilbert objected. Sir Isaac explained that Gibson was the only witness who saw David remove the corpse and his client had no intention of denying its removal; there were just a couple of points that needed to be established. Gilbert retracted his objection and Sergeant Gibson returned to the stand wearing civilian clothes. Sir Isaac didn't waste any time; he'd done his research on the soldier the previous night.

"Could you tell the jury what regiment you are in Sergeant." Without any delay the Sergeant replied. "6th Parachute Regiment, Sir."

"But surely you're in the SAS, Sergeant?" Sir Isaac glared at the witness, Gibson swallowed hard. SAS operatives never revealed they were in the regiment. If it were known publicly his cover would be blown, even when they wore the famous beret they were still anonymous except to those in the same unit.

"6th Paras, Sir." Gibson was a good liar. He had to be to survive under cover.

"Come on, Sergeant, you are under oath," Sir Isaac said. "Are you not the Sergeant Gibson who won the DSM for your behind the lines work in the Falklands War?" The Sergeant began to sweat. "Are you not the man who led a unit of SAS on to an Air Lufthansa Aircraft at Lusaka and shot dead four hijakers who were holding one hundred and twenty people hostage?" The sergeant couldn't believe where Goldstein could possibly have got such information from. "And only recently," continued Sir Isaac, "you have returned from duty in Northern Ireland, Belfast in fact, where you have been working under cover on a building site. Do you want me to name the owner of the building site?" Goldstein's old boys brigade had come up trumps again. He knew if Gibson refused to answer or continued to deny his involvement with the SAS he could easily discredit the only witness to the crime and ask His Lordship for a dismissal. He stared hard at Gibson who was caught between two loyalties. If he continued to lie and Goldstein could prove his involvement with the SAS, he would be found in contempt of court and would be discredited, not to mention his cover would be blown.

"Would you please answer the question," insisted Goldstein. "Are you in the SAS?" His voice was disconcerting. Gibson looked round the court in a quandary. Goldstein played his trump card. "I could easily supena the builder you have been working for in Belfast. Surely you would not want me to expose this man as it would put his life in extreme danger." Gibson cracked.

"Yes I am in the SAS." His undercover career had just ceased, the brigade had lost a good operative. Goldstein strolled into the middle of the court and spoke calmly.

"Your Lordship, due to the inconsistency of this witness who has deliberately lied under oath on two occasions, I would like to ask for an immediate end to this ridiculous affair." Lord Clover looked across at the prosecutor's bench where Peregrine Gilbert sat dejected.

"Can you offer any more evidence than this man's testimony?" Gilbert stood up.

"No, Your Lordship." Goldstein smiled. Lord Clover continued. "Sergeant Gibson, you have purged yourself under oath and normally I would have you arrested but I sympathise with your problem. However, you have discredited yourself as a reliable witness and I have no recall but to end this trial. The prisoner is free to go."

Sir Isaac had his Rolls sent round to the front door and the small group pushed and fought their way through the bustling photographers to the waiting car. Sir Isaac had reserved a table at Jacomelis Restaurant in Chelsea, a tradition he followed after every successful case.

Chantille and her parents and David and Sir Isaac and his two associates all attended the celebration meal. David was happy but also a little sad. "I would have liked to have explained why I moved the body and several other things but I never got the chance," he said to Sir Isaac after thanking him for what he'd done. Chantille had already given him his cheque for fifty thousand which he took without a word.

"Tell your story, ma boy, sell it to the tabloids. Tell it for Mrs. Peters and Superintendent Redburn. Tell a fairy story but take their money and take this nice young lady off on a world tour and don't come back. Enjoy." He held his glass of champagne high into the air and gulped its contents down in one go. He could see David was still pondering things over in his mind and he leaned across and whispered in his ear.

"Sergeant Gibson was your only way out you know. The fact, for whatever reason, is you still moved the body. Ah! we would have got a lot of sympathy from the jury when you told the sad story of Madam Peters but Lord Clover would have had to instruct the jury to find you guilty."

Richard Normans stood outside the newspaper offices in Fleet Street. He smiled to himself as he pushed the letter through the door. It was two am and the cold rain was beating down. He pulled up the hood on his anorak and walked back to the small tourist hotel where he was staying about half a mile away.

James Delany sat at his editor's desk and fumbled for a cigarette in his drawer. A pile of letters were thrown haphazardly onto the desk and one of them caught his eye. He thought he recognised the handwriting on the envelope and then he saw there was no stamp. 'My God!' he thought to himself as he slipped the paper knife under the flap and opened the letter. It began:

'Dear Mr. Delany,

As you read this letter several people will be in the last throws of life. Two days ago I placed several drops of ricin in three full kegs of Samuel Braithwaites Brewery in Tadcaster. I owed Lord Bradbury a promise. By now the barrels will be lying empty in some publican's cellar. I do hope you haven't been up to Yorkshire recently, my little joke. As you can see I am alive and well and if you check the handwriting on the other letters I'm sure you'll find it's the same. Anyway, I'll have to write off now because I have a few demand notes to write to other breweries. I need the money, we could do with another jet. Do you know where we could buy one, Gadaffi perhaps? Anyway I will keep you informed of my progress.

Signed Anthony Heyes.'

Delany darted through the outer office and into the room lined with cabinets. He opened the drawer marked Heyes and rummaged through for one of the previous letters. He checked them, all scrutinising every letter, every word, till he finally stopped. His mouth was open and his face ashen. A young reporter came into the room and saw him standing as if in a trance.

"What's wrong, Chief? Are you alright?" Delany turned and looked at the young woman.

"He's alive, the bastard's not dead, he's alive."

"Who's not dead?" inquired the woman.

"Heyes, Anthony Heyes. He's just sent me another letter, He's done it again, the Poisoner, he's alive."

Back at his hotel Richard was writing out demand letters to several top breweries.

'Dear Sir,

As you, no doubt, will see we have resumed our operation of poisoning chosen brewers, the latest being Samuel Braithwaites of Tadcaster. I presume our short association with Braithwaites will end up with the company going into liquidation. This need not have happened, nor Lord Bradbury's tragic death. We offered him immunity from our services if he would pay a small once only fee of £100,000. We are prepared to purport to your company also this once only fee, offering complete immunity forever from our services. However, if this letter is publicised or handed to our oppostion, namely the police, our offer of immunity will be withdrawn and your name will go onto our list for a possible visit. If you are prepared to accept our offer please fly your company's flag upside down and we will contact you with regard to payment details.

Yours faithfully,
Anthony Heyes.'

Richard proceeded to list all the breweries from the London Yellow Pages. There were seventeen in the metropolitan area. That's one million seven hundred thousand pounds. He was glad Tan had suggested he translated Tan's letters into his own words.

"Do it on the train journey and then if anything happens to me you can continue the fight." Richard had used the last of the ricin to substantiate his letter to the Chronicle. Pity though, but he knew all the companies would pay up, there was just too much money involved, after all Joseph Bottomley's in Leeds had long since closed. Richard stopped what he was doing for a moment and looked out of the window and pondered. 'I wonder how much flying lessons cost?'

THE END